Praise for Jayne Ann Krentz's

SHARP EDGES

"A fast-paced mystery. . . ."

—*Chicago Tribune*

"Entertaining. . . . The dialogue in Krentz's twelfth novel cuts through with . . . sarcasm and snappy double entendres. . . ."

—*People*

"Eugenia and Cyrus are endearing curmudgeons, old-fashioned in their loyalty and guts, and even though we know they have to triumph, we don't want to miss a word."

—*Publishers Weekly*

"Krentz's usual lilting, charming prose and slightly eccentric characters. . . ."

—*Kirkus Reviews*

"Strong characterizations, clever dialogue, and touches of humor make for a fast-paced read that is trademark Jayne Ann Krentz."

—*Rendezvous*

"If there is one thing you can depend on, it is the humor, passion and excitement of a Jayne Ann Krentz novel. Clear your schedule and settle in for a wonderful read."

—*Romantic Times*

Books by Jayne Ann Krentz

Deep Waters
The Golden Chance
Silver Linings
Sweet Fortune
Perfect Partners
Family Man
Wildest Hearts
Hidden Talents
Grand Passion
Trust Me
Absolutely, Positively
Sharp Edges

By Jayne Ann Krentz writing as Jayne Castle

Amaryllis
Zinnia
Orchid

Published by POCKET BOOKS

JAYNE ANN KRENTZ

SHARP EDGES

POCKET STAR BOOKS

New York   London   Toronto   Sydney   Tokyo   Singapore

This book is a work of fiction. Names, characters, places and incidents are products of the author's imagination or are used fictitiously. Any resemblance to actual events or locales or persons, living or dead, is entirely coincidental.

A Pocket Star Book published by
POCKET BOOKS, a division of Simon & Schuster Inc.
1230 Avenue of the Americas, New York, NY 10020

Copyright © 1998 by Jayne Ann Krentz

Originally published in hardcover in 1998 by Pocket Books

All rights reserved, including the right to reproduce
this book or portions thereof in any form whatsoever.
For information address Pocket Books, 1230 Avenue
of the Americas, New York, NY 10020

ISBN: 0-671-52409-7

First Pocket Books paperback printing September 1998

10 9 8 7 6 5 4

POCKET STAR BOOKS and colophon are registered trademarks of
Simon & Schuster Inc.

Cover art by Tom Hallman

Printed in the U.S.A.

For my editor, Linda Marrow,
who knows what a good story
is all about.
My thanks.

"Forged in fire, neither liquid nor solid, capable of transmitting or reflecting light, glass is proof that there is magic in the world."

—from the introductory notes of the
Catalog of the Leabrook Glass Museum,
by Eugenia Swift, Museum Director

"The finest glass is a glass that's filled with really good beer."

—Cyrus Chandler Colfax,
Private Investigator

Prologue

Three years earlier . . .

Cyrus Chandler Colfax watched Hades pursue Persephone as she fled Hell with the seeds of spring in her hands. The torment on the face of the Lord of the Underworld struck a chord. He knew exactly what the poor guy was going through. He wanted to give him some advice.

Sure, it was nice to have a woman around, especially in a place like Hell. Good to have someone who laughed politely at your lousy jokes. Someone you could take on vacation, assuming you ever got to go on vacation. Someone who maybe even knew something else you could do with tuna fish besides make a sandwich out of it.

But what good was having a woman who did not want you?

Cyrus took a closer look at the desperate face of Hades. *Forget her. She probably faked her orgasms, anyway.* He knew firsthand what the fraudulent kind felt like. Katy had gotten very good at them.

"Incredible, isn't it?" Damien March's perfect white smile glinted in the shadows that surrounded the display pedestal. "Fourth century. Roman, of course. The absolute apogee of glass-cutting in antiquity."

"Uh-huh." Cyrus could feel his eyes start to glaze over already. Damien was particularly grating when he went into his lecturing mode.

"The technical term is *diatreta*. Most examples of the art are deep bowls such as this one. The experts refer to them as cage cups because of the way the carved figures stand out from the background. It almost looks as if they are attached by a net. Or trapped in an invisible cage."

"Yeah." Cyrus tuned Damien out while he studied the ancient object.

Hades and Persephone looked as if they were struggling to spring free of the small bridges of glass that bound them to the bowl. Caught in the narrow beam of the light suspended above it, the cage cup glowed a dozen hues of fiery amber. The color of the fires of Hell? Cyrus wondered. The figures were so exquisitely carved that they appeared to be living creatures frozen forever in the translucent medium.

It wasn't just the brilliance of the carving that riveted his attention. It was the fact that it was so old. It gave him a strange feeling to know that he was looking at an object made of glass that had survived for nearly seventeen hundred years.

"Our client got it in a private auction." Damien walked out of the shadows to stand on the opposite side of the glass case that enclosed the cage cup. "A very private auction. None of the bidders knew the identity of the others, and none of them knew who had put the cup up for sale. Everything was handled with complete discretion and a guarantee of anonymity."

Cyrus looked up. "Are you telling me that it was an illegal sale?"

"How could it possibly be illegal?" Damien was clearly amused. "The experts will tell you that the Hades cup no longer exists. The last official records of it date from the early 1800s. It is presumed to have been destroyed sometime during the Victorian era. But in reality it went into a series of private collections."

"And that's where it's been all these years?"

"Rumor has it that it has surfaced only a handful of times. Always in the underground art market." Damien gazed at the ancient bowl with rapt interest. As he bent forward the light gleamed on his prematurely silver hair and etched the aristocratic lines of his patrician face. "It has garnered a certain reputation."

"What kind of reputation?"

Damien's mouth curved in the condescending way that had become increasingly irritating during the past few months. "Legend has it that every time it goes from one owner to another, someone dies."

Cyrus raised his brows. "That kind of reputation, huh?"

"Not unusual for an object of such great antiquity. Things this old have a certain power. Those who are sensitive to it can feel it."

Cyrus did not like the intent manner in which Damien stared at the old glass. An uneasy chill moved through him, but it had nothing to do with the age of the Hades cup. "Come off it, March. You don't believe that kind of crap."

Damien did not respond directly. "No one knows much about it, you know. It has never been studied by the experts because it has always been hidden away in private collections. Impossible to say exactly how the ancients achieved the amazing colors, for example.

Was there gold or some other metal in the original batch of glass that came out of the furnace? Or was the effect achieved simply by chance?"

Cyrus was well aware that he was no expert when it came to art. Damien was the authority on this kind of stuff for the firm of March & Colfax Security. Nevertheless, he did not think that anything about the ancient bowl had occurred by mere chance. Even he, with his untrained eye, could see that the thing was too brilliantly executed, too detailed, too carefully crafted to allow for the fluke factor.

"I doubt if it was an accident," he said.

Damien lifted his head. His ice blue eyes held a gleam of mockery. "Do you?"

The firm of March & Colfax Security was six months old as of last Monday. Cyrus did not think that the partnership would last another six months. In spite of what Katy believed, he knew he had made a mistake going into business with Damien.

He had told himself that he did not have to be close friends with a man in order to have a working relationship with him. But not only did he not like Damien March very much, he no longer trusted him.

As his grandfather, Beauregard Lancelot Colfax, used to say, no point trying to do business with a man you can't trust as far as you can piss.

It was true that Damien had offered a valuable entrée into the big time of the private security business. He had connections to the elite social world where wealth and power formed a closed biosphere.

On the surface, the business arrangement appeared to work well. March knew how to socialize with the monied crowd. He knew how to talk to them. He could bring in the big accounts.

Cyrus's part of the deal was simple. He had the

instincts, the training, and the sheer, dogged tenacity that it took to get results for the clients.

Transporting the Hades cup safely to its new owner was one of the most important jobs March & Colfax had undertaken to date. The billionaire collector who had hired them had demanded absolute discretion. He wanted no rumors about the cup leaked to the art world or to the press. He was obsessed with protecting his anonymity and was willing to pay well for the privilege.

Cyrus knew that for the moment he was stuck. He could not end the partnership with March tonight. He had made a commitment to see that the cup got where it was supposed to go. He never walked away from a commitment.

But now as he stood looking down at the ancient bowl that seemed to burn with the fires of Hell itself, he made his decision. Once the thing was safely in the hands of the reclusive Texan who had hired March & Colfax, he would dissolve the business relationship with March. Effective immediately.

He had never liked the highbrowed, affected, arty type, anyway.

Katy would be appalled and furious. Cyrus knew she had dreams of moving in the same world that Damien inhabited. But some dreams, as Grandpappy Beau used to say, weren't worth the price of admission.

"The Hades cup has some interesting properties," Damien continued in his pedantic tones. "In transmitted light, such as this, it seems to be made of amber flames."

"So?"

"Watch what happens when I angle the light so that it's reflected off the surface of the glass rather than passed through it."

He reached up to adjust the lamp that hung over the glass case.

"I'll be damned." Cyrus stared, briefly fascinated.

In reflected light the Hades cup changed colors. It was now a deep, dark red. The color of blood.

"We had better be on our way." Damien released the lamp and stepped back into the shadows. He shot the cuff of his Italian-made gray suit and glanced at his gold-and-black-steel Swiss watch. "Our rich Texas friend will be anxiously awaiting our arrival."

Cyrus checked his own watch, which had a leather strap and a nice picture of a parrot on the face. The colors of the bird's plumage matched the bright hues of the turquoise, red, and yellow aloha shirt he wore. "We're on schedule."

Damien's mouth twitched in another of his supercilious smiles. "Timing is everything in life and in business."

"Grandpappy Beau used to say something like that."

It wasn't until two hours later when the bullet came out of the darkness behind him that Cyrus was forced to acknowledge just how bad his timing had been.

He should have ended the partnership with Damien yesterday, he thought, as he was spun around and slammed into the ground. But the knowledge came too late. The shot had already ripped a path through his left shoulder. The color-splashed tropical shirt was rapidly soaking up his blood.

His only consolation was that he knew the bullet had been aimed at his spine, not his shoulder. It had been his instincts, a hunter's instincts, that had given him the subtle warning. They had been ingrained in him from the cradle by his grandfather, and they had saved his life.

* * *

Cyrus survived the bullet and the night. But when he woke up in the hospital the following day he discovered that his whole world had changed.

His wife, Katy, was dead. The victim of a carjacking, the police said.

Damien March had vanished with most of the liquid assets of March & Colfax Security, leaving the company on the brink of ruin.

And the Hades cup had disappeared.

One

$\mathcal{I}$t took all of the considerable self-control Eugenia Swift had at her disposal to hang on to her temper, "For heaven's sake, Tabitha, the last thing I need is a bodyguard."

Tabitha Leabrook smiled with the sort of poised confidence reserved for those who have grown up with money, social influence, and very high self-esteem.

"Think of him as a precaution, Eugenia," she said. "A prudent preventative action. Rather like wearing a seat belt."

"Or getting a flu shot," Cyrus Chandler Colfax offered helpfully.

Eugenia tightened her fingers in a reflexive movement. The fresh-off-the-press invitation to the Leabrook Glass Museum's annual Foundation Reception crumpled in her hand.

She wondered what the penalty was for strangling very large men who wore tacky aloha shirts, khaki chinos, and moccasin-style loafers. Surely no judge or jury would convict her, she thought. Not when they saw the evidence.

Colfax had said very little thus far, obviously content to wait as the argument swirled like a waterspout in the center of the room. He was biding his time, letting Tabitha wear her down. She sensed his plan as clearly as if he had written it out for her to read. He intended to loom in the shadows until she had been sufficiently softened up. Then he would step in to deliver the coup de grâce.

Dressed in the splashy blue, green, and orange shirt, he should have looked ridiculous against the oriental carpet and warmly paneled walls of her expensively furnished office. Unfortunately, he did not appear even slightly out of place. He clashed terribly with the expensive decor, of course, but he did not look out of place.

It was the room that looked somehow prissy and too elegant.

Eugenia was not fooled by the beachcomber ensemble. Not for one minute. She had a talent for being able to look beneath the surface. It was a gift that had led her into a successful career, first as an assistant curator at the Leabrook and now as its director.

She could see very clearly that Colfax was going to be a problem.

The cryptic tropical attire could not conceal the reality of Cyrus Colfax. He looked as if he had just ridden in off the range with a pair of six-guns strapped to his hip and was prepared to clean up the town.

Slow-moving and slow-talking, he had the feral, ascetic features of an avenging lawman of the mythic West. He even had the hands of a gunman, she thought. Or at least, the sort of hands she imagined a gunslinger would have. Strong and lean, they were a highly uncivilized combination of sensitivity and ruthlessness.

There was an aura of great stillness about him. He made no extraneous movements. He did not drum his fingers. He did not fiddle with a pen. He simply occupied space. No, Eugenia thought, he controlled space.

She estimated his age at about thirty-five, but it was difficult to be certain. He had the kind of features that only toughened with the years. There was a hint of silver in his dark hair, but nothing else to indicate the passing of time. There was certainly no evidence of any softening around the middle, she noticed.

But what disturbed her the most were his eyes. They were the color of thick, heavy glass viewed from the side, an intense, compelling green that was cold, brilliant, and mysterious. It was a color that was unique to a material forged in fire.

Eugenia tossed aside the crushed invitation and folded her hands together on top of her polished cherrywood desk. This was her office and she was in charge. She glared at Tabitha.

"What you are suggesting is highly inefficient and a complete waste of time," she said. "Besides, I'm supposed to be on vacation."

"A working vacation," Tabitha reminded her.

She knew she was losing the battle, but it was her nature to fight on, even when defeat loomed. It was true that she was the director of the museum, but Tabitha Leabrook was the chief administrator of the Leabrook Foundation. The Foundation endowed the museum and paid the bills. When push came to shove, Tabitha had the final say.

Ninety-nine percent of the time the chain of command created no major problems for Eugenia. She had a great deal of respect for Tabitha, a small, dainty woman in her early seventies. Tabitha had a seemingly unlimited reservoir of public-spirited energy, refined tastes, and a good heart. She had a penchant for face-lifts and the money to afford them. She also had a will of iron.

For the most part Tabitha demonstrated a gratifying respect for Eugenia's abilities and intelligence. Since appointing her director of the Leabrook, she had given Eugenia her head when it came to the administration of the museum.

Tabitha and the Board of Directors of the Leabrook Foundation had been delighted with Eugenia's achievements. Under her direction, the Leabrook had swiftly shed its stodgy image and achieved a reputation for an outstanding and exciting collection of ancient and modern glass.

It was unlike Tabitha to interfere in Eugenia's decision-making. The fact that she was doing so today indicated the depths of her concern.

"I will feel much more comfortable if Mr. Colfax accompanies you to Frog Cove Island," Tabitha said. "After all, if there is some question of murder here—"

"For the last time," Eugenia interrupted, "there is no question of murder. The authorities declared Adam Daventry's death an accident. He fell down a flight of stairs and broke his neck."

"The lawyer who is handling the Daventry estate called me an hour ago," Tabitha said. "He told me that the executors insist that Mr. Colfax make some inquiries into the matter."

"So let him make inquiries." Eugenia spread her hands. "Why do I have to be involved in them?"

Colfax stirred at the edge of the beam of light cast by the Tiffany lamp on the desk. "The estate wants everything handled very quietly. Very discreetly."

Eugenia eyed his bright, palm-trée-patterned aloha

shirt. "No offense, but somehow I don't see you as the soul of restraint and discretion, Mr. Colfax."

He smiled his slow, enigmatic smile. "I have many hidden qualities."

"They are extremely well concealed," she agreed politely.

"It will be an undercover operation." Tabitha's eyes gleamed with enthusiasm. "Rather exciting, don't you think, Eugenia?"

"I think," Eugenia said carefully, "that it sounds like a lot of nonsense. I read the articles in the *Seattle Times* and the *Post-Intelligencer*. There was no mention of any suspicion of foul play in Daventry's death."

Tabitha peered at her over the rims of her reading glasses. "I must remind you, Eugenia, that the sooner the executors are satisfied, the sooner the Leabrook will be able to move the Daventry glass collection here to the museum."

Tabitha was right, and Eugenia knew it. Adam Daventry had left his magnificent collection of glass to the Leabrook. For most of his time as a collector he had focused on seventeenth- to twentieth-century glass. But a few months before his death, he had also begun to acquire some ancient glass.

Eugenia was eager to get her hands on the collection, but that was not the real reason she planned to spend her summer vacation on Frog Cove Island.

Adam Daventry's death had made the Seattle papers for two reasons. The first was that he was the last direct descendent of the Golden Daventrys, a prominent Northwest family that had made its early fortunes in timber and then moved on to amass even more cash in Pacific Rim shipping.

The second reason Daventry's death had garnered a mention was that five years earlier Adam Daventry had moved to Frog Cove Island off the Washington coast and established an art colony. The island had become a popular summer weekend destination for Seattlites, tourists, and others who liked to browse the local galleries. The annual Daventry Workshops Festival, held in June, had become a major summer event that drew large crowds.

Although Daventry had plastered his name on the art colony and the summer festival, he, himself, had always avoided the public eye. The rare photos that had been taken of him showed an elegantly lean, dark-haired, middle-aged man with smoldering eyes and Faustian features.

Eugenia had met him six months earlier when he had come to Seattle to consult with her in her professional capacity. She had quickly discovered that she had something in common with Daventry, namely an abiding passion for glass. But in spite of that, she had come away from the encounter with a one-word description of him. The word was *bloodsucker*.

"I don't understand why you're so upset about this arrangement, Eugenia," Tabitha said. "It's not as if you both won't have plenty of privacy. From what the lawyer said, Glass House is quite large. Three stories and a basement. There are any number of bathrooms and bedrooms, apparently. So many, in fact, that the executors plan to sell it off to a hotel firm to be converted into an inn."

"Yes, I know, but—"

"The only thing you and Cyrus will have to share is a kitchen," Tabitha concluded.

"Don't worry," Cyrus said. "I'll bring my own food and do my own cooking, Ms. Swift."

Eugenia chose to ignore that. She pitched her voice to a soothing tone, the sort she used when she urged possessive private collectors to donate their finest pieces to the Leabrook.

"No one's going to stop you if you want to go to Frog Cove Island, Mr. Colfax. But I fail to see why you should stay at Glass House with me, even if it is big enough to be an inn."

"Because I need open, unquestioned access to the place, Ms. Swift. Among other things, I want to go through Daventry's papers and files. It's going to take time to do a thorough investigation. The easiest way to handle it is for me to stay at the house."

Eugenia drummed her fingers on the desk. "I suppose that the estate has every right to hire an investigator. And I really don't care what you investigate, Mr. Colfax. But I fail to see why you have to attach yourself to me."

"It's a perfectly logical move," Tabitha insisted.

Eugenia clenched her fingers around the pen. Tabitha was a great fan of murder mysteries. She was obviously thrilled by the prospect of aiding and abetting a real-life private detective.

"I've got a job to do on Frog Cove Island," Eugenia said steadily. "I'm going to inventory Daventry's collection. Make arrangements to have it all crated and shipped back to Seattle. I don't have time to play Nancy Drew."

"You don't have to assist in the investigation," Tabitha assured her. "That's Mr. Colfax's job. But he needs a cover in order to do his work."

"Why on earth can't he just be up-front about what he's doing?" Eugenia retorted. "Why can't he tell people he's looking into Daventry's death?"

"I just told you, I'm supposed to be discreet," Cyrus said. "Besides, the island community is a small one and very insular. It's not likely that any of the locals would talk freely to a private investigator if they knew who he was and what he was doing."

"I'm sure Mr. Colfax won't get in your way," Tabitha said with an encouraging smile.

Eugenia eyed Cyrus with brooding dismay. He most definitely would get in her way. She could tell that much just by looking at him. One could not simply ignore a man like this. The shirt alone made it impossible.

In the normal course of events, his presence would not have constituted a serious problem for her. An irritation, perhaps, but not a major problem. As Tabitha had pointed out, Glass House was reputed to be quite large. But the business she intended to pursue on Daventry Island did not come under the heading of normal.

She had her own agenda at Glass House, and that agenda had nothing to do with inventorying the Daventry glass collection.

Twenty-four hours after Adam Daventry had fallen to his death, his lover, Nellie Grant, had drowned in a boating accident. Her body had never been recovered.

The official verdict was that she had been washed overboard into the icy waters of Puget Sound. There had been some speculation that, despondent over her lover's death, she had committed suicide.

Eugenia did not believe that Nellie had taken her own life, and she knew her friend had been experienced with small boats.

The problem was that she could not come up with any other logical explanations for Nellie's death at sea. She only knew she would not be able to sleep well until she got some answers.

She was, after all, the one who had introduced Nellie to Adam Daventry. Any way she looked at it, Eugenia knew that if Nellie had never met Daventry and gone to Frog Cove Island, she would probably still be alive.

"Mr. Colfax can go to the island as a tourist," she suggested in what she hoped was a calm, reasonable tone. "He can browse through the art galleries or hang out in the local taverns. Isn't that the way a *real* professional investigator would go about worming information out of people?"

Colfax did not even wince at the thinly veiled insult, she noticed. But Tabitha's surgically tight jaw became even tighter.

"Mr. Colfax is a very real professional investigator," she said. "He has his own firm, Colfax Security, with two offices on the West Coast, including one in Portland."

"We're planning to expand to Seattle this year," Cyrus said easily.

"Is that so?" Eugenia narrowed her eyes. "Tell me, why does the Daventry estate suspect foul play in Adam Daventry's death?"

"It's not a matter of suspicion," Cyrus said. "It's more a case of what the executors feel was an inadequate investigation by the local authorities. They just want a second opinion, that's all. And they want it done quietly."

"But what possible motive could there have been?" Eugenia demanded.

"Haven't got a clue," Cyrus said.

Eugenia made herself count to ten. "I hesitate to ask, but do you perhaps have any suspects?"

"Nope."

She sighed. "You've asked the Leabrook to provide cover for you, Mr. Colfax. Just exactly how do you expect us to do that? What sort of excuse am I supposed to use in order to explain why I'm spending my summer vacation with you at Glass House?"

Tabitha spoke up before he could respond. "I thought we could send him along as your assistant."

"My *assistant?*" Eugenia swung around in her chair. "Trust me, Tabitha, no one is going to believe for one moment that Mr. Colfax is an assistant curator or anything else involved in the museum business."

Cyrus glanced down at the palm trees on his chest. "Is it the shirt?"

She refused to acknowledge the question. She kept her pleading gaze fixed on Tabitha. "This is not going to work. Surely you can see that."

Tabitha pursed her lips in thought. "He does have a certain eccentric style, doesn't he? Perhaps we could pass him off as a photographer hired to take pictures of the Daventry glass collection. Photographers are inclined toward eccentricity."

"I have never," Eugenia said between her teeth, "met one who looked this eccentric."

"A photographer cover is too complicated, anyway," Cyrus said. "I'd have to bring along a lot of fancy equipment that I wouldn't have time to figure out. Furthermore, there's always the risk that a real photographer on the island might want to talk shop. In which case I'd probably give myself away in the first five minutes. I'm not real good with gadgets."

"Good grief." Eugenia closed her eyes. "It's hopeless."

"Cheer up," Cyrus said. "I have an idea that I think might work."

"Lord spare me." Eugenia cautiously opened her eyes. "What is it?"

"We can go to the island as a couple."

She gazed at him, uncomprehending. "A couple of what?"

"Of course." Tabitha bubbled over with excitement. "A *couple*. That's a wonderful idea, Mr. Colfax."

He gave her a modest smile. "Thanks. I think it has possibilities."

Eugenia froze. "Wait a second. Are you talking about you and me? Together? As a *couple?*"

"Why not?" He gave her what was no doubt intended to pass for an innocent, earnest expression. "It's the perfect excuse for us to spend some time alone together at Glass House."

"Oh, you won't be entirely alone," Tabitha said helpfully. "There's a sort of caretaker-butler on site. The lawyer said his name is Leonard Hastings. He used to work for Daventry. The estate kept him on to look after things, especially the glass collection."

Eugenia knew the name. The box she had received that contained Nellie Grant's clothes and personal effects had been sent back to Seattle by someone named Leonard Hastings.

She planted her hands on her desk and pushed herself to her feet. "This is beyond ludicrous. It's insane. Anyone with a slice of brain can see that it will never work."

Tabitha tilted her head. "I don't know, Eugenia, I think it's a very clever plan."

"Simple, too," Cyrus said. "I'm a big believer in keeping things as simple as possible."

Eugenia realized that the situation was deteriorating rapidly. "It's simple, all right. Simpleminded."

"Everyone's a critic," Cyrus said.

Eugenia tried hard not to grind her teeth. In spite of the abundant evidence to the contrary, she was very sure that whatever else he was, Cyrus Chandler Colfax was not simple.

Her eyes met his, and for a few seconds everything came to an abrupt halt. A frisson of awareness brought all of her nerve endings to full alert.

She knew this sensation. It was the same feeling she got when she looked into one of the first-century B.C. Egyptian glass bowls on display in the Ancient Glass wing of the museum. There was power here. It drew her even as it set off alarms.

In fairness to a civilized society, Colfax should have been required to wear caution flags and a lot of flashing red lights to warn the unwary against approaching too close. The Hawaiian shirt did not do the job.

She was certain that Cyrus's laid-back ways were a facade. She knew that as surely as she knew the difference between fourteenth-century Islamic glass and Chinese glass from the early years of the Qing dynasty. His strong, ruthless hands and enigmatic green eyes told the real truth. Even as she tried to assess him, he was sizing her up with a hunter's focused interest and intelligence.

She was sure that he did not intend for her to learn anything more about him than he wanted her to know.

Two could play at that game, she thought.

Which meant they had a standoff.

She made one last stab at warding off the inevitable. "Tabitha, you can't possibly expect me to work under these conditions."

"Nonsense." Tabitha's shrewd eyes burned with the fires of excitement. "Where's your sense of adventure? Why, if I didn't have so many commitments here in Seattle during the next few weeks, I'd be tempted to go in your place."

Not a chance, Eugenia vowed silently. She had no intention of allowing anyone, not even Tabitha Leabrook, to go to Frog Cove Island in her stead. But she needed to be free to pursue her own plans, and that meant she had to be in charge of the situation. From what little she had seen, Colfax did not appear to be the easily managed type.

She picked up the plump, 1930s-era fountain pen she used to sign official correspondence and lounged back in her chair. "What happens if I simply refuse to cooperate in this fiasco?"

"Easy." Cyrus shoved his hands into his pockets and smiled benignly. "I tell the Daventry estate folks that you won't assist the investigation."

She waited for the other shoe to drop. When Cyrus did not say anything else, she rolled the fat pen between her palms.

"That's it?" she asked.

"Well, not quite," Cyrus said slowly. "After I tell the estate executors that the Leabrook was uncooperative, they will probably instruct their lawyers to tie up the assets of the Daventry estate as long as possible."

Eugenia closed her eyes.

"I figure that a good legal team could probably arrange to keep the Daventry glass collection out of the hands of the Leabrook for four or five years," Cyrus continued. "Maybe longer."

A cold chill went through Eugenia. She opened her eyes and sat very still.

Tabitha's mouth dropped open in shock. "My God, we can't risk that. We must have that glass. It's an incredible collection."

Eugenia watched Cyrus closely. "He's bluffing, Tabitha."

Cyrus raised his brows.

He was not bluffing, Eugenia thought. If she did not cooperate, he would convince the executors to tie up the estate. The Leabrook could wind up spending a fortune fighting for the bequest in court.

"That's blackmail," she said.

"Eugenia, really, that's going much too far," Tabitha chided. "Mr. Colfax is not issuing a threat. He's merely telling us what the executors' reaction will be if he isn't allowed to conduct his investigation."

"Like heck he is. He's threatening us, Tabitha."

Tabitha made a tut-tutting sound. "You're over-reacting, my dear. And it's all moot in any case. I've already agreed to assist him, and not just because it will please the Daventry estate."

"I know, I know," Eugenia said wearily. "You're worried about me."

"I'm being cautious." Tabitha's expression turned serious. "If there is a possibility that Adam Daventry was murdered, the motive might very well have had something to do with his art collection. I do not want you staying alone with all that valuable glass and only that caretaker person for protection."

Eugenia knew when she was beaten. "All right, Tabitha, if you insist, I'll go along with this idiotic scheme."

Tabitha beamed. "Thank you, my dear. It will be a tremendous load off my mind to know that you'll have Mr. Colfax with you at Glass House."

"There is one small stipulation," Eugenia added gently.

Cyrus's gaze sharpened fractionally. "What's that?"

"I get to choose the cover story we use," Eugenia said briskly. "Given the extremely limited range of options, I'll have to settle for the one in which you pose as my assistant."

There was a beat of silence.

"Don't think that one will work real well," Cyrus said.

"Too bad." She glared at him. "It's the only one I'm prepared to consider."

Cyrus nodded. "Mind if I ask why you chose that one instead of the one in which we pose as a couple on vacation?"

She eyed his shirt. "I would have thought it was obvious. It's going to be difficult enough to pass you off as my assistant. But I can absolutely guarantee that never in a million years would it be possible to convince anyone that we were a couple."

"I get it," Cyrus said. "You're trying to tell me that I'm not your type."

She thought about the unsubtle threat he had issued a moment ago. "No," she said. "You're definitely not my type. And there's one more thing I want clear here. I don't know much about private investigators, but I've noticed that on TV they always carry guns."

"I'm a real-life investigator, Ms. Swift, not a TV private eye."

"I trust that means you don't actually carry a gun around with you. I absolutely refuse to share a house with a strange man who carries a gun. I detest guns."

"So do I." Cyrus moved his left shoulder slightly. "I once had a nasty experience with one."

At six-thirty that evening, Eugenia poured herself a glass of chilled sauvignon blanc and went to stand at her living room window. Her condominium was located midway up in a high-rise building in the heart of the city. She had paid extra for the view of Elliott Bay, but she considered the money well spent. Something about vast expanses of water was soothing to her soul.

She had spent the last four months engaged in a major remodeling project, which was finally complete. She had ordered the architect to tear down every wall except those needed for privacy in the bath and bedroom. The background color was white, a perfect foil for her growing collection of West Coast studio glass art. The contemporary glass sculptures glowed on carefully lit pedestals arranged around the room.

An arched entry divided the hall from the white-carpeted living room. A low, white sofa and white leather chairs together with some glass tables comprised the furnishings.

The only color in the room besides the brilliantly hued glass sculptures was around the gas fireplace.

Eugenia studied the hand-painted amber and green tiles that formed the fireplace surround. Nellie Grant had designed them for her.

The last time she had seen Nellie was here in this very room. The remodeling had been in its final stages. The wall beside the fireplace had still been open and tiles had been stacked on the floor, when Nellie appeared at the front door. That had been the morning after Adam Daventry had fallen to his death.

Rather than wait for the private ferry that served Frog Cove Island, Nellie had used Daventry's launch to get to the mainland. She had rented a car and driven an hour and a half into Seattle.

She had definitely not been grieving.

> *You were right, Eugenia. He was a bastard. I should have listened to you. I'm not sorry he's dead. I know that sounds awful, but it's the truth. I have to return to the island this afternoon to get the rest of my stuff, but after that I never want to see the place again.*

Eugenia glanced at the painting above the recently completed fireplace. It was one of Nellie's works, the first in a series called *Glass*, she had explained. It depicted a late-nineteenth-century French vase from the Daventry collection. Nellie had captured the rich, vibrant colors and the enthralling effects of light shining through the glass.

> *Daventry said that since he had no children for me to paint, he wanted me to do some portraits of*

*his favorite glass pieces. I did four of them before
he died. Now that he's gone, I figure they belong to
me. I want you to have this one, Eugenia. Sort of
a housewarming gift. You've been terrific about encouraging my work.*

Nellie had been eager to get her career as an artist
under way. Eugenia suspected that was one of the
reasons she had fallen victim to Daventry's charm. He
had convinced her that he could introduce her to the
right people and get her work hung in the most prestigious galleries.

Eugenia walked, slipper-shod, across the new white
rug. She paused beside a pedestal and gazed into the
swirling green depths of a whimsical glass sculpture
that had been created by a young artist in Anacortes.

Watching the play of light on beautiful glass always
helped her to clarify her thoughts.

After a moment she reached for the phone on the
table beside the sofa. She flipped open a card file and
found the home number of her friend at Mills & Mills,
the firm that handled the Leabrook's security.

The same intuition that she relied on so heavily
when it came to art was sending small warning signals
concerning Cyrus Chandler Colfax. It told her that he
was not what he seemed.

"Sally? Eugenia. I need a favor from you."

"It's nearly seven." Sally Warren sounded startled.
"Are you still at the museum?"

"No, I'm home." Eugenia sank down onto the arm
of the sofa. "I'm going out of town the day after tomorrow. I need some information."

"Finally going to take a vacation, huh? About time.
I'll bet you can't even remember the last one you
took."

Eugenia frowned. "Of course I do. I went to England two years ago."

"And spent all of your time in the glass collections at the Ashmolean and the British Museum. But we'll let that pass. What do you need?"

"Mills & Mills has been in the security business for a long time, right?"

"Thirty years," Sally agreed.

"You must know all of the other major security firms on the West Coast."

"Probably. Why?"

"I met one of your competitors today. Cyrus Chandler Colfax. Ever heard of him?"

There was a short, startled silence on the other end of the line.

"Colfax?" Sally sounded distinctly cautious.

"Yes. Do you know him?"

"I've never met him, but I've heard about him. I wouldn't call him a competitor. He doesn't go after the same business. Mills & Mills specializes in museum security. Colfax usually does corporate and private stuff. Very exclusive. Very expensive."

Eugenia tightened her grip on the phone. "What can you tell me about him?"

"Wait a second, you're not thinking of moving the Leabrook account to Colfax Security, are you?"

"No, of course not. But I want to know whatever you can get on him."

"It will take me a while. Mind if I ask why you need to know about Colfax?"

"Because I'm going to spend my summer vacation with him."

· 2 6 ·

Two

"*L*evel with me, Cyrus, what kind of pressure did you use on Jake to get him to show up for Rick's graduation?" Meredith Tasker held wisps of blond hair out of her eyes. "Did you threaten to turn him in to the IRS for income tax evasion? Tell him you'd sabotage his latest business negotiations, maybe? Or did you go for the more direct approach and hire some professional leg-breakers?"

Cyrus leaned back against the fender of his dark green Jeep. He folded his arms and studied the scene in the crowded high school parking lot.

It was a clear, warm day in Portland. Perfect weather for a graduation, he thought. The ceremony had ended a few minutes earlier. Parents, some vastly relieved, others triumphant, stood in small groups and congratulated each other on having survived the experience of getting a teenager through high school. Their exuberant, newly graduated offspring, glorying in their sense of immortality and unlimited futures, clustered in various energetic flocks. Laughter and elated shouts drifted across the grounds.

"I don't know what you mean, Meredith. Jake wouldn't have missed Rick's graduation for all the high stakes deals in Southern California."

"That son of a bitch missed his own mother's funeral because some business came up in New York that required his personal attention. Come on, I was his wife. I know him better than anyone. What did you do to get him here today?"

Cyrus shrugged. "Nothing much. I had my secretary call his office last week to remind him of the date."

There was no need to add that as soon as his secretary had gotten Jake Tasker on the phone, Cyrus had taken over the call. The conversation had been short and to the point.

"I told you, I can't make it," Jake Tasker said from his L.A. office. "I've got business. Rick will understand."

"Let me put it this way, Tasker. Either you put in an appearance at Rick's graduation, or my next phone call will be to Harry Pellman."

Tension hummed over the line. "What do you know about Pellman?"

"I know he's one of your biggest clients."

"What of it?"

"He owes me a favor," Cyrus said softly.

A year ago he had retrieved an exquisite and extremely valuable seventeenth-century Flemish tapestry that had been stolen from Pellman's private collection. There had been complications because the thief happened to have been Pellman's recently discarded lover. Pellman had wanted the matter handled with absolute discretion.

Colfax Security prided itself on absolute discretion.

"What the hell are you talking about?" Jake asked warily.

"If I suggest to Pellman that he find himself a new broker, he'll pull his account from your firm and transfer it to one of your rivals in about ten seconds flat," Cyrus said.

"Christ, I don't believe this. You'd tell Pellman to dump me just because it's not convenient for me to go to Rick's graduation ceremony?"

"Yeah. That about sums it up. I'm glad we understand each other, Tasker."

"You are a real bastard, you know that?"

"I'll look for you in the audience."

Cyrus pushed the memory of the conversation aside and gave Meredith a reassuring smile. "Like I said, Jake wanted to come."

Meredith's mouth curved faintly, but her eyes remained grave. "All right, I won't push it. I'll just say thank you, the way I've thanked you over and over again for the past five years. I don't know what I would have done without you, Cyrus. I owe you more than I can ever repay."

"You don't owe me anything."

"That's not true, and you know it. Every time I think of how you stepped in after Jake walked out . . ."

"I'm Rick's uncle, remember? I had a right to step in and lend a hand."

Meredith looked across the parking lot. Cyrus followed her gaze and saw Jake Tasker and Rick moving toward them through the crowd.

"You were only married to Katy for two years," Meredith said quietly. "Hardly enough time to saddle you with a sense of obligation toward her family."

"Whatever I did, I did because I wanted to do it,"

Cyrus said. "Not because I felt obligated. Don't ever forget that."

She glanced at him quickly with a troubled expression. "Rick was so excited when Jake showed up today. He hasn't seen him in months. You know how it is, the out-of-town act always gets the most applause."

"It's okay, Meredith." Cyrus looked at Rick and wondered, not for the first time, what it would be like to have a son of his own.

"Rick is still very young," Meredith went on earnestly. "When he matures a little and looks back on his teenage years, he'll understand that it was you, not Jake, who got him to manhood without any major disasters. He'll be grateful."

"I said it's okay, Meredith. I don't want Rick's gratitude. Hell, I'm grateful to him. We had some good times together."

"I know that he hasn't paid much attention to you today, but it's only because Jake showed up with his usual flashy gifts. That kind of thing is distracting to a kid that age. You mustn't think that Rick doesn't appreciate all you've done."

"Forget it."

She grimaced. "When I think of how you spent what little vacation time you had with him these past few years and most of your weekends, too—"

"Like I said, good times. Guy stuff." Cyrus smiled fleetingly at the memories of the camping and rafting trips, the karate classes, and the dive lessons.

He and Rick had done the kind of things that fathers and sons were supposed to do together. His own father had not stuck around to do them with him, and his mother had died in a car crash a few months after he was born. But he'd been lucky, he thought. He'd had his grandparents.

Back in Second Chance Springs there had been no money for karate classes and dive lessons, but that was beside the point. Beau had taken him fishing and hunting from the time he could walk. Cyrus had learned how to shoot, how to track game, how to survive in the desert, and how to find his way through the mountains without a map.

He no longer hunted, but the lessons he had learned had stayed with him. He still did some fishing when he got the chance. There was something about the long silences and the stillness of fishing that suited him. Fishing was important, even when you didn't catch anything.

His grandmother, Gwen, had taught him how to read, how to grow roses in the desert, and about fifty different ways to prepare tuna fish.

He knew he'd learned other things from his grandparents, things that were less easily put into words but that were infinitely more important. Things that some people thought were old-fashioned and out of place in the modern world.

They were things that were rooted in the very center of his being and that, on the rare occasions when he happened to be in an introspective mood, he realized defined him in some elemental way.

Katy had never comprehended or understood that deeply embedded part of him. Few people ever had.

There were some who would claim that the stuff Beau and Gwen had taught him was not especially suited to life in the modern world. But Cyrus knew better. He knew that it was the things he had learned from his grandparents that had made it possible for him to survive in that world.

"You claim that you were there for the good times with Rick," Meredith said. "But I'll never forget that you were there for the bad times, as well. I almost lost him, Cyrus. We both know that. He took the divorce hard."

"He was only thirteen. Tough age for a kid to go through his parents' divorce."

"There is no good age. He went wild those first few months after Jake left. Staying out all night. Hanging out with kids who were using drugs and alcohol. Shoplifting. It seemed like he was either moody or angry all of the time. I was scared to death."

"It's over, Meredith. He's graduated high school with honors and he's off to college in September."

"Because of you." She grimaced. "I still shudder when I think of the time the police called to tell me he had been picked up and taken to the station."

Desperate, panicked, and alone, Meredith had turned to Cyrus that night. It was Cyrus who had climbed out of bed to handle the aftermath of the incident that had involved alcohol, a fast car, and a group of kids who were growing up too fast and too hard without adult supervision.

At the start of their association, Rick had been filled with a deep, cynical distrust. Cyrus was his uncle, but only by virtue of the recent marriage to his aunt, Katy.

"Why did you come to get me?" Rick demanded as they walked out of the police station. "Where's Mom?"

"She's at home."

"She should have come, not you."

"I'm your uncle."

"Bullshit. You only married Aunt Katy six months ago. You hardly know me."

"Something tells me we're going to get better acquainted real quick." Cyrus unlocked the car door. "Get in."

"I'll take the bus home."

"It's two in the morning." Cyrus did not raise his

voice. He never raised his voice. "Get into the car. You've given your mother enough grief for one night."

Rick hesitated. The streetlight caught the sheen of frustrated anger in his eyes. Cyrus knew the kid wanted to find strength and fortitude in his lonely defiance, but it had been a long night.

"Screw it," Rick said. He flopped down onto the passenger seat.

Cyrus walked around the front of the car and got in behind the wheel. "You're lucky," he said as he turned the key in the ignition. "You got picked up by well-trained, professional cops."

"You call that lucky?"

"I was sixteen when I got pulled over by a sheriff back in my hometown. He beat the crap out of me before he let me go."

Rick stared at him. "You serious?"

"Yeah."

"Did your folks sue?"

Cyrus smiled grimly. "Spoken like a true child of the modern age. No, my folks didn't sue. My father wasn't around. He disappeared before I was born. My mother got killed by a drunk driver when I was only a few months old. That left my grandparents. They didn't have the money to file a lawsuit."

"So what did you do?"

"Learned a valuable lesson." Cyrus pulled away from the curb. "Made sure I didn't get stopped by a cop again."

"No, I mean what did you do to make that sheriff beat you?"

"I dated his daughter."

Rick gaped at him. "He arrested you just for going out with her?"

"Officially, Sheriff Gully stopped me for speeding.

But we both knew he was pissed because he'd found out that I had spent the evening with his precious Angela."

"But why would he beat the shit out of you for that? I mean, it was just a date. Big deal."

Cyrus slowed to a halt at a stoplight and turned to look at Rick. "It wasn't quite that simple. I'd convinced Angela to go out with me because I knew her father would be pissed if she did it. And I was right."

"You *wanted* to piss him off?"

"Yeah."

"How come?"

"Because a few days earlier I'd heard him tell old Earl Dart down at the grocery store that I'd never amount to anything. That part didn't bother me much because I'd never figured the sheriff for being too smart, anyhow."

"So what was it he said that made you mad?"

"He went on to tell old Earl that he felt sorry for my grandparents, but everyone knew that no one could expect much from me because my mother had been a tramp who'd gotten herself knocked up at eighteen. He said my father had probably been married or something because she had never told anyone who he was. Then Gully said that he sure wouldn't want his daughter getting involved with me."

Rick whistled softly. "So you asked Gully's daughter to go out with you as a kind of revenge?"

"Yeah. I knew that Gully would be furious when he discovered what had happened."

"If you knew this Gully bozo that well," Rick said slowly, "you must have figured that he'd probably beat the crap out of you when he found out you'd dated Angela."

"Sure."

"So why'd you do it?"

"I couldn't think of any other way to balance the scales."

"What about Angela?" Rick asked. "What did she think of all this?"

"That's a very good question. The answer is that she wanted to go out with me because she was mad at her steady boyfriend and wanted to teach him a lesson."

"So she was using you?"

"We used each other," Cyrus said. "Neither one of us was seriously interested in the other."

"Damn." A shudder went through Rick. "You were willing to let that Gully guy beat you up in order to balance the scales?"

"Okay, so I wasn't as bright at sixteen as you obviously are at thirteen," Cyrus said. "The good news is that I've learned a lot since then."

Rick looked unwillingly fascinated. "Like what?"

"Nowadays when I decide to even the score, I'm a lot more careful. I try real hard not to get the crap beaten out of me if I can possibly help it."

Cyrus eased the memories of that first serious conversation with his nephew aside as he watched Rick and Jake approach the Jeep. He was aware of Meredith's tension as she waited beside him.

"I think Rick hated me for a while at first," she whispered.

"He didn't hate you."

"He blamed me for the divorce."

"He was thirteen. He was mad. He needed a target, and you were the only one around. Kids that age aren't rational or logical about that kind of thing. Hell, most adults aren't, either."

"Except you." Meredith snatched a tissue from her purse and hastily dabbed at her eyes. She gave Cyrus a watery smile. "You're always calm and rational. Always in control. Were you born that way?"

He smiled slightly. "As Grandpappy Beau used to say, there are only two ways to go through life. You're either in control or out of control. I picked the former."

"Solid as a rock. No wonder Katy wanted to marry you the day after she met you."

"The feeling was mutual."

The image of Katy slid through his memories. It was a picture of a woman who could have stepped straight out of a Renaissance painting. There had been an ethereal quality about her. He had taken one look at her and known that she needed to be protected from the world.

But in the end he had failed to keep her safe. Damien March had used her and then murdered her in cold blood. Officially, Katy had died at the hands of an unknown carjacker, but Cyrus had never believed that story. He was certain that March had killed her because she had known too much about his plans to disappear with the Hades cup.

"It's so unfair that you and Katy had so little time together," Meredith said.

"Don't think about the past, Meredith. There's no profit in it. You've put your own personal life on hold long enough. Tell Fred you'll marry him and put him out of his misery. He's a good man."

"Maybe I'll do that."

"Hey, Mom, Uncle Cyrus, guess what?" Rick came to a halt in front of them. His eyes flashed with excitement as he glanced at his distinguished-looking father. "Dad says he's going to buy me a car at the end of summer so that I can have it when I go to college in the fall. I won't have to take your old Honda, Mom."

Meredith raised her brows. "It's not that old."

Jake avoided Cyrus's eyes as he clapped Rick on the shoulder. "The kid will need his own transportation at college. I'll check back in August to make the final arrangements."

"Fine," Meredith said. "I'm sure Rick will have picked out the car he wants by then."

Rick laughed. "You can say that again."

"It's settled, then." Jake glanced at his wristwatch. "Hell, look at the time. I'd better be on my way. My flight back to L.A. leaves at three."

Disappointment doused the excitement and pleasure that had been in Rick's eyes a second earlier. "You're leaving already, Dad?"

"Got to run." Jake gave a what-can-you-do shake of his head. "I have a meeting with some people in Newport Beach this evening. You know how it is."

"Yeah." Cool acceptance replaced the disappointment in Rick's expression. "I know how it is. Glad you could make graduation."

"Wouldn't have missed it. Not every day my only son gets out of high school. Take care of yourself. Good luck with the summer job. I'll give you a call when I get a chance."

"Sure."

A short silence descended on the three people left standing beside the Jeep as Jake turned and walked off toward his rental car.

"Got plans for tonight?" Cyrus asked finally.

"What?" Rick swung back around to face him. "Oh, yeah. Alan and Doug and some of the others are coming to the house this evening. Mom said we could have a party."

Meredith winced. "I'm going to dinner with Fred. I don't think I could take a house full of kids celebrating graduation. Want to join us, Cyrus?"

"I'll take a rain check," he said. "I'm going out of

town for a while. I've got some business to take care of tonight before I leave."

"Where are you going?" Rick asked.

"Frog Cove Island."

"Never heard of it."

"It's in Puget Sound. One of those little islands off the coast. A lot of artists live there."

Rick nodded. "How long will you be gone?"

"I'm not sure. A couple of weeks, maybe."

Meredith smiled. "Are you finally going to take a vacation, or is this a job?"

"It's a job."

"Sorry to hear that." Meredith gave him a speaking glance. "You could do with a vacation, Cyrus. I can't even recall your last one."

"I've been a little busy for the past three years."

Her mouth twisted in rueful acknowledgment. "I know."

"See you when you get back?" Rick asked in a seemingly offhand manner.

"Sure," Cyrus said. "We'll go fishing."

"Okay, then." The last of the coolness vanished from Rick's eyes. "Guess I'd better get out of this stupid hat and gown."

"I expect to find the house in one piece when I return tonight," Meredith said.

"Don't worry." Rick started to turn away.

"Don't forget our deal," Cyrus said softly.

Rick grinned. "Not a chance." The long folds of his gown flapped around him as he whirled and started off toward his friends.

Meredith glanced at Cyrus. "What deal?"

"No booze and no getting into a car with anyone who's been drinking."

"I don't know what I would have done without you, Cyrus." Meredith stood on tiptoe and kissed him lightly on the cheek. "You know, one of these days you should take a real vacation."

The following afternoon Cyrus eased the Jeep into one of the two short lines of cars waiting for the small, privately operated ferry to Frog Cove Island. It took him less than sixty seconds to spot Eugenia Swift.

She was in the silver Toyota Camry at the front of the other row of vehicles. Her window was rolled down. He could see that she was speaking to someone on a cellular phone. There was no way to overhear the conversation at this distance, but he could tell that she was very intent on it.

He studied the boldly sculpted planes of Eugenia's face while he punched in a number on his own phone. She was not especially pretty, let alone beautiful, but there was a striking vitality about her that made it hard for him to look away. Her dark hair was pulled back into a sleek knot at the nape of her neck. She wore a close-fitting, long-sleeved black pullover that accentuated her slender, lithely built frame. She had fine-boned wrists and high breasts.

He was too far away to see the color of her eyes, but he remembered that they were a very rich shade of amber.

Sleek and smart. Wore a lot of black. Liked long scarves.

The arty type. Probably wouldn't know what to do with a can of tuna fish.

The impression he had formed at their first meeting held firm. She looked like a lady cat burglar.

The ringing on the other end of the line stopped.

"Quint here."

"This is Colfax." Cyrus watched the way Eugenia's elegantly shaped fingers curved competently around the steering wheel. "What have you got for me?"

"Nothing to get excited about," Quint Yates said. "I hate to disappoint you, but the lady seems to have led what used to be called a blameless existence."

"Nobody leads a completely blameless existence." Cyrus kept his eyes on Eugenia as he spoke to his assistant. "Give me what you have."

"Very little beyond what you already know. Graduated from the University of Washington with a degree in Fine Arts and an expertise in glass. Studied in Venice for a while. Went to work for the Leabrook Museum as an assistant curator. Endeared herself to Tabitha Leabrook the first year on the job when she persuaded Dorothy McBrady to put her collection of fifteenth-century Venetian glass on permanent loan in the museum."

"Go on."

"Our Ms. Swift sailed on to new heights a year later when she detected a forgery in a collection of early-Roman cameo glass that had been loaned to the museum for an exhibition. She pulled off the same trick again six months later when she curated a display of eighteenth-century Chinese glass."

"She found another fraud?"

"Yep. After that, her reputation was made. Major glass collectors routinely consult her."

Cyrus was not surprised. He had known she was good. During the past three years he'd made it his business to be aware of the art experts who specialized in glass. "Anything else?"

"Two and a half years ago Tabitha Leabrook promoted her to the position of Director of the Leabrook Museum and gave her a whopping budget. You know the rest."

"Yeah." The museum's collection of ancient and modern glass was well on its way to becoming one of the best in the nation. Even the big European museums respected the Leabrook for its depth and quality. A new wing featuring contemporary studio glass art had recently been completed.

"She gets job offers from other institutions all the time," Quint said. "But she routinely turns them down."

"I have a hunch it's because she enjoys the authority she has at the Leabrook." Cyrus watched Eugenia through the window. "She pretty much gets to run the whole show there. Something tells me she's the kind who likes to be in charge."

"That's it on the professional side."

"What about the personal angle?"

"Not much there, either. Thirty years old. Never been married. Oldest of three children. Brother and sister both went into academia. One teaches at a college here in Oregon. The other is an assistant professor at a school in California."

"Parents?"

"Also academic types. They divorced when Eugenia was fourteen. Her mother went back to school to get her Ph.D. She now teaches in the women's studies department at a college back East. Her father is in the sociology department at a Midwestern university."

Cyrus groaned. "That fits."

"With what?"

"With the way she looked down her nose at me the first time we met. She's one of those highbrowed intellectual types."

"Could have been your shirt."

"Nah, couldn't have been the shirt. I wore my best one. Any lovers?"

"Couple of relationships that lasted a while, but nothing serious for the past year and a half. She has what you might call business dates, but that's about it. Actually her sex life reminds me a lot of yours. Nothing very interesting going on."

"You can skip the editorial remarks. No one is more aware of my boring sex life than me. Anything else?"

"Not much. She lives alone and apparently likes it that way. Her idea of a vacation is a trip to a world-class museum."

"Okay, that's all for now as far as Ms. Swift is concerned."

"Right."

"Anything new on the Connoisseurs' Club angle?"

"I've got all of the names and addresses. I'm starting the background checks."

"You know how to reach me if you come up with anything." Absently, Cyrus severed the connection. He did not take his eyes off Eugenia Swift. She was still on the phone.

Something important, he decided. He could feel the intensity of the conversation from here. Funny how much you could tell just by watching a person's body language.

Eugenia was annoyed. Irritated. Impatient. Frustrated. He smiled to himself. She was drumming her fingers on the steering wheel. Some people could not sit still for more than five minutes at a time.

He, on the other hand, could stay still for hours when necessary. His grandfather had taught him the secret of stillness. It was a hunter's trick.

Cyrus considered his quarry in the Toyota. According to Quint, she was unlikely to be arguing with a lover because she did not have one. Therefore, by process of elimination, he was forced to the conclusion that she was probably discussing him.

The fierce battle that she had fought to keep him from accompanying her to Frog Cove Island raised a lot of interesting questions. He had been mulling them over since the meeting in her office.

If her only goal on the island was to combine a vacation with the task of inventorying the Daventry glass, she should not have had the reaction she'd had when she'd discovered that he was going to accompany her.

It would have been understandable if she had been merely annoyed or put out by the prospect of sharing Glass House with him. But Eugenia had been genuinely alarmed. He'd seen the brief flare of real panic in her eyes before she'd managed to conceal it.

He was a major problem, not a minor nuisance, for her.

He wondered why.

There was, of course, one all-too-obvious explanation. It was just barely possible that Eugenia had picked up the same rumors that he had. If she was on the trail of the Hades cup, he had some very big problems, himself.

He opened the door of the Jeep, got out, and walked toward Eugenia's car.

"I understand that you don't have too much, Sally." Eugenia narrowed her eyes against the glare of sunlight on water and watched impatiently as the small ferry prepared to take on passengers and vehicles. "Just give me what you've got."

"The most interesting thing is that Colfax was once half-owner of a company named March & Colfax Security."

"What's so interesting about that?"

"Three years ago the firm collapsed after something went very wrong on a transport job. Armed robbery. The details are amazingly scarce. I couldn't even find out the name of the client, let alone what got stolen. But Colfax was shot in the process."

Eugenia sucked in her breath. "*Shot?* As in, with a *gun?*"

"Yes. It gets worse. While he was in the hospital, his wife was the victim of a carjacking. She was killed. The cops found her car but not the murderer."

"My God."

"Damien March, the other partner in March & Colfax Security, disappeared at about the same time."

"What do you mean he disappeared? Was he killed, too?"

"That was the conclusion of the authorities, but they never found the body. The object, whatever it was, that was stolen in the course of the robbery vanished, too."

Eugenia frowned. "What about insurance claims?"

"None were filed."

"This is getting a little bizarre, Sally."

"My thoughts precisely. Look at it this way, maybe you'll have something interesting to write home about after this year's summer vacation."

Eugenia ignored that. "Anything else on the personal side?"

"Just basic stuff. Mother died shortly after he was born. No info on his father. Colfax was raised by his grandparents. Dropped out of college to take care of them during the last year of their lives. After they died, he worked as a cop in a medium-sized town in California for a while. Eventually quit to go into business for himself as a private investigator. That's about it on the early years."

A large, dark object loomed between the open car window and the bright sun. Eugenia suddenly found herself in dense shadow. Her fingers closed convulsively around the phone. She turned her head quickly and jumped when she saw Cyrus Colfax looking down at her. The glare off his mirrored sunglasses nearly blinded her.

"I've got to go, Sally."

"Not so fast. This is beginning to sound interesting. What's he like?"

"Who? Colfax?"

"We're not talking about Santa Claus."

"You can say that again." She did not take her eyes off Cyrus. "The only thing I can tell you at the moment is that he drives a Jeep, and he wears aloha shirts and those tacky mirrored sunglasses."

"Uh-oh. Not your type, huh?"

"Definitely not."

"Oh, well," Sally said. "Try to enjoy your vacation, anyway. You need one."

"I'll try." Eugenia pushed the button to end the connection. She summoned a superficially polite smile. "Hello, Mr. Colfax. Lovely day, isn't it?"

"I think we'd better talk."

"Certainly. But not now. The ferry is boarding." She put on her own sunglasses, a green-tinted, oval pair that had a well-known designer's name embossed on the frame.

She turned the key in the ignition, put the Toyota in gear, and without another glance at Cyrus, drove quickly down the ramp.

Three

The passenger-side door of the Toyota opened shortly after the ferry pulled away from the dock. Cyrus settled down on the seat beside her. He left the door ajar and kept one moccasin-shod foot on the deck.

"Let's try this conversation again," he said a little too pleasantly.

He was right there in the car with her. Much too close for comfort. Eugenia realized that her breathing had become shallow, as if he had somehow sucked out most of the oxygen in the vicinity. She was torn between a sudden urge to get out of the car and the equally strong impulse to find out what brand of aftershave he used.

This was insane.

Shocked by her reaction, she froze for a few seconds. Like a computer locked up by a jolt of lightning, she thought, disgusted and a little horrified.

But Cyrus was overwhelming at close quarters. In

the mirrored sunglasses, he was no longer an avenging gunslinger of the Old West. He was now an avenging lawman from the far more dangerous future.

She wondered if he had brought along a pair of handcuffs.

Damn, damn, damn. The fact that she was fantasizing about him like this was definitely not a good sign, she thought. She had not had any really interesting fantasies about a man for a very long time. In fact, lately, she had started to think about getting a cat.

Cyrus looked at the door handle on her side. He said nothing, but she sensed his amusement.

She was annoyed to discover that she had a death grip on the handle. Very deliberately she released it and draped her hand casually over the steering wheel.

In her professional capacity as the director of the Leabrook she routinely dealt with wealthy, powerful, influential people. She was not about to let one lone private detective in an aloha shirt fracture her composure.

An ancient bit of wisdom whispered through her head. *Keep your friends close, but your enemies closer.* She could not avoid Cyrus for the next two weeks. Therefore, the only smart thing to do was keep a close watch on him. It was in her own best interests to learn as much about him as possible.

She stared straight ahead at the offshore fog bank that concealed Frog Cove Island. "I realize you must get asked this question a lot, but I can't resist. Why the aloha shirts?"

"I'm on vacation. Just like you."

"Frog Cove Island isn't exactly Hawaii, and I thought you said you were going there to investigate Daventry's death, not take a vacation."

"Funny you should mention the subject of vacations," Cyrus said. "I've been wondering why a hard-working museum director like you would spend her time off on a project that could be handled just as easily by one of the Leabrook's other curators."

"The Daventry glass is an extremely important acquisition for the Leabrook. I wanted to inventory it myself."

He shrugged. "The executors of the Daventry estate want to be satisfied that Daventry's death was an accident. What's more, they're willing to pay well for answers. It should be a simple, straightforward job. Thought I'd combine my time off with the opportunity to make some easy money."

She knew that he was lying to her. He wasn't even bothering to be earnest or clever about it. It was as if he didn't care if she believed him. And she, of course, was lying to him. She supposed that evened things out in a peculiar way.

She wrenched her gaze from the rapidly approaching fog bank and made herself look at Cyrus with a degree of professional detachment. It occurred to her that she might be able to learn something about the process of investigating a possible murder from him. She would have to be subtle about it, she reminded herself.

"If you're a genuine investigator, you must have read the reports and talked to the police who investigated Daventry's death," she said. "What do you think happened to him?"

"Frog Cove Island doesn't have what you'd call a professional police department. From what I could find out, it's got someone called Deputy Peaceful Jones."

Eugenia considered that. Not the name on the report that had been filed on Nellie. Her death had been investigated by the team from the mainland that had conducted the search-and-rescue effort.

"Interesting name," she murmured.

"Yeah." Cyrus's mouth curved fleetingly. "At any rate, he's the one who wrote up the report on Daventry. There was a party at Glass House the night Daventry died. Lots of alcohol, and reading between the lines of Deputy Peaceful's report, I'd guess some other drugs as well."

On her last visit to the condo the day after Daventry's death, Nellie had mentioned his taste for designer drugs, Eugenia reflected. *When he was on them he felt like a god. Tried to act like one, too.*

"I see." Until she discovered what Cyrus's real agenda was, she did not dare let on that she knew anything about Daventry or that she was looking for a woman who had been at the party the night of the accident.

"No one actually saw Daventry take a header down the stairs," Cyrus continued. "But there's no reason to think that it wasn't an accident."

She blew out a breath and tightened her hand on the steering wheel. "In other words, you aren't really going to Frog Cove Island to look for evidence of a murder."

"Let's get something straight here, Ms. Swift. I promised my clients peace of mind. That's what I intend to give them."

She drummed the fingers of her right hand on the back of the car seat. "I wonder who put the notion of possible foul play into the minds of the Daventry estate executors."

"Are you implying that I talked them into hiring me?"

"Did you?"

"Now, why would I do that?" he asked softly.

"Gee, I don't know." She saw her own reflection in the mirrored sunglasses. "Maybe the security business is a little slow this time of year. Maybe this looked like an easy way to bill the estate for a lot of excessive fees. Maybe you're the private detective equivalent of an ambulance-chasing lawyer."

"Come, come, Ms. Swift. No need to be polite. Why don't you just come right out and say what you think?"

His failure to take offense at the insult emboldened her. "I don't even want to imagine the bill the estate is going to receive after you waste a couple of weeks puttering around Frog Cove Island supposedly looking into Daventry's death."

"Don't worry, the estate has plenty of money to pay for my services."

She pounced. "So you admit that this is some kind of expensive scam you're running. You're wasting the estate's money on a sham of an investigation."

"For the record," Cyrus said very deliberately, "I always endeavor to give satisfaction to my clients. The Daventry estate executors want reassurance. They'll get it."

She did not have to be psychic to figure out that she had crossed some invisible line. It had taken a lot of pushing, but she had finally managed to annoy him with the accusation that he intended to fleece his clients.

She had crawled far enough out on this limb, she thought. Time to ease her way back to a safer position.

"What happens if you don't learn anything more than what this Deputy Peaceful person already came up with in his report?" she asked, genuinely curious.

"Then I tell the executors that Daventry's fall really was an accident."

She wished she could see his eyes. Then again, maybe it was better that they were concealed behind the tacky shades. "What's your best guess?"

His mouth twitched at the corner. "My best professional guess is that it was an accident."

"Why am I not surprised?"

"I'm getting the impression that you don't trust me, Ms. Swift."

She wondered if she should worry about the prickling sensation at the nape of her neck. "I can't imagine where you got that idea."

He uncoiled from the seat with a deceptively lazy movement that did not quite camouflage the economic grace of the action. He closed the door, braced one hand on the roof of the car, and leaned down to talk to her through the open window.

"The interesting part," he said, "is that I feel pretty much the same way about you."

Outrage swept through her. "What's that supposed to mean?"

He smiled. "I don't trust you, either, Ms. Swift. But I will give you some free advice. Don't make the mistake of underestimating me."

"I don't place a lot of value on stuff I get for free. You know what they say, you get what you pay for."

He nodded once, apparently accepting her decision. "Okay. If you want to pay full price, be my guest. But I don't intend to make the same mistake with you."

"Is that right?"

"You bet. I have great respect for your professional expertise. You did a hell of a job with that exhibition of ancient glass at the Leabrook last spring."

That stopped her cold. "You saw 'Through a Glass, Darkly'?"

"Flew up from Portland three times to take it in. You had both quality and depth in the collection. What's more, you managed to create the kind of publicity excitement that pulls in the crowds." He paused. "I especially liked the fourth-century Roman pieces."

"Yes. Well, thanks." She was chagrined by the warming effect his blatant flattery had on her. She was also baffled. "You toured the exhibition *three* times?"

"Yeah. Brought my nephew, Rick, with me once. He liked it, too. Good for a kid that age to think about the past a bit."

She squelched the treacherous little bubbly sensation that threatened to override common sense. If Cyrus had switched tactics from unsubtle warnings to outright compliments, there was a reason. She had to be on her guard.

"I didn't realize you had a personal interest in old glass," she said coolly.

"I've only been into it seriously for about three years. There's something intriguing about objects made out of such fragile material that have survived for so long, isn't there?"

The three years rang a very loud bell. According to Sally Warren, Cyrus had been wounded in the course of a robbery three years ago. His wife had been killed in a carjacking. His partner had disappeared and was presumed dead. And the stolen object, whatever it was, had vanished.

And it had all happened three years ago.

It didn't require her several academic degrees and her assortment of professional credentials to deduce that something was very, very wrong here.

"Glass is an amazing substance," she said, carefully. "And not necessarily fragile. It can be made tough enough to withstand the impact of a bullet."

"Like Grandpappy Beau used to say, it just goes to show that strength comes in a lot of different forms." Cyrus straightened as if he intended to walk back to his Jeep. But he paused when a sudden thought seemed to occur to him.

"You said you don't put a lot of stock in free advice, but there's something else you should know about me."

"Really?" She smiled blandly. "What's that?"

"When I take a strong personal interest in a project, I tend to be a little obsessive. Smart people do not get between me and what I want."

Cold, ghostly fingers touched the back of her neck. "We're back to threats, I see. Somehow they suit you better than the chitchat about ancient glass."

"Any chance of an honest truce, here? Life will be simpler and far more pleasant if we don't spend all of our time going for each other's jugulars."

"You surprise me. I would have thought you thrived on other people's jugulars."

"Only as an occasional snack, not as a regular diet. Guess this means no truce, huh?"

"Guess so." There could be no truce with a man who was not telling her the truth.

"Your boss wanted you to think of me as a precaution."

"Yes, I know," Eugenia said politely. "Rather like a flu shot."

He nodded. "Yeah. Or a condom."

She glowered at him. "Whatever Tabitha thinks, I do not need a bodyguard, and furthermore, I do not like the way you went about convincing her that I might need one."

"Okay. Have it your way." He turned and walked back down the aisle between the two lines of parked cars.

Eugenia sat back and folded her arms. *Arrogant bastard.* He had deliberately tried to intimidate her. The bad news was that he had almost succeeded.

The question was, why had he gone to the effort?

She studied him in the rearview mirror as he re-turned to his car. He moved with the unhurried, gliding stride of a man who did not know what it was like to be off-balance either mentally or physically. She wondered what it would take to make him move fast.

It would have to be something really, really important, she decided.

As if he knew that she was watching him, he glanced back at her when he opened the door of the Jeep. Light glared fiercely on the surfaces of his mirrored sunglasses. She quickly averted her eyes, but she knew that he had seen her. She had not missed his faint, satisfied smile.

The small ferry plowed into the wall of fog. A featureless, gray mist closed around the craft and its passengers, sealing them off from the sunlight and the rest of the world.

Eugenia listened to the slap of the waves against the hull of the boat and wondered how she was going to share a kitchen with Cyrus Chandler Colfax.

Four

The man who had once been Damien March reclined in a white lounger positioned on a gleaming white tile deck at the edge of a turquoise blue pool. He sipped a gin-and-tonic from a nineteenth-century Baccarat glass and surveyed the expanse of azure Caribbean sea that lay beyond a profusion of brilliant red frangipani.

All his life he had worked toward the goal of surrounding himself with beauty and perfection. He lusted after the beautiful and the perfect the way other men lusted after sex. Money, he had discovered long ago, was the key to possessing both. Money bought power, and power could purchase many beautiful, perfect things.

Here on this remote island he had come very close to creating paradise for himself. For the most part he was satisfied with his pristine, private world.

The government of the small, independent island he had chosen for his new home prided itself on being extremely accommodating. The attitude of the local officials was that money and those who possessed it should not be subjected to the sort of irritating rules and laws that interfered with the natural flow of business.

Here in paradise, for a price, one's privacy was completely protected. Discretion was the watchword. Banking and investment transactions were never questioned. One's business associates were not subjected to embarrassing investigations or humiliating searches at the local airport.

Best of all, the government was happy to issue its own passport in any name one chose to anyone who was willing to pay the price. The current fee was one million dollars. A bargain as far as the man who had once been Damien March was concerned. Indeed, he had been so pleased with the deal that he had insisted upon giving the helpful officials a gratuity of five hundred thousand dollars.

But every paradise, he had discovered, even his, had its serpent. The disloyal viper who had stolen the Hades cup from him had paid for his crime. His body had washed up onto the beach just below the white villa not long after the cup had disappeared.

The former Damien March had been extremely annoyed by the death of the thief. Obviously the person or persons who had bribed the creature to steal the cup had wanted him dead before he could be found and made to talk.

The murder had been a very intelligent move on the part of those who had arranged the theft of the cup, but it had left the ex-Damien March with virtually no clues and no trail.

Fortunately he knew of a private investigator who was not only remarkably talented when it came to getting results, but who was also, at least in this case, awesomely motivated to find the Hades cup.

"Another drink, sir?"

The ex-Damien March looked at the woman who stood in front of the lounger. She wore only the bottom half of a small, white thong bikini. Her breasts were high and full. Enhanced, he decided, but the surgery had been well done. Her hair was the color of gold, and her eyes were as blue as the sea. Contact lenses, he thought, but what the hell. When it came to human beings, nothing was one hundred percent perfect, no matter how much one paid. That was why he preferred art to people.

"No, my dear. I have some work to do. Ask the chef to serve lunch out here by the pool."

"Yes, sir." She turned and walked back into the cool shadows of the villa.

The former Damien March studied the twin globes of her buttocks. He couldn't be certain from this distance, but he feared that they were starting to lose some of their buoyancy. He would have to start thinking about a replacement. He did not look forward to the task. Good help, *perfect* help, was so bloody hard to find.

He put down the gin-and-tonic, sat up on the edge of the lounger, and reached for his laptop. It was time to get a status report on the missing Hades cup.

He booted up the computer and checked the encrypted messages from his people on the West Coast. They were short, but encouraging.

. . . Colfax has made contact with the director of the Leabrook Glass Museum in Seattle. They have both gone to Frog Cove Island (off coast of Washington). Staying in a private home. Former owner of the house, Adam Daventry, collected glass. Died in a fall last month. Apparent accident . . .

Interesting. Colfax was on to something at last. The ex-Damien March smiled to himself and took another sip from his glass of gin-and-tonic. Cyrus Chandler Colfax reminded him of the old saying about the mills of the gods. Colfax ground slowly, but he ground exceedingly fine.

He had put the right investigator on the case, the ex-Damien March thought. If anyone could find the Hades cup, it would be Colfax. Once Cyrus had recovered the cup, he would be relieved of it. And then he would be killed. This time, the ex-Damien March thought, he would make certain of the results.

He had always known that sooner or later he would have to get rid of Colfax. It was the old story of the tortoise and the hare. Eventually, through sheer, dogged persistence, the tortoise always caught up with the fleeter, smarter hare, leaving the hare with no choice but to make turtle soup.

Assured that things were moving forward on the main front, the ex-Damien March opened another computer file. For the past three years he had kept his eye on a politician from California who had shown excellent potential.

Zackery Elland Chandler II was now running for the Senate. It was a very tight race against an incumbent, but Chandler was two points ahead in the polls.

The man who had once been Damien March had owned many fine things in his life, but he had never owned a U.S. Senator. It was time to think about adding one to his collection.

The blackmail note was waiting for Zackery Elland Chandler II when he booted up his computer to read his e-mail.

Old sins cast long shadows. The young woman from Second Chance Springs died a long time ago, but her connection to you has survived. I'm sure you'll be happy to know that the link to your past can be kept quiet. For a price.

Zackery stared at the screen in disbelief. A crank, he thought. It had to be a crackpot. He double-checked the e-mail account to see if he had accidentally accessed the wrong one. He maintained two. One had an address that was widely available to the public. The second was for his business and personal use.

He was in his private account, the one with the address that was not widely circulated.

He read the note again. Politicians got a lot of strange mail. Most of it could be ignored. It would have been easier to dismiss this message if it were not for the reference to Second Chance Springs. The name of the small spot in the road near the California-Mexican border rang a very distant bell.

There had been a woman once, a student at the small college he had attended his freshman year. She had worked part-time as a waitress in a coffee shop near the campus. He had dated her for a while. Slept with her a few times. He could not recall her name, but he had a vague recollection of her telling him about her boring life in a place called Second Chance Springs and how she yearned to escape.

She had made him nervous, however, when she talked about her future. He had made it clear that she should not look to him for help with her plans. He had his own agenda, and it definitely did not include marriage for several more years.

He had not spelled out the rest of it, which was that when he did marry, his bride would not be an unsophisticated little nobody from a place like Second Chance Springs.

His goals had been mapped out for him by his father at a very early age. Zackery was headed for a law career followed by public office.

When he was young, Zackery had done everything he could to please his impossible-to-please father. But by the time he went off to college he had internalized the elder Chandler's goals. Zackery wanted the future that had been decreed for him. After the death of his father, he had wanted that future with even more fervor.

He had achieved the first goal with a lucrative law career. When the time had come, he had moved into the political arena. He had used his success in California state politics to establish a reputation that, according to the polls, could take him into that most exclusive of all clubs, the U.S. Senate.

It had all been astonishingly easy up to this point. He was fifty-four years old, and he was doing what he had been born to do. There had been no serious setbacks in his life, no major tests, no hard choices to make.

Maybe it had been too easy.

He tore his eyes off the computer screen and looked at the framed picture of his wife, Mary, and his son and daughter.

The coffee shop waitress from Second Chance Springs had been nothing more than a brief fling at the end of his freshman year. Jesus, he'd only been nineteen years old.

He had transferred to an East Coast college the following fall and never looked back. He had made certain to leave no forwarding address at the coffee shop.

Damn. He could not even remember her name, let alone what she had looked like.

Five

Cyrus dropped his duffel bag and two of Eugenia's expensive-looking red leather suitcases onto the front steps of Glass House. He eyed the massive, stainless steel doors that guarded the structure.

Glass House was well named, he thought. It was all bright, reflective surfaces and see-through walls. Heavy glass blocks formed a frame for the gleaming doors. Beyond the doors the house was mostly walls of thick, double-paned glass that revealed the building's steel skeleton. There was one solid portion that ran the length of one side of the third story. A veranda with clear acrylic panels wrapped the lower story.

Glass House was perched on an isolated bluff at the far end of Frog Cove Island. The exotic architecture should have resulted in a light and airy appearance, Cyrus thought. He wondered why it didn't look like a big, gossamer-winged butterfly sitting here overlooking the Sound. What it actually resembled was a large, squat beetle armored in a glass carapace.

He studied the electronic code box next to the door. "Daventry believed in top-of-the-line security."

"Not surprising." Eugenia set her red leather garment bag and red leather cosmetic case down beside the rest of the matched set of luggage. "He had a fortune in glass to protect."

"I can see a lock like this in the city, but it seems a little extreme for Frog Cove Island. It's not like they've got a crime problem around here. I checked. Last major event was a boat stolen out of the marina. That happened eight years ago."

"I should think you would appreciate expensive security systems." She glanced around at the looming trees. "I wonder where the caretaker is. He was supposed to be here to meet us and let us inside."

"Maybe he went into Frog Cove to pick up groceries or something."

"No problem." Eugenia opened the flap of her sleek leather shoulder bag. "I've got the code."

He took the piece of paper from her and glanced at it. Written in bold, flowing handwriting, which could only have been Eugenia's, was a string of numbers and the words *Daventry house security code*.

He cleared his throat politely. "Anyone ever point out that it's generally not a good idea to carry around a key code that's clearly labeled like this? Someone steals your purse, he's got instant access."

She smiled a little too brightly. "More free advice?"

"Forget it." He turned to punch in the code. "You knew Daventry, right?"

"We met." Her voice was suddenly very cool.

"Ever been here to Glass House?"

"No." She hesitated. "What made you ask?"

"I heard he liked to throw big parties. Invited the local art crowd and some off-island friends from the art world. Just wondered if you'd ever been one of his guests."

"No, I was never one of his guests, and I resent the interrogation."

"Just curious." He watched the green light wink on in the code box. There was a series of clicks as the lock disengaged. "Daventry's last lover was someone who used to work at the Leabrook. Her name was Nellie Grant."

"My, my. You have done some homework."

"Did you know her well?"

"I knew her, yes."

Her brittle tone brought all of his instincts to full rev. He pushed open one of the twin steel doors. "See much of her after she came out here to stay with Daventry?"

"No, I did not. She died the day after Daventry did. Washed overboard on her way back here to the island." Eugenia hoisted her garment bag and cosmetic case and prepared to step past him. "Don't waste your breath on any further questions, Colfax. You can't put me down in your notebook as a contact to prove how industrious you were to your clients. I have no intention of participating in your fraudulent investigation."

Nellie Grant's name definitely meant something to her. The link between the Leabrook's former employee and Adam Daventry had been worrying Cyrus. But a small piece of the puzzle had just clicked into place. He had never been a big believer in coincidence. Now he was more certain than ever that Eugenia's involvement in this situation was anything but coincidental.

He wondered if she had known Adam Daventry far more intimately than she had implied. She claimed that she had never been on the island, but she might have lied. When he had launched his initial inquiries, one of the first things he had discovered about Daventry was that the man had had a long string of lovers. All of them had been either artists or women who were closely connected to the art world.

The possibility that Eugenia might have been one of those lovers could not be overlooked. He had a strong suspicion that a mutual fascination with old glass would have been a powerful lure for her. When she chose a lover, he thought, she would seek out a man who shared her interests. The arty, highbrowed, sophisticated type.

Daventry definitely had fit the profile.

Cyrus wondered if Eugenia and Nellie Grant had been rivals for Daventry's affections. Nothing beat a lovers' triangle for complicating a situation. Throw in an extremely valuable object such as the Hades cup, and you had a real sorceror's brew.

Be a hell of a twist, he thought, if it turned out that Daventry actually had been murdered. But he'd already run that possibility through his brain and examined it from every angle. It didn't work.

When you got right down to it, shoving a man down a flight of stairs was simply not a reliable way to kill him. There was a high probability that the victim would only break an arm or a leg, instead of his neck. As murder went, it was sloppy and unprofessional.

If there was one thing Cyrus thought he could be nearly one-hundred percent sure about it was that anyone clever enough and resourceful enough to attempt the theft of the Hades cup would be a real pro.

No, Daventry's death had to have been an accident. It was the only thing that made sense. That meant that the odds were high that the Hades cup had not been stolen the night Daventry died. It might still be hidden here in Glass House.

He felt the adrenaline sleet a little more quickly

through his blood. After three long years, he was closing in at last. He knew it with that certainty he always felt when a case was coming together.

He punched in the code and opened the door. Hoisting the duffel bag and the two red suitcases, he stepped aside to allow Eugenia into the hall. When he made to follow, he nearly collided with her. She had come to an abrupt halt on the other side of the threshold.

"Good heavens," she whispered, awed. "Daventry really did like glass."

Cyrus removed his sunglasses and examined the gleaming, three-story atrium hall. A monumental chandelier was suspended from the ceiling. It was a many-tiered waterfall of peridot green glass. The walls of the hall were mirrored from floor to ceiling. The mirrors reflected an elegant, curved staircase fashioned of glass bricks and stainless steel. There was an elaborate, decorative pattern traced in glass mosaic tiles beneath Cyrus's feet.

There was also a small, engraved sign just inside the hall.

Visitors are asked to kindly
remove their shoes.

A small stack of paper slippers sat next to the little sign.

"Yeah, I guess he did," Cyrus said.

"This is incredible." Eugenia put down her bags and stepped out of her shoes. She gazed around in amazement.

Cyrus was amused by her wonderstruck expression. "Looks like a very expensive carnival fun house, if you ask me."

"It's spectacular," she breathed. "It will make a fantastic inn."

"Each to his own, I guess."

He trailed after her as she walked slowly down the hall. When she reached the kitchen entrance, she halted once more and glanced inside with an apprehensive air. Then she visibly relaxed.

"Thank God," she said. "An espresso machine."

Cyrus looked over her shoulder. "Hot damn, an electric can opener."

Rain, the steady summer kind, struck shortly before midnight. Eugenia was aware of the time because she was sitting up on one side of her bed, gazing at the glowing numerals on the face of the French cut-glass clock that sat on the glass nightstand.

After nearly two hours of determined effort, she had abandoned the attempt to sleep. She was restless and strangely tense after spending the evening alone in the house with Cyrus. Leonard Hastings had not put in an appearance.

Given the atmosphere of watchful challenge that existed between herself and Cyrus, dinner had actually gone surprisingly well. Both of them had brought sacks of groceries. Hers had been filled with pasta, little jars of pesto sauce, bottled spring water, a loaf of good Seattle bread, and a couple of bottles of sauvignon blanc and zinfandel wine.

His had been loaded with a dozen cans of tuna fish, frozen microwavable dinners, and a couple of six-packs of Pacific Express beer.

"I probably shouldn't ask," Eugenia said, "but what do you intend to do with the tuna fish?"

"You'd be amazed." He removed a plastic-wrapped bag of sandwich bread from one of the sacks. "A little mayonnaise, some pickles, and a couple of slices of bread and you've got dinner."

"It sounds more like a tuna fish sandwich."

"Same thing." He eyed the package of pasta in her hand. "What are you planning to eat tonight? Macaroni and cheese?"

"Not exactly." She put the pasta down on the counter and reached back into the sack. "It's been a long day. I think I'll just whip up something quick. Maybe some fresh asparagus and pasta with pesto sauce."

"Fresh asparagus, huh?"

The wistful note in his voice made her glance up quickly. She frowned when she saw the way he was looking at her asparagus. "Don't get any ideas."

"Your asparagus is safe." He sounded hurt. "I promise I won't steal any of your pesto, either." He turned to stack his tuna fish cans in a cupboard.

Eugenia flushed. If he had tried to make her feel churlish, she thought, he had succeeded. "I suppose there's enough asparagus for two."

"I wouldn't think of taking some of it. Besides, I don't know any recipes for tuna and asparagus."

She glared at his broad back as he continued to stack cans of tuna. "Oh, what the heck. I've got enough pesto sauce for both of us. If you like, I'll cook dinner tonight."

Cyrus paused, a can of tuna in his hand. He did not turn around. "That's real nice of you."

"But you have to clean up afterward."

He finally turned to face her. He looked sincere and grateful, but there was a suspicious gleam in his green eyes.

"Deal," he said.

She wondered if she had just been had.

At the end of the meal, he had surprised her with

his apparently genuine appreciation. She was tempted to ask him when he'd last had a good, homecooked meal, but she had ruthlessly crushed the nurturing instinct. Her intuition warned her that she must not show any weakness around Cyrus Colfax. He would be quick to take advantage.

They had broken bread, her excellent chewy sourdough, not the cheap, aerated white stuff that he had brought with him, in relative harmony. After two glasses of zinfandel and a couple of cans of Pacific Express, they had reached the mutual decision to delay a detailed exploration of Glass House until the following day.

Eugenia had gone to bed exhausted, but she was too keyed up to sleep.

She got to her feet and went to the massive armoire on the far side of the room. The black jeans she had unpacked earlier were draped over a hanger inside. She took them down and stepped into them. Next she pulled on a black top and slipped her feet into a pair of black ballet-style slippers.

She reached inside a suitcase for the small flashlight she had packed. Better not to turn on any lights, she thought. Cyrus might wake up and start asking questions.

The truth, she thought wryly, was that she had no idea what she was doing. She did not know how to conduct an inquiry into a murder. She only knew that she had to start somewhere, and that Glass House was the obvious place.

It was ironic that she found herself sharing the house with a professional investigator, but she did not dare ask Cyrus for help.

Cautiously, she opened her bedroom door and walked to the balcony rail. She looked down into the atrium. Darkness cascaded in waves down the staircase.

For a moment she hesitated, uncertain how to satisfy the restlessness that had kept her from sleep.

She remembered that Nellie had once mentioned in passing that she had used a room on the third floor of Glass House as a studio. If she had left her mark anywhere in this house, it might be there.

It was as good a place to start as any other.

Eugenia turned and walked along the balcony toward the staircase. Her slippered feet made no noise as she tiptoed past Cyrus's door.

She had almost reached the staircase when she saw that the darkness down below was not nearly so absolute as it had been a moment ago.

At first she thought that her eyes had adjusted to the tomblike atmosphere. But her instincts did not buy that easy explanation. Neither did her common sense.

A chill shot through her.

She switched off the flashlight and went to the railing to peer down. There was a slender wedge of light angling from a crack in the door that opened onto the basement stairs.

Even as she watched, the light shifted slightly. Someone with a flashlight was standing at the top of the basement stairs.

Anger poured through her. There was only one other person who could be creeping around Glass House tonight. Cyrus had waited until he thought she was asleep, and then he'd set out to explore on his own.

She'd known from the beginning that he was up to no good.

She leaned as far out over the railing as possible. "What do you think you're doing, Colfax?"

The light from the basement winked out abruptly. Whirling, Eugenia dashed to the staircase.

"How dare you sneak around like this in the middle of the night?" she yelled as she pattered swiftly down the stairs. "I knew you had something up your sleeve."

She reached the floor of the hall and raced to the basement door. It was closed now. She yanked it open and stumbled to a halt at the top of the steps. Thick darkness severed only by the beam of her own flashlight greeted her. Cyrus was lying low in the shadows.

"Come out of there, Colfax. I knew Tabitha should never have trusted you. I don't care what the Daventry estate lawyer said."

She groped for the wall switch and found it. But when she turned it on, nothing happened.

She started cautiously down the steps, her flashlight trained on the floor below.

"Don't you dare try to frighten me, Cyrus. It won't work. I want to know what's going on here. What do you think you're doing?"

A large, powerful hand closed around her shoulder from behind. Eugenia was so shocked, she could not even scream.

"I was just about to ask you the same thing," Cyrus said from the step above her.

"Cyrus." She froze and then turned around so quickly she hit him in the midsection with the flashlight.

"Umph." His hand went to his ribs.

He had obviously just gotten out of bed. His hair was tousled and his chest was bare. She could not help but notice that it was a very broad chest. The triangle of curling hair on it tapered down over a flat, hard stomach and disappeared into a pair of chinos.

Eugenia stared at him, eyes widening. "Oh, my

God. If you're up here with me, then that means someone else is down there."

"Brilliant deduction." Cyrus snapped the flashlight out of her hand as he moved past her. "Stay here."

He plunged down into the darkness at the bottom of the stairs.

"Oh, no, you don't," Eugenia muttered. "You're not going anywhere without me. I don't trust you one bit, Colfax."

Six

He would have enforced his instruction to Eugenia to stay put in a more emphatic manner if it had not been for the cold draft that swirled through the cavernous basement. It told Cyrus his quarry had already escaped.

He came to a halt at the bottom of the stairs and braced himself as Eugenia, hard on his heels, plowed straight into him.

"What in the . . . ?" She recoiled from the collision and grabbed the wooden bannister. "Why did you stop? He'll get away."

"You don't follow orders very well, do you?" He found a second light switch and snapped it. This one worked. A fluorescent tube winked on overhead, revealing a long passageway between rows of storage rooms. "I told you to wait at the top of the stairs."

"I've always felt that following orders showed a sad lack of creativity."

"Or common sense."

She ignored that as she straightened and swept a sultry mass of hair out of her eyes. "Where is he?"

"Gone. Whoever he was, you scared him off." Cyrus surveyed her with a sidelong glance.

She looked more than ever like a cat burglar tonight. Her jeans fit her as if they had been hand-tailored. The denim fabric hugged her hips and nipped in at her waist, emphasizing her sleek frame. He wondered what kind of store sold tailored jeans. A very expensive one, no doubt.

Her black pullover looked just as pricey as her jeans. Trained, experienced investigator that he was, he noticed immediately that her firm breasts shifted easily beneath the fabric. *Ah-hah, Watson. The lady is not wearing a bra.*

That observation immediately raised the issue of whether or not she had bothered to put on a pair of panties beneath the snug jeans. That was the thing about his chosen career path, he thought. In his line of work one question always led to another.

She had apparently used only her fingers to comb her thick, dark hair. It billowed, soft and loose, around her shoulders.

Not just any cat burglar, he decided. A very sexy cat burglar.

"How can you be sure the guy is not hanging around here somewhere?" she demanded, staring past him down the hall.

"Feel that damp air? It's from outside. The door at the far end of the basement is open." Cyrus walked forward along the passageway. "He went out through the pantry."

"Damn." She hurried after him. "I'll bet he was after my glass."

"*Your* glass?"

"The Daventry glass belongs to the Leabrook now," she said austerely.

"That doesn't make the glass yours."

"You know what I mean."

"I'm getting a fair idea," he said. "Are you this possessive about everything you consider yours?"

"There's no need to get sarcastic just because I take my job seriously." She frowned. "We'd better check the glass vault."

"I want to take a quick look outside first. Just in case."

"Just in case what?"

He glanced back at her. "Just in case he was dumb enough to hang around."

"Good lord." Her eyes widened. "You can't go chasing out of the house after him. It's past midnight. There's nothing but forest out there, and in case you haven't noticed, the rain is still coming down very hard."

"I noticed."

"Whoever he is, he knows his way around, and you don't. It would be a complete waste of time to rush out into the woods to look for him. Not to mention a little stupid."

"Yeah, but it's the sort of bold move that impresses clients."

She glared. "Your clients aren't here at the moment."

"Good point. Speaking of stupid moves," he added laconically, "I should mention that a few minutes ago you didn't hesitate to pursue our visitor down here into the basement."

"That's when I thought he was you."

"Which reminds me, I want to thank you for that little display of trust."

She had the grace to blush. "Okay, so I assumed

that you were up to no good. What was I supposed to think under the circumstances?"

"Beats me. Maybe that I was upstairs asleep in my room?"

"I had no reason to assume that you were innocently asleep," she said.

"Especially given the fact that you were not innocently asleep, yourself. Which brings up a very interesting question. Just what are you doing running around at this hour of the night?"

"I couldn't sleep," she muttered. She glanced at the gleaming stainless steel door on the right. "What if he got into the glass vault?"

Cyrus glanced at the code box beside the vault door. "Relax. It's still locked."

"You're right." Her eyes narrowed as she studied the unblinking green lights. "But whoever he was, he obviously knew his way around the house. This may not have been his first visit."

"I'd say that's a certainty."

"For all we know, he's been raiding the glass vault on a nightly basis since Daventry's death. When we open that door we may discover that there's not a single piece left inside. Damn, we should have checked it when we first arrived this evening."

"Take it easy. Leonard Hastings was here to keep an eye on things, remember?"

"Yes, but there's no sign of him tonight."

For some reason he felt compelled to try to soothe the rising anxiety he could hear in her voice. "We'll take a look in a few minutes."

He was not overly concerned with the contents of the glass vault. Logic and common sense told him that Daventry would not have stored an object as dangerous and as valuable as the Hades cup in a collection that was frequently shown to visitors and guests. If the cup was here at Glass House, it would be well concealed.

"We'll need to get all the house locks reprogrammed first thing tomorrow." Eugenia sounded as if she were jotting down notes. "I wonder if Leonard Hastings knows how to do it, or if we'll have to send for a computer locksmith from the mainland."

"I know this brand. I can reprogram them."

"You can?" She sounded surprised and somewhat dubious.

"You know, a lesser man might be easily crushed by your lack of respect for his professional skills."

"Something tells me you don't crush very easily." She paused, frowning. "I just had another thought. Whoever was down here tonight had to know that the house was occupied. Both of our cars are parked in the drive."

"I don't think we're dealing with a very smart burglar here."

"It's a big house. Maybe he assumed it would be safe to enter it, even knowing it was occupied. Burglars break into inhabited homes every day of the week."

"Little did he know that you'd be prowling around in the middle of the night waiting to pounce on him."

Her chin came up swiftly. "I was not prowling."

"What would you call it? You sure as hell weren't sleepwalking." He came to a halt in front of a door that stood ajar. Cold night air poured through the crack. He could see the shadows of the unlit pantry at the top of the narrow flight of stairs. "Are you sure you don't want to tell me why you were taking a midnight tour of the house?"

"There's nothing to explain. I just wasn't sleepy, that's all." She examined the door. "So this is how he entered and left."

"Looks like it."

She gave him a worried glance. "He knows the house security codes, Cyrus."

"Yeah."

"Who would have access to them?"

"Could be anyone, I guess, but there is one real obvious suspect."

She searched his face with a quizzical expression. "For heaven's sake, who?"

"Leonard Hastings."

She blinked a couple of times. "Good thinking. Of course, he would know the codes. You're right, he's definitely a suspect."

"I can't tell you how much your good opinion means to me."

"Very funny. You know, the fact that he wasn't here to let us into the house is very strange. Downright suspicious, in fact. I wonder if he planned to steal the Daventry glass before we arrived and didn't quite finish the job."

"Let's not leap to any more conclusions. Hang on while I take a look around."

He went up the steps and pulled the pantry door fully open. Another door, the one that opened onto the veranda, was flung wide. He contemplated the darkness and the dense forest that loomed just beyond the edge of the clearing. Rain dripped steadily from the eaves.

"Be careful," Eugenia called as she climbed the basement stairs behind him.

"You're a fine one to talk. But don't worry, I'm not going out there." He closed the door on a gust of wet air and relocked it. "No point in it. The rain will have wiped out any footprints. Our man is long gone, and like you said, he knows his way around and I don't."

"I suppose we ought to report this to that Deputy

Peaceful person you mentioned." She frowned. "But I'm not sure how much good it will do."

"I think it's safe to say it won't do any good at all. This kind of crime rarely gets solved, especially if nothing was taken."

"I'll go get the security code for the glass vault. I want to see if there's any sign that the intruder got into the Daventry collection." She went past him into the pantry. "I'll be right back."

Cyrus listened to her retreating footsteps. Interesting that she did not have the security code with her even though she was up, dressed, and busily sneaking around in the middle of the night, he thought. It implied that whatever her goal had been, she had evidently not planned to pay a midnight visit to the glass vault.

He wondered where she had been going when she'd spotted the intruder.

And just to complicate things, he wished that she had been headed toward his bedroom.

He sighed as he walked back along the basement hall toward the glass vault. Obviously his prolonged stretch of celibacy was beginning to impact his thinking processes. He knew that he was capable of controlling himself and the situation, but that knowledge did nothing to ease the tightness in his lower body.

She was not his type, he reminded himself. He did not go in for lady cat burglars. Furthermore, there was far too much riding on the outcome of this project to screw it up by screwing around with a woman he could not trust. He had to keep his priorities straight. The Hades cup came first.

A moment later she appeared at the top of the basement stairs. She looked flushed and breathless from her hasty trip to and from the second floor.

"I've got the code." She hurried down into the

basement. "I swear, I don't know what I'm going to do if we open that door and discover that all of the Daventry glass is missing. What a catastrophe that would be. Tabitha would never get over it."

Cyrus could not resist. "You could always hire a trained professional investigator to find it for you."

She gave him a speaking glance as she halted in front of the steel vault door. "I suppose the next thing you're going to tell me is that you're available to take on the job?"

"I might be able to make room in my schedule. Assuming that we could agree on a fee, of course."

"Don't hold your breath." She unfolded a piece of paper and studied the numbers written on it. Then she raised her eyes to the security lock. "Okay, here goes."

Cyrus glanced down the intersecting passage and saw a winking red light. "Hold it."

She paused, one finger hovering over the code box. "What's wrong?"

"This door is still locked, but the one at the end of that hall is not."

She moved away from the steel door and walked to the intersection. "I didn't notice that door earlier."

"Neither did I." Cyrus led the way to the door at the end of the hall.

It was stainless steel, just like the door of the glass vault. It was tightly closed, but the code box indicated that it was unlocked.

"The lawyer gave Tabitha a code for one room down here, not two," Eugenia said. "Maybe that lock takes the same code as the glass vault."

"I doubt it."

"But why would there be two security-coded doors?" Frowning, she stepped briskly around him and hurried down the passage.

She stopped in front of the steel door and tugged on the handle. The door opened slowly. Cyrus came up behind her as she looked through the widening crack.

"It's a wine cellar," she announced. "I should have guessed. Daventry considered himself a connoisseur of wines as well as art. There's probably a fortune in old vintages down here." She wrinkled her nose. "What on earth is that awful smell?"

The stench that spilled from the opening was all the warning Cyrus needed. "Oh, shit. Wait, don't—"

He clamped a hand around her shoulder to pull her back, but he was too late. Eugenia had already found the light switch on the inside wall.

She stiffened beneath his hand, her face twisted with shock as she stared into the wine cellar. *"Oh, my God."*

Cyrus jerked her out of the doorway and stepped into the opening. The wine cellar was mirrored like all the other rooms in Glass House. Light from the overhead fluorescent tube gleamed dully on hundreds of dusty wine bottles.

It also shone coldly on the body that lay crumpled facedown on the floor.

Cyrus took a handkerchief out of his back pocket. He crouched down beside the dead man and carefully tugged the wallet out of a worn back pocket.

He flipped it open and studied the driver's license inside. "We've found Leonard Hastings."

Eugenia wrapped her hands around the hot mug of tea that Cyrus had placed in front of her. "I can't believe it." She realized she had said that several times in the past ten minutes. "I just can't believe it. I wonder how long he's been there?"

"A while. Three or four days, at least." Cyrus

plucked the tea bag out of his mug and tossed it into the clear acrylic trash container. He walked across the kitchen and sat down at the glass table opposite Eugenia.

He had put on a shirt. This one had brilliant orange and pink birds of paradise all over it. Eugenia told herself she was glad he had covered himself, but she knew she was not going to be able to forget the sight of his bare chest anytime soon.

"When I talked to him on the phone a few minutes ago, Peaceful Jones said it was probably a heart attack."

Eugenia frowned. "How does he know that?"

"He said his wife is the local doctor. She's been treating Hastings for a bad heart for years. Apparently Hastings took a lot of medication. According to his license, he was seventy-three."

Eugenia took a swallow of tea. Her eyes met his over the rim of the mug. "Know what I thought when I first saw him lying there?"

"Yeah." Cyrus leaned back in his chair. "That he'd been murdered. Don't feel bad, that was my first thought, too."

She shuddered. "Did Jones say how long it would take him to get out here?"

"About forty minutes. He's bringing his wife, the doctor, with him. He said there's one first aid car on the island. They'll use it to take Hastings back to the clinic."

"Then what?"

Cyrus shrugged. "He said there's no funeral home on the island. Usual procedure is to call an air ambulance service to transport the body to the mainland. He said his wife handles that end of things."

"I feel terrible." Eugenia gulped tea. "Here I was

thinking what a lousy caretaker Leonard Hastings was."

Cyrus studied her with an enigmatic expression. "We've got about half an hour before Deputy Peaceful and the first aid car arrive. I think we'd better go over our story."

She stared at him, bewildered. "I beg your pardon?"

"It's been an eventful evening. We've got a dead body down in the basement, and we chased a prowler out of the house tonight. That kind of stuff tends to be a little stressful even if you're used to it. And I don't think you are."

Eugenia bristled. "If you think I'm going to fall apart when Deputy Peaceful gets here and blow your stupid cover story, relax. I can handle it."

"I'm not so sure about that. I think you're playing out of your league, Ms. Swift."

A trickle of panic whispered through her. How much did he know, she wondered. How much had he guessed? Why did he care? She made herself take several deep breaths.

"What do you mean by that?" she asked as calmly as possible.

He put down his mug, sat forward, and folded his arms on the table. His green eyes were coldly intent, deadly serious. "I've had enough of the fun and games. Let's put our cards on the table. I'll show you mine if you'll show me yours."

She narrowed her eyes. "So you admit you've got a secret agenda here?"

"Yeah. And I know damn well you've got one, too. Tell me why you're really here on Frog Cove Island. We may be able to work together."

"What makes you think I'm here for anything other than a working vacation?"

His mouth curved faintly, but his eyes stayed cold. "As Grandpappy Beau used to say, just because a man moves a little slow and talks a little slow, it doesn't mean that he thinks a little slow. You're here because of the Hades cup, aren't you?"

Her jaw dropped. "The Hades cup?"

"Skip the innocent act. We don't have time."

She swallowed. Maybe she had a bigger problem on her hands than she had realized, she thought.

"Are you speaking of *the* Hades cup?" she asked carefully.

"There's only one that I know of."

"As in the fourth-century A.D. cage cup that's supposed to have been brought back to England from Italy by the Earl of Radstone in the early nineteenth century?"

Cyrus raised his brows. "I see you're familiar with it."

"Are you crazy?" She was beyond stunned surprise, she realized. She was beginning to get downright scared. She was sitting alone in a very weird house with a dead body in the wine cellar and a large delusional man in the kitchen.

"No, Eugenia, I'm not crazy. Neither are you. Talk to me. Fast."

She wet her lips with the tip of her tongue. *Don't lose it now.* The deputy and the doctor would be here in a few minutes. All she had to do was keep Cyrus talking until they arrived.

"I know a little something about the legend, of course," she said. "But the cup, itself, hasn't been seen by a reliable witness since the early eighteen hundreds. Most experts think it was destroyed in the last century."

"It exists," Cyrus said. "It's been in a series of private collections. I saw it myself three years ago."

Three years ago. When he had been shot. When his wife had been killed. When his partner disappeared. When an extremely valuable object had vanished.

Impossible.

"You probably saw a forgery," she suggested gently. She strained to hear the crunch of tires on the graveled drive.

"It was the real thing. My partner, Damien March, and I were hired to see that it got to our client. But March set me up. He stole the cup, and then he murdered my wife, Katy, to cover his tracks."

She tightened one hand in her lap. "Are you telling me that it was the Hades cup that you and your partner were hired to protect three years ago?"

Cyrus looked mildly impressed. "I see you've done some research on me."

In a horrible kind of way, his story fit with what Sally Warren had managed to dig up on him. She stared at him, trying to decide if he was sane and dangerous or a candidate for a locked ward in a mental hospital. Neither possibility had a soothing effect on her nerves.

"Let me get this straight," she said. "Are you here because you think that Adam Daventry owned the cup?"

"He bought it a few months ago when it came up for auction on the underground art market."

"My God." *The Hades cup.* If it really existed, it might be sitting downstairs right this very minute. Eugenia pushed back her chair and leaped to her feet. "The vault . . ."

"Forget it." Cyrus looked coldly amused by her sudden excitement. "Assuming it's still here in the house, it will be well hidden. Only a fool would have kept it on display with the rest of his art collection. Daventry was no fool."

"This is too bizarre to be believed." Sanity returned. The Hades cup did not exist. Everyone in the world of glass knew that. She sank slowly back down into her chair.

"You said the Daventry estate hired you to look into Daventry's death." She searched his face. "Are you telling me that was true? Do you think he was murdered for the cup?"

Cyrus hesitated. "No. I don't. Odds are, the fall was an accident."

"What makes you so sure?"

"No pro would have tried to commit murder with such an uncertain method," he said calmly.

"You're saying that anyone who was after the Hades cup would be a pro?"

"Yeah. That's what I'm saying."

His steady, unwavering gaze convinced her that he believed everything he was telling her. He might be crazy, but he was not deliberately lying to her.

"So you did con the estate into hiring you," she whispered. "You needed a cover to get into this house to search for the cup."

"I picked up the rumors that the cup had resurfaced a few weeks ago. It took me a while to trace the leads. By the time I realized that Adam Daventry had bought it, he was dead, the Leabrook was preparing to acquire his collection of glass, and the estate was getting set to sell the house. I had to move quickly, and I didn't have many options."

She tensed. "What makes you think the cup is still here?"

"I don't know for certain that it is here," he admitted. "It's possible that it was stolen by one of the other members of the Connoisseurs' Club the night he died, but I doubt it."

"Why?"

"Daventry didn't trust his friends. The members of the Connoisseurs' Club enjoyed showing off their acquisitions to each other, but the bottom line was that they were all rivals. He would not have told any of them where he hid the cup."

"Why is it so important to you to find the Hades cup? Do you intend to sell it?"

"I don't want the damned cup." His eyes were frozen pools of green ice now. "I want the man who stole it three years ago."

A fresh wave of unease rolled through her stomach. "I see."

"I need the cup to find him. It's the only thing that will lure him out of hiding."

She swallowed again. "You really believe that your ex-partner stole it, don't you?"

"I don't think it was Damien March. I know it." There was not an ounce of doubt in his voice. "He murdered my wife in the process."

"Dear God, Cyrus. Are you sure? Do you have any proof? I understood your wife was killed in a carjacking."

A flicker of surprise came and went on his gunslinger's face. "You really did do your research, didn't you? The carjacking was staged by March to cover his tracks. The only way to prove any of it is to get my hands on him. And to do that, I need the Hades cup."

"You're sure March is still alive and that the cup was recently stolen from him?"

"Every scrap of rumor points in that direction. This is the first solid lead I've had in three years. I have to follow it to the end."

"What makes you think that the cup will bring him out into the open?"

"March will do whatever he can to get it back. He

was obsessed with it three years ago, and obsessions like that don't change."

He sounded as if he knew what he was talking about, she thought. Maybe he did. He was obviously obsessed with finding Damien March.

Cyrus watched her steadily. "Okay, I showed you my hand. Now it's your turn. Tell me where you fit into this. And don't give me that garbage about being here to inventory the Daventry glass collection."

She raised her chin. "I certainly didn't come here because of the cup. I only have your word that it exists. Personally, I think you're on the trail of a fantasy."

Her gaze was uncompromisingly steady. "I'd like to believe that you're not after the cup. It would simplify matters."

"I don't care if you believe me or not." It had been a long day. Her anger and frustration boiled over without warning. "You want to know why I'm here? I'll tell you. I'm here because of Nellie Grant. The authorities say that she was washed overboard during a storm, but I think she may have been murdered."

He looked at her, obviously dumbfounded. "Nellie Grant? Daventry's last lover?"

Abruptly she realized she had said more than she had intended. But it was too late to retreat. "Yes."

"What the hell makes you think she was murdered?"

Eugenia hesitated. After a few seconds she got to her feet and carried her empty mug to the sink. "Nellie grew up on the water. She knew boats, and she was big on following the safety rules. I think it's highly unlikely that she would have taken a small boat out in bad weather, let alone get washed overboard by accident."

Cyrus was quiet for a few seconds. "You're sure about her skill with boats?"

"Yes." Eugenia whirled around and braced herself against the sink. "There's more. She came to see me the morning after Daventry died. She was in a very strange mood. Agitated and restless. She told me that she was going back to the island that afternoon to pack up the rest of her things, and then she planned to return to Seattle."

Cyrus considered that. "Anything else?"

Eugenia began to pace the kitchen. "She told me that in the weeks before his death, Daventry had grown tense and more secretive than usual."

"Go on."

"There isn't much else to tell. I don't have anything concrete. Just a feeling."

"Just a feeling?" he repeated neutrally.

"Yes." She frowned. "And don't you dare ridicule my intuition. Everyone knows I have very good instincts."

He lounged back in his chair, scepticism plain in his eyes. "Any idea of a motive here? Why would someone want to kill Nellie Grant?"

"I don't know how to explain this. But her anxious mood the day after Daventry died made me wonder if she'd seen something the night of his death. She hinted that Daventry used a lot of drugs. I wondered if maybe—"

"She'd witnessed a drug deal and someone wanted her dead?"

"Well, yes." She shoved her hands into her back pockets, turned, and paced in the other direction. "You have to admit it's a possibility."

"Uh-huh. A possibility. A real remote one."

He didn't believe her, she thought. In all fairness,

she had to admit that she had not exactly leaped to accept his story at face value either.

Cyrus watched her as she paced. "Mind telling me why you've decided that it's your job to find out what happened to Nellie Grant?"

"She worked for me. She handled graphic design in the Leabrook's publicity department."

"How long did she work for you?"

"Almost a year."

"Do you always go rushing off to investigate when something happens to one of your employees?"

The ache in her jaw warned her that she was clenching her teeth. "No. But Nellie was my friend as well as my employee. She was an artist. She came from a very unhappy background. She was fragile."

"A lot of people have it tough. A lot of them are fragile. A lot of them come to bad ends." Cyrus's hand closed around the edge of the table. "Tell me why you feel you have to know what happened to this particular woman."

Eugenia halted facing the window. She shut her eyes. The words she had not yet spoken aloud welled up in her throat "I'm the one who introduced her to Adam Daventry. If it hadn't been for me, she would never have met him. If not for me, she would never have fallen in love with him. She would never have come here to Glass House. She would never have died."

Cyrus whistled softly. "Well, hell. So that's how it is. You blame yourself."

Eugenia heard the distant rumble of an automobile engine. She opened her eyes, turned, and looked straight at Cyrus. "I have to know what happened to her. It's as important to me as finding the Hades cup is to you."

"In that case," he said, "I think that you and I can do a deal here."

"A *deal?* What kind of a deal?"

"You may be one hell of a museum director, but I doubt if you've had much experience with the private investigation business."

"So?" The vehicle was in the drive. Eugenia could hear the crunch of gravel under tires.

"So here's my best offer. If you agree to keep quiet about the Hades cup and everything else I've told you tonight, I'll help you investigate the circumstances surrounding Nellie Grant's death."

She hesitated.

"For free," Cyrus added deliberately.

Outside, van doors slammed. Eugenia could feel the pressure that Cyrus was applying. It lapped at her in waves. He needed her cooperation badly. But he was willing to trade for it.

"I've told you what I think of free stuff," she said.

Voices on the veranda. A man and a woman.

"When it comes to this kind of thing, I'm very good," Cyrus said.

A knock on the door.

Decision time.

"All right," Eugenia said. "It's a deal."

Deputy Peaceful Jones shook his head in a sorrowful manner as he hoisted one end of the body bag. "A real shame about poor old Leonard."

Cyrus nodded, his hands full with the other end of the body bag that contained poor old Leonard. "Yeah. Real shame."

With his gray ponytail, beads, and a T-shirt embroidered with a picture of the Milky Way Galaxy and a little sign that read *You Are Here,* Peaceful was definitely not your stereotypical lawman. But he seemed solid enough to Cyrus.

"I reckon it's no surprise, eh, Meditation?" Peaceful looked at his wife as she held open the door of the van.

Dr. Meditation Jones, dressed in a long, flowing gown and a beaded headband, smiled a serene smile. "No. His aura had grown very weak in recent months." Her high, breathy voice made her sound much younger than one would have guessed from her gray braids. "His time had come."

Cyrus caught Eugenia's eye as he helped ease the body bag into the van. He could not be certain, but he could have sworn that, in spite of the macabre scene, her mouth twitched. He realized he was having to work to suppress a grin.

Peaceful slammed the van door and squinted at Cyrus through a pair of small, round spectacles. "Too bad you folks had to be the ones to stumble over old Leonard like this. But I guess someone had to find him."

"I take it no one had noticed that he was missing?" Cyrus asked.

"Old Leonard didn't have what you'd call any close friends," Peaceful said.

"He had a very disturbed aura," Meditation confided gently. "It made people unconsciously want to avoid him. I tried to get him to meditate and fast in order to clear his essence, but he refused."

Eugenia came down the steps. "It must be hard on a doctor when her good advice is ignored by the patient."

"Yes," Meditation said. "But in the end we are all responsible for our own auras. All a doctor can do is point the way. It's up to the patient to walk the path."

Cyrus looked at her. "Sounds like something my grandfather would have said."

She smiled. "Your grandfather must have been a very wise man."

"Yeah," Cyrus said. "He was." He looked at Peaceful. "Something else happened this evening. We had an intruder earlier. That's what got us out of bed."

Peaceful frowned. "Anything taken?"

"Not as far as we can tell. We scared him off. I'll recode the locks in the morning."

"Can't hurt," Peaceful said. "I wouldn't worry too much about it, though. Probably just some local kids fooling around. We haven't had a genuine burglary on this island in years. Frog Cove is the kind of place where people never lock their doors."

"Daventry locked his doors," Cyrus pointed out.

Peaceful squinted against the glare of the van's headlights. "Mr. Daventry was a little different. He wasn't really one of us, if you know what I mean. I hear you folks are here on vacation?"

"A working vacation," Eugenia said smoothly. "I'm here to inventory the Daventry glass collection. I'm the director of the Leabrook Glass Museum."

Meditation looked quietly pleased. "I heard that Mr. Daventry left his collection to the Leabrook. I'm so glad. His glass should be in a museum. Perhaps the gesture will help his aura find serenity on the other side of the veil."

Peaceful studied the birds of paradise on Cyrus's shirt. "I take it you're a friend of Ms. Swift's?"

"He's my assistant," Eugenia said very firmly. "He's going to help me with the inventory."

Peaceful did not take his eyes off Cyrus's shirt. "Assistant, huh?"

"I live to serve," Cyrus said.

Seven

*E*ugenia surveyed the closed doors that lined the right side of the balcony. "Any more dead bodies in those rooms and I'm outta here."

The tour of Glass House had been disappointing from her point of view. A few minutes ago they had walked through the studio that Nellie had used. But the room was bare except for an easel and some old acrylic paints. Cyrus had shown a keen interest in the library on the second floor, with its extensive collection of books, papers, and files. Eugenia doubted that she would find anything in it that would assist her in her quest.

She was already having doubts about the wisdom of her late-night bargain with Cyrus. This morning he seemed suspiciously cheerful and easygoing, a little too complacent for her peace of mind. She had a nagging feeling that she had allowed herself to be manipulated.

She reminded herself that although they had struck

a bargain, the truth was they each had entirely separate agendas here on Frog Cove Island.

"Come on, be a sport. Where's your sense of adventure?" Cyrus opened the first door on the right with a small flourish. "What are the odds that there's more than one dead body in this house?"

"I don't know. I was never very good at math." She went to stand beside him. The bedroom was typical of the others they had encountered on the tour. Lots of reflective surfaces, frosted glass tables, and white-on-white furniture.

Cyrus looked up at the mirrored ceiling. "On a sunny day you'd have to wear shades in here."

"I admit his designer may have gone a bit overboard with the mirrors." Eugenia started toward the next room. "I wonder who the architect was."

Cyrus looked suddenly thoughtful. "That, Ms. Swift, is an excellent question."

She glanced back at him, surprised by his serious tone. "Why do you say that?"

"Because if the Hades cup is hidden in this house, it will no doubt be in a concealed safe, which would have been engineered into the original design."

She stopped at the next door and paused with her hand on the knob. "You really do believe that cup exists and that Daventry had it, don't you?"

"You really do believe that Nellie Grant was murdered, don't you?" he asked dryly.

She'd asked for that, she thought. "You think I've cooked up a fantasy to explain her death."

"My professional opinion? Murder is a very outside possibility here. There's no obvious motive. Nothing more to go on than your intuition, when you get right down to it."

"You're the one who's following a few rumors

about an old legend. In my professional opinion, the Hades cup doesn't exist."

He held her eyes. "All I need from you is your silence, not your expert opinion."

"And all I need from you is your professional expertise."

"You got it."

"This is crazy," she muttered. "Both of us think that the other is on a wild goose chase."

"Not exactly the basis for a good working relationship, but what the hell," Cyrus said. His eyes were very green. "We have a deal, right? I'll help you find out what happened to Nellie Grant if you'll keep quiet about the real reason I'm here."

"Yes." She shoved open the door. "We've got a deal."

She glanced into the room, expecting to see yet another mirrored ceiling, chrome bed, and lots of glittering glass surfaces.

Thick darkness spilled out of the chamber.

Eugenia was amazed. "Well, what do you know. A room in Glass House without any windows."

"Interesting." Cyrus reached around her to find a light switch.

There was a click. A series of pinpoint lights came on in the stygian gloom. The dramatic illumination revealed a maze of black glass pedestals. Each display stand was topped with a glass case that contained a work of art.

The lights had been arranged so that only the objects in the display cases were visible. All of the space between and around the stands was lost in inky shadow. A handful of paintings, also illuminated with pinpoint lights, hung on the walls.

"An art gallery." Curious, Eugenia walked into the

heavily shadowed room. "But this one isn't devoted to glass."

"I wonder why it wasn't kept locked like the basement vault?"

Eugenia paused in front of one of the pedestals. She studied the sculpture of an oversized set of male genitalia.

"Probably because the contents aren't particularly valuable," she said.

Cyrus walked over to look at the large penis and scrotum. "That's your opinion."

She grinned in spite of herself. "I was referring to the quality of the artwork, not the subject matter."

"I'm relieved to hear that."

It was too dark to see his face, but she sensed that he was smiling.

His arm brushed against her shoulder. She felt the firmness of muscle beneath skin. Having him this close filled her with an odd restlessness.

She was intensely aware of him. And proximity was definitely not dulling the effect. In fact, it was having just the opposite impact. Even his scent intrigued her. She sniffed surreptitiously and confirmed what she had already learned. He did not wear aftershave.

Her nose tingled with the fragrance of soap and warm masculinity. She wondered why the combination made her toes curl. It wasn't as if she had not smelled both before in her life.

She made herself concentrate on the small plaque in front of the sculpture. It read *Essence of Man,* followed by two dates separated by three months. Beneath the dates was an inscription. She bent closer.

Possessed Only Average Artistic Ability
But She Gave Exceptionally Good Head.

"Good grief." Eugenia straightened abruptly.

The top of her skull collided with Cyrus's chin.

"Ouch." He rubbed his jaw. "Not the usual sort of art note, I take it?"

"No, it isn't." She could feel the heat in her face. Thank heavens for the deep gloom, she thought. She moved quickly to the next pedestal.

A narrow beam of light shone on a series of interlocking metal rings. Cautiously she read the plaque. The title of the work, *Worlds,* was followed by two dates three weeks apart. The inscription below was blunt enough to make Eugenia wince.

Below Average Talent in Both Art and Bed.

"There aren't any artists' names," Cyrus observed. He stood looking down into a neighboring glass case. "Just titles, dates, and a sexually oriented inscription."

"I get the feeling that the notes refer to the artists, not the objects inside the cases." Eugenia wandered through the dense shadows between rows of pedestals. "I wonder what this room is all about?"

"You want the professional conclusion of an experienced investigator trained to observe minute details?"

"Why not? I've always wondered what one of those conclusions sounded like."

"I have a hunch that we're standing in a gallery devoted to the work of Daventry's ex-mistresses. According to my information, the guy liked to sleep with artists."

Eugenia shivered as she moved deeper into the gloom. She recalled the way Daventry's eyes had glittered when she had introduced him to Nellie. "Your information is correct. He had a thing for artists."

She was about to turn back toward the door when

she caught the glint of glass at the far end of the room. Automatically, she went toward it.

She came to an abrupt halt a yard away from the last pedestal and stared at the object inside.

It was as if she had walked into a haunted crypt. Her blood ran cold. Her stomach tightened. Her palms became damp.

"My God."

"Something wrong?" Cyrus moved toward her through the shadows.

"That *thing* inside the case." It was hard to get the words out.

She found it literally painful even to look at the sculpture. It was composed of broken glass and bits of rusted metal. Everything about it was twisted and warped. It writhed with the artist's rage and madness, a monstrous creation that tainted the space around it.

"Take it easy." Cyrus put an arm around her shoulders. "Granted, I wouldn't want it sitting on my mantel, but it doesn't look any worse than a lot of modern art."

"It's horrifying."

"Yeah, it is kind of ugly, isn't it?" He leaned forward to read the plaque. "It's called *Flower*."

Eugenia shuddered.

"The dates are from five and a half years back," Cyrus said.

"Just before Daventry moved here to Frog Cove Island."

"The inscription is a little more flattering than most of the others, but not much. *Talented But Not Worth the Price.*"

Eugenia took a deep breath, absurdly grateful for the heavy, comforting weight of his arm. "Whoever created that . . . that *thing,* was filled with fury. She must have been more than a little crazy, too."

"No offense, Eugenia, but I think you're letting your imagination get the better of you."

"No." She shook her head. "Not my imagination. When it comes to art, I rely on my intuition. And I'm almost never wrong."

She had gone for the deal.

Cyrus was not sure if that was good news or bad news. He had taken a calculated risk when he had told her his real agenda. But with the local law knocking at the door last night and a dead man in the basement, he had made a gut-level decision.

It was not as if he'd had a lot of options, he reminded himself later that morning as he stood at the counter of Burt's Gas & Grocery. He needed Eugenia's willing cooperation, even if she was lying through her teeth to him.

"Understand you folks stumbled across Leonard Hastings out at Glass House last night." The slightly built man behind the counter stuffed a half-gallon of skim milk into a sack. The name on his apron announced that he was the Burt of Burt's Gas & Grocery. "It's all over town that old Leonard's ticker finally gave out on him."

"That seemed to be the general consensus of opinion." Cyrus pulled cash out of his wallet. "Dr. Jones said he took a lot of medication for his heart problems."

"That's a fact. Well, hate to say it, but I doubt if anyone will miss old Leonard too much."

Eugenia looked up from a display of wilted fresh produce. "Why not?"

"Meditation Jones will tell you that he had a dirty aura." Burt made a face. "Hell, maybe she's right. All I know is that no one else except Daventry would have hired him. Old Leonard was kind of creepy. But, then, so was Adam Daventry. In a more high-class way, if you know what I mean."

"I didn't realize people around here thought Daventry was creepy." Eugenia walked toward the counter with a red pepper and some lettuce in her hands. "Did you know him?"

"Not hardly." Burt snorted. "Daventry didn't have time for us local folks. Did his shopping on the mainland. Claimed he couldn't get his fancy food here."

Cyrus was amused by the hint of red in Eugenia's cheeks.

"I see," she said stiffly.

"I ain't complainin', mind you," Burt continued. "If it hadn't been for Daventry we wouldn't have all these artists livin' here, and I'm makin' as much money off the tourists as everyone else. But just because his art colony idea worked don't mean Daventry was a nice guy."

"I understand Daventry gave some wild parties out at Glass House," Eugenia murmured.

"Yep. Deputy Peaceful had to go out there a time or two. Word is there was drugs and stuff at those parties. Couldn't prove it by me. The only ones who got invited were the artists and those friends of his who used to come from off-island."

Cyrus looked at him. "Did you see his guests from the mainland?"

"Sure. Same ones every time. Used to come in on the ferry. Five of 'em. Never stopped in town. Just went straight out to Glass House. Stayed the night and left the next day. Reckon they won't be coming back now that Daventry's pushing up daisies." Burt smiled. "I hear you two are here on vacation."

"A working vacation," Eugenia said glibly. "Daventry left his glass collection to the Leabrook Museum. I'm the museum's director. I decided to spend my time off inventorying the glass before it's packed and shipped back to Seattle."

"Uh-huh." Burt did not sound impressed. "Heard you worked for some little museum in Seattle."

"The Leabrook may be small compared to some museums," she said coolly, "but I assure you that when it comes to glass, it can hold its own with institutions several times its size."

Cyrus was amused by the haughty note in her voice and the arrogant tilt of her chin. She wore a pair of hunter green trousers topped with a rakish, military-style green shirt. A wide leather belt set off her slim waist. Two small circles of beaten silver gleamed in her ears.

Her proud, self-possessed composure intrigued him at the same time that it challenged him. There was strength in this woman. He had learned long ago that strength was frequently used to conceal or control powerful passions.

He wondered what kinds of passions simmered beneath Eugenia's sleek facade. He also wondered whether or not she had told him the truth last night when she claimed that she was here to find out what had happened to Nellie Grant.

He was still pondering the first question, but when it came to the second, there were two distinct possibilities. The first was that she had not lied, in which case she suffered from an overdeveloped sense of personal responsibility.

The second was that she had lied, in which case the odds were good that she was after the Hades cup.

He had to admit that she had been very convincing with the Nellie Grant story. Not many people lied that well. But he had known one or two who could. Damien March came to mind.

"Haven't been inside a museum since I was a kid."

Burt rested one arm on top of his cash register. "Whenever I get a chance to go to Seattle these days I try to take in a ball game. Don't have time to mess around with that boring cultural stuff, y'know?"

"Really?" Eugenia said.

Cyrus winced. The icicles that hung from the single word would have frozen the marrow in most men's bones.

Burt, however, appeared oblivious to the chill in the air. He turned back to Cyrus with a quizzical look. "Deputy Peaceful says you're Ms. Swift's assistant?"

The skepticism in Burt's eyes was very similar to the look Cyrus had seen in Deputy Peaceful's gaze last night. No one was buying the cover story. It was time to fine-tune it.

"I'm not exactly her assistant." Cyrus gave him a deliberate, man-to-man wink. "More like a real close friend. Between you and me, the only glass I care about is the kind that can hold beer."

Burt guffawed. "I'm with you there."

"Genie, here, talked her boss into letting me come along on this inventory trip. Thing is, this was the only two weeks that we could arrange to get off together this summer. Figured we'd better grab 'em."

"That makes sense." Burt surveyed the pineapples on Cyrus's teal green shirt. "Couldn't quite figure you for one of them arty types."

"You got that right." Cyrus was aware that Eugenia had gone rigid beside him. He glanced at her. "Ready, honey? Better be on our way. Almost lunchtime."

Amber fireworks flashed in Eugenia's eyes. He wondered briefly if she would lose her temper and blow the altered story to smithereens. He'd hate to lose the cover, but the explosion just might be worth it.

She rallied quickly, however, and even managed a

brittle smile. "I'm ready. But I'm beginning to think this vacation of ours was a serious mistake."

Burt gave her a sympathetic look. "I know it must have been kind of a shock finding old Leonard the way you did. But don't let it give you a bad impression of Frog Cove Island, Ms. Swift. Heck, we're just gettin' fired up for the big art festival. Starts at the end of the week, y'know. Real popular event."

"Genie's looking forward to it, aren't you, honey?" Cyrus said.

Eugenia bared her neat, white teeth in a brilliant, utterly fraudulant smile. "Yes, indeed. Wouldn't miss it. Definitely the highlight of my vacation."

She whipped her sunglasses out of her purse, pushed them onto her nose, and stalked toward the door.

Burt watched her with a small frown.

"She's a little high-strung," Cyrus explained. "You know these arty types."

Burt relaxed and chuckled. "I know what you mean."

Cyrus picked up the groceries and strolled leisurely toward the door.

By the time he reached the sidewalk, Eugenia was several steps ahead. He refused to break into a trot. A man had his dignity to consider. Cradling the sack in one hand, he took his sunglasses out of his left pocket and put them on.

Eugenia turned her head to glower at him over her shoulder. "What did you think you were doing back there in the store? You're supposed to be my assistant, not my . . . my—"

"*Lover* is the word you're searching for."

"Don't put words in my mouth."

"The cover story wasn't working." He looked up at the colorful banners hanging over the street. *Daventry Workshops Festival* was printed on them in bold graphics. "Peaceful Jones didn't buy it last night and Burt wasn't buying it today. I had to switch to the other cover story."

"You should have discussed it with me before you did anything so drastic."

"There wasn't time."

She strode ahead of him along the sidewalk in front of a row of small boutique shops. "I liked you much better as my assistant."

"Probably because it gave you the illusion of being in charge."

"This isn't a joke."

"Genie, be fair. I didn't have a choice. I'm supposed to be running an investigation for you. I had to make an executive decision." Cyrus nodded politely at a small knot of people who were staring curiously from the post office steps. "You heard what Burt said. I just don't look like the arty type. Maybe it's the shirt."

"Yes," she said tightly, "maybe it is. You never exerted any real effort to make the assistant curator story work, did you? You deliberately sabotaged it, leaving me no option but to go along. I hate being manipulated, Cyrus. I will not tolerate it."

The argument felt strange, Cyrus thought. People rarely questioned his decisions. They did not always like them, but they rarely questioned them. "I had to think on my feet back there in the grocery store."

"If that's a sample of how well you think on your feet, we're in bad shape."

"Not impressed, huh?"

"No, I am not the least bit impressed."

"I told you back at the beginning that the museum story was weak." The tension in her elegant spine was starting to worry him. "I'm sorry I had to spring it on you like that. I thought you'd understand. You saw the way Burt was looking at me. We don't want to arouse any more curiosity around here than necessary."

"Your dumb version of a cover story is going to be even harder to sell than the assistant curator bit," she fumed. "One look at the two of us, and it's obvious to any dimwit that we couldn't possibly be involved in a . . . a relationship."

"I don't know about that."

"I do."

The lady doth protest too much, he thought with a flicker of hope. Or maybe that was just wishful thinking on his part. Yeah, probably wishful thinking.

"Genie, I apologize. But what's done is done. We have to go forward from here."

"Do you always do things this way?"

"What way?" he asked, surprised by the question.

"Make decisions without bothering to consult anyone else?"

The accusation startled him. It was true, he was accustomed to being the one who made the decisions, he realized. It was second nature to him. From the day he had dropped out of college to take care of his ailing grandparents, he had been making decisions. The knowledge that others depended on him had been with him long before that.

For as long as he could recall, there had been people who needed him. In the beginning there had been Beau and Gwen Colfax who had depended upon him to fill the void left by the death of their only child, his mother, Jessica. After them had come a long line of people who had also needed him. Crime victims, clients, his wife, Katy, Meredith and Rick Tasker, his employees. The list was endless.

Of course he made decisions, he thought. He had to make decisions. People expected him to make decisions. His one attempt at sharing decision-making power, the partnership with Damien March, had been a disaster.

"I did what I thought was best," he said finally.

"Bad excuse." She fell silent for a few strides.

He was not the only one in the vicinity who was in the habit of making decisions, he thought.

"I think one of the problems we have here is that you're as accustomed to being in command as I am," he said. "I can respect that."

"Can you, really?" she asked in scathing tones.

"Yes, but if we're going to accomplish our mutual objectives, we'll have to learn to work together." He paused and then added as humbly as he could, "I promise to discuss things with you in the future."

He could feel her mulling over the logic of the situation. She was furious with him, but she still had her own agenda to pursue. He was betting that she would not put it at risk just because he'd made the small alteration in the cover story.

"All right, we're stuck with the situation," she said. "But I swear, Cyrus, if you call me Genie or honey again, I won't be responsible for my actions."

He breathed a silent sigh of relief. "I'll keep that in mind."

"And the next time you come up with some bright little surprise, talk to me about it first."

He considered that. It would be a novelty, if nothing else. "Deal."

She stopped and turned around, one hand on her hip, the other gripping her leather shoulder bag. "And for heavens sake, stop dawdling."

"Yes, ma'am."

He circled around a cluster of gallery browsers, who had just walked off the noon ferry, and caught up with Eugenia. She ignored him when he fell into step beside her.

They passed a craft boutique that featured little hand-carved orca whales and a gallery that sold locally designed wooden furniture.

Cyrus focused on dinner. It was unlikely Eugenia would agree to cook again tonight after the unpleasant scene. The knowledge was vaguely depressing. Last night had been a night to remember, he thought. It was the first time someone else had cooked dinner for him outside of a restaurant in a very long time.

"Did you hear what Burt said about the drugs at Glass House?" Eugenia asked.

"Yeah, I heard."

"It fits with what Nellie told me about Daventry's use of designer drugs," Eugenia said thoughtfully.

"Maybe. But I think you can ditch the theory that Nellie was murdered because she witnessed a drug deal."

Eugenia threw him a quick, frowning glance. "Why?"

"Because if Daventry was involved with drugs, it's highly unlikely he'd do his deals here on Frog Cove Island, where people tend to notice strangers. He'd buy the stuff back in Seattle or L.A. Someplace where he and the dealers would all be anonymous."

"What about those regular guests who came on the ferry to attend his parties? The ones Burt mentioned?"

"Probably the other members of the Connoisseurs' Club."

She sighed. "I hate to admit it, but there's some logic in what you said about its being unlikely that Daventry conducted his drug deals here on the island."

"I try to do something logical every once in a while, just like I try to do something dashing."

"To impress the clients?"

"Right." Cyrus halted beside the Jeep. He opened the passenger door and held it for Eugenia. "Tell me something. What are you going to do if you don't get your questions about Nellie Grant answered?"

Her brows rose above the rims of her sunglasses. "But I will get them answered. I'm working with you now, and you're a hotshot investigator, remember?"

"Yeah, that's right. Guess it slipped my mind."

"My turn. What happens if you do manage to locate the Hades cup and you succeed in drawing Damien March out of hiding?"

He shrugged. "When I'm finished I'll return the cup to its rightful owner."

She leaned back against the side of the Jeep and crossed her arms beneath her breasts. "It occurs to me that if the Hades cup actually exists, and I'm not ready to admit that it does, it's part of the Daventry glass collection."

"Oh, no, you don't," he warned softly. "Don't get any ideas about claiming it for the Leabrook. The Hades cup goes back to the client who paid March & Colfax to transport it to him three years ago."

Eugenia snapped off her dark glasses and fixed him with a cool look. "How did your client get the cup in the first place?"

"He bought it at auction."

"Did you see the paperwork? Bill of sale? Record of ownership?"

Cyrus smiled faintly. "The Hades cup hasn't ever changed hands on the open market. The kind of people who have owned it haven't been the type who bother with official bills of sale and transaction records."

"Then there is no solid provenance to prove ownership?" she asked briskly.

"Don't go any farther down that road, Eugenia. I

told you, the cup belongs to my client. I'm going to see to it that he gets it. What he does with it after that is his business."

"From what you've told me, the cup may have been stolen any number of times in the past. Your client's claim may be no more legitimate than Daventry's was. In which case, it seems to me that the Leabrook has a clear right to it."

Cyrus gripped the edge of the roof and leaned very close to Eugenia. "Forget it," he said softly.

She did not so much as flinch. "I'll talk to Tabitha about the situation, if you like. And I'll also check with our lawyers. But the more I think about it, the more I think we can make a strong case for the cup going to the Leabrook. Assuming you ever find it, of course."

"The hell you will. We had a deal, Ms. Swift."

She gave him an overly bright smile. "Rest assured I have no intention of reneging on it. If you find the cup, I'll authorize you to use it to try to lure Damien March out into the open so that you can turn him over to the police. But I can't make any promises beyond that."

"Eugenia, pay attention. The cup goes back to my client."

She pursed her lips. "The Leabrook will have to arrange for proper security of the cup while you're setting up your scheme to find March."

He set his teeth. "I am a professional security consultant. I will arrange security for the Hades cup."

"I hate to point this out, Cyrus, but from all accounts, the last time you had charge of the cup the security sucked."

He became aware of a dull roar in his ears. "I think you'd better get into the Jeep. Now."

"It would be the find of the decade in the glass

world. No, make that the find of the century." Excitement lit her eyes. "I mean, I still can't quite bring myself to believe it exists, but, lord, if it does, well, the sky's the limit. I could organize an entire exhibition around it. Play up the legend angle. People love that kind of thing."

"Get into the damn Jeep," he said. "Or I will put you into it."

"Take it easy, Cyrus." She gave him a placating smile. "I'm getting into the Jeep." She slipped into the front seat. "See? There, I'm in the Jeep. Are you happy now?"

She looked up at him with the same patronizing expression he could imagine her bestowing on a difficult, temperamental artist.

Very carefully, he closed the passenger door. He walked around the front of the Jeep, opened his own door, and got in behind the wheel. He sat there for a few seconds, wondering if he should risk turning the key in the ignition. The experts claimed it was unsafe to drive when one was not in full control.

And he was definitely not in full control.

He stared straight ahead through the windshield. "You were right when you said that the last time I had the Hades cup, the security sucked. The next time I get my hands on it, I intend to take very good care of it. When I'm finished with March, I will return it to my old client. The Leabrook has no claim on it."

"I understand that you're concerned about your business reputation, but I think this is a matter for the lawyers to hash out."

Very deliberately, he removed his sunglasses and met her eyes. "I have some more free advice for you, Eugenia. Don't get in my way."

She stilled. "I could give you the same advice."

She was not going to back down, he realized. She

would go toe-to-toe with him until one of them hit the mat. He had never met a woman like this one. She would drive him crazy before it was over.

"Cyrus?" She frowned. "Are you all right? You look a little strange."

The roaring in his ears exploded into flames that leaped through his veins. He had just enough common sense left to recognize that he could no longer distinguish between the sexual and the personal challenge she offered. The dangerous part was that he was not sure he even cared about the difference.

"No." He reached for her. "I'm not all right."

He pulled her close and kissed her hard.

Eight

Without warning, Eugenia's insides turned to molten glass. She suddenly realized that if she had not been sitting down, she would have learned the true meaning of the phrase *weak in the knees*.

Hormone city.

And to think she had been wondering lately if she should take more vitamins or start drinking ginseng tea.

"Good grief." Her words were muffled because Cyrus's mouth was crushed against her own.

No man had ever kissed her this way. There was a sense of overwhelming heat. A great torrent of it rolled toward her. There was nowhere to run. Nowhere to hide.

As if she would even want to escape, she thought. A strange euphoria sang in her veins. She wanted to throw herself into the powerful, onrushing tide. As far as she was concerned, it was not moving fast enough.

She clenched one hand in Cyrus's hair.

"Son of a—" The words ended in a hoarse groan as he tightened his grip on her.

This was probably a blatant attempt to control her with cheap sex tactics, Eugenia thought. If so, it was a ruthless maneuver. Just the sort of thing she should have expected from Cyrus. She was outraged. He should know that she was far too intelligent and too mature to succumb to this approach.

On the other hand, she was hotter than the inside of a glassmaker's furnace.

She wrapped her arms very tightly around his neck. The curiosity factor was kicking in fast. No man had ever before tried to control her with tawdry sex tactics. Or, if he had, she had been unaware of the effort, which, in turn, was overwhelming testimony to the failure of the attempt.

Cyrus flattened one hand on her back and held her securely against his chest. His other hand clamped around her upper thigh.

She would chew him out later, she vowed.

Much later.

Right after she sampled a few more degrees of the sexual heat he gave off in waves. Why should she deprive her hormones of the only real stimulation they had enjoyed in ages?

"Damn," Cyrus muttered when he finally came up for breath. "I should have known better than to do this."

"Don't think it will change anything."

"Trust me, I'm not thinking at all at the moment," he said with heartfelt conviction.

"And don't get the idea that you can use sex to control me."

"I should be so lucky." His mouth closed over hers again, hot and deep and demanding.

Apparently he did nothing in a hurry, she thought. But he was certainly thorough.

She flexed her fingers on his broad shoulders, savoring the sleek, muscled feel of him. He was as solid as a rock. Stubborn as a brick, perhaps, but definitely solid. The kind of man who did not bend or waver or run from a woman who was as strong as himself.

Cyrus muttered something unintelligible, then twisted and eased her against the back of the seat. He leaned into her.

Eugenia's head swam. He was big. With shoulders that blocked out the sun when he bent over her. She moved one hand to his leg. Her groping fingers curved over a very hard object that bulged beneath the fabric of his chinos.

"Christ." He sucked air.

"Sorry." She shifted again, and this time her arm struck another hard object.

The Jeep horn blared loudly.

"Oh, shit." Cyrus raised his head. "I don't believe this."

Eugenia opened her eyes and came back to reality with a sickening thud. Sunlight danced on the hood. She blinked against the glare. That was when she noticed the handful of grinning spectators who had stopped to watch the activities taking place in the front seat of the Jeep.

"Good lord, this is insanity." She straightened quickly and yanked at her shirt, which had come out of the waistband of her trousers. "I haven't been this embarrassed since I accidentally spilled champagne over one of the Leabrook Foundation board members at last year's annual reception."

"Nice to know where I rank on the spectrum of embarrassing incidents in your life." Something dangerous still burned in his eyes.

"You've got a nerve, acting as if I've offended you."

He picked up his sunglasses and put them on with a deliberate, economical movement of his hand. "Should I be flattered to know that you're humiliated because you were seen kissing me?"

An odd little chill went through her. She gazed at the impenetrable mirrored shields that concealed his gaze. The futuristic lawman was back.

"What did you think you were doing just now, anyway?" she demanded.

"I was about to ask you the same thing."

"You started it."

His mouth twisted. "Now that's a real adult comment. I could have sworn that what happened here a minute ago was a mutual effort."

That brought her up short. He was right. She always accepted responsibility for her own actions.

"Yes. It was mutual. Not real smart, but mutual." She found her sunglasses and shoved them onto her nose with a sense of relief. At least they were more evenly matched now. "For heaven's sake, let's get out of here."

"Just as soon as I find the keys."

"What happened to them?"

"In all the excitement, I must have dropped them." He leaned down to grope around on the floor of the Jeep.

"Some security expert." She tried to ignore the amused stares of those passing by the car. "Can't even keep track of car keys."

"Has anyone ever told you that women who refrain from slashing a man's ego to ribbons generally get more dates?"

"An ex-boyfriend once said something to that effect."

"But you didn't pay any attention, right?"

"Let's just say that since I didn't particularly want to date him anymore, I saw no reason to restrain myself."

"I think I could almost feel sorry for him." Keys jangled. "Ah, here we go." Cyrus sat up and reached toward the ignition.

"Hurry. I feel like we're on display in a zoo."

She was reaching for her seat belt when she saw the framed picture in the window of the art gallery across the street. Shock doused the sparks of embarrassment, anger, and sexual impulse.

"My God. *Cyrus.*"

"Now, what is it?" The lenses of his sunglasses gave him a look of well-chilled menace. "I'm trying to start the damn Jeep."

"That painting. Over there."

He scowled at her abrupt change in mood. Then he turned to gaze out his own window. "Which painting? There are two of them."

"The one with the sixteenth-century Venetian goblet set against a backdrop of green-tinted glass." She glanced at the sign painted on the window of the shop. "In the Midnight Art Gallery. See it?"

"Okay, okay, I see a picture of a fancy-looking bowl with a little pointy thing on top of the lid. What about it?"

"Nellie Grant painted that picture. I would stake my life on it."

Cyrus snapped his head around. "How the hell can you tell that?"

"Because I've seen her work. I'm in the art business, remember?"

"I thought you were an expert on glass."

"I am." She shrugged impatiently. "But the feeling I get when I'm looking at an artist's work is pretty much the same, regardless of the medium."

"What do you mean?"

She frowned, uncertain how to explain. "There's a sense of identity. It's sort of like someone's voice. Once you've heard it, you recognize it."

He watched her closely. "You're sure that painting was done by Nellie Grant?"

"If it's not one of hers, it's one heck of a forgery. Why would anyone bother to forge the work of an artist whose paintings were not yet considered valuable? To my knowledge, Nellie hadn't even sold any of her work before she died."

"Is that a fact?" Cyrus took another look at the picture in the window.

Eugenia leaned around him, studying the painting with a mounting sense of urgency. "I've got a picture hanging above my fireplace that Nellie gave me the day after Daventry died. She told me it was one of a series of four she called *Glass*. I'd be willing to bet every piece of Venetian glass in the Leabrook that the picture in that window is another in the same series."

"Okay, okay. Take it easy. Maybe the Midnight Gallery handled Nellie's paintings here on the island."

"I'm sure Nellie would have told me if she had started selling her work through a local gallery." She reached for the door handle.

"Eugenia, wait, let's talk about this before you go rushing off . . ."

She had opened the door and got out before he could finish the sentence. "I want to know when and how that gallery got her painting."

Cyrus muttered something that she did not catch. It had not sounded helpful or encouraging. She slammed the door and started around the Jeep.

The onlookers who had been enjoying the show went back to browsing in shop windows as Eugenia slipped between parked cars.

Cyrus got out from behind the wheel. He took two long strides and managed to grab her arm before she reached the middle of the street. She tried to shake him off but was not surprised when she failed to do so. It would take a lot to get rid of him, she reflected.

"The first rule in the detective business is to be cool," he growled in her ear.

"Don't try to stop me. I'm on to something here. I can feel it."

He tightened his grip, slowing her headlong rush to a more casual pace. "We have a deal. If you want my help in finding out what happened to Nellie Grant, you'll have to do things my way."

"Okay, I'm cool, I'm cool." She made herself stop straining at the manacle that was his hand.

"Smile," he ordered softly. "Try to look like a typical gallery browser who's spotted something of interest in a shop window."

"Got it." She made herself smile. "Any other tricks of the trade I should know?"

"Don't head straight for the painting that you think Nellie Grant did. Show some interest in the one next to it, first."

"Why should I waste any time on it?" She broke off as his logic sank in. "Oh, I get it. We don't want to appear too obvious, right?"

"That's the general idea."

When they reached the sidewalk, he drew her to a halt in front of the Midnight Gallery window. Out of the corner of her eye, Eugenia studied the painting she was certain had been done by Nellie. She frowned when she realized she could not read the signature. The name was a small, indecipherable scrawl in the lower left-hand corner.

"We're supposed to be looking at the other picture, remember?" Cyrus muttered.

"I'm looking at it." She turned away from Nellie's to contemplate the other painting in the window.

It was an underwater ocean scene featuring whales and dolphins frolicking beneath the surface of an impossibly blue sea.

"Generic, trivial, and completely uninteresting," Eugenia said.

"You don't like whales and dolphins?"

"I love whales and dolphins. I just don't like pictures of them that look as if they've been mass-produced."

"Are you always this critical?" Cyrus said.

"For heaven's sake, I can't show real interest in that picture. I'm sure the gallery owner will know who I am. Everyone else on the island does after what happened last night. Whoever owns this shop will expect me to have more demanding tastes, to say the least."

"All right, let's try it another way," he said patiently. "I'm the one who doesn't know anything about art, and because you're sexually obsessed with me, you've decided to educate me."

She whirled around to stare at him. "I beg your pardon? Sexually obsessed?"

"After that little exhibition in the front seat of my Jeep, I think it's safe to say it's a believable story. Given the fact that no one inside this gallery could have missed the show, we'd better go with it. Besides it fits in nicely with our basic cover."

It was all she could do not to grab him by the collar of his pineapple print shirt and shake him. The only thing that stopped her was the knowledge that he was too big to move in any direction he was not already inclined to go.

"I am *not* sexually obsessed with you."

"Whatever you say. But I don't think you have to worry about no one buying our new cover story."

Jayne Ann Krentz

"What. Do. You. Mean?"

"Earlier, you were worried because you didn't think anyone would believe that you and I were a couple. You said it was obvious I wasn't your type." His mouth curved with lethal amusement. "Now everyone on the island knows exactly what you see in me."

This time she did take hold of his collar. With both hands. "Don't get any ideas about playing out some version of *Lady Chatterley's Lover* here."

He looked down. "You're wrinkling my shirt."

Eugenia did not trust herself to speak. Without a word she released him, turned on her heel, and strode toward the door of the gallery.

"Remember what I said," Cyrus murmured behind her. "Take a look at some of the other paintings before you ask about the one you think Nellie Grant did."

"How hard can this private eye stuff be? None of the detectives in any of the mystery novels I've read seem overly bright. They just stumble around until they trip over a clue."

"At this rate, I'm not going to have any ego left by the end of this job."

"Something tells me you'll survive." She jerked off her sunglasses as she swept through the door.

There were three other people inside the small gallery. They were busily examining an array of bland watercolors that featured morose-looking seagulls perched on top of chunks of gnarled driftwood.

Eugenia did not see anyone behind the counter. A black curtain concealed the opening to the back room. Someone was moving behind it.

Cyrus took a look around and then sauntered over to a framed picture of storm-tossed surf and leaden skies. He examined it without removing his dark glasses.

"What do you think about this one, sweetheart?" he asked. "Don't you think it would look great over my fireplace?"

Eugenia ground her teeth at the *sweetheart,* but she made herself join him in front of the picture. "I don't think so. You don't really want that seascape in your living room."

"What's wrong with this picture?"

Good question, Eugenia thought grimly. *A lot of things if we're talking about the picture that includes you and me. Dear God, what if I am sexually obsessed with this man?*

She had never been obsessed with any man. She liked men and she enjoyed their company. But she had always kept a certain distance between herself and the male of the species, even on those rare occasions when she had gotten romantically involved with one.

A therapist would no doubt say that she was afraid to trust a man because her father had proved weak and self centered, she thought. And maybe the therapist would be right.

She only knew that it was important to keep a safe distance. Deep down she wanted to avoid the risk of trusting someone who ultimately could not be trusted. She wanted to stay far enough away to ensure that she would not be hurt and disappointed when she discovered the inevitable weakness beneath the surface. Far enough away to keep her heart out of the danger zone.

Far enough away to be certain that she was always in control.

She told herself not to panic. What she had experienced out there in the Jeep was nothing more than the explosive results of a volatile mix of long-suppressed sexual energy, adrenaline, and anger. A heady brew when one was unprepared, but she was back in command of herself now. It would not happen again.

She concentrated on the seascape Cyrus was admiring. "There is nothing wrong with that picture. It's just that I don't think you'd enjoy it for long. It's insipid. After a while you'll get bored with it."

"Insipid? I thought it was kind of colorful. And it's just the right size for the mantel."

He was deliberately taunting her now, she thought. She wondered just how obnoxious he was going to be. "It has a superficial decorative quality, but it's flat. Like wallpaper."

"Wallpaper, huh?" Cyrus's sunglasses gleamed as he tilted his head slightly to get another view of the seascape. "You know what I think, honey?"

She forced a frozen smile. "No, darling. I haven't got a clue."

"I think that your ability to appreciate nice pictures like this one has been ruined by the influence of post-modernism."

She gazed blankly at him. "Huh?"

Cyrus fitted his hands to his hips. "The insecurities imposed on the artistic establishment by twentieth-century minimalism and the modernists were bad enough. But now we're dealing with a whole generation of art critics and curators whose sensibilities have been savaged by the confusion of post-modernism."

Eugenia glanced uneasily around, aware that everyone in the shop was listening. "Uh, Cyrus—"

"It's created a quagmire, that's what it's done. Until the art world finds a way to redefine the condition of contemporary art, no one can move forward. Oh, sure, people like to talk about post-post-modernism, but give me a break. That's a meaningless concept. Nothing but static . . ."

Eugenia considered how he would look with the

frame of the seascape around his shoulders. "Speaking of meaningless static . . ."

The curtain behind the counter shifted. "That's an interesting observation you just made on post-post-modernism." A tall, fine-boned woman in her early forties stepped out of the back room.

She had sharp features and eyes that were an unusual shade of blue. Fine lines radiated out from the corners. Her curly, auburn hair was strikingly streaked with silver. She wore it in a long, cascading fall anchored with a large clip at the back of her head. The folds of an exotically patterned caftan flowed around her. Heavy earrings fashioned of metal and semiprecious stones hung from her ears. They matched a broad necklace.

She smiled at Cyrus. "The problem of self-definition is always a complicated one, isn't it?"

Cyrus looked pleased. "You can say that again."

Eugenia drummed her fingers on a nearby frame. "My friend, here, has recently decided to take an interest in art."

The auburn-haired woman gave Cyrus a frankly appraising look as she moved around the end of the counter. Then she smiled at Eugenia. "Glad to hear it. Wish more people would. It would be good for business. I'm Fenella Weeks, by the way. I own this gallery."

"I'm Eugenia Swift. This is Cyrus Colfax."

"Pleased to meet you." She raised her brows. "You're the couple who are staying out at Glass House, aren't you? The ones who found Leonard Hastings last night?"

"That's right," Cyrus said. "News travels fast around here."

Fenella laughed. "You'd better believe it."

"Did you know Hastings?" Cyrus asked.

"Not well. I'm new on the island. I moved here and opened the gallery a few months ago. Leonard never came in. I don't think he was interested in art." She looked at Eugenia. "You're with the Leabrook, aren't you?"

"That's right."

"We have a couple of glass artists on the island. Unfortunately, I don't have any of their pieces in the gallery at the moment. But I'm expecting to get something from Jacob Houston in a day or two. You might want to take a look at his work. Rather special."

"I'll look forward to it," Eugenia said politely.

Fenella sighed. "It's so important for an artist to catch the attention of the right curators, dealers, and collectors. I do my best to get the local artists some exposure, but it's impossible for a small, out-of-the-way gallery like this one to exert any real influence."

Eugenia gave her a commiserating smile. "I understand."

The facts of life in the art world were harsh. The value of a piece of contemporary art was established by the complex interplay of collectors, dealers, and museums. The right exposure meant everything. An artist's career depended entirely on getting his or her work into the most prestigious galleries and on having that work purchased by the most important collectors and museums.

Eugenia was well aware that the situation was especially difficult for glass artists. She found it endlessly frustrating to know that glass was still not accepted as a medium for high art in some circles.

Historically, those who worked in glass had been viewed as craftsmen, not artists. Their creations, no matter how exquisite, were considered examples of craftsmanship, not art, in many quarters. If she had her way, the Leabrook would help change that image.

Fenella turned to Cyrus. "Are you interested in that painting?"

He grimaced. "Guess not. But I still think it would look great over my fireplace. That wall needs something and it needs it bad."

Eugenia seized the opening. "If you're serious about a painting for your living room, why don't you take a look at the one in the window?"

Cyrus brightened. "The one with the whales and dolphins?"

She wondered if she should strangle him now or later. "No. The one with the old goblet and the mirrored-glass backdrop."

He looked dubious. "You really like that one?"

"Yes, I do," Eugenia said firmly. She glanced at Fenella. "A local artist?"

"That's right." Fenella's huge earrings chimed as she walked to the window display. "Her name is Rhonda Price. This is a new direction for her. Nice technique, don't you think? A wonderful sense of light and color. That bowl seems to glow."

"Rhonda Price?" Eugenia was stunned. She glanced at Cyrus, who merely raised his brows behind his shades. "Have you got anything else by her?"

"Not yet, but she promised to bring in another one soon." Fenella picked up the painting and turned it around so that Eugenia and Cyrus could examine it more closely. "I just put this one on display yesterday. The price is three hundred dollars."

"I'll take it." Eugenia saw Cyrus's mouth tighten slightly and knew that he was not pleased with her impulsiveness. She ignored him.

"I thought we were going to buy a picture for my living room, not yours," he said.

"Don't worry, we'll get you something with seagulls in it before our vacation is finished." Eugenia stared at the small signature in the bottom right corner of the painting. She was close enough to read it now. Rhonda Price.

But this was Nellie's work. She was certain of it.

"Do you want to see the next one Rhonda brings in?" Fenella asked as she carried the painting to the counter.

"Yes. Definitely." Eugenia followed her. "Any chance of meeting Rhonda Price?"

"Don't see why not." Fenella pulled a long sheet of brown paper off a roller and fitted it to the painting. "She took the ferry into Seattle yesterday. When she gets back, I'll tell her you'd like to meet her."

"Thank you." Eugenia opened her purse and took out her wallet. "I would appreciate it."

Cyrus strolled over to the counter. "Ask her if she ever does pictures of seagulls and waves."

Cyrus stood at the counter of the gleaming, high-tech kitchen and poured a glass of sauvignon blanc. "All right, out with it." He looked at the painting Eugenia had set up near the window. "You've been stewing since you bought the damn thing. What's going through your brain?"

"I know Nellie painted this picture."

He studied her as he carried the wineglass and a can of Pacific Express across the kitchen. The discovery of the painting in the Midnight Gallery had riveted her attention. He could feel the focused energy and intelligence pulsing through her as she studied the picture.

"If you're right—" he said.

"I'm right."

He smiled faintly. "Then you've come up with what we in the detective business like to call a genuine lead. The next step is to talk to Rhonda Price."

"I hope she returns to the island soon. I've got a

lot of questions for her. I have to know how she got
hold of this painting and why her name is on it."

"If this Rhonda Price knew your friend well enough
to try to pass her work off as her own, she may have
been involved with Daventry, too," Cyrus said quietly.
"In which case, I've got some questions of my own."

Eugenia glanced at him. "What do you mean?"

"I'm interested in anyone on this island who knew
Daventry well."

"This is getting complicated."

"True. But as you pointed out to me only this afternoon, how hard could the detective business be? Even
a guy like me can get a license."

She flushed. "I was annoyed."

"Yeah. I know. Don't worry about Rhonda Price.
We'll find her. In the meantime, what do you say we
take the drinks out onto the veranda? It's a nice evening. Weather report said there would be no rain
until tonight."

She hesitated, obviously reluctant to leave the
painting, even for a short while. Then she exhaled
slowly. "Fine. I guess there's nothing I can do until
tomorrow."

"Right." He led the way out through the French
doors.

The late summer day was fading swiftly, victim of
the thickly wooded hillside that rose behind the house.
The looming trees cut off the last rays of the sun long
before it actually set behind the Olympic Mountains.
Standing on the veranda, Cyrus could hear the deep,
cold waters of the Sound lapping at the base of the
bluff.

He set Eugenia's glass down on a small table and
settled into one of two chrome and white leather
loungers. He leaned back, propped his feet on the
railing, and took a swallow of his beer.

Without a word, Eugenia sat down beside him. She picked up her wine and took a sip.

Cyrus wondered what it would be like to be here on a real vacation with her, to know that she would sleep in his bed tonight.

"I suppose I should do some work in the glass vault tomorrow morning," Eugenia said after a while. "Tabitha will expect a complete inventory when I get back to Seattle."

"She doesn't know the real reason you volunteered to spend your vacation here at Glass House?"

"No." Eugenia leaned her head against the back of the lounger. "She's sure the authorities are right about Nellie's having been lost at sea. I think I'm the only person in the whole world who cares about what really happened to her."

"Nellie didn't have any family?"

"Not that I know of."

"What happened to her stuff?"

"Leonard Hastings packed it up and sent it to me." Eugenia hesitated. "I was going to give it to charity, but I couldn't bring myself to do it until I was sure about what had happened. I put it into storage for a while."

Cyrus felt a flicker of interest. "Any papers or letters that might tell us what was happening here at Glass House during the last few weeks?"

"No. Nellie didn't write letters. She didn't keep a journal or make notes. I couldn't find anything useful in her things. Believe me, I looked."

He considered that for a while. Then he took another swallow of beer. "I want to go through the files Daventry stored in that room that adjoins the vault. We can work together in the morning."

She cradled her wineglass in her hands. "I never thought I'd say this, Cyrus, but I'm glad you're here.

Finding Hastings's body last night and knowing there was an intruder in the house was bad enough. Now there's this weird business with Nellie's painting. All in all, I'm getting a creepy feeling about this whole thing."

"I like to think that I come in handy once in a while."

She groaned. "I'm sorry I insulted your professional expertise this afternoon."

"Forget it."

"No, I had no right to make that stupid comment when you dropped the car keys, and I shouldn't have implied that private detectives aren't bright. It was uncalled for."

"I said, forget it. Hell, in the course of my professional career I have done lots of things that weren't real bright. And hard as it may be for you to believe, I've even had people say worse things about me than you did."

She smiled wryly. "Thanks. You're too kind."

"We can't ignore what happened today," he said after a while.

"We certainly can't," she agreed with gratifying speed.

He settled back. "We should probably talk about it."

"Fine with me. Since you brought up the subject, I may as well tell you that I found Rhonda Price's number in the phone book. I thought I would start calling her tomorrow after the first ferry arrives from the mainland."

He closed his eyes and held on to the reins of his patience. "I wasn't talking about Rhonda Price. I meant we can't ignore what happened between us in the front seat of my Jeep this afternoon."

"Oh, that."

He opened his eyes. "I wasn't trying to control you with sex. I started out pissed as hell, and things sort of took off from there."

"I understand." Her voice was tight. "It was as much my fault as it was yours. We're both under pressure. We're in a very stressful situation. Perfectly understandable."

"Uh-huh."

"After all, we found a dead body together."

"Some people would consider that a bonding experience," he suggested.

She was silent for a couple of heartbeats. "Yes, I suppose it is. The thing is, we're both trying to walk a very fine line here. We've agreed to cooperate on some issues, but we have separate goals. It makes for a lot of tension and natural conflict."

"Should have guessed you'd have it all nicely rationalized by now."

"We're both adults," she continued, warming to her theory. "We're capable of dealing with this in a mature fashion. I, for one, certainly intend to do so."

"Does this mean you aren't sexually obsessed with me?"

She choked on her wine. "Of course, I'm not sexually obsessed with you." She sputtered. "I've never been sexually obsessed with anyone in my life. I don't have relationships based on sexual obsession."

"I see." He downed another swallow of Pacific Express. "I've never actually had a relationship based on sexual obsession, either."

She gave him a sharp glance. "You haven't?"

"No." He paused. "It might be kind of interesting."

"I think it would be extremely superficial, shallow, and short-lived."

"Yeah, probably that, too." He shifted a little in his

chair. "So what do you usually base your relationships on, if not sexual obsession?"

She cleared her throat, took another sip of wine, and settled back in the lounger again. "The usual. Compatibility. Shared professional interests. A certain similarity in matters of taste. That kind of thing."

"Similarity of taste, huh? Damn. It's the shirt, isn't it? You can't get past it."

Her mouth curved in an unexpected grin. "No. It's not the shirt."

"You're sure?"

"Positive."

He realized that her response made him feel much more optimistic than he had felt in a long time. "Well, if you don't want to talk about sex, how about dinner?"

"What about it?"

"Just wondered what you were going to fix for yourself," he said very casually.

"I don't know." She crossed her legs. "I brought some radicchio and arugula with me. Maybe I'll do a little goat cheese salad and some zaru soba."

He cocked a brow. "What's a zaru soba?"

"Cold buckwheat noodles and some special dipping sauce. How about you?"

"Don't suppose you know any interesting recipes for tuna fish, do you?"

"The only kind of tuna I eat is sushi-grade ahi grilled medium rare with a little wasabi on the side."

Morosely he regarded the spectacular view. "I was afraid of that."

Eugenia hesitated a minute. "I've got enough goat cheese and radicchio for two. And plenty of noodles. If you want to make the same deal as last night—?"

"Sure, I'll clean up. No problem." He thought about it. "I'm good at cleaning up. It's what I do."

Nine

The gin-and-tonic arrived in a late-nineteenth-century English rock-crystal glass. The man who had once been Damien March savored the sumptuous feel of the heavy glass in his hand. It was a Thomas Webb piece. It looked as if it had been hewn from a solid chunk of quartz rather than crafted in a glass workshop.

The ex-Damien March contemplated the new e-mail messages he had just received from his West Coast people. Colfax was definitely on the trail of the Hades cup.

With matters under control on that front, it was time to contact the future Senator from the great state of California again. The secret to successful blackmail was to create the aura of a partnership between blackmailer and victim. Once the victim had accepted the fact that the person who threatened him the most was the only one who could save him, he became cooperative.

The ex-Damien March looked out over the sun-bright Caribbean and thought about how much he was enjoying himself. He had launched this game with some uneasiness. For all his insufferable, laid-back manners, his slow, methodical ways, and his amused disdain for what he considered affected behavior in others, Cyrus Colfax was both smart and dangerous.

It always gave the ex-Damien March an uneasy sensation to acknowledge that he and Colfax had so much in common. Nevertheless, it was the truth, and he had recognized it from the start. They had both come from nothing, the bastard sons of fathers who had never acknowledged their existence. They were both self-made men. They were both intelligent and willing to stay focused on an objective for as long as it took to achieve it. And they were both capable of a degree of ruthless determination.

But there was one significant difference between the two of them. The ex-Damien March knew that ultimately it separated the winner from the loser. While he had used his natural gifts to achieve a lifestyle that was very close to perfection, Colfax had shackled himself in the chains of an arcane code of honor. It was this code that would, in the end, destroy him.

Exactly what he deserved. The former Damien March tightened his hand around the rock crystal glass. Three years ago he had thought that he was free of Cyrus Chandler Colfax. He had been wrong. The damned son of a bitch had been tracking him for the whole of that time, drawing relentlessly closer and closer.

Eventually, the ex-Damien March knew, he would have awakened one morning to find Colfax on his doorstep.

Perhaps this business of losing the Hades cup was an act of fate, he thought. It would force the inevitable confrontation, but that confrontation would take place on his terms, not Colfax's.

One thing had become clear during the past three years. As long as Cyrus Colfax was alive, paradise was not safe.

The ex-Damien March allowed the rage to flow freely through him for a time. It gave him strength and power.

When he had himself back under full control, he reached for his laptop computer.

Zackery Elland Chandler II shut down the computer. He sat quietly for a moment behind the teak desk that his father-in-law had given him the day he announced his bid for the Senate.

The newest message from the blackmailer had gotten down to specifics.

> . . . Old Sins Cast Long Shadows: You may relax, our business arrangement is not about money. It will be simply politics as usual. After November you will be in a position to do occasional favors for someone who has only your best interests at heart. . . .

There were few people on the face of the globe who wielded more influence than a United States Senator. The blackmailer was not interested in a cash payoff. He wanted access to power.

All he had to do was agree to the bastard's terms until after the elections, Zackery thought. A scandal of this magnitude blowing up before November could ruin his chances at the polls. He'd seen lesser revelations crush other candidates.

Once he was in office, he thought optimistically, it would not do nearly as much damage. If he played his cards right, the news of his long-lost son would be stale gossip by the time the next election rolled around.

Unless, of course, some journalist discovered that blackmail had been paid prior to the election. Rumors of a coverup, Zackery knew, would never be allowed to die.

He had to face the truth. If he paid blackmail now, he would end up paying it for the rest of his career.

Damn it to hell.

He had so many things he wanted to accomplish. So many vital, important things. But in order to make a contribution to the future of the country, he had to win this election.

And in order to win the election, he might have to sell his soul.

He looked at the photograph of Mary, Jason, and Sarah. They believed in him. They were proud of him. They loved him. The news of a son he had never acknowledged would have a stunning impact on all of them. Would they believe him when he said that he had never even known about his supposed offspring? Especially if the son he had never known chose to tell a different version of events?

If they ever discovered that he had paid blackmail, would they understand why he had lied to them?

He got up and walked to the window. The bright, hot Southern California sun created a dazzling glare on the windows of the nearby buildings. For a moment all he could see was an endless vista of mirrored glass. His future ricocheted endlessly, uselessly, from one reflective surface to the next until it was lost in infinity.

With an effort he pulled himself together. He had to start thinking logically. He needed facts. At this point he had only the blackmailer's word that there was a son. The first thing to do was discover the truth. Then he would make his decision.

He went back to the desk and picked up the phone. It was while he was in the middle of dialing his lawyer's number that he was struck by a disturbing possibility.

The mysterious blackmailer could be his own son.

On the heels of that thought came another that was even more unsettling. He wondered what the kid looked like.

No, not a kid. Not any longer.

If he existed, his son would be thirty-five years old. A man, not a boy. And quite possibly he would be angry, bitter, and dangerous.

Ten

Two days later Cyrus put down the folder he had been studying. He leaned back in his chair, stretched out his legs, and contemplated the view through the door that divided the glass vault from the records storage room.

Eugenia was hard at work inventorying the Daventry glass, but he knew that she was not in a good mood. She was, in fact, getting extremely restless. Rhonda Price had not returned to Frog Cove Island.

The records storage room was a bit cramped, but as far as Cyrus was concerned, it was more comfortable than the vault. The rest of Glass House could hardly be described as restful, but the interior of the glass vault disturbed his senses in some elemental way.

He had never considered himself the overly imaginative type—just the opposite, if the truth be known. But to him, gazing into the vault was like looking into a crystal jungle where the leaves of the exotic plants were shards of glass and the eyes of the predators were faceted crystal.

Daventry had really outdone himself with the glass vault, Cyrus thought. Everything in the room where Eugenia was working glittered and dazzled.

Unlike the dramatically lit gallery on the third floor, the vault was not done in classic museum style with lots of dark, shadowy space between display cases. Instead, it had a surreal quality. The walls and ceilings were all mirrored, and the display cases were made of glass. The result was that objects inside the cases were reflected endlessly.

But the most unpleasant aspect of the room as far as Cyrus was concerned was the lighting. The entire chamber was infused with a pale acid green tint from the colored fluorescent tubes imbedded beneath the glass block floor.

The glass on display in the specially lit cases glowed as brilliantly as if it had all been fashioned of pure gemstone. Eugenia was surrounded by topaz vases, ruby bowls, turquoise bottles, and emerald ewers. The pieces that were made of clear glass looked especially bizarre in this setting. To Cyrus, they appeared to be so many beakers, cups, and pitchers created for ghosts.

Eugenia stood on the far side of the windowless room. The sight of her bent over a large glass paperweight made him smile.

The cat burglar was back this morning.

Eugenia wore another in what appeared to be an endless supply of sleek black tops. This one had an austere round collar and long, snug sleeves. She padded around in the little black slippers she wore inside Glass House.

The intensity of her expression fascinated him. He watched her turn the paperweight in her hand. From where he was sitting in the small anteroom, it appeared to be crammed full of small, brilliant crystal flowers.

"Is it valuable?" he asked, idly curious.

"It's all relative." She did not look up from her inspection. "It's Clichy millefiori. Quite lovely. Worth several thousand on the open market. But it's not a particularly important addition for the Leabrook. Our paperweight collection already has several fine examples."

"I see." He studied the graceful curve of her body as she made a note in a log. When he became aware of the stirrings of a hunger that had nothing to do with food, he made himself look away for a while. The small exercise in self-control was good for him, he thought. It probably built character. Besides, there was no point getting sexually obsessed by a woman who was not sexually obsessed with him.

"Any luck with the files?" Eugenia asked.

"Not yet." He glanced at the one he had set aside. "Just the usual paperwork you'd expect to back up a collection of valuable art. Letters of authenticity, sales receipts, photographs, histories. But I've only gone through a third of the drawers. Got a long way to go."

"Maybe I'll try Rhonda Price's phone again."

"You've called her half a dozen times. She's obviously not on the island. No point calling her again until the next ferry arrives."

Eugenia's mouth pursed in a mutinous expression. Then she sighed. "I suppose you're right." She set the paperweight carefully back inside a display case and removed a large, heavily decorated goblet. "Recognize this one?"

He studied it. "That's the goblet in the picture you bought at the Midnight Gallery the day before yesterday, isn't it?"

"Yes." She glanced around the sparkling, neon-green-tinted chamber. "Nellie obviously used this room as a backdrop for it. She used the same green background for the first one in the series. The one she gave me."

"You said there were four altogether?"

"That's what she told me. I've accounted for two of them. I wonder what happened to the other two."

"Maybe she never got a chance to finish them," Cyrus suggested as gently as possible.

"No, she distinctly said she had painted four of them." Eugenia picked up an enameled perfume bottle. "Nice. Very nice."

"What is it?"

"A bottle by Émile Gallé." She touched it reverently. "He was a major figure in the Art Nouveau movement in France."

"Expensive?"

"Mmm. Very." She turned a page in the log. "According to Daventry's records, he acquired it seven years ago at auction."

"Tell me about Daventry," Cyrus said softly.

She looked up, startled. "What do you want to know?"

"How did you meet him?"

"I told you, he came to me for a professional consultation."

"What kind of information did he want?"

Very carefully, she put down the Gallé bottle. "He asked me to evaluate a small Roman glass bowl that he had bought in England." She indicated a display case on the other side of the chamber. "That piece on the right. He had decided to begin acquiring ancient glass, and he wanted some advice."

"He came to you for a consultation?"

"Yes." She shrugged. "Since he had already arranged to leave his entire collection to the Leabrook, I was happy to help him."

Cyrus watched the way the mirror-reflected light gleamed on her dark hair. He remembered what she had said about her criteria for relationships. "Shared interests."

"I beg your pardon?"

"Nothing." He looked at the Roman bowl. It was a dingy, clouded green. There was an odd patina on the surface. "That iridescent sheen is a result of having been buried in the ground, isn't it?"

Eugenia's brows rose. "Yes. The bowl was probably once part of a cache of grave goods. The Romans made vast quantities of glass objects. An amazing amount has survived."

"You don't have to look dumbstruck just because I recognized the cause of the iridescence. I told you, I've done some research on ancient glass during the past three years."

"So you said."

"The Hades cup doesn't have that sheen. And it's incredibly detailed. Persephone's features are so vividly cut you'd swear you can almost tell what she's thinking."

She gazed at him with deep, thoughtful eyes. "What about the face of Hades? What kind of expression does he have?"

"He's pursuing Persephone as she tries to escape the Underworld. He looks pretty much like you'd expect him to look under the circumstances."

"Enraged? Furious?"

"No." Cyrus glanced at her. "He looks desperate."

She frowned. "Desperate?"

"Sure. How else would he feel?"

"I don't know." She hesitated. "He's the Lord of the Underworld. Powerful. Dangerous. Accustomed to getting his own way. I would have thought he'd have been infuriated by Persephone's defiance.''

"Whoever crafted the cup understood Hades's reaction," Cyrus said softly. "If he loses Persephone, he loses the woman who can bring light into the darkness of his realm."

"Well, maybe." She paused. "You really did see some kind of cage cup three years ago, didn't you? Are you sure it wasn't a forgery?"

"Positive." He settled deeper into the chair. "We're getting off target here. Let's go back to Daventry."

Eugenia closed the lid of the case that contained the Gallé bottle. "What more do you want to know?"

"Whatever you can tell me." He took a stab in the dark. "Did you date him?"

"Yes." She gazed through the lid of another case into the depths of a blue, heavily etched vase. "But not for long."

He was startled by the twisting sensation in his stomach. She had been involved with Daventry. *Damn.*

"Why did you stop seeing him?" He kept his voice neutral. "I'd have thought that he'd be the perfect match for you."

She turned around to look at him. Her eyes were wide with surprise. "What in the world gave you that idea?"

"As far as I can tell, he met all of your requirements. He was interested in glass, well-educated, cultured, classy background. My research tells me that women found him attractive. What went wrong?"

"It's hard to explain."

"Was it because you introduced him to Nellie? Did he drop you to go after her?"

She shot him a scathing glance. "You're not very subtle, are you?"

"Depends. I can be. But sometimes subtlety doesn't pay. Tell me what happened between you and Daventry."

"Why should I? It's my private business."

"Look, Eugenia, I'm trying to do a job here. We're supposed to cooperate, remember? The more I know about Daventry, the easier it will be for me to figure out if Nellie's death was connected to something going on in his life."

"Hah." She made a face. "You want to know about him because you think it might help you to find what he did with the Hades cup."

"That, too."

"All right." She folded her arms beneath her breasts. "I'll tell you why I stopped seeing Daventry. But don't blame me if it doesn't make sense. I'm not sure I fully understand the reason, myself."

"I'm listening."

"Daventry was a bloodsucker."

Cyrus stilled. "You want to enlarge on that point?"

"What I'm trying to say is that Daventry used people. He had charm and charisma, and he employed both to suck whatever he needed or wanted from his victims."

It seemed to Cyrus the temperature in the crystal room plunged at least thirty degrees. "What did he want from you?"

"Information."

"What kind of information?"

Eugenia turned away from the display case and began to prowl through the glittering cases. Her slipper-clad feet made no sound on the glass block floor.

"I told you, he wanted to know about ancient glass. He had just begun to collect it, and he was very enthusiastic about it. You could almost say passionate."

"Passionate, huh?"

"He hung on every word I uttered. To tell you the truth, it was rather flattering at first. Do you realize how rare it is for a woman to go out with a man who listens to her? I mean, really listens?"

For some obscure reason, Cyrus felt obliged to defend his gender. "Maybe you've been dating the wrong men."

She grimaced. "Maybe I have. At any rate, by the third date, I was having a few second thoughts. And by the fourth date, I knew I had to stop seeing Daventry."

"Did he—" Cyrus broke off, searching for a tactful way to phrase the question. "Was he, uh, sexually aggressive?"

"He used charm, not aggression to get what he wanted," Eugenia said crisply. "Although, toward the end of our association, I got the distinct impression that he would have been willing to use force to reach his objective if he thought that was the most efficient way to do it."

Cyrus felt the tension hum in the muscles of his shoulders. "Did he say or do anything that led you to believe that he could turn violent?"

"No. Not exactly." Eugenia quickened her pace and hugged herself more tightly. "But there was something about the way he looked at me when he didn't think I noticed. Something cold and calculating. It was hard to catch him at it because he could turn on the charm in an instant. When I tried to explain that to Nellie, she said I was crazy. No, she said I was jealous."

Cyrus could not help it, he had to know. "Did you sleep with Daventry?"

She gave him an exasperated look. "When, exactly, do you use subtlety? Be sure to let me know, because I wouldn't want to miss it."

"Sorry. Couldn't think of a more genteel way to ask."

"Did you even try?"

"Sure. But it's one of those awkward questions."

"It certainly is. And if I had slept with Daventry, I would refuse to answer it." She raised her eyes briefly to the mirrored ceiling. "But since I didn't, I guess there's no harm in telling you that the relationship never progressed to that point. It remained on a professional level."

"I see. It stopped there because you decided he was some kind of human bloodsucker?"

"I didn't like the feeling that I was being used."

"Understandable."

Eugenia stopped in front of a large case. She peered at a black and gold glass pitcher inside. "But to tell you the truth, I don't believe it would have gone any farther, even if I had been attracted to him."

"Why not?"

"I think Daventry was sexually attracted to artists. Women like Nellie. He was gallant and charming to me for a while because he wanted to drain me of whatever I knew about fourth-century glass. But I don't think he found me very exciting." She stared very hard at the black and gold pitcher. "In a physical sense, if you know what I mean."

"Yeah. I know what you mean." Cyrus studied the delicate curve of the nape of her neck. A deep, aching need settled into his lower body. "I find it hard to believe that he didn't want to seduce you."

She gave him a speaking glance.

"Not that you would have gone along with it, of course," he added quickly.

The corner of her mouth twitched. "Thank you for that vote of confidence."

"You're welcome. Got another personal question."

"I was afraid of that."

Cyrus exhaled slowly. "If he had so much charm and charisma, and if the two of you had so much in common, how did you manage to see past the blinding glare of his perfections?"

"Intuition," she said. "I'm very good at detecting fakes."

At five o'clock that afternoon, Eugenia dropped the gleaming chrome phone back into its cradle and glared at Cyrus. "Rhonda Price is still not answering her phone."

"She's probably not back on the island yet," Cyrus said from the windowed wall where he was watching rain move across the waters of the Sound.

"There's one more ferry at six and that's it for the day."

"A good private investigator has to have patience." She drummed her fingers on the arm of her chair. "I don't have all summer to find out what's going on here."

"This is only our fourth night on the island," he pointed out.

"And so far the only thing I've discovered is that someone named Rhonda Price is trying to pass off Nellie's paintings as her own."

"You've had more luck with your case than I've had with mine." Cyrus turned toward her. "I think we both need a break. What do you say we take a leisurely evening drive around the island and then have dinner in town?"

"Where do you want to eat?" She was chagrined by the churlish note in her voice. "This isn't Seattle. I counted exactly two restaurants in town, including the Neon Sunset Café. I refuse to eat there. It's the kind of place that serves day-old doughnuts and greasy hamburgers."

"Guess that leaves the fish house at the marina."

It was a reasonable suggestion, and she knew it. "All right. Maybe it would be good to get away from here for the evening. I like glass more than most people, and this place is interesting, architecturally speaking, but it's a bit much after a while."

"Yeah, that's for damn sure."

For some reason that made her laugh. "It's not that bad. Come on, let's go to town." A thought struck her as she pushed herself up out of the chair. "We can drive by Rhonda Price's house on the way."

"Don't get any ideas." Cyrus eyed her warily. "If you think I'm going to help you break into her place so that you can have a look around, think again."

"Never crossed my mind." Eugenia widened her eyes. "I just thought that we might discover that she's home after all and simply hasn't been answering her phone."

"Sure. And if I believe that, you've got a nice glass bridge you can sell me, right?"

"Are you always so suspicious?" she demanded.

"Goes with the territory."

At eight-thirty that evening Eugenia decided that she was feeling infinitely less waspish. She sat with Cyrus at a secluded window table in the Marina Restaurant and polished off the last of her pan-fried razor clams with enthusiasm.

"Okay, I admit it." She put down her fork. "This was a good idea. I'm glad we got out of the house for a while, even if you didn't let me break into Rhonda Price's cabin on the way here."

His failure to support her in the half-formed scheme had been a disappointment. Cyrus had agreed to cruise slowly past Rhonda's small cottage, but when they had seen no sign of anyone inside and no car in the drive, he had adamantly refused to let Eugenia get out of the car.

"I knew you'd hold that against me for the rest of the evening," Cyrus said.

"You could have been a little more cooperative. I just wanted to look in the windows."

Cyrus's eyes gleamed with amusement. "Trust me, you'll thank me in the morning."

"I thought you tough, private eye guys were very big on sneaking around in order to look for clues."

"Those of us who want to retain our licenses and our businesses try to avoid breaking and entering charges."

A waitress paused to scoop up the empty plates. When she was gone, Eugenia propped her elbows on the well-worn table and rested her chin on her hands. She was aware of a deep and growing curiosity about Cyrus.

"How long have you been in the security business?" she asked.

"Since my late twenties."

"You were a cop before that, weren't you?"

"Yeah."

She tipped her head slightly to the side. "Why did you quit police work?"

He hesitated. "I don't function well in a bureaucracy. I'm not much of a team player. I'm more of a loner. I needed to be my own boss."

"You like to give orders, not take them."

"I guess that about sums it up," he agreed.

"So you started your own business?"

"It was a one-man operation at first. Then I hired Quint Yates. He's incredible with a computer. A lot of modern investigation depends on computers. I started to expand into corporate work. That's when Damien March contacted me. He had his own company, too. He suggested we merge and go after the high-end private market."

"Did it work?"

"No." Cyrus's eyes were clear and cold. "I realized almost from the start that I had made a mistake. For Katy's sake, I tried to make it fly. But within six months I knew I would have to end the partnership. Unfortunately, the Hades cup job came along before I made my move."

"You really think Damien March stole the cup and set you up to take the fall."

"I don't think he did it," Cyrus said. "I know it."

"Where does your wife come into this? Why do you believe that he killed her?"

"Earlier today you told me that Adam Daventry was a user. A kind of vampire who sucked what he wanted out of others. March was one of those, too."

"What do you mean?"

"My wife was a very gentle woman. Very beautiful. Very delicate. Very innocent. She never stood a chance against March."

Eugenia frowned. "I still don't understand why you think he killed her."

"I told you, she knew too much. She was a liability. He had to cover his trail."

"But how did your wife learn his plans? Did she see something she shouldn't have seen? Overhear a phone conversation that incriminated March?"

"No. Not exactly." Cyrus looked down into the depths of his coffee. "As I said, he was a user. He needed Katy's help to carry out the plans for the theft of the Hades cup. So he seduced her."

Eugenia nearly fell off her chair. "He *seduced* her?"

"He took advantage of her naïveté to set me up. And when he no longer needed her, he got rid of her."

Eugenia was speechless. "Wait a second here. Let me see if I've got this straight. You're telling me that your wife had an affair with your business partner, aided and abetted him in his criminal scheme, and then got murdered by him when he covered his tracks."

Cyrus's gaze turned fierce. "March took advantage of her gentle, trusting nature. He deceived her and then he destroyed her."

"Gentle, trusting nature, huh? So sweet and naïve that she didn't know the difference between right and wrong? So delicate that she couldn't be expected to respect her wedding vows?"

"What the hell are you saying?"

"Cyrus, I'm sorry for your loss. You obviously cared for her very deeply. But I think you've allowed your old feelings for her to blind you to the obvious. It sounds to me like your wife cheated on you, plain and simple."

He tossed his napkin down on the table "I think it's time to leave."

"I don't care how you wrap it up and tie it with a ribbon, the woman you married lacked character, backbone, and a sense of honor."

"Goddamn it, don't you dare say that about Katy."

"It's the truth from where I sit. Where was her loyalty to you, her husband, in all this?"

He looked very dangerous now. "You don't know what you're talking about."

"Did you ever cheat on her?"

"*Never.*"

"Why not?"

Seething anger burned in the depths of his eyes. "She was my *wife.*"

"You were her husband. She was supposed to be loyal to you." Memories of the day her father had given her his mealy-mouthed reasons for filing for a divorce flashed in Eugenia's head. "Even if, for some reason, she no longer loved you, that is no excuse for her weak, dishonorable, self-indulgent behavior."

"Damn it, Eugenia—"

"I have no patience with people who have no sense of responsibility and personal integrity. And to think that you've spent three years tracking her killer. She didn't do anything to deserve such loyalty from you."

"If you say one more word—"

"I won't." She shot to her feet, aware that her hands were trembling. "Excuse me, I have to make a trip to the ladies' room."

"Sit down."

"Don't worry, I'll be right back. You've got the car keys. I certainly don't intend to walk home, and I doubt if there's a taxi on the island." She swung around on her heel and started off through the crowd of diners.

She did not look back. She knew that if she did she would see the rage in Cyrus's face. As it was, she could have sworn that she felt the heat of it clear across the restaurant.

Stupid. Ridiculous. Why on earth had she let herself get carried away like that? It was none of her business if Cyrus thought his wife had been an angel. The man was entitled to his view of the past. She had no right to deprive him of whatever comfort his memories gave him.

What she had done was inexcusable.

When she went back to the table she would apologize.

She hurried down the narrow hall marked *Restrooms,* found the door labeled *Mermaids,* and pushed it open. She was relieved to see that she had the facility to herself. She walked to the mirror and stared bleakly at herself.

What in the name of heaven had come over her? She'd gone bonkers out there because of something that did not even concern her. She *never* lost her self-control like that.

The restroom door opened behind her. Eugenia tensed, half-afraid that Cyrus had followed her with the intention of continuing the argument.

In the mirror she watched as a small, gaunt woman of about thirty walked into the room. She was dressed in faded, paint-splotched jeans and a scruffy sweater. Lanky blond hair fell straight down her back, framing thin, angular features and pale eyes.

"I'm Rhonda Price. Fenella Weeks says you're looking for me."

"Yes." Eugenia whirled around. "Yes, I want to talk to you. It's about your paintings. My name is—"

"I know who you are." Rhonda clenched her spidery fingers into fists. "I came here to tell you to stay away from me. Do you understand? I don't want to talk to you about my work. I don't want to talk to anyone about it."

"Please, I have to ask you some questions."

"Leave me alone, damn you. Don't come near me." Rhonda whipped around, jerked open the restroom door, and ran out into the hall.

Unable to think of anything more productive to do, Eugenia launched herself away from the counter and raced after Rhonda. She reached the hall in time to see the other woman turn to the left and flee toward a door at the back of the restaurant.

Rhonda went through the opening and vanished into the night.

Eugenia dashed after her. Outside she found herself

on a dark, poorly illuminated section of the old pier. The smell of dead fish warned her that she was standing downwind of the restaurant's huge garbage bins.

Light, running footsteps sounded. Rhonda was going around the rear of the restaurant. Probably headed toward the parking lot, Eugenia thought. There might be time to catch her.

Without the least notion of what she would do or say if she did catch Rhonda, Eugenia broke into a run. She was very glad she had not worn high heels.

A short, sharp cry sounded at the back of the pier. It was cut off abruptly. A second later, Eugenia heard an ominous splash.

She hurried around the rear corner of the restaurant. There was no sign of Rhonda. She went to the edge of the pier and looked into the water.

There was just enough light to see Rhonda floating facedown. She was not struggling.

Eugenia glanced around frantically and spotted an old, doughnut-shaped life preserver hanging on the railing. Next to it was a rusted metal ladder that descended into the cold, black water.

"Get help," she yelled at the top of her lungs as she kicked off her shoes. "There's a woman in the water."

She prayed that one of the busboys or someone sleeping on a boat in the marina had heard her. There was no time to wait for assistance. Rhonda Price was drowning.

Eugenia kicked off her shoes. She grabbed the life preserver and scrambled awkwardly down the old ladder. It groaned beneath her weight.

She heard footsteps on the pier above her. Not coming to help. Receding into the distance.

"Wait," Eugenia shouted. "Get help."

But the fleeing footsteps faded into the night.

The ladder gave out another wrenching, grinding groan. Metal scraped on metal. The rung on which Eugenia was balanced gave way.

She fell the remaining three feet.

The shocking cold of the water hit her with the force of icy lightning.

Eleven

"So much for not needing a bodyguard." Cyrus stopped in front of the mirrored fireplace to stoke the blaze with short jabs of the poker. "I can't even let you go to the ladies' room by yourself."

"I'll get it right next time, I swear I will." Eugenia's eyes gleamed with amusement above the rim of a mug of hot tea. "All I ask is another chance to prove that I can go to the restroom and get back on my own. I swear I've got it figured out."

"I'm glad you find it amusing. Wait until Tabitha Leabrook hears about this."

"I vote we don't tell her."

He exhaled slowly. "Good plan. She'll only worry."

"And she'll start asking questions," Eugenia said dryly. "I'm supposed to be inventorying the Daventry glass collection, not investigating Nellie's disappearance. As far as Tabitha knows, you're the one who's looking into a possible murder, not me."

"Yeah. Things are getting messy, aren't they? Are

you sure you're warm enough?" Cyrus set the poker into the chrome stand.

"I'm fine. I wasn't in the water very long, thanks to you. By the way, how did you manage to be at the head of the pack that came charging out of the restaurant?"

"A busboy started yelling that there were two women in the water."

"And you naturally leaped to the automatic conclusion that one of them was me?"

He shoved his hands into the pockets of his chinos. "As you were not in sight, it was logical to assume you might be one of the women in trouble. I had a sudden, blinding image of Tabitha Leabrook demanding to know how the hell I had managed to screw up the supposedly simple job of keeping an eye on you."

"Ah." She nodded as if in sudden comprehension. "So it was the thought of your business reputation going down the tubes that galvanized you."

"Let's just say that I was inspired to move a little more quickly than usual." There was no point telling her about the chill that had zapped him when he had heard the busboy shouting for assistance. He had known, before he had even seen her clinging to the ladder, one arm cradling the unconscious Rhonda, that she was in trouble.

"Well, you can stop worrying about me, Cyrus. You heard Dr. Jones. I don't show any signs of hypothermia. Rhonda was the one who was hurt. Meditation said she must have hit her head when she lost her balance and went over the side of the pier. Peaceful agreed with her."

"I know." Cyrus gazed down into the flames. He could not forget how cold and shivery Eugenia had been when he had climbed down the ladder to haul her and Rhonda to safety. The icy water of Puget Sound could kill a person in less than half an hour.

At least Meditation Jones's small clinic had looked like a medical clinic was supposed to look, he thought. He had been half-afraid he would find a shadowy, incense-laden room stocked with strange herbs and candles.

He had been greatly relieved to see a lot of shiny, high-tech equipment and bright, clean surfaces. Meditation had actually worn a white coat over her long, loose dress. There had even been some framed paperwork from the University of Washington medical school hanging on the wall.

Meditation had examined Rhonda first and then called for an air ambulance to take the unconscious patient to a mainland hospital. She had then turned her attention to Eugenia, who had been huddled in a blanket.

Cyrus had hovered.

Meditation had finally given him one of her serene smiles and offered her own brand of medical reassurance.

"Calm yourself, Mr. Colfax. Eugenia is fine. Her aura is as strong as your own. The colors are bright and true and clear. All she needs is a good night's rest."

He decided that was Meditation's version of "Take two aspirin and call me in the morning."

He had been settling Eugenia, still wrapped in a blanket, into the front seat of the Jeep, when he heard the *whump-whump-whump* of the helicopter's rotor blades. Rhonda had been on her way to a hospital before Cyrus had gotten Eugenia back to Glass House.

He had to admit Eugenia did look all right. No, he corrected himself, she looked better than all right. She had taken a shower and put on a thick, white terry cloth bathrobe. Her dark hair, amber eyes, and striking features were a sultry, dramatic contrast to the snowy robe and the crystal room.

"You saved Rhonda Price's life," he said. "I wonder if she'll be grateful."

"I doubt it. Before she went running off down the pier, she made it very clear that she did not want anything to do with me." Eugenia grimaced. "I won't be able to talk to her until she gets out of the hospital. What if she doesn't come back to the island when she's released?"

Cyrus went to the nearest bank of windows and stood looking out into the night. "If she skips, I'll find her for you."

"You will?"

"Yeah. I've got a few questions for her, myself."

"What questions?" Eugenia asked swiftly. "According to you, my theories about Nellie's death are just fantasies born out of my over-developed sense of responsibility."

"I told you I'd help you investigate, and I will." He swung around and leveled a finger at her. "But no more taking matters into your own hands the way you did tonight. Is that clear?"

"I didn't set out to take matters into my own hands. It all just sort of happened."

"Uh-huh. Something tells me things just sort of happen like that a lot around you."

"Now, Cyrus—"

"You should never have confronted Rhonda alone. You know nothing about questioning people who have things to hide. What the hell did you think you were doing?"

"I didn't have much choice," Eugenia pointed out. "She confronted me, remember?"

"Damn it, I don't care which one of you started it. All I know is that you ended up in the water with her. It could have been a very dangerous situation."

"It was dangerous for Rhonda, but not for me."

"Is that right? You could have been the one who hit her head and got knocked unconscious when you went running to the rescue. That pier was still slippery from the rain this evening—" Cyrus broke off abruptly.

This was crazy. He was overreacting, and he knew it. What he did not understand was why. He was amazed to realize that his temper was suddenly on simmer, just as it had been earlier at dinner.

He wondered morosely what it was about Eugenia that got to him so easily. She had a talent for sabotaging his self-control in a way that no one else had ever been able to do.

"I'd rather you didn't lecture me anymore tonight, Cyrus." Eugenia patted a small yawn. "I haven't got the energy for a knock-down-drag-out fight. Maybe in the morning."

"I don't want a fight." He flexed his hands slowly. "I just want the facts."

She leaned her head against the back of the sofa and watched him through half-closed lids. "You heard me tell Deputy Peaceful the whole story."

"The hell I did. You gave him the short, simple version."

"The short, simple version?"

"The one in which you told Rhonda that you wanted to talk to her about her art, and she said she didn't want to discuss it. The one in which she just turned and ran out of the restaurant for no apparent reason. You remember that version?"

"But that's exactly what happened." Eugenia frowned. "I never even got a chance to mention Nellie's name to her. Rhonda told me to leave her alone, and then she took off. I went after her. When I got outside on the pier, I stopped because I couldn't see her. Then I heard a scream and the splash."

Cyrus rubbed the back of his neck. "While you were with Meditation Jones I talked to the busboy who saw you and Rhonda run out the side door. Fortunately, he confirmed that Rhonda left ahead of you and that you were standing in plain sight just outside the door when she screamed from the far end of the pier."

Eugenia gave him a quizzical look. "What do you mean, fortunately he confirmed all that?"

He shrugged. "It simplifies things."

"How does it simplify things?"

He glanced at her, exasperated. "It makes it real clear that you didn't get into a shoving match with Rhonda at the edge of the pier."

Her mouth dropped open as the implications hit her. "My God. You mean someone might have concluded that I pushed her into the water?"

He braced one hand on the mirrored mantel. "Why do you think Deputy Peaceful was asking all those questions at the clinic?"

"Good grief." Outrage lit her eyes. "I never realized that he thought that I might have shoved Rhonda off the pier."

"I'm not saying he did believe that. He was just checking out the possibilities. Like I said, the busboy's version of events coincides with yours, and that takes care of the problem."

"Of all the nerve." Her expression went from angry to appalled in the blink of an eye. "Don't tell me that you had a few doubts, too?"

"No." He smiled. "Not for a minute."

"Well, thank goodness for that much." She shuddered. "It's infuriating to think that anyone could have thought for a second that I would do such a thing."

"Don't worry about it." Cyrus tried for a soothing tone. "Peaceful knows that the fall was an accident. He told me that Rhonda has always been a little high-strung and that lately she's been acting even more anxious than usual."

"Is that so?" Eugenia's gaze was suddenly very intent. "Did he have any theories about why she might have started acting more nervous lately?"

"I got the impression that he thinks she might be doing drugs, although he didn't come right out and say it." Cyrus cleared his throat. "He mentioned that Meditation had noticed that Rhonda's aura had become a little pale and thin lately."

Eugenia wrinkled her nose. "Oh, well, that explains everything. Everyone knows that a pale, thin aura can make a person extremely tense."

Cyrus grinned. "Yeah. Common knowledge. Peaceful also told me that for years the town council has promised to build a railing on that old pier. Apparently Rhonda's not the first person to fall off it."

Eugenia gave a ladylike snort. "First time some tourist goes over the side there's going to be a major lawsuit."

"Probably."

"You said a busboy heard Rhonda's scream and raised the alarm?"

"He says he heard the scream, but he didn't know what had happened until he heard you shout for help. Then he rushed into the restaurant and started yelling."

"Hmm. That explains it, I guess."

"Explains what?"

She stared thoughtfully into the fire and tapped one

finger against the tea mug. "It must have been his footsteps I heard."

"Footsteps?"

"They came from somewhere near the garbage bins." Her brows drew together in a considering expression. "But I could have sworn that the person was running away down the pier, not going back inside the restaurant for help."

"It would have been difficult to be sure one way or the other. You were pretty busy at the time."

"True, I did have other things on my mind. It was right about then that I lost my footing on the ladder. What with trying to hang on to the life preserver and grab Rhonda, matters got confusing." A tremor went through her. "And the water was so cold."

He felt her shiver as if it had gone down his own spine. "Do you want more tea?"

"No, thanks." She looked up. "The only thing I didn't tell Deputy Peaceful was that I suspected that the painting I bought at the Midnight Gallery was Nellie's work, not Rhonda's. And the reason I didn't tell him that was because I can't prove it and Rhonda will deny it."

"You think Rhonda knew the real reason you wanted to see her?"

Eugenia hesitated. "Yes. Definitely. It was obvious she was scared. I'm sure she had guessed that I suspected she had passed off Nellie's work as her own. Why else would she have acted the way she did?"

"Who knows? She may be seriously neurotic or even paranoid. Especially if she's doing drugs."

"This was more than neurotic, Cyrus. She was scared and angry. She was probably afraid that I would expose her. I'm sure Rhonda knows something about Nellie." Eugenia narrowed her eyes. "She may even know how she died."

"Don't go off into fantasyland with this. She may simply have taken advantage of Nellie's death to steal her work and sell it for whatever she could get."

"Maybe." Eugenia looked unconvinced. "You know, Cyrus, Meditation told me that Rhonda may be in the hospital for two or three days."

"You never give up, do you?"

"I beg your pardon?"

"Don't give me the innocent act," he said. "You're still working on figuring out how to talk me into helping you take a look around her cottage."

"I wouldn't dream of asking you to get involved with anything that might possibly be construed as illegal."

He smiled faintly. "Like hell you wouldn't."

She raised her brows. "So?"

He exhaled deeply. "I'll think about it."

"You know," she said brightly, "if we're going to do it, we probably ought to do it tonight."

"No," he said with great conviction. "We are not going to do it tonight. I want to think about this a little more before we do anything really stupid."

"But, Cyrus . . ."

He released his grip on the mantel and went to the couch. He leaned down and planted his hands on the white cushions on either side of her shoulders, caging her. He brought his face very close to hers.

"I said, not tonight, Ms. Swift."

She blinked, and then sparks of laughter lit her amber eyes. "You know, if you're any kind of example, you private investigators aren't nearly as spontaneous and adventurous as I have been led to believe."

"Your concept of what constitutes spontaneous and adventurous sends cold chills through me." He inhaled the scent of her freshly scrubbed body and felt his insides clench. With an effort, he straightened. "It's been a long night, and I'm getting a little old to be fishing my dates out of the water. Time for bed."

"All right, be that way. See if I care." The humor faded from her expression. She set her mug down on the glass end table with great care. "But first I have an apology to make."

"If you're going to say you're sorry because you got both of us wet tonight, forget it."

"It's not that." She looked at him with clear, somber eyes. "I want to apologize for what I said earlier at dinner. About your wife. I had no right to say all those unpleasant things about her. I don't expect you to forgive me, but I want you to know that I'm sorry."

He felt the same twisting sensation in his gut that he had experienced at the restaurant when she had talked so passionately of love and honor and loyalty. He turned back to the fire.

Deliberately, he stripped his voice of all inflection. "Are you apologizing because you've changed your opinion of her?"

She cleared her throat. "My opinion of her behavior is not what's important here. You loved her, and I had no right to trample on your feelings for her. It was rude and cruel and inexcusable."

He glanced at her over his shoulder. "So why did you do it?"

She closed her eyes. "You pressed a couple of my hot buttons from the past. My parents were divorced when I was fourteen. My father was a professor of sociology at a small college at the time. He had an affair with one of his graduate students."

"I see."

"The divorce, itself, was bad enough. But the worst part was having to listen to all of my father's rationalizations, justifications, and so-called reasons why it was such a good idea for the whole family."

Cyrus remembered Rick's disgust with Jake Tasker's elaborate explanations for breaking up the Tasker family. "Yeah. I know what you mean."

"Dad managed to avoid being the one to tell me and my brother and sister about the divorce. He made Mom do the dirty work. But I went to his office one day and asked him why he was doing it. I told him we wanted him to stay with us." Her hand curled into a fist. "I told him we needed him. I pleaded with him."

Cyrus heard the self-disgust vibrate in her voice. "What happened?"

"He gave me a lot of garbage about how people grow apart and change and how everyone has an obligation to pursue his or her own happiness. How people have a responsibility to themselves to find fulfillment. He said that someday I would understand."

"Did you?"

"Certainly." Eugenia smiled wanly. "But I didn't have to wait to grow up in order to figure it all out. I learned everything I needed to know that day in his office."

"What did you learn?"

"That my father was weak." She gazed into the fire with shadowed eyes. "That he lacked a strong sense of honor and loyalty and that he could not make a lasting commitment or accept real responsibility. That I could not depend on him for anything important."

Cyrus could feel old, long-buried emotions shifting ghostlike in the mists of his memories. "You learned all that?"

"Yes. I was hurt and angry at the time, but I was careful to keep it all beneath the surface. I had to stay in control for Mom's sake. She had enough trouble on her hands. She needed my help. I didn't want to be another problem for her. And then there was my brother and sister. I had to be strong for their sakes, too."

He thought about how he had grown up with a need to be in control. From his earliest years he had been conscious of his responsibility toward his grandparents. They needed him. He could not take the risk of causing them any more grief than they had already endured.

"It was like that for me with my grandparents," he said. "Somewhere along the line I guess the control thing gets to be a habit."

She looked at him. "You know, it's strange. But when I look back now I feel a sense of pity for my father. It's hard to remain angry with someone who is simply weak in the ways that truly count."

He had a sudden, vivid image of Katy. Lovely, fragile, *weak* Katy. "Anger is a powerful emotion. It can crush and destroy. You have to be careful where you aim it."

"Yes. All I know is, that day in his office I promised myself that whatever else I did in life, I would not allow myself to be weak the way my father was. And still is, for that matter."

"So you became strong."

She grimaced. "Some people would say I've overdone it."

"Which people?"

"A couple of ex-boyfriends, among others."

"Ninety-pound weaklings, I'll bet."

She smiled. "You may be right." The amusement faded. "How did you get to be strong, Cyrus?"

"What makes you think I'm strong?"

"I can feel it. You radiate strength and power the way ancient glass does."

The quiet certainty in her voice gave him a strange feeling. The conversation had taken a turn toward the bizarre, he thought. He'd never talked to a woman this way. Hell, he'd never talked to *anyone* like this.

"You sound like Meditation Jones," he growled. "All that crap about auras."

Eugenia drew her knees up beneath the white robe and rested her chin on her folded arms. Her eyes were deep, luminous pools of gold in the firelight. "You make your own rules, and you live by them. You don't bend them when it's convenient. That takes strength."

"Rules?"

"Your wife betrayed you, but she was your wife." Eugenia's gaze did not waver. "You feel you have a duty to avenge her memory, even though she was unfaithful. You're following your own code. Of course, there are some who would call it a good working definition of an obsession."

He winced. "What do you call it?"

"A sense of honor. An example of your own brand of strength."

He took a deep, steadying breath. The twisting sensation inside him eased. "Some people would say that your determination to discover what happened to Nellie Grant is an obsession."

She searched his face. "What would you call it?"

"A sense of responsibility. Loyalty. Honor. You're following your own rules, too, aren't you? The ones you made for yourself the day you vowed that you would not grow up to be weak like your father."

Her mouth curved into a small, knowing smile. "Does it occur to you that you and I may be a little out of touch with the modern world?"

He walked back to the sofa and stood looking down at her. "Does it occur to you that you and I may have a little more in common than you first thought?"

"Yes." She looked at him very steadily. "The thing that worries me the most at the moment is that I seem to be apologizing to you on a fairly frequent basis. First because I insulted your professional expertise and tonight because of the remarks I made about Katy."

"Why does that worry you?"

"I suspect that if one person is always apologizing to the other in a relationship, it's safe to assume things are not balanced."

He put one knee on the sofa beside her and lowered himself slowly so that her mouth was close enough to kiss. "I've been hoping you'd use that word."

"Apology?"

"No. Relationship."

"Oh. That word." She put her arms around his neck and brushed her mouth lightly against his.

He groaned, aware that her silent invitation was having the same effect on his senses that a flame-thrower had on dry kindling. He crushed her slowly against the back of the white sofa and covered her mouth with his own.

She muttered something that was lost in the translation and clutched fiercely at his shoulders. Cyrus felt the heat radiating between their bodies. He caught her head between his hands and deepened the kiss. Together they slid sideways along the back of the sofa.

When the free fall was halted by the cushions, Cyrus found himself sprawled on top of Eugenia, one leg firmly lodged between her thighs. She felt sleek and resilient beneath him. The sash of her robe had loosened, revealing the high curves of her breasts.

He levered himself up slightly, just far enough so that he could push the terry cloth garment out of the way.

She put her hands beneath his shirt and spread her fingers across his chest. "This is probably not a good idea."

"I thought you wanted spontaneous and adventurous."

"Spontaneous and adventurous is one thing. Dangerous is something else."

"Don't worry." He drew a deep breath as she flattened her palms against his skin. "I'll take care of everything. I've got a condom in my pocket."

"That wasn't the kind of danger I was talking about," she whispered.

And then she kissed his shoulder.

He felt her teeth and her tongue. He squeezed his eyes shut for a few seconds, fighting for control. When he thought he had it, he bent his head and took the nipple of her right breast into his mouth. He bit down gently.

"*Cyrus.*" She came up off the sofa with a gasp, straining against him.

He put an arm around her waist and rolled to the side.

They tumbled off the edge of the low sofa and landed on the inch-thick carpet. This time she wound up on top of him. She unbuttoned his shirt and began to kiss his chest with hungry enthusiasm.

He gave a low, husky laugh. "What are you trying to do? Eat me alive?"

"Worried?"

"No." He traced her graceful spine to the divide that separated her firm, rounded buttocks. "I just want to be sure you realize that we get to take turns."

"Okay by me." She nibbled on his throat.

Excitement pounded through him. He realized that her robe was wide open now and so were her legs. He looked down the length of her as she straddled him. She was smooth and sinuous, he thought. Not flashy or bold. The neat, elegant definition of her breasts, waist, and hips made him want to stroke her.

"You're beautiful," he breathed.

She went very still. Her head came up. "Thank you. So are you."

He grinned. "You think I'm beautiful?"

"Yes." Her smile was slow and sexy. "Or, as we say in the museum business, a real work of art."

"Are you telling me that I remind you of a nice glass vase?"

"No." She stopped smiling. "Glass vases have a tendency to shatter under pressure. Something tells me you wouldn't break, regardless of how much force was applied."

He saw the undisguised hunger in her eyes. He knew then that she wanted him.

He reached down between her legs. When his fingers slipped through the dark, silky nest, he discovered that she was already wet and hot. So very, very wet and hot. Her clitoris was swollen and tight. When he drew his finger across it Eugenia shuddered.

"I take it back," he said. "You aren't just beautiful. You are spectacular."

She kissed him. "You make me feel incredible."

He knew he would not be able to hold himself together much longer. He unzipped his pants and dug the condom out of his back pocket.

When he was ready, Eugenia took him into her hands. Cyrus thought he would explode. He shifted position, turned her in his arms, and pushed her flat on her back.

"Yes," she whispered. She reached for him.

He was surprised by the taut, snug feel of her.

"Oh, my God," she muttered. "I knew you were big, but I hadn't realized—" She broke off on another gasp.

And then he was inside and she was sinking her nails into his back. Her knees lifted. Her thighs pressed against him. He reached down between her legs once more, found the full, plumped nubbin, and slid his finger beneath it.

If he had been surprised by the tight clutch of her body, he was stunned a moment later by her small, shocked scream of release. But then she was convulsing in his arms, and he was beyond the point where he could speak, let alone frame an intelligible question.

"You okay?" he asked when he could breath normally again.

"Umm-hmm." She sounded like a purring cat.

"You, uh, sort of screamed there at the end," he said. "I didn't hurt you, did I?"

"No. I was just a little startled, that's all. I've always wondered what it felt like to have one of those without a vibrator."

He knew a lot about being needed, he thought.

Being needed was something he understood It was familiar. Grandparents, clients, Katy, Rick and Meredith. Lots of people had taught him how it felt to be needed.

But until tonight, he had never really known how it felt to be wanted.

Twelve

"**W**hat's up, Quint?" Cyrus cradled the phone between his left shoulder and his ear while he lathered his face with shaving cream.

Eugenia had left his bed ten minutes ago to go back to her own room. She was probably already in the shower, he thought. If she had not bounced up as soon as she awakened and dashed off down the hall, he might have found a way to persuade her to use his bath facilities.

Ah, well. There was always tomorrow morning.

At least, he hoped there would be a tomorrow morning. He and Eugenia had not gotten around to discussing the short-term future last night.

The day had dawned overcast and gray, but he was feeling as good as if he had awakened on a beach on Maui. He studied his image in the mirror and noticed that he was grinning like a fool. He would wear the green and purple palm tree shirt today, he decided. It was one of his favorites.

"Did I wake you?" Quint asked.

"No." Cyrus picked up the razor.

"Thought maybe I got you out of a warm bed." There was a cheerfully lascivious note in Quint's voice.

"I was already up."

"How are things going there? Anything interesting happening?"

Cyrus angled the razor against his jaw. "Depends on your definition of interesting."

"You and Ms. Swift getting along all right?"

"I'm not paying you to pry into my private life, Quint."

"I know. You pay me to pry into other peoples' private lives." The teasing disappeared from Quint's voice. "Actually, that's why I'm calling. Your private life."

Cyrus stopped grinning. "What have you got? Something on this case?"

"No. This has nothing to do with your case." Quint hesitated. "It's the ZEC file."

The razor stilled in Cyrus's hand. "Are you sure?"

"Positive. You know those triggers you had me put in place a few years back?"

"What happened?"

"One of them got tripped. I found a red flag on the file when I booted up the computer this morning."

Cyrus lowered the razor very carefully. The ZEC file contained all the information he had on his father, Zackery Elland Chandler II.

Several years ago, he had asked Quint to create a system that would give him an early warning in the event that Chandler ever went looking for him.

Cyrus was not certain how he felt about the prospect of meeting Chandler face-to-face, but he had known one thing for sure. He did not want to be taken by surprise. He wanted to be alerted well in advance so that he could control the situation.

But after the triggers had been put in place, nothing had ever happened. Chandler had never come looking.

Until now.

After all these years, it was unlikely that Z. E. Chandler II had suddenly decided to seek out his long-forgotten son, Cyrus decided. Something else must have tripped the computer trigger.

Maybe his father had died.

Cyrus's stomach went cold.

No, he would have heard it on the news. Z. E. Chandler II was a high-profile politician, after all. Belatedly it occurred to Cyrus that he had not listened to any news broadcasts since he had arrived on Frog Cove Island.

"Cyrus?" Quint sounded uneasy. "You still there?"

"I'm here." He gripped the edge of the sink with one hand and adjusted the phone with the other. "Tell me about the red flag."

"You're not gonna believe this. Looks like someone sent an investigator to Second Chance Springs to ask questions about your family. The guy works for Chandler's private attorney."

He's asking questions.

"Chandler's all right?"

"Sure. Far as I know. What do you want me to do on this end?"

"Nothing." Chandler was not dead. He was asking questions. In Second Chance Springs. Cyrus took a deep breath. "Just sit tight and monitor the situation. Call me right away if anything new develops."

"Right." Quint paused briefly. "Uh, you okay with this, Cyrus?"

"Yeah. Stay on top of it. Let me know if the investigator gets any closer." Cyrus hung up the phone.

He stared at himself in the mirror for another minute or two before he raised the razor slowly to his face.

After all these years, Zackery Elland Chandler II had hired someone to trace his son. His *other* son.

"Why?" Cyrus asked the green-eyed man in the mirror. "And why now?"

Thirteen

"If you're going to whine," Eugenia said, "you can go back to Glass House. I can handle this on my own."

"I am not whining. And if you think I'm going to let you look around Rhonda Price's cottage all by yourself, you're crazy. I merely pointed out that there was a risk and that we need to be careful."

"Okay, okay. You've made your point. We'll be careful."

He was in a strange mood this morning, Eugenia thought as she stalked determinedly through a stand of dripping fir. She did not know quite what she had expected from him after last night, but the return to the cool, self-contained hunter was not it.

But, in all fairness, her own mood was not exactly one of light, breezy good cheer, she admitted. It was complex. Rather like the bizarre situation in which she found herself.

The truth was, she could not figure out how she

ought to react this morning or what she ought to feel. But it did not take a degree in psychology to figure out that introducing sex into the equation on Frog Cove Island was bound to create a host of complications.

She still found it hard to believe that she had plunged headfirst into what was clearly destined to be a brief, sexual fling with a man who was definitely not her type.

She did not have flings, Eugenia reminded herself. She had had a very limited number of reasonably serious, carefully controlled relationships over the years. She had never had anything that could be labeled a wild fling.

On the other hand, she had never met a man like Cyrus. Last night she had gotten a look at what lay behind the barrier of self-containment that he had fashioned for himself. That glimpse had confirmed what her intuition had already told her. The strength she had sensed in him went all the way through to the bone.

She wondered morosely if Cyrus was having second thoughts. She studied him out of the corner of her eye. He was in full Western lawman mode. Cold-eyed, watchful, steel-jawed. She half expected him to flash a badge.

She doubted that the fact that they had gone to bed together was what was bothering him this morning. She knew that he had reveled in the passion, just as she had. But a man who was accustomed to keeping much of himself concealed behind a wall of self-imposed control might seriously regret having allowed anyone a glimpse past the barricade.

She surveyed the dense, wet trees that surrounded them. "Are you sure we're going the right way?"

"I'm sure."

She shoved her hands deeper into the pockets of her black windbreaker. The plan had been a simple one, she thought. Park the Jeep well away from Rhonda Price's cabin so that it would not be noticed, and then hike in through the woods. But she had begun to feel disoriented as soon as she lost sight of the road.

"Maybe we should have brought a map," she said.

"We don't need a map."

She gazed around with a sense of growing unease. "All these trees. It's hard to tell which way we're walking."

"Relax. We'll be there in another few minutes."

"People get lost in the woods every year. Sometimes they're never found."

"This is an island, remember?" He looked briefly amused. "A small one, at that. The terrain slopes gradually downward to the water from the highest point. If you get lost, you just keep moving downhill. Sooner or later you'll hit Island Way Road."

She felt like an idiot. "I knew that."

"Look, if you want to change your mind about this—"

"I am not going to change my mind."

"Fine. Then we keep walking."

Eugenia decided it would be best if she kept her mouth shut for a while. Nothing intelligent was coming out of it, anyway.

The cottage came into view a short time later, a lonely, rundown cabin that should have appeared quaint and rustic, but that looked forlorn and sad, instead. *Rather like its tenant,* Eugenia thought, recalling the thin, desperate Rhonda.

Cyrus halted at the edge of the clearing.

Eugenia stopped beside him. She gazed at the small cabin. The windows were grimy, the curtains faded and tattered. The log walls needed to be restained. Bits and pieces of a low rockery indicated that someone had once attempted a garden, but the effort had been abandoned long ago.

"I only talked to Rhonda for about a minute and a half last night," Eugenia said. "But I felt kind of sorry for her."

"Yeah?" Cyrus studied the cottage from the shelter of a large fir. "Why?"

"I don't know. There was an air of desperation about her. I think she was scared."

"She had good reason. She was afraid you were about to expose her fraud."

"Yes, but the real question is, why was she trying to pass off Nellie's work as her own in the first place?"

Cyrus looked at her. "Simple. Rhonda's probably a lousy artist. She found Nellie's stuff, figured Nellie didn't need it anymore, and decided to claim it as her own."

"Maybe. Well, we're not accomplishing anything standing around out here. Let's go inside and see if we can find the other two paintings in Nellie's *Glass* series. You're the expert. How do we do this?"

"The simplest way possible," Cyrus said.

He took the lead, moving quietly through the trees until they reached the rear of the cabin. A stack of firewood, a battered plastic garbage can, and a hose guarded the door.

Cyrus went up the two wooden steps and knocked.

Eugenia frowned. "You do know how to pick locks, don't you?"

Humor gleamed in his cool gaze. He pulled a handkerchief out of his pocket. "First, we try it the easy way." He wrapped the square of cloth around the doorknob and twisted.

Eugenia watched, astonished, as the door swung inward. "It's not locked."

"You heard what Deputy Peaceful said the night we found old Leonard. Frog Cove Island is a small-town kind of place. Most folks don't even lock their doors." Cyrus leaned inside. "Anybody home?"

A heavy silence poured through the open door. Cyrus paused a few seconds. There was an air of stillness about him, as if he were listening to sounds that no one else could hear.

Eugenia felt herself growing increasingly tense. "What are you waiting for?"

"Nothing. Just making sure that we're alone." He walked into the cottage.

Eugenia followed quickly.

"Don't touch anything," Cyrus warned.

"Believe me, I won't." She gazed around the minuscule kitchen. It contained an ancient stove, an even older refrigerator, and a badly cracked sink. The linoleum on the floor was stained and torn.

"Very atmospheric," she said.

"Also very cheap."

"That too." Eugenia looked at him, uncertain how to proceed. "Where do we start?"

"You tell me. This was your idea."

She glared. "I've never done this before."

"Hang around with me, lady, and you will experience all sorts of new adventures. First time without a vibrator, huh?"

Heat washed through her. She knew she was turning red. So much for hoping that he had not recalled that less-than-sophisticated remark.

"I think I'll start with her studio," she said. "Every artist, even a bad one, has a studio."

"All right. Use this to open closets and drawers." He tossed her the handkerchief. "As long as I'm here,

I might as well take a look at her files. I'm not having much luck with Daventry's."

She glanced down at the handkerchief. "What will you use?"

"These." He took a pair of transparent plastic gloves out of his pocket. They made snapping sounds as he molded them to his hands.

Eugenia stared. "Good grief. Sometimes you scare me."

"The feeling is mutual." He went through the door that opened onto a small living room.

Eugenia trailed after him. "What sort of files would someone like Rhonda Price have?"

"Everyone has files." Cyrus came to a halt in the center of the room. "Phone bills, credit cards, bank statements. Paperwork is as necessary to modern life as food and shelter. You can't live without it. And it always leaves a trail."

"Rather like the paperwork that provides a provenance for a work of art."

He glanced at her. "Exactly like that."

Eugenia looked around the shabbily furnished front room. There was an easel near the window. Next to it was a stand full of tubes of acrylic paints. Two old mayonnaise jars containing brushes were arranged on the table.

Rhonda Price's studio.

There were several canvases stacked against one wall. Eugenia headed for them first, wondering if she would get lucky straight off. She sorted through them quickly and saw immediately that things were not going to be as simple as she had hoped. None of the pictures bore any trace of Nellie's talent.

"You were right when you said that Rhonda was probably a lousy artist. No wonder Fenella Weeks said the painting I bought represented a new departure for her."

Cyrus studied the painting she held out. "More than just a departure."

"Yes." Eugenia looked at a poorly executed abstract scene that featured a lot of muddy colors and meaningless shapes. There was no sense of form or substance. No sensation of depth. "You know, as an experienced gallery owner who had seen Rhonda's earlier work, Fenella must have noticed the difference in technical skill as well as the new subject matter."

"For all you know, she was well aware that the painting she sold to you wasn't Rhonda's work." Cyrus eased open a drawer in the battered desk near the window. "Maybe the two of them had an arrangement."

Eugenia looked up quickly. "You mean, Fenella agreed to sell the painting, split the money with Rhonda, and not ask any questions?"

"Why not?"

Eugenia considered that. "It makes sense as far as it goes, but there wasn't a lot of cash involved. I only paid three hundred dollars for Nellie's picture."

Cyrus glanced meaningfully around the decrepit cottage. "Three hundred bucks would go quite a ways around here."

"True. Especially if Rhonda was feeding a drug habit on top of everything else. You know, Cyrus, I think I'd better have another chat with Fenella."

"What good will that do? She'll deny that she knew the painting wasn't Rhonda's. She'll just play the role of innocent gallery owner who was duped. It's not as if you caught her trying to pass off a forged Cézanne or Picasso. No one's going to be real upset about any of this."

"Except the artist's friend."

Cyrus flipped through a sheaf of phone bills he had found. "But the artist's friend has no proof that the painting she bought in the Midnight Gallery was done by anyone other than Rhonda. Another piece of free advice. Be careful before you start flinging around accusations you can't back up. In my experience, people get real ticked."

"Damn. You're right." Eugenia leaned the paintings against the wall. "This is so frustrating. All these questions and no answers."

"It's always like this at the beginning of a case," Cyrus said.

"How do you stand it? Doesn't it drive you crazy?"

"You get used to it. The key is to have patience. Lots and lots of patience."

She remembered what he'd said about being on the trail of the Hades cup for three long years. "I'm not the patient type."

The remote, self-contained expression in Cyrus's eyes slipped again. An unnerving hint of pure, masculine complacency appeared in its place.

"Yeah. I've noticed," he said.

She knew that he was recalling her enthusiastic passion last night. *Dignity,* she reminded herself bracingly. She must focus on maintaining her composure. She could be just as cool and controlled as he was. Deliberately she turned her back on him.

She wandered down the short hall and went into the tiny bedroom. An aging bed, a threadbare rug, and a sagging dresser constituted the furnishings.

She got down on her hands and knees and surveyed the floor beneath the bed. The search revealed only a stack of old art journals and some dust bunnies.

She brushed the dust off her hands, stood, and went to the closet. When she opened the door with the aid of the handkerchief, she found several paint-stained shirts and a couple of pairs of faded jeans.

The dresser drawers offered underwear, socks, and some folded sweaters.

She was about to give up in disgust when she glanced behind the dresser and saw the faint gleam of a black metal frame. Excitement flooded through her. *"Cyrus."*

He came to stand in the doorway. "Find something?"

"There's a painting here." She wriggled her arm behind the dresser and groped for the edge of the frame with the handkerchief. "I can only think of one reason why Rhonda would put it back here."

"Yeah, it is kind of obvious, isn't it?"

His ironic tone annoyed her. "What do you mean?"

"It strikes me that if I wanted to hide a painting, I'd pick a more discreet location. Not some place where anyone could find it within five minutes."

"You forget, Rhonda didn't intend to hide it. Not for long, at any rate. She planned to pass it off as her own work." Eugenia dragged the painting carefully out into the open. "My guess is that she simply stored it here as a temporary measure after she ripped it off."

Cyrus studied the painting as Eugenia turned it toward him. "Well, you're right about one thing. Even to my untrained eye, that looks like your friend Nellie's work."

Eugenia examined the three enameled glass flasks arranged against the neon green background. The painting was infused with Nellie's trademark sense of light. "More items from the Daventry collection."

Cyrus frowned. "You recognize those pieces?"

"Yes. Three of the eighteenth-century Venetians. I saw them yesterday." She bent closer. "Look, Nellie's signature is still on this painting. Rhonda hasn't had a chance to alter it."

"All right, you've made your point. It does look as if Rhonda helped herself to at least two of Nellie Grant's paintings."

"And I've got the third in this series hanging in my condo. That means there's only one more to find." Eugenia drummed her fingers on the edge of the frame. "I'm going to confront Rhonda with this as soon as she gets out of the hospital. She knows something, Cyrus. I'm sure of it. I'm still afraid she'll disappear as soon as she's released."

"I told you, I'll find her if she doesn't come back to the island."

"I know, but . . ."

"You don't have a lot of faith in my talents, do you?"

She flushed. "I've already apologized once for my remarks on that subject."

"Don't worry, my ego is getting accustomed to being sliced and diced."

She felt her jaw tighten. "Let's be honest here, Cyrus. You've agreed to help me because you want my cooperation. But you've made it very clear that the only thing you really care about is the Hades cup."

Cold light doused the amusement in his eyes. "We have a deal." The words were shards of glass, sharp and dangerous.

Eugenia shivered. "Sorry," she said stiffly. "I didn't mean to imply that I doubted your word." Damn, damn, damn. She was apologizing to him again.

"You want a written contract?"

Her cheeks were flaming hot now. "No, forget it. I never meant . . . Oh, the heck with it. Let's change the subject."

"Fine by me."

Eugenia felt as if she'd had a narrow escape. This was what came of introducing sex into the situation, she thought. Everything between herself and Cyrus had become infinitely more complicated. She could not even get mad at him in quite the same way that she had before they had gone to bed together.

She took a deep breath. "I just thought of something. If Rhonda was so familiar with Glass House that she knew where these paintings were stored, she may have known other things about what went on there."

"Yeah."

The single, softly spoken word riveted Eugenia. She stared at Cyrus. His eyes were colder now than they had been a moment ago.

"Don't tell me, let me guess," she said carefully. "You're wondering if Rhonda might be able to give you a lead on the Hades cup."

"The possibility has occurred to me."

"Oh." No wonder he was so willing to help her keep track of Rhonda Price, she thought glumly. Once again, the paths that led to their individual agendas were intertwined.

Cyrus looked at her. "While you're worrying about my real motives for helping you keep tabs on Rhonda Price, there is one other thing you might want to consider."

"What's that?"

"Try this for a shot in the dark. What if Nellie Grant isn't dead? What if she's alive and working with Rhonda?"

For a second she did not think she had heard him correctly. "What on earth are you talking about?"

"It's a small island. All the artists attended Daventry's parties. It's reasonable to assume that Nellie and Rhonda knew each other."

"Yes, but what does that have to do with it? The authorities said that Nellie is dead."

"They never found a body."

"No, but . . ." It was too much to take in all at once. Eugenia tried to think. "Impossible. If Nellie were alive, she would have contacted me."

"Maybe. Maybe not. If Nellie decided that she had to disappear for some reason, she could have faked the lost-at-sea bit. You said she knew her way around boats, right?"

"Yes," Eugenia whispered. "That's why I doubted that she'd been washed overboard by accident. I assumed she'd been murdered and someone had made the killing look like a boating disaster. But I never considered that she might have deliberately disappeared. I still think she would have contacted me by now if she were alive."

"Go with me on this. If she were alive, it's possible that she arranged for Rhonda to sell the paintings in order to raise some quick cash."

More questions without answers. Eugenia folded her arms very tightly beneath her breasts. "We have to talk to Rhonda."

"I think," Cyrus said, "that what we need right now is some coffee."

"No, thanks," Eugenia said.

"At the Neon Sunset Café," Cyrus added. "It's the closest thing to a coffee house that this island has, and everyone knows that artists like to hang out in coffee houses. Rhonda may have spent some time there."

"You're right." Eugenia brightened. "Someone who works there might be able to tell us a lot about Rhonda. Good idea, Cyrus."

"Thanks, but I can't take credit for it. I got the idea from chapter five of the detective manual."

"What detective manual?"

"The one that came with the correspondence course I took to get my PI license."

"A correspondence course, hmm? Nice to know I'm working with a real pro," Eugenia said.

The Neon Sunset was almost entirely deserted. A teenaged waitress dressed in a T-shirt and jeans lounged against the counter, flipping through a copy of a magazine that featured a malnourished model on the cover.

"Ten o'clock in the morning is not a fashionable hour for the artistic crowd." Eugenia sat down at a small table. "They go in for late nights."

"That means that the waitress will be bored. Bored people love to talk."

Eugenia watched Cyrus remove the worn leather jacket he had put on over his aloha shirt and lower himself into a chair. Every action was carried out with the slow, unhurried masculine grace that never failed to intrigue her.

After all this time with him, she still had not seen him make any fidgity or restless movements. He didn't drum his fingers or swing a foot or tap a toe the way she often did. He never fiddled with spoons or refolded paper napkins into new shapes. He simply commanded the space he inhabited. The man in the photographer's vest seated at the next table was a lot bigger and bulkier, but it was Cyrus who dominated the room.

"How do we get the waitress onto the subject of Rhonda Price without being obvious?" Eugenia asked.

Cyrus watched the waitress approach. "Something tells me that won't be a problem."

Eugenia frowned. "Why not?"

"You're an overnight celebrity."

" 'Morning." The young woman came to a halt beside the table. She looked at Eugenia with keen interest and snapped her gum. "You're the lady who jumped into the marina to save Rhonda Price last night, aren't you?"

"Uh, yes. That's right." Eugenia caught Cyrus's eye. He looked amused. She turned back to the waitress. There was a small name tag on her shirt. It read *Heather*. "Are you a friend of Rhonda's?"

"Not exactly. I know her, though. Everyone does. She comes in here a lot. Likes to pretend she's a real hotshot artist, but I've heard Fenella Weeks say she can't even draw a straight line."

"I don't agree," Eugenia said smoothly. "I bought one of Rhonda's paintings. It's very, very good."

Heather shrugged with complete disinterest. "I'm not, like, really into art, y'know? I just work here."

"No kidding." Cyrus smiled at her. "I thought maybe you were an artist, yourself."

"Nah." She blushed. "Not hardly. My Dad says if I get mixed up with that crowd while I'm workin' here, he'll make me quit my job."

"He doesn't approve of the local bohemian community?" Eugenia asked.

"Don't know about bohemians, but he doesn't think much of artists. Says they're all lazy. Won't get real jobs. He says the only thing they want to do is get high and party. Says the island was a nicer place before Adam Daventry set up the art colony. Personally, I think it was kind of a boring place."

"Does Rhonda like to party, too?"

"Oh, sure. She used to go up to Glass House all the time," Heather said. "She and Mr. Daventry had a thing going for a while. Boy, was she pissed when he dropped her to take up with that artist from Seattle. But that didn't stop her from going to his parties."

"Rhonda had an affair with Daventry." Eugenia folded her arms and watched Island Way Road untwist in front of the Jeep. "It makes sense. Another artist's scalp for Daventry's belt."

"Yeah. It also raises some new questions."

"It certainly works against your theory that Rhonda and Nellie were friends. The waitress implied that Rhonda was jealous of Nellie. Maybe she stole the paintings to get even."

"We can't be sure of that. Friendships can form under some unusual circumstances." Cyrus slanted her an assessing glance. "Just like other kinds of relationships."

Eugenia stiffened. Did he mean that he wanted to talk about their relationship? "I suppose we should discuss things."

He had the grace not to pretend that he did not have a clue. "I vote we don't. Call me intuitive, but I have a hunch that if we try to talk about it, we'll get into serious trouble."

Disappointment settled heavily in the pit of her stomach. "You may be right."

"You ever been involved in one of these before?"

"An affair?"

"An affair with a man you figure is all wrong for you," he clarified. "Someone like me who doesn't fit the profile."

"No."

"Guess that explains it."

She frowned. "Explains what?"

"Why you're so tense."

"I am not tense."

"You've been acting like a cat that got its tail caught in the screen door on Halloween, as my Grandpappy Beau used to say."

"I am not tense."

"Hell, you're making me tense."

She did not believe that for a moment. It was impossible to imagine Cyrus tense. She turned abruptly in the seat to face him.

"You just got through saying that it would probably be best if we did not discuss this," she said.

"Yeah, I did, didn't I?" He sounded morose.

She hesitated and then gave in to the impulse. "Do I fit the profile of the kind of woman you generally get involved with?"

"Nope, you sure don't."

"I see." She was amazed at the depressing effect that bit of news had on her. It was not as though she had not already known the answer, she thought. "Well, that makes us even, at any rate."

"Yeah." The cellular phone rang. Cyrus reached for it. "This is Colfax." He frowned. "Rick? Where are you?" There was a brief silence as he listened. "What happened to the summer job? All right, stay where you are. I'll come and get you."

Eugenia glanced at the phone as he set it down. "Who was that?"

"My nephew, Rick Tasker." Cyrus braked to a smooth stop. "He just arrived on the ferry. Says he wants to spend a couple of days here with me."

Surprised, Eugenia considered. Then she shrugged. "It's all right with me, if that's what's worrying you. There's plenty of room."

"Thanks, I appreciate it. But that's not the big problem."

She tilted her head slightly, trying to read him. "What is the problem?"

"I know Rick pretty damn well. Something's wrong."

Fourteen

"**W**hat happened to the job at the video arcade?" Cyrus asked.

"The guy who hired me said he wouldn't need me for another couple of days." Rick was monumentally casual.

"So you just blew off the whole concept of a summer job?"

Eugenia glanced at Cyrus as she set two cans of soda down on the small chrome tables. The almost paternal note of criticism in his voice surprised her. He sounded more like an irritated father than an uncle related only through a very short marriage.

"Don't sweat it. I'll go back to Portland day after tomorrow. The job is still there." Rick picked up one of the soft drink cans and popped the top. "So, is it okay if I stay?"

"Yeah. Sure. It's okay. But we agreed you'd work this summer. The idea was that you would buy your own books in the fall, remember?"

"I remember." Rick swallowed some of his cola.

Eugenia sank down onto the padded chrome lounger and took a sip of the bottled spring water she had opened for herself. She studied Cyrus and Rick as they talked together. This was one of the clearest glimpses she'd had yet into Cyrus's personal life. It made her realize that she was hungry for any small insight she could get.

Physically, the two males had little in common. The lack of a blood relationship was obvious. Next to Cyrus, Rick was the epitome of the young, modern, suburban aristocrat, well-bred, well-dressed, and handsome in the manner of such beings.

His slender, youthful build was rapidly maturing into the sort of trim, athletic figure that would one day look terrific in power suits and silk ties. His teeth had been straightened to perfection. His light brown hair had been cut and styled in an expensive salon. Anyone could see that BMWs, designer labels, tennis, and good schools were in his genes.

Rick was fated to go through life with jackets that always fit well, Eugenia reflected. She was pretty sure that money for college textbooks would not be a genuine problem in the fall. This talk of getting a job had to do with principle, not financial necessity. Cyrus wanted Rick to contribute toward his own education.

What fascinated Eugenia was not the superficial differences between Cyrus and Rick, but the more subtle similarities. They spoke volumes about the relationship between the two.

Rick's easy, relaxed position in the lounger was nearly identical to Cyrus's. The heels of his pricey sneakers were stacked on the railing in an exact echo of the way Cyrus had propped his own moccasin-shod feet. Rick even held a can of soda the way Cyrus held his, fingers circling the rim with negligent control.

"Does your mom know you're here on Frog Cove Island with me?" Cyrus asked.

"Yeah." Rick gazed out at the waters of the Sound with the sullen, sulky expression unique to those on the brink of adulthood. "Sure."

"Rick . . ."

"I left her a note, okay?"

"A note." Cyrus took a swallow of his drink. "I don't think a note really cuts it. Go call her and tell her where you are."

An angry, mutinous look flashed across Rick's face. But he got up without an argument and walked into the house.

Cyrus waited until Rick was out of earshot before he turned to look at Eugenia. "Sorry about this."

"It's all right."

"He's going off to college in the fall. Hasn't made up his mind what he wants to study yet, though."

"No reason to rush the decision."

Cyrus frowned. "Can't put it off for long. He needs to get focused."

"He's only eighteen, Cyrus. There's plenty of time for him to settle on a career path."

"I think he should go into computer science. That's where the jobs are these days."

"Some of them. But not all of them."

"Things aren't the same as they were when I was his age. Back then, you could hustle a job if you had guts and determination. Today that's not enough. You've got to have technical expertise of some kind."

Eugenia smiled to herself. "That sounds like something my grandmother once said to me."

Cyrus shot her a frowning glance. Then his mouth quirked in a rueful line. "Is that a polite way of telling me that I'm coming across as an old codger?"

Eugenia thought about the heated lovemaking that

had kept her awake for a good portion of the night. "Actually, you're pretty spry for an old codger."

His brows rose. "Spry?"

"If I think of a better word, I'll let you know."

"You do that." Cyrus took another swallow from the can and leaned his head back against the lounger. "I wonder what really happened to the video arcade job."

Rick came out onto the veranda. His face was set in stubborn lines. "Mom wants to talk to you, Cyrus."

"Figured she would." Cyrus exhaled deeply, took his feet down off the rail, stood, and went indoors.

Rick glanced warily at Eugenia as he sat down. "Is he mad?"

"You know him better than I do."

"Sometimes it's hard to tell what Cyrus is thinking."

Eugenia smiled. "I know. For what it's worth, I don't think he's mad."

"But he's not real thrilled to have me show up on the doorstep like this."

"He's worried about your summer job."

"Not a problem." Rick's fingers clenched around the rim of the can. "It's still there, waiting for me when I get back day after tomorrow."

Eugenia said nothing. She and Rick sat in silence for a while. After a time, Cyrus reappeared. His eyes were grim.

"I think we'd better talk, Rick."

Eugenia glanced at Rick and saw the stiffness in his shoulders. She stood quickly. "If you'll excuse me, I'm going to do some work in the glass vault."

Neither Cyrus nor Rick took any notice of her as she slipped inside. She closed the French doors behind her, aware of the brooding weight of the stillness that settled on the veranda in her wake.

The phone rang just as she started to descend the

stairs into the basement. She picked it up on the third ring.

"Hello?"

"I'm trying to reach Cyrus Colfax," a brusque male voice announced. "He there?"

"Yes." Eugenia hesitated, glancing toward the glass-paned doors. She could see that Cyrus and Rick were locked in tense conversation. "He's a little busy at the moment. Can I take a message?"

"Better interrupt him. This is important. He'll want to hear what I have to say."

Eugenia scowled at the phone. "May I say who's calling?"

"Tell him it's Quint Yates."

"Excuse me." She infused her voice with the brisk, cool tone she used when she dealt with telephone solicitors. "I'll be right back."

Eugenia put down the phone and walked back to the glass doors. She saw Rick gesture wildly with the hand that held the soda can. His young face was suffused with anger and pain. Cyrus sat stoically in his chair, feet propped once more on the railing.

She opened the door cautiously.

"I'll tell you how I found out." Rick's voice rose with impassioned rage. "I overheard Mom talking to Dad on the phone. They were arguing about money again. I heard her tell him that she knew you'd forced him to come to my graduation. She said you must have threatened him or something. Is that true?"

Eugenia opened the door wider. "Excuse me, there's a phone call."

Cyrus ignored her. "There was a mix-up in your father's schedule. I just gave him a call and reminded him of the date of your graduation. No big deal."

"That's not what Mom said."

"Your mother did not overhear the conversation I had with your father."

Eugenia tried again. "Cyrus, the phone."

"Dad only came to my graduation because you made him come," Rick said fiercely. "Admit it. He never wanted to be there. No wonder he didn't hang around. What did you do to get him to fly in from L.A. for the day?"

"Let it go, Rick."

A suspicious glitter of moisture appeared in Rick's eyes. He blinked furiously. "I just want to know what it took to make my Dad come to my graduation. What kind of threat did you use? Tell me. I want to know the truth, damn it. Is that asking too much?"

"What your Dad and I talked about is our personal business," Cyrus said without inflection.

"Like hell. I'm involved here, y'know."

Eugenia cleared her throat. "Don't know about you, Rick, but speaking personally, I can tell you that I would have paid someone like Cyrus big bucks and not asked any questions if he had promised to get my father to attend my high school graduation. And I would have paid him double if he could have found a way to get Dad to my brother's and sister's graduations."

Rick jerked in his chair. He turned to glare at her. His face was flushed, his eyes, wary. "Huh?"

"My father didn't come to my graduation because he was assisting his new wife in childbirth classes. He told me on the phone that he wanted to experience every aspect of fatherhood the second time around."

"No shit," Rick said, clearly taken aback.

"He didn't make my brother's graduation because he had to deliver a paper at a sociology seminar on new directions in the American family. And he missed my sister's because it was on the same date as his new son's birthday."

Rick stared at her.

Eugenia turned to Cyrus. "There's a phone call for you. Someone named Quint Yates."

"Right. Daily report time." Cyrus got to his feet.

"What kind of a dad would have to be forced to go to his own son's graduation?" Rick demanded of no one in particular.

"Who knows?" Eugenia said. "Probably the kind who had a bad father, himself. At least, that's the usual explanation. It has to do with repeating bad parenting patterns or something."

Rick frowned. "But if a guy had a bad father, he should figure out that he ought to do things differently with his own kid."

Eugenia was impressed. "You're right. Unfortunately, not everyone looks at things that clearly." She paused. "And sometimes people are just too weak to make the effort to change the pattern. They won't accept the responsibility."

Cyrus paused briefly in the doorway. "At least you two grew up with a father somewhere in the picture. I've never even met mine."

He walked into the house and closed the door very quietly behind him.

Eugenia gaped, dumbstruck.

Rick was equally stricken.

"What was that all about?" Eugenia finally asked.

Rick shifted uncomfortably. "Mom told me once that Cyrus's father took off before he was born. His parents weren't even married. That's about all I know. Cyrus never talks about it."

Eugenia dropped down onto the lounger and picked up her bottled water. She sat for a moment, gazing out over the cold Sound.

"Sort of puts things in perspective, doesn't it?" she said after a while.

"Yeah." Rick grimaced. "Cyrus has a way of doing that."

Cyrus halted at the top of the staircase and glanced at his watch. The glowing dial revealed that it was ten minutes after one in the morning. The house had been quiet since ten-thirty, when its three occupants had disappeared into the privacy of their own rooms.

He had lain on the top of his bed, staring at the ceiling for a while, and thought about how Eugenia had gone off to bed without giving him a clue to her mood. He had not even been able to tell if she wanted him to go to her room.

One thing had become clear as the minutes ticked past. She had no plans to come to his room.

He decided that, as a trained detective, it was simple to deduce two possibilities. The first was that he and Eugenia had experienced a glaring failure to communicate. The second was that she had deliberately used Rick's presence in the house as an excuse to hide out in the safety of her own room.

Last night she had wanted him. She had left him in no doubt on that point. But he also knew that she was wary of getting involved with a man who did not fit her image of a suitable mate. A man whose motives she did not entirely trust. A man who could make her lose control.

Yeah, now that he thought about it, it was obvious why she was avoiding him tonight.

On top of that, Rick was pissed at him, and Zackery Elland Chandler had hired a private investigator.

And just to finish off the list, he was afraid that he was no closer to finding the Hades cup than he had been when he arrived on the island.

All in all, not one of his better days.

The brooding feeling had grown steadily heavier as the night deepened. When he had finally accepted the fact that he was not going to get any sleep, he put on a pair of pants and his blue pineapple shirt and decided to do something productive. Like check the house locks.

He went down the glass block staircase barefooted, listening to the sounds of the night. He did not need the flashlight he had brought with him. Moonlight streamed through the wall of windows that overlooked the Sound. It formed colorless pools on the floor and glimmered on shiny, reflective surfaces.

At the bottom of the stairs he crossed the cold tiles to the front door. The security-coded lock was set.

He turned and walked methodically through the shadowy rooms. One by one he checked windows and doors.

He was in the front room, trying the French doors next to the mirrored fireplace, when he heard the soft movement behind him. He knew that it was Eugenia who stood there even before he turned around and saw her revealed in a puddle of silvery moonlight.

"Cyrus?" She held the lapels of her bathrobe closed at her throat with one hand. "I thought I heard you in the hall. Is anything wrong?"

"No. Just checking the locks. You must have been awake if you heard me leave my room."

"Couldn't sleep."

"Thinking about Nellie?"

"No." Her eyes were mysterious, shadowed and deep. "I was thinking about you."

This was good, Cyrus told himself. Thinking about him had kept her awake. This was a very encouraging sign.

"What about me?"

"I was wondering what happened when you finally tracked down your father."

He should have seen that one coming, he thought. But he hadn't. He'd been too busy wondering if she had followed him downstairs in order to invite him into her bed. So much for his ability to detect clues. Probably ought to go back and reread chapter thirteen of the detective manual.

He walked to the next set of French doors. Checked the lock.

"What makes you think I traced him?" he asked.

"Let's just say that I can't see you *not* looking for him. You would have wanted to find the answers. Close the books."

He stood looking out through the glass panes of the French door. "I guess you could say that he was my first missing persons case. I went looking for him a few months after my grandparents died. I was two years older than Rick is now. I didn't know how to do things efficiently in those days. Took me a while. A year and a half."

"But you finally located him?"

"He lives in Southern California. Used to be a partner in a big law firm. Married. Two kids. Both went to private schools. Both became lawyers. Just like their father."

"I see."

"He belongs to a country club where some of the stars play golf. His family had money, and his wife's had even more of it. So he went into politics."

"Do I know his name?"

"Zackery Elland Chandler."

Eugenia whistled softly. "The congressman?"

"Yeah. He's running for the U.S. Senate at the moment. Right from the start of his career he based his campaigns on his support for old-fashioned family values and the need for individuals to take personal responsibility."

"Ouch."

"Sort of ironic, isn't it?"

"Did you introduce yourself?" she asked.

"Didn't seem to be much point in it. He never came looking for me so I figured he'd just as soon I didn't show up on his front doorstep."

"From what I've read, Chandler is in a very tight race."

"Yeah."

"You'd be one heck of a threat to his political career. I can see the headlines now: *Conservative candidate's abandoned son holds press conference.*"

"I don't think I'll be holding a press conference."

"No," she said. "Well, at least you know who he is. He's not a total mystery."

Cyrus studied the way the trees shouldered together to prevent the moonlight from reaching the forest floor. "Funny you should say that. There's a lot of mystery left."

"What do you mean?"

"I found out today that Chandler sent a private investigator to my hometown. I think he's trying to find me."

Eugenia was silent for a while. "Do you want to be found?"

"I don't know. I may not have a choice. The real question is, why is he looking for me now, after all these years?"

"Any ideas?"

"I've been thinking. There's one possibility that leaps to mind."

"What's that?" Eugenia asked gently.

"Something has happened to make him believe that I'm a potential threat to his political future. He may be trying to find me in order to try to deal with me now rather than have the situation blow up in his face."

"Deal with you? What do you mean?"

"Maybe he'll offer me money to deny the relationship. There's no paperwork that can link us. My mother did not put his name on the birth certificate. She died without revealing it to my grandparents or anyone else."

"There are genetic tests," Eugenia said.

Cyrus smiled grimly. "Maybe he wants to pay me not to submit to them."

"You're working on sheer speculation here, Cyrus. Maybe it's not what you think. Maybe your father is looking for you because he wants to get to know you."

"If he had wanted to know me, he would have come looking long ago. There's a reason why he's searching for me now. I need to know what it is."

"All right, I understand. But in the meantime, why don't we go to bed?"

He turned around to face her. "What?"

She smiled and held out her hand. "It's late. Let's go upstairs. You need your sleep, and so do I."

He felt the warmth seep back into him. It drove out the cold that had settled deep inside. "Are we talking one bed or two?"

"One bed."

He started toward her, aware of his erection pressing hard against his zipper. "Yours or mine?"

She laughed, a soft, welcoming sound that flowed over him like a sparkling stream.

"Surprise me," she said.

"Thought you'd never ask." A fierce, exultant sensation cascaded through him. He scooped her up in his arms and carried her out of the front room.

Eugenia smiled again as he started up the elegant

staircase with her. "I think I saw this scene in a movie once."

"Yeah? The guy have as much style as me?"

The sexy alchemy of feminine anticipation gleamed in her sultry eyes. She touched the front of his pineapple aloha shirt.

"Not by half," she said.

She awoke at dawn, aware that Cyrus was sitting up on the edge of her bed. The first thing she saw when she opened her eyes was the vicious scar on the back of his shoulder. She had felt it with her fingertips during their lovemaking, but this was the first time she had actually seen it. Yesterday morning when she had left his bed the sheet had still covered him.

"Cyrus." She levered herself up on her elbow and touched the old wound very gently. "This was where Damien March shot you, isn't it?"

"You know about that, too?"

"Yes. The information came with the other data Sally Warren dug up on you."

He caught her hand, turned it over, and kissed her wrist. "I told you I'd once had a nasty experience with a gun."

"Nasty is right. It must have been incredibly painful."

He grimaced. "And not especially sexy. I should have worn a shirt to bed."

"Don't be ridiculous." She sat up and folded her legs, tailor-fashion, beneath the sheet. "If I had an old wound like that, would the sight of it bother you?"

He looked startled. "No, of course not."

"Then you know how I feel about seeing your scars," she said impatiently. "What bothers me is realizing how much it must have hurt. This is the first time I've seen the extent of the damage. It's a miracle you weren't killed."

His face relaxed. "It's all right. It was a long time ago."

"It was only three years ago."

His smiled. "Calm down, I'm okay."

"He shot you in the *back,* Cyrus. He not only tried to kill you, the bastard did it in the most treacherous, cowardly way possible."

"Hush." Cyrus put his fingertips over her mouth. "You'll wake Rick."

"But—"

He took his fingers away from her lips and kissed her until she fell back against the pillows. He followed her down, crushing her gently into the bedding. The solid, warm weight of his body sent delicious tingles of awareness all the way to her toes.

"Remember what I said about how you could never control me with sex?" she murmured.

"Yeah." He cradled her face between his hands. His eyes gleamed in the dawn light. "Change your mind?"

"Not exactly." She ran her fingers through his hair. "But I was wondering if maybe you'd like to try it again?"

He laughed softly, a rich, dark, sensual laugh that wrapped her in warm honey. "Like my Grandpappy Beau used to say, if at first you don't succeed . . ."

"Try, try again?"

He grinned. "Sounds like you knew my grandfather."

"It was just a wild guess. I told you, I've got excellent intuition."

"I remember." He glanced out the window. "As much as I respect my grandfather, I think my next try had better wait until tonight."

With obvious regret he eased away from her and got to his feet.

She watched him scoop up the aloha shirt that had been tossed onto the floor during the night. His broad shoulders moved with easy power as he slipped into it.

It gave her a strange feeling to have him in her bedroom like this. She could not take her eyes off him as he pulled on his pants. The quiet, confident masculinity that emanated from him riveted all her senses.

"You're going back to your own room because of Rick, aren't you?" she asked.

"I'm sure he's figured out that you and I are sleeping together, and that's okay." Cyrus picked up his moccasins. "But I want him to know that there is such a thing as discretion and common courtesy. A man doesn't flaunt his lover in front of an eighteen-year-old kid."

She smiled. "Is that something else Grandpappy Beau taught you?"

"I figured that one out for myself." He started toward the door.

"Cyrus?"

He turned back, waiting.

"About this eighteen-year-old kid," she said slowly.

His expression darkened. "Don't remind me. I've got to find a way to make things right between Rick and me today. But I'm not sure how to do it."

"Try letting him know that you don't think of him as a kid anymore."

Cyrus studied her intently for a long moment. "You think that's part of the problem?"

"I get the impression you've been a father figure to him for so long that you may not have realized you've done your job."

"My job?"

"You've made a man of him. I think he wants to be treated like one."

Cyrus was silent for a while. Then he nodded. "I guess you're right. Maybe he doesn't need me anymore."

The strange echo of a deeply buried wistfulness in his voice made her frown. "He may not need you to protect him or show him how to be a man, but I can guarantee that there's something else he needs from you a whole lot more. And he's going to want it for the rest of his life."

"What's that?"

"Your respect."

Cyrus gazed at her for a long moment. "Okay, I get the point. See you at breakfast."

Fifteen

*E*ugenia stood near the window of the Midnight Gallery and held the brilliant yellow, red, and turquoise glass sculpture in both hands. Light blazed through the seductive, sinuous curves.

"Beautiful," she murmured, more to herself than to Fenella, who watched from behind the counter.

"A lovely thing, isn't it? He calls it *Sun*."

Eugenia glanced at her. "A local artist?"

"Yes. Jacob Houston. I mentioned him to you when you came in the other day. He has a house and workshop out on Creek Road."

Eugenia carried the sculpture to the counter and set it down very carefully. "I'll take this, please."

Fenella chuckled. "Going to put it into the Leabrook?"

"No. This one is going into my own personal collection. But I think I'll show it at the annual exhibition of contemporary studio glass at the Leabrook this fall."

Fenella's eyes widened. "The Cutting Edge exhibition?"

"That's right." Eugenia opened her wallet and took out her credit card. "I'd love to take a look at some other Houston pieces."

"You're serious, aren't you?"

"Very." Eugenia handed over her credit card.

"Jacob will be thrilled." Fenella worked the cash register as she talked.

"I'd like to speak to him." Eugenia watched Fenella cocoon the glass sculpture in numerous folds of heavy brown paper. "Can you give me directions to his workshop?"

"Creek Road is about a mile out of town. When you see the sign, turn left. Jacob's place is about half a mile from there. But be prepared. He's the temperamental type. Flies off the handle at the least provocation. Except when he's working the glass. Then he's as cool as iced tea on a summer day."

"Thanks." Eugenia picked up the package.

"Enjoying your stay out at Glass House?"

"Very much. Fantastic views."

"So I've heard."

Eugenia looked at her. "You've never been there?"

"Adam Daventry only invited *artists* to his parties." Disgust glinted in Fenella's eyes. "He was obsessed with them. Liked to surround himself with them, sleep with them, watch them work."

"I see." Be subtle, Eugenia thought. She had a sudden mental image of the dark gallery filled with art created by Daventry's old lovers. "I admit I've heard a few of the tales. Apparently he, uh, had a number of affairs."

"Slept with just about every female artist on the island and a few of the men, too."

This was, Eugenia realized, a perfect opportunity to confirm Heather's gossip about Rhonda Price. "Including the artist who painted the picture I bought?"

"Poor, silly Rhonda didn't last long," Fenella said flatly. "Daventry decided she had no real talent. He only wanted to sleep with talent. But he didn't know real talent when he saw it."

"If what you say is true, he was a fool, wasn't he?" Eugenia said softly. "After all, he failed to recognize Rhonda Price's incredible ability."

A startled look appeared in Fenella's eyes. It was followed by a brief flash of what could have been rage. It was quickly suppressed.

"Yes, he did."

"Sounds as if Daventry was a little sick."

Fenella's mouth tightened. "Well, he's gone now. It'll be interesting to see how long it takes the Daventry estate to sell Glass House. I doubt if there are too many buyers around for a place like that."

"I suppose not." Eugenia walked to the door and opened it. "Very expensive to maintain."

She stepped outside onto the sidewalk. She was surprised by the odd sense of relief she felt as soon as she was out of the gallery. Although they had a lot in common, she could not warm to Fenella. There was a lot of anger there, Eugenia thought. And some of it had been directed at Daventry. Fenella had obviously felt slighted by the fact that he had not invited her to his infamous parties.

Eugenia glanced toward the pier and noticed that the small private ferry had just docked. Five vehicles and a handful of walk-on passengers were preparing to disembark. The first wave of morning tourists was about to hit the island.

She crossed the street beneath the Daventry Workshops Festival banner and walked to where she had parked her Toyota. She opened the door and got behind the wheel. Very carefully she set the Jacob Houston sculpture down on the passenger seat beside her.

She was in the process of inserting the key into the ignition when the small flurry of ferry traffic trundled past. She froze when she caught a fleeting glimpse of a familiar-looking blond-haired woman behind the wheel of a small compact.

Rhonda Price was back on the island.

So much for Colfax Security's professional expertise, Eugenia thought. Rhonda Price was supposed to be in the hospital.

She slammed her car into gear and prepared to follow Rhonda.

She waited until Rhonda had driven to the end of the street and turned onto Island Way Drive. Then she eased her own car away from the curb and pursued her quarry at what she hoped was a discreet distance. There was no reason to follow too closely. It was obvious that Rhonda was headed toward her small cottage.

There would never be a better opportunity to confront her with questions about Nellie's *Glass* paintings.

Twenty minutes later she drove along the narrow, rutted road that ended more or less at Rhonda's front door. The compact was parked in the drive. The trunk was open.

Eugenia stopped her car next to Rhonda's, got out, and walked to the front door. It stood ajar.

She paused on the step and peered into the tiny front room. The sound of drawers crashing in the bedroom told her that Rhonda Price was frantically packing.

Eugenia knocked once. When there was no response, she stepped into the house. She went to the door of the bedroom.

Rhonda was inside, shoving clothing willy-nilly into two battered suitcases

"Leaving so soon?" Eugenia asked politely.

Rhonda gave a stifled scream and spun around. Genuine terror flashed in her eyes. It was replaced by anger when she saw Eugenia.

"You."

"Me." Eugenia propped one shoulder against the door frame and folded her arms. "I'm the one who went into the marina after you."

"If you expect me to thank you, don't hold your breath." Rhonda turned back to the dresser and jerked open another drawer. "I don't have time to express my undying gratitude. I've got to make the next ferry."

"Why?"

"Why?" Rhonda pulled some sweaters out of the drawer. "Because someone tried to kill me the other night, that's why. And I don't intend to hang around waiting for whoever it was to try again."

"Are you telling me that you think someone pushed you into the water?"

"I'd call it a little more than a push." Rhonda touched the bandage on her head. "I don't care what everyone thinks. I didn't fall and accidentally knock myself unconscious on the way over the side. Someone hit me first."

Eugenia straightened. "Did you see anyone?"

"Only you."

"I swear I didn't hit you."

Rhonda gave her a disgusted look. "I guess not. You wouldn't have jumped into the water to pull me out if you had wanted me to drown. But I'm sure that what happened to me was no accident."

Eugenia remembered the footsteps she had heard that night. "Do you remember anything at all?"

"No. The doctor at the hospital in Bellingham said something about it being common to lose some memory of events during the last few minutes before a head injury."

"Who would want to kill you?"

"I don't know." Rhonda went to the closet and started yanking shirts off hangers. "And since I can't prove that someone did try, I'm going to do the smart thing and disappear for a while."

"The same way Nellie Grant disappeared?"

Rhonda swung around, clutching the shirts. Her eyes widened. "Nellie Grant didn't disappear. She's dead."

"So they say. And you passed off at least one of her paintings as your own, didn't you?"

"That's a lie." Rhonda's eyes flickered toward the chest of drawers.

"I'm in the art business, remember?" Eugenia said gently. "I can recognize an artist's style and technique. I've seen Nellie's work. I've got *Glass I* hanging over my fireplace at home."

"So that's what happened to it," Rhonda muttered.

"What are you talking about?"

"Nothing." Rhonda raised one thin shoulder in a shrug. "You can't prove a damn thing."

"That's debatable. But we'll let it slide if you'll tell me why you took her paintings."

"I'm not going to tell you anything."

"Come on, Rhonda, you owe me something for pulling you out of the water."

Rhonda hesitated and then sighed. "What the hell? When he dumped me, Daventry made a point of telling me how *genuinely talented* my replacement was. So after they were both gone, I decided to help myself to those *brilliant* works of art."

"Why?"

Rhonda gave her a scathing look. "The usual reason. I needed the money."

"How did you get into Glass House? Leonard Hastings was supposed to keep an eye on the place."

"Leonard was old. His hearing was so bad he wouldn't have heard a train wreck if it had happened next to him. Besides, he had to sleep sometime, didn't he? I went in at night. I knew my way around because I'd stayed there for a while. I had the security codes for the doors."

Eugenia felt a piece of the puzzle click into place. "You used the pantry entrance, didn't you?"

Rhonda looked startled. Then she scowled. "Yes."

"When did you enter the house to get the paintings?"

"It took me a while to work up my nerve. But when I heard that some people from Seattle were coming to stay at Glass House, I knew I had to make my move." Rhonda's eyes slid away. "I went in a couple of nights before you got there."

"Was it the same night that Leonard Hastings collapsed with a heart attack?"

"How should I know?" Rhonda shuddered. "I never saw him. He may have been dead when I went in through the basement, but I swear I never saw him."

"You're sure?"

"Of course I'm sure. Be hard not to notice a dead body. I grabbed the two paintings I found in the studio that night and left."

"You came back, though, didn't you?" Eugenia said slowly. "The night that Cyrus and I arrived on the island."

Rhonda grimaced. "All right, yes. I took a chance. I told you, I only found two of the *Glass* series the first time. I knew there were four. When Fenella told me that she thought she could get at least three hundred for the first one, I decided it was worth the risk of going back to search for the others."

"Even though Cyrus and I were there?"

"It's a big house. Like I said, I knew my way around. Thought I could manage it. But I had just opened the door at the top of the basement stairs when I heard you shouting from the balcony above. I ducked back inside and took off."

Eugenia pursed her lips. "Well, that answers a couple of questions. How did you learn that there were four paintings in the *Glass* series?"

"Daventry told a friend of mine about them." Rhonda's face twisted. "Adam was so damned proud of his newest little artist, you see. Said he was having her paint portraits of his glass because he didn't have any children for her to paint. He said his glass collection would be his legacy."

"What's the name of your friend?"

Rhonda's jaw tightened. "None of your business. I'm not going to drag him into this."

"I just want to talk to him. Please, Rhonda."

"Forget it. I don't want him to get into trouble." Rhonda smashed the shirts into the suitcase. "The ferry will be leaving soon. I've got to get out of here."

"Tell me about Nellie Grant."

"There's nothing to tell."

"You were jealous of her."

"Not for long." Rhonda's mouth twisted. "As far as I'm concerned, she was just one more of his victims. He considered himself a connoisseur of artists. He liked to discover them, the same way he enjoyed finding a new piece of glass for his collection. When he had sucked everything he wanted out of them, he threw them aside."

"I know."

Rhonda spun around. "You knew Adam Daventry?"

"Briefly. It was a business relationship, not a personal one." Eugenia paused. "I was the one who introduced Nellie to Daventry."

"You didn't do her any favors, did you?"

"No." Eugenia took a breath. "Now she's gone, and I need to know what happened to her."

"Don't look at me." Rhonda hauled the suitcases off the bed and stood them on the floor. "As far as I know, she was washed overboard on her way back here to the island. But since you were such a terrific friend of hers, I'll give you the other *Glass* painting I found. It won't do me any good now."

Eugenia watched her go to the dresser and reach behind it. "Rhonda, don't you have any idea of who might have hit you the other night?"

"No." Rhonda hauled the painting out and leaned it against the wall. "But I've come to the conclusion that it may have had something to do with what happened at Glass House the night Daventry died. And that means I want no part of it."

"You were at that last party?"

"Sure. Everyone was there. Every last one of his naïve little pet artists. We all hoped we'd get discovered by one of Daventry's damned Connoisseurs, you see. We were such fools."

Slowly, Eugenia picked up the painting. "What did happen that night?"

"Adam Daventry fell down the stairs and broke his neck."

"Yes, I know. It was an accident."

"Think so?" Rhonda seized the suitcases. "I wouldn't be surprised if someone helped him take that fall down those stairs."

"Why would someone kill him?"

"Wrong question, Ms. Swift. The right question is,

who wouldn't want to kill him?" Rhonda lurched toward the bedroom door with her suitcases.

Eugenia followed her down the hall. "Do you think someone tried to kill you because you saw something you shouldn't have seen that night at Glass House?"

"Maybe." Rhonda set the suitcases down in the living room and began to toss paints and brushes into a cardboard box. "Those parties up at Glass House got pretty wild. It would be easy to slip in during the middle of one, shove Adam down the staircase, and then leave without anyone noticing."

"What do you know that makes you dangerous to the killer?"

Rhonda gave her a scornful look. "If I knew that, I'd be able to figure out who cracked my head open and shoved me into the water the other night." She picked up the box of paints and brushes and carried it outside to the car.

Eugenia went to the doorway and watched Rhonda set the box into the open trunk.

"There's someone I'd like you to talk to," Eugenia said when Rhonda brushed past her to get the suitcases. "A private investigator. He owns a security firm. He can help you."

"Forget it." Rhonda dragged the suitcases out the front door. "I'm not talking to anyone. I'm getting out of here."

Eugenia opened her purse and dug out one of her cards. "Look, if you change your mind, call me at Glass House. I'll arrange for my friend to assist you."

Rhonda narrowed her eyes. "Your friend is the guy who's staying with you at Glass House, right? The big dude who wears the dippy aloha shirts?"

"Uh, yes. That's him. But I wouldn't draw too many conclusions about him based on his taste in shirts, if

I were you. He really does own a very successful security firm. Honest."

Rhonda's mouth curved into a sneer. "No offense, but I think I'll pass on the offer."

She slammed the lid of the trunk, scrambled into the front seat, and fired up the compact. Without a backward glance, she roared out of the driveway.

Eugenia watched, frustrated, until Rhonda had vanished around the bend. Then she walked over to her Toyota and opened the door. Gently she rested Nellie's painting behind the front seat.

She caught sight of the package she had left on the passenger seat just as she fitted the key into the ignition. There was something wrong with the shape of it.

It had been smashed flat.

Slowly Eugenia reached out to pick it up. Her stomach fell away as she listened to the broken shards of the ruined glass sculpture shift ominously inside the brown paper wrapping.

Whoever had crushed the Jacob Houston piece had left a note. It was scrawled in large block letters on a sheet of paper that had been torn from an artist's sketch pad.

The message was simple and to the point:

Stay away from her. Leave the island while you still can.

Sixteen

$\mathcal{T}$he instant he saw Eugenia standing in the driveway of Rhonda Price's cabin with what looked like a large, crumpled paper sack in her hands, Cyrus knew that something very unpleasant had happened.

As usual with Eugenia, his worst fears were confirmed.

She looked up at the sound of the Jeep engine, a deeply troubled expression on her face.

"Damn." He brought the Jeep to a halt and shoved open the door. "What the hell are you doing here?"

"I was about to ask you the same question. Rhonda Price came back to the island."

"I know. I just passed her driving hell-for-leather back toward town."

Eugenia narrowed her eyes. "How come you didn't know she had been released from the hospital?"

"I got a call from Quint about twenty minutes ago." Cyrus eyed the package in her hands as he went toward her. "He said she walked out of the hospital this morning."

"No offense, but it would have been nice to have had a little advance warning from your hotshot security team. As it was, I was lucky to see her as she drove off the ferry. Five minutes either way and I would have missed her."

"Rhonda didn't bother to check herself out of the hospital, she just walked off through the emergency room entrance. No one noticed that she was gone for a while. By the time Quint was alerted, she was already on board the ferry."

Eugenia's brows lifted. "How much do you pay your people, Cyrus?"

"Too much, apparently." There was no point telling her how he had chewed Quint into small bite-sized pieces when he had got the news of Rhonda's unscheduled departure. He rarely lost his temper with his staff. The fact that he had done so over a relatively minor screwup this morning was just one more disturbing indication that he did not have this situation under full control.

Eugenia frowned. "How did you know where to find me?"

"Elementary, my dear Swift. When I heard that Rhonda was headed back here, I put that fact together with the fact that you had gone shopping for groceries. I then got what you might call a blinding flash of the obvious."

"I don't understand."

"Let's just say that, given my luck lately, it was inevitable that the two of you would cross paths in town. I also knew that if you saw Rhonda, you would confront her. When I didn't spot either of your cars parked on Waterfront Street, I drove out here to see what was happening."

She nodded. "Logical."

"I thought so. Now tell me what the hell went on here."

"Well, among other things, I learned that Rhonda was the intruder we chased out of Glass House the first night."

"Damn." He decided to ignore the note of cool one-upmanship in her voice. She was entitled. "Are you sure?"

"She admitted it. Said it was the second time she'd snuck into the house since Daventry's death. She was after Nellie's *Glass* paintings. She knows that there are four of them. She got two."

He considered that briefly. "So three of the four are now accounted for."

"Right. The one hanging in my condo, the one I bought in the Midnight Gallery, and the one Rhonda just gave me."

"Why did she give you the third one?"

Eugenia grimaced. "I think she's concluded that anything to do with Glass House is bad luck."

"She may have a point. She say anything else interesting?"

"She's concluded that Daventry's death might not have been an accident. She thinks someone hit her on the head and pushed her into the marina because she saw something she shouldn't have seen at Glass House the night he died."

"I see. And does she have any idea of what it was she might have seen?"

Eugenia gave him a disgruntled glare. "Well, no."

"In other words, she's concocted a neat little conspiracy to explain her own fall into the marina. That's why she's on the run, I take it? She's afraid someone's out to kill her?"

Eugenia sighed. "It does sound a little improbable, doesn't it?"

"Sounds neurotic as hell, is what it sounds." He leaned back against the Jeep fender and folded his arms. "It's about as improbable as Nellie Grant being murdered for similar reasons."

Eugenia widened her eyes. "You sound somewhat serious. Don't tell me you're starting to buy into my theory of how Nellie died."

"Let's just say that, given the weirdness of this whole mess, I'm keeping an open mind. Might be interesting to see where Rhonda goes now and what she does next."

Eugenia smiled much too sweetly. "Think Colfax Security is up to the challenge of keeping track of Rhonda Price this time?"

"It better be up to it, or I may have to hire you and put you in charge of the business." He looked at the package she held. "What's this? Something from Fenella Weeks's gallery?"

"It is. Or was. This is the crowning jewel of my morning's detective work." She turned the package in her hand. Glass tinkled.

"You broke it already?"

"I had some assistance. It was on the front seat of my car. Someone smashed it while I was inside the cottage. Whoever did it very kindly left a note explaining why he went to all the trouble."

With a flourish, Eugenia handed him a sheet of torn paper.

Cyrus looked down at the note. He went cold. "Oh, shit."

"Succinctly put. What do you make of it, Sherlock?"

"Nothing good, that's for damn sure." He looked up. "But whatever else it is, it's personal."

Eugenia raised her brows. "I figured that out right off. The note was lying on the front seat of my car."

"That's not what I meant. It says *stay away from her.* Whoever wrote this isn't just warning you away from the island. He's trying to protect Rhonda."

"Well, yes, I can see that." She gave him a narrow-eyed, quizzical look. "Why do you keep saying *he?*"

"Could be a woman," Cyrus admitted. "But I doubt it. Looks like a man's writing. Either way, there's an implied relationship. Quint said no one visited Rhonda in the hospital, but a man called twice to check on her condition."

Eugenia frowned. "She mentioned a friend. Said Daventry had told him about Nellie's *Glass* portraits. That's how she knew there were four of them."

"She give you a name?"

"No. She said she didn't want to get him involved in this."

"Another artist?"

"Yes, I think so." Eugenia tapped the package in her hand with one finger. "That message is written on paper that was torn from an artist's sketch pad."

They both looked at the note.

"An artist, then," Cyrus said slowly, thinking it through. "Someone local. Someone who must have been in town and saw the ferry arrive and followed the two of you out here."

Eugenia examined the crushed package. "Whoever he is, he owes me. He destroyed my Jacob Houston."

"Who's Jacob Houston?" Cyrus asked, distracted.

"The artist who made this. Or what's left of it. Fenella Weeks mentioned him, remember?"

"Vaguely. A glass artist?"

"Yes. He's very, very good. I want to see more of his work before I leave the island. I'd like to display some of it in the Leabrook's Cutting Edge exhibition in the fall. Houston's got an incredible sense of intuitive, organic design. He's also got a master's technical expertise. The way he works color in the glass is phenomenal—" She broke off. "Am I boring you, Cyrus?"

"Sorry. Were my eyes glazing over?"

"I think so."

He shrugged. "It happens sometimes. I think I'd better have a talk with the guy who wrote this note."

"How will you find him?"

"I figure he must have been waiting for the ferry in town."

She scowled. "So? Oh, I see what you mean. He must have been in town when I was in Fenella's gallery."

"Yeah."

"Frog Cove is a very small place." Excitement kindled in her expression. "If Rhonda had a close relationship with someone, any number of people probably know about it."

"Yeah."

"It should be simple to figure out who he is."

"Piece of cake." Cyrus smiled. "And because it is so simple, I think I can just about handle it. I'll go into town and get a name."

"I'll come with you."

He braced himself. "I think it will work better if I do this alone."

"What possible difference could it make if I come with you?"

"It might not make any difference at all. But I'd rather do this by myself. I have a hunch it will look a little less obvious that way."

"Nonsense." She opened the door of her car, slipped behind the wheel, and slammed the door shut. "I'll follow you."

"Sure." He gripped the edge of the Toyota roof. "That's real subtle. We both drive into town and start asking pointed questions about Rhonda Price and her boyfriend. You don't think anyone will notice?"

"I can be subtle."

"Forget it, Eugenia. Leave this to me. You've done more than enough today. If you keep blundering around the way you did this morning, you'll blow the whole case apart before we find out anything useful. Let me have a crack at this. It's what I do, remember?"

"Are you afraid that if I ask too many questions about Nellie, I'll screw up your search for the Hades cup?"

He tightened his fingers around the unyielding metal with such force he wondered that he did not punch holes through it. "Your lack of faith in me does not bode well for a good working relationship."

"Our relationship works just fine, if you ask me." She turned the key in the ignition with a crisp, irritated motion. "I know exactly what you're after, and I know exactly where I stand with you."

"I could say the same thing about you. I'm not the only one with a separate agenda here."

Fire flashed in her eyes. "What is that supposed to mean?"

"It means that you're willing to sleep with me, even though you don't trust me. I'd like to know why."

"Why you—" She broke off, rendered momentarily speechless by outrage. "Don't you dare tell me that you believe I'm sleeping with you because I think it will make you more . . . more cooperative."

He clenched the car roof as if he could hold the vehicle in place with sheer muscle. "Then why the hell *are* you sleeping with me?"

She gave him a very dangerous smile. "I thought you had already answered that question to your own satisfaction. You're the one who came up with the theory that I'm sexually obsessed with you, remember?"

"I still like the theory, but I think there may be a few holes in it."

"Brilliant observation. Tell me, Mr. Holmes, how did you arrive at that dazzling deduction?"

He narrowed his eyes. "Somehow, I don't see you sleeping with a man you don't trust, even if you are sexually obsessed with him."

"No, no, no, my dear Holmes, you've got it all wrong." She snapped the shifter into reverse. "I might make the mistake of sleeping with a man I couldn't trust. Any woman could make that sort of mistake."

"Yeah?"

"Damn right. But I sure as hell would not have an orgasm with him."

She trod hard on the accelerator. The Toyota roared into reverse. Cyrus unclenched his fingers very quickly and stepped back before his shoulder was wrenched out of its socket.

"Try not to make me look any worse than I already do, Quint." Cyrus spoke into the phone as he negotiated the narrow, winding strip of blacktop that led back into town. "I have to tell you that so far Colfax Security has not left a terrific impression on Ms. Swift."

"Don't worry, we'll find Price. Stredley's on his way to Seattle even as we speak."

"Too bad we haven't got the Seattle office open yet."

"We can cover this out of Portland, Cyrus. Don't worry about it."

"Let me know as soon as you've traced her."

"Got it." Quint paused. "Sorry about the foul-up this morning."

"Forget it. Just make sure it doesn't happen again."

"It won't."

Cyrus hesitated. "Anything new on the ZEC file?"

"Chandler's investigator left Second Chance Springs yesterday. Looks like he's on his way back to L.A. By now he knows that Jessica Colfax had a baby thirty-five years ago. It won't take him long to trace you."

"I've been thinking about this," Cyrus said. "There's only one logical reason why Chandler would suddenly decide to look for me after all this time. He's concluded that I'm somehow a threat to his election chances."

"What would make him think you've suddenly become a danger to him after all these years?"

"Maybe someone's blackmailing him."

There was a short, hard silence on the other end of the line. "You're the only one in a position to blackmail him, and we know damn well you aren't doing that."

"Someone else may have stumbled onto the truth and decided to use the information," Cyrus said.

"Maybe. But not real likely. You know, it doesn't sound like you're having a really great vacation, boss."

"Whatever gave you that idea? I'm having a wonderful time. Remind me to send you a postcard." Cyrus hung up the phone.

I might make the mistake of sleeping with a man I couldn't trust. But I sure as hell would not have an orgasm with him.

Cyrus concentrated hard on the convoluted logic in Eugenia's enigmatic statement. The effort proved frustrating. The best he could come up with was that she trusted him up to a point. Like until he found the Hades cup.

He could live with that, he decided. For a while.

He was still pondering the complexities of Eugenia's

thinking patterns when he reached Frog Cove. He refocused his attention on finding a parking space. It was not hard.

He pulled next to the curb in front of the Neon Sunset Café and leisurely got out of the Jeep. A glance at the dock told him that the ferry carrying Rhonda Price away from the island had already departed. He could see the outline of it on the horizon.

He turned and walked into the café. The young, ponytailed waitress was busy serving lattes to two tourists. He remembered that her name was Heather. She smiled at him as he took a seat at the counter.

"Be with you in a second," she called cheerfully.

He waited patiently until she was free to take his order.

"I remember. Just plain coffee, right?" she asked when she came back around the end of the counter.

"Right. I'm not real big on all those fancy coffee drinks with espresso and milk in them." He glanced at the heap of pastries stacked beneath a clear plastic dome. "Those doughnuts fresh?"

She wrinkled her nose. "Sort of."

"I'll risk one."

"Okay." She whisked off the plastic dome. "Help yourself."

"Thanks."

He was not in the mood for a doughnut, but he had learned long ago that, for some obscure reason, people were more inclined to chat with you if you had food in your mouth. He selected a plain one and took a bite.

"Where's your friend?" Heather asked casually as she poured coffee. "Thought I saw her earlier."

"She was doing some shopping. But she had to go back to Glass House. My nephew is visiting."

She brightened. "Is he that really cute guy that got off the ferry yesterday afternoon?"

Cyrus smiled around a mouthful of doughnut. "You see everyone who gets off the ferry, don't you?"

"Can't miss 'em."

"Did you see Rhonda Price this morning?"

"Uh-huh. But she left again on the last ferry."

"Didn't stick around long, did she?"

"No." Heather set the coffee mug down in front of him. "Kind of sad."

"What was sad about it?"

"Well, he was here, y'know? He saw her drive off the boat, and he waved and all, but he couldn't get her attention as she drove past. And now she's gone again."

"Someone was here, waiting for her?"

"Jacob Houston. The glass artist, y'know? I feel kind of sorry for him in a way. He really cares about her, but she just treats him like a friend. You can see it tears him up inside."

Some days the information came more easily than others, Cyrus reflected. He wondered if Jacob Houston had known that he had smashed his own work of art.

He also wondered if Houston's sense of protectiveness toward Rhonda Price had led him to shove Adam Daventry down a flight of stairs.

That was about as likely a possibility as the other scenario he had been thinking about lately. That was the one in which Nellie Grant had faked her own death in order to disappear because she had killed Daventry.

There suddenly seemed to be a lot of suspects in a murder that was supposed to have been an accident, he thought.

Eugenia was still fuming when she walked into the mirrored atrium hall. She was irritated with Cyrus, but furious with herself. The orgasm crack had come out of nowhere. What in the world had possessed her to say such a thing?

Cyrus had a very weird and unpredictable effect on her temper, she thought. In the future, she would have to be more cautious.

"Rick?" She paused at the foot of the staircase. "Where are you?"

"Up here." His voice drifted down from the second floor. "Is Cyrus back yet?"

"No. He stopped in town." Eugenia put down the grocery sacks and climbed the stairs. At the second floor she turned and walked along the balcony, following the sound of Rick's voice. "I bought the makings for black bean tacos. Okay with you?"

"Sure. Get some chips and salsa, too?"

"Naturally." She came to a halt in the doorway of the library. "What are you doing?"

"Helping Cyrus."

Rick was seated cross-legged in front of a lateral file drawer. He was poring over the tabbed file folders. There was a pen and a notebook on the floor beside him.

"How are you helping Cyrus?"

Rick looked up. "I'm going through some of these files for him. Making notes of what's in them. He said it would save him some time."

"I see." She walked farther into the long room. "You're creating an index of the contents of the files?"

"You could call it that. Cyrus gave me a list of the kind of stuff he's looking for."

"He's really determined to find the Hades cup, isn't he?"

"Are you kidding? After what happened three years

ago, he'll do anything to find the cup. And his ex-partner."

Eugenia sank down slowly onto a window seat. "You must have been about fifteen when Cyrus's wife was killed."

"Uh-huh. Cyrus didn't talk about it very much, but you could tell it hit him hard. Mom told me once that she thinks he feels responsible for Aunt Katy's death."

"Because he failed to protect her?"

"Something like that. But it wasn't his fault. Some carjacker shot her in cold blood. They never found the guy. Cyrus was in the hospital at the time. There wasn't anything he could have done to save her."

"No," Eugenia agreed. "There wasn't anything he could have done."

Katy had betrayed Cyrus. In doing so, she had put herself in harm's way, Eugenia thought. But Cyrus would not rest until he had seen justice done.

Eugenia knew that she had to accept that nothing was more important to Cyrus than tracking down Damien March. He was obsessed with finding the near-mythical Hades cup because he believed it would help him accomplish that goal.

Rick shifted position to open another file drawer. "You and Cyrus known each other long?"

"No, not long."

"Just wondered." Rick kept his eyes on the files. "He seems sort of serious about you."

That news startled her more than anything else that had happened that day. "How can you tell?"

"I dunno. Just something about the way he talks to you."

"The way he *talks* to me?"

"Yeah. You know, sort of normal."

"You're losing me here, Rick. What's normal with Cyrus?"

Rick paused in his filing. His brow creased in concentration as he struggled to explain. "For as long as I've known Cyrus he's always been kind of quiet around most people. Not quiet in a shy way, but in a listening, waiting sort of way."

She thought about her first impression of Cyrus. Remote, detached, but very aware of his surroundings. "I think I know what you mean."

"When he does talk, he's always real cool."

"Cool as in always in control?"

"Yeah. In control." Rick appeared pleased by her quick uptake. "He never loses his temper. Even when he's really, really pissed, he's cool. In fact, the way you know he's mad is because he just gets colder. Mom says he needs to get in touch with his feelings."

Eugenia thought about the depths of fierce, vital emotion she had glimpsed on rare occasions in Cyrus's eyes. And then she remembered the molten green heat she had seen in his gaze when he had made love to her. "Hmm."

"Cyrus says that just because a man doesn't burst into tears every time he hears some dippy sad song doesn't mean he doesn't have feelings."

"I'll go along with that."

"Cyrus says a man has a right to privacy when it comes to that kind of thing."

"Okay, I'll buy that, too."

Rick nodded, satisfied. "You have to know Cyrus pretty well to be able to tell when something's bothering him."

"I don't know about that. He seems pretty obvious to me."

"That's what I meant when I said he was different with you. He seems more relaxed or something."

"Think so?"

"Yeah." A contemplative look crossed Rick's face. "He even teases you. He never teased Aunt Katy."

"I see." Eugenia was not sure she wanted to hear a lot about Katy.

Rick sat back on his heels. "It's been a while, but I remember how he was with her. Always calm and careful. Like she was made of glass."

"You mean he was gentle with her?"

Rick nodded. "Mom says Katy was fragile. Delicate. She needed someone to lean on. But with you, Cyrus is different. I'll bet he could lose his temper with you."

"He never lost his temper with your aunt?"

"Never. At least, I don't think he ever did. Mom says he was a rock for Aunt Katy, and he's been a rock for her since Dad—" Rick broke off abruptly. "Well, you know."

"Yes," Eugenia said. "I think I do."

"I went a little crazy right after Dad divorced Mom. Got into a lot of trouble. One night the cops picked me up at a wild party. Mom fell apart. She didn't know what to do. So she called Cyrus."

"And he took care of things."

"Yeah. After that, he was just always around." A reflective look appeared in Rick's eyes. "I never thought much about it. But now when I look back, I realize how much stuff we did together. He took me camping. Got tickets to ball games. Sat in the stands with Mom when I competed on the swim team. Helped me learn how to drive. Just sort of hung out with me a lot."

"Sounds like he stepped into your father's shoes for a while."

"I guess he did." Rick exhaled deeply. "I shouldn't have blown up at him just because he made Dad come to my graduation."

"Oh, I don't know. Maybe back in the beginning it

was okay for Cyrus to protect you. But I think you're old enough to take care of yourself now, don't you?"

Rick glanced at her quickly and then looked away. "I know he was only doing what he thought was best, but I don't want him trying to fix things for me the way he did when I was younger. I'm not a kid anymore."

"Tell him that," Eugenia said. "He'll understand."

"You think so?"

"Yes."

Rick looked dubious. "It's hard to get Cyrus to change his mind after he decides what's best in a situation. He's kind of like an aircraft carrier."

"An aircraft carrier?"

A grin flickered briefly at the edge of Rick's mouth. "Not what you'd call real maneuverable. Hard to turn. Sets a course and just keeps going."

"I know what you mean." Eugenia thought about Cyrus's determination to find the Hades cup. "Still, I think if you remind him that he's done a pretty good job of helping you become a man and that you're ready to set your own course because of what he taught you, you might get through to him."

"Maybe you're right. Maybe I'll just come right out with it."

The familiar sound of Cyrus's Jeep rumbled through the open window. Eugenia swiveled around on the wide seat and glanced down into the drive.

"He's back." She got to her feet and started toward the door. "About time. He'd better have the name I want, or I'm going to see about getting myself another professional detective for a partner."

Rick chuckled. "Don't worry. Cyrus always gets results."

"We'll see about that."

Eugenia flew down the staircase and went out onto

the veranda. She stopped at the railing, gripped it with both hands, and watched Cyrus mount the steps.

"Well?" she said.

"I got the name of Rhonda's good buddy here on the island." He smiled wryly. "Take a guess."

"I haven't got a clue."

"Jacob Houston."

"Houston?" Startled, she examined that for a few seconds. "He smashed his own work in an effort to frighten me off? I don't believe it. It takes a lot to make any artist destroy his own creation."

"I doubt if he knew what was inside the package."

That gave her pause. "You're right. He couldn't have known." She eyed him with deep suspicion. "You didn't confront him by yourself, did you?"

"No. Thought we'd do that together." Cyrus came to a halt at the top of the steps. *"Partner."*

"We can go out to his workshop right now." Eugenia turned swiftly. "I'll get my purse. I can't wait to hear what Houston has to say for himself."

"Not so fast." Cyrus reached out to catch hold of her arm. "We're going to have a little strategy session before you go flying off half-cocked again."

"Who needs a strategy session? I want some answers."

"We'll get them. But we're not going to rush this. We're going to think first and then act. After extensive experience in the business, I can guarantee you that it will work better that way."

She whirled around. "If you think I'm going to waste time chitchatting about strategy when I could be grilling Houston . . ."

"Uncle Cyrus?" Rick spoke from the doorway.

Cyrus looked past Eugenia. "What have you got, Rick?"

"You said to keep my eyes open for anything that

looked unusual. I found these. Think they might be useful?"

Eugenia saw that Rick was holding several rolls of faded blueprints. "What are they?"

"Architectural drawings of Glass House," Rick said. "I found them stashed in the back of a closet in the library. Looks like whoever stuck them in there forgot about them a long time ago."

"Let me see those." Cyrus plucked one of the rolls from Rick's arm and unfurled it quickly. He whistled softly. "As-builts. These are the final versions of the drawings that were used to build this house of mirrors. Rick, remind me to call my lawyer in the morning and have him put you into my will."

Rick grinned. "All I want is the Jeep."

"Don't get greedy."

Eugenia glanced at the drawings. "What good will these drawings do you?"

Cyrus raised his eyes from the faded blueprint. His smile bordered on wolfish. "Don't you get it? Daventry must have had the Hades cup hidden somewhere in this house. He needed a secret safe for that. These drawings may show me where it is. If my luck holds, the cup will still be there."

Seventeen

"**I**s it okay if we talk while we do this?" Rick asked an hour later.

"Yeah." Cyrus walked to the far end of the library, tape measure in hand. He crouched to mark the length of the floor. "You want to chew me out again because your dad showed up at your graduation?"

"No."

Cyrus was relieved. "I appreciate that."

Rick grasped the end of the tape and held it steady on the opposite side of the room. "Eugenia says I should just be up front with you."

Cyrus looked up warily. "What the hell does Eugenia have to do with this?"

"She and I talked a little before you got back here this afternoon."

"This sounds ominous."

Rick smiled wryly. "Nah. She just helped me get some of my thoughts straight."

"Twenty-four feet, six inches. What thoughts?"

"Hang on while I write that down." Rick scrawled the numbers on the pad. "I know why you made Dad come to my graduation."

"I thought this wasn't going to be about your father."

"I'm not mad at you anymore about that." Rick made a face. "I have a feeling it wasn't the first time you helped Dad remember an *appointment* with me."

Cyrus straightened and took the tape to the window seat. "Look, your dad got some of his priorities mixed up somewhere along the line. All I did was straighten him out on a couple of occasions."

"I'll bet you did."

Cyrus concentrated on noting the length of the window seat. "Six feet, three inches. One of these days, he'll probably get his priorities straight again all by himself."

"Maybe. Maybe not. In the meantime, all he cares about is the next deal he's got cooking. I know that. Hell, Cyrus, I've always known it."

"Remember, when you have a kid of your own, you don't have to set your priorities the same way your father did."

"I won't," Rick said quietly. "I'm going to set them the way you did."

Cyrus stared at the numbers on the tape measure. They suddenly made no sense. "Yeah? Well, I may not be the best example to follow."

"You're the best example I had. So you're the one I'm going to follow."

Cyrus could not think of anything to say. A curious warmth rose inside him. He focused hard on the tape measure. "Width of the window seat is three feet exactly."

"Got it." Rick wrote busily.

A short silence came and went. Cyrus rewound the

tape measure, aware that Rick was spending an inordinate length of time writing down the new measurements.

After a while Rick cleared his throat. "Anyhow, about what I wanted to say."

"I'm listening."

"When I talked to Eugenia earlier, it hit me that you've done a lot of things for me since that night you came to get me at the police station. I guess I just took you for granted. I never thought about how busy you must have been, especially during the past three years when you had to rebuild your business."

Cyrus swung around to face him. "Rick, whatever I did, I did because I wanted to do it, okay? You're a great kid. If I ever have a son, I hope he turns out like you."

Rick flushed a deep shade of crimson. "Yeah? Well, thanks."

"So what did you want to talk about?"

Rick sighed. "The kid thing."

"Kid thing?"

"I'm not one anymore, Uncle Cyrus." Rick met his eyes across the width of the room. "It was one thing to do stuff like you did with Dad and graduation when I was younger. You wanted to protect me. But I don't need you to do it anymore, okay?"

Images from the past five years flitted through Cyrus's mind. He saw himself teaching Rick how to build a campfire. How to paint a room. How to use a condom. Most of all, how to control the anger and the pain that Jake Tasker's careless betrayal of his responsibilities had created. Yes, he had wanted to protect Rick. Rick had needed him.

But it looked as though Rick didn't need him anymore.

"Okay," he said.

"You've told me that a man has to be able to handle the fact that other people don't always live up to his expectations. You said the important thing was to set your own expectations for yourself and do your damnedest to meet them. You said that was the only way I'd be able to face myself in a mirror for the rest of my life."

Cyrus frowned. "Did I really say all that?"

"About a million and a half times."

"Damn. That sounds like something Grandpappy Beau used to say to me. Maybe I am turning into an old codger."

Rick ignored that. "I can take care of myself now, Uncle Cyrus. You gave me the tools to do the job. Let me handle it."

"Does this mean you aren't going to borrow my Jeep anymore?"

Rick grinned. He looked as if a great weight had been lifted from his shoulders. "I said I could take care of myself. I didn't say I would have any quality of life without occasional access to your Jeep."

Cyrus relaxed. Rick was not the only one who felt as though a burden had been lifted, he thought. "I was afraid of that. Let's get back to work. How are the measurements matching up to the dimensions on the floor plan of this room?"

Rick glanced at the drawing and then at his notes. "Everything's the same in here."

"No room for a hidden vault, then. Let's go try the master bedroom."

"Sure." Rick picked up the notebook and followed Cyrus out of the library. "I get the feeling Eugenia doesn't think you're going to find the Hades cup. She thinks you're wasting your time."

"That's one of the interesting things about Eugenia," Cyrus said. "She's not shy about giving you her opinion."

Eugenia held her patience until after dinner. When she had polished off the last taco, she sat back in her chair and regarded Cyrus and Rick across the remains of the feast. "All right, you two have had your chance to do your thing. I take it you haven't found any discrepancies between the actual measurements and those on the drawings?"

"Not yet," Rick said. "It's amazing how hard it is to measure every single dimension in a room."

"We haven't even done the basement yet," Cyrus added. "Thought we'd get to it tonight after dinner."

"No way." Eugenia glared at him. "It's my turn. Let's talk about how we're going to deal with Jacob Houston."

"Oh, yeah. The strategy bit."

"Yes. The strategy bit."

Cyrus smiled benignly. "Don't worry. I'll deal with him in the morning."

"No, you will not." Eugenia had had enough. She pushed herself up out of the chair. "I'll deal with him tonight. With or without your professional advice on strategy. He's an artist. I know how to deal with artists."

"I said I'd handle it."

"Hah. You haven't paid any attention to my case since Rick produced those house plans this afternoon. All you can think about is finding some mysterious hidden chamber."

"I'm not ignoring your case, I'm just taking things in logical sequence. I'm staying focused."

She gave him her brightest smile. "Focus on this, Mr. Detective." She waggled her fingers in a mockery of a good-bye salute, turned her back, and grabbed her keys off a Venetian glass mosaic table.

"Damn." The rubber-tipped legs of Cyrus's chair squeaked on the tile as he shoved it back. "I told you, this kind of thing takes patience."

"I've waited all afternoon for you two to finish fiddling with those drawings. I'm not going to wait any longer."

"You're not going to see Houston alone." Cyrus pursued her toward the hall.

"You're free to come with me." She threw him a cool smile over her shoulder as she stepped into her black loafers at the front door. "If you can tear yourself away from your hunt for secret vaults and hidden passages, that is."

"Okay, okay, I'm coming." Cyrus looked at Rick. "You want to go with us or stay here?"

"I'll come with you." Rick was already on his feet. "Is the detective business always this interesting?"

"No," Cyrus said. "Luckily for me."

The view through the glory hole in the side of the glass furnace was a window into the heart of a miniature volcano. Eugenia stood in the doorway of Jacob Houston's workshop and watched as the glassmaker eased a blowpipe through the opening and dipped it into the molten glass inside the crucible.

Cyrus and Rick gazed curiously over her shoulder, briefly silenced by the scene before them.

She understood their fascination. In the course of her career she had watched glass worked many times, but the process never failed to enthrall. The contradictions and mysteries of a substance that retained its characteristics as a liquid even while it took solid shape, a substance that could be transformed into endless shapes and that could transmit and reflect light, compelled and fascinated her.

The ancient history of glassmaking, a craft and an art with roots that reached back thousands of years, was an inescapable part of the allure, she thought. Tonight, Jacob Houston used a blowpipe to work glass in a manner that would have been familiar to Roman artisans two thousand years ago.

She had often thought that if it weren't for the fact that glass was so common, more people would see it for the amazing material that it truly was.

Jacob was unaware of his audience. His entire attention was concentrated on his work. Fenella had been right about one thing, Eugenia reflected as she watched him; Jacob was sure and steady when he practiced his art. But this was the same man who had smashed the package on the front seat of her car that morning, she reminded herself. He had a quick temper.

"Jacob Houston?" she called over the roar of the furnace.

"I'm busy." Jacob did not turn to see who stood in the doorway. He was focused on gathering a quantity of molten glass on the end of the pipe.

"I spoke to your friend, Rhonda Price, today," Eugenia said.

"What the hell—?" Jacob turned, mouth open in shock. His eyes narrowed quickly. Something that could have been fear appeared in his gaze. The glob of molten glass on the tip of his blowpipe glowed white-hot.

Eugenia concluded that Jacob was in his mid-forties. He had lost most of the hair on the top of his head. The remainder was gathered into a small, thin ponytail. He was a heavy-set man with bearlike features and massive hands.

"You're that woman from the Leabrook." He scowled at her. "The one who upset Rhonda. I don't have anything to say to you. Get out of here."

"Take it easy, Houston." Cyrus moved to stand beside Eugenia. "We're not leaving until you give us some answers."

Jacob's eyes flew wildly from Eugenia to Cyrus. "I said, I'm trying to work, goddamn it. I don't want to talk."

"My name is Cyrus Colfax. This is my nephew, Rick Tasker. Apparently you already know Ms. Swift."

Jacob squinted uneasily at Eugenia. "So?"

Eugenia gave him the smile she reserved especially for temperamental artists. "I'm a great admirer of your work, Mr. Houston. In fact, the package that you crushed today in my car contained your piece, *Sun*. I had just purchased it from the Midnight Gallery. I wanted it for my personal collection."

"*Sun?* Jacob stared at her, shaken. "That was my *Sun* in that package?"

"I'm afraid so." Eugenia said gently. "It was incredible. A brilliant fusion of color and design. You captured the essence of the medium. Power and delicacy. Color and light. I loved it the minute I saw it."

"Christ." Jacob wiped his brow with the back of one bare, hairy arm. "I can't believe it. My beautiful *Sun.*"

"Smashed to smithereens." There was cold-blooded good cheer in Cyrus's voice. "Nothing left but little itty-bitty pieces of glass."

Eugenia shot him a quelling look, but it was too late. She saw the tears well in Jacob's eyes. They rolled down his cheeks.

"I think we'd better talk," Cyrus said.

Jacob's one-room cabin was a gloom-filled cave studded with three glass sculptures that glowed like huge, brilliantly cut gems. Eugenia had a difficult time keeping her attention focused on the interview. Her gaze kept wandering to the three pieces of studio glass. Each was a magical construct seemingly fashioned out of pure light and color.

The most irresistible of the three was an elegant bowl conjured out of pale green glass. The color was the same inimitable green hue as Cyrus's eyes, Eugenia thought.

Cyrus faced Jacob across a battered formica table. "Why are you trying to protect Rhonda?"

"She says someone hit her and pushed her into the water." Jacob sat with his elbows on the table. He propped his head in his big hands. "Don't you understand? She thinks someone's tried to kill her."

"Do you believe that?" Eugenia asked quickly.

"I don't know." Jacob wiped his broad face with his palm. "I just don't know. Maybe."

"Why did you try to frighten Ms. Swift?" Cyrus gave him a disgusted look. "She's the one who went into the water after Rhonda."

"I knew Rhonda didn't want to talk to her. She didn't even want to see her. When I saw Ms. Swift follow her from the ferry dock, I went after her and smashed the package and left the note. I just wanted to make her go away and leave Rhonda alone."

Eugenia felt a wave of pity for the big man. She stepped in again before Cyrus could continue the questioning. "I understand why you did it, Jacob, but there was no need. I know why Rhonda tried to avoid me. It had to do with Nellie Grant's pictures. We talked it out. I don't think Rhonda is afraid of me anymore, but she is definitely afraid of someone else."

"The person she thinks tried to kill her," Jacob moaned.

"Why would anyone want to murder her?" Cyrus asked.

"I don't know." Jacob stared at the top of the table between his arms. "But she thinks it's because she saw something she shouldn't have seen the night of Daventry's last party."

Eugenia leaned closer. "What did she see?"

"That's the hard part." Jacob heaved a huge sigh. "She doesn't know. We've been over it a hundred times and neither of us can figure out who or what she might have seen that put her in danger. And we can't figure out why the attempt was made on her life now rather than right after the party."

"Were you at the party?" Cyrus asked.

"Sure. We were all there. Every artist on the damned island was invited. Daventry used us, you see. He served us up at his Connoisseurs' Club parties as if we were hors d'oeuvres. And we let him do it, God help us, because we all wanted a chance to promote our careers. His friends had money. Lots of it. They were important collectors."

Eugenia frowned at Cyrus. Then she turned back to Jacob. "Did you know Nellie Grant?"

"Nellie?" Jacob nodded. "Sure. I met her. Felt sorry for her in a way. She hadn't figured Daventry out yet. She still thought he could do big things for her career. It was the same garbage line he had fed Rhonda until he got tired of her."

"Rhonda told me today that she thinks Daventry may have been murdered," Eugenia said carefully.

"I know. She started wondering about that in the hospital." Jacob massaged his brow. "It was the only thing she could think of that would explain why someone's out to kill her."

"Assuming someone is out to kill her," Cyrus said dryly.

Jacob sighed. "I hear what you're saying. It's possible that someone shoved him down those stairs. But it's just as likely that he tripped and fell. I'm sure he was doing his special dope that night. Rhonda says it made him feel real powerful. Totally in control. Hell, maybe he stood at the top of that staircase and decided he could fly."

"Speaking of dope, what about his guests?" Cyrus lounged back in his chair and stretched out his legs. "Were they using the designer stuff, too?"

"Hell, no." Jacob's face twisted into a grimace. "The booze flowed freely, but that was it. I'm not saying there aren't a few people from the local crowd who wouldn't have said yes to the offer of some interesting pharmaceuticals. But Daventry kept the shit for himself. He didn't even give it to the members of his club. They all made do with fifty-year-old Scotch and French champagne."

Rick spoke up for the first time. "Was Daventry paranoid about getting busted because of the dope?"

Jacob jerked at the sound of his voice. He turned his head to look at Rick with a faintly baffled expression. "I don't think so. He always considered himself exempt from the rules. He thought he had enough money to buy his way out of any mess. Rhonda says he kept his own private stock of drugs because it was one more way of making himself feel special. Unique. He liked possessing things that no one else possessed."

Cyrus stirred slightly. "That fits."

Eugenia glanced at him, aware that he was thinking about the Hades cup.

Jacob scowled. "I've answered all your questions. Now, what about Rhonda?"

"What about her?" Cyrus asked.

"Whether or not someone is out to get her, the fact is, she's scared to death. She thinks she's in danger."

"I told her to call me if she decides she wants protection," Eugenia said.

Cyrus raised his brows. "Why in hell would she call you?"

Eugenia cleared her throat discreetly. "I said that I would arrange for your firm to help her if she decided she wanted help."

"Well, hell," Cyrus murmured. "Nice of you to drum up business for me."

Jacob's head swiveled on his large neck as he looked first at Eugenia and then at Cyrus. "What's this about you providing help?"

"I own Colfax Security. We do that kind of work." Cyrus gave Eugenia an irritated look. "I was trying to keep that fact quiet here on the island."

"Is this on the level?" Jacob demanded.

"Of course it is." Eugenia frowned at Cyrus. "Give him one of your cards."

"Cyrus is my uncle," Rick said. "I can vouch for him. Show him your private investigator's license, Uncle Cyrus."

Jacob gazed at Cyrus with a mute, beseeching expression.

"Okay, okay." Cyrus dug into his pocket and tugged out a worn leather wallet. He flipped it open to display an official-looking piece of paper. Then he pulled a card from one of the small pockets and handed it to Jacob.

Jacob closed his huge hand around the card. "Does this mean you'll help Rhonda?"

"Maybe." Cyrus's mouth was a hard line. "Assuming she wants help."

A faint ray of hope gleamed in Jacob's eyes. "I might be able to convince her to trust you."

"Don't go out of your way. I'm a little busy at the moment." Cyrus got to his feet. He looked at Eugenia

"I think we've accomplished more than enough here tonight. You've managed to blow my cover, and, lucky me, it looks like you've found me a new client who probably can't afford my fees. Let's get out of here before you do me any more favors."

"All right." Eugenia stood. "Just one more thing, Jacob."

He watched her anxiously. "What's that?"

"The Leabrook has an annual exhibition of Northwest studio glass in the fall."

"I know. Cutting Edge. I went into Seattle to see it last year. Fantastic show."

"I'd like to display some of your work in this year's exhibition."

"My work?" Jacob blinked several times. "In the Leabrook?"

She eyed the impossibly green glass sculpture on the mantle. "And I'd also like a piece for my personal collection to replace the one that was on the front seat of my car."

"Yes. Sure." Jacob glanced at her and then at the vase. He surged to his feet with an abrupt, awkward motion that knocked over his chair. "You can have that one, if you like."

"Oh, yes." Eugenia gazed hungrily at the piece as he lifted it down from the mantel. "I like."

Rain dripped from the eaves of Glass House and pounded on the windows. Eugenia lay alone in bed, listening to it.

Rain had a lot in common with glass, she thought. A transparent substance that transmitted and reflected light when light existed around it. Like glass it became opaque when there was no light.

It was midnight. There was no light in the rain that sheeted against the windows.

She turned, pushed aside the covers, and sat up on the side of the bed. Cyrus had not come to join her. She did not know if it was because he had decided to sleep alone tonight, or if he was still prowling through the glass-and-mirror rooms with his blueprints and his tape measure.

She sat very still, listening for the sound of his footsteps outside her door. She was aware that she had been waiting for those footsteps for the past hour.

When she heard nothing she got to her feet, pulled on her robe and slippers, and opened her door. She stepped out into the hall. No light showed from beneath either Rick's or Cyrus's door.

Tightening the sash of her robe, she walked toward the stairs. A faint glow from the first floor confirmed her intuitive feeling that Cyrus was still awake.

She went quietly down the stairs, crossed the hall, and saw that a single lamp had been left on in the living room. There was no sign of Cyrus.

She continued on through the house to the door of the sunroom. Inside the glass-walled chamber, all was in darkness. She sensed Cyrus's presence before she heard his voice.

"What's the matter, Eugenia? Couldn't sleep?"

"No." She walked into the room and waited for her eyes to adjust to the depths of the darkness.

She finally saw him. He lounged in one of the chrome and white leather chairs, gazing into the night-shrouded forest. His legs were stretched out in front of him, his fingers steepled.

"You couldn't sleep either, I take it?"

"I've been doing some thinking," he said.

She closed the door behind her, walked forward, and sat down in the chair beside him. The rainy night closed around them.

"Come to any conclusions?" she asked after a while.

"It has occurred to me that there are a couple of ways to look at this mess."

"By mess, I take it you mean my case?"

"Yeah. The mess. I admit that the most likely scenario is that the authorities were right when they declared Daventry's death an accident. But what if they were wrong?"

She was startled. "You're starting to believe he might have been murdered?"

"Maybe. Logic tells me that if Daventry actually was killed, the most likely explanation would involve the Hades cup, though. Not drugs. God knows, people have died in the past because of that damned piece of glass."

She knew he was thinking of his dead wife. "So you said."

"The thing that works against that possibility is that a shove down a flight of stairs is a crime of opportunity, not a planned event. And the outcome would be unpredictable."

"You said that anyone out to steal the Hades cup would be a pro."

"Right. So what if we start from another angle. What if we assume that Daventry was killed for some reason that had nothing to do with either dope or the Hades cup?"

"What does that leave?"

"A very personal reason," Cyrus said.

She frowned, thinking about it. Everyone agreed that Daventry had enemies. "You mean, what if he was killed because someone who hated him saw a golden opportunity to get rid of him and took it?"

"Maybe you've been right all along. Maybe your friend Nellie actually did see something she shouldn't have seen—"

"Daventry's murder?"

"Or something that convinced the killer that she might be able to identify him or her. And maybe Rhonda Price saw something, too."

Eugenia took a deep breath. "There's some logic to that. Nellie was supposedly washed overboard the day after Daventry died. But why would anyone wait this long to go after Rhonda?"

"I don't know. But I think it's safe to say that the one factor that changed in the equation is the appearance of the *Glass* paintings."

Eugenia glanced at him, startled. "You're right. Rhonda was shoved into the marina within a couple of days after she put one of them up for sale in the Midnight Gallery. But what could the pictures have to do with Daventry's death?"

"Beats the hell out of me," Cyrus admitted. "I'm just trying to view this from a fresh perspective. I'm looking for something to tie all the loose ends and three deaths together."

"Three? There have only been two. Daventry and Nellie."

"You're forgetting Leonard Hastings," Cyrus said softly.

"But he died of a heart attack."

"There was no autopsy. His physician of record was satisfied that it was a heart attack, and he had a long history of health problems. No one bothered to ask any questions."

"But how could a killer have made his death look like a heart attack?" Eugenia asked.

Cyrus shrugged. "Hastings took a lot of medications. Someone could have swapped one of his regular pills for something else, maybe one of Daventry's designer drugs. Lord knows what it would have done to him."

"That's a very strange thought, Cyrus."

"I know. I'm just kind of letting things flow, looking for a new angle."

Eugenia smiled to herself. "That's what any artist does. It's called the creative process."

"Just call me Michelangelo."

Eugenia studied his shadowed form, trying to make out his expression. It was impossible. "Do you realize what you're saying? If there is a killer, he or she may be one of the locals. Someone who lives right here on the island. Someone with a personal grudge against Daventry."

"Apparently there's no shortage of people around here who disliked Daventry."

She shivered. "Where does this new theory leave us?"

"It leaves me thinking that I want you off the island. You can go back to Seattle with Rick on the ferry tomorrow. I can have Stredley meet you. He'll keep an eye on you until I get this thing settled."

She was so startled that it took a few seconds for the outrage to hit her. "Oh, no, you don't. You're not getting rid of me that easily."

"I don't like the feel of this thing," Cyrus said. "I've got work to do, and I can't do it if I have to worry about you."

"Who says you have to worry about me? I've been taking care of myself for a long time."

"Maybe, but you haven't had to protect yourself from a killer."

"The killer, assuming there is one, isn't after me. He's after someone who might have seen something the night of Daventry's murder."

"Yeah. And maybe he'll decide to go after people who ask too many questions about Daventry's death, also. I want you out of the way."

"I appreciate your concern," she said stiffly. "But I'm not leaving this island."

"Eugenia," Cyrus said very softly, "I know its unchivalrous, crude, and tacky to point this out, but when push comes to shove around here, I'm a lot bigger than you are."

"You may be bigger, but I'll bet I'm a lot faster."

He moved so quickly she never even realized he had come up out of the chair until she found herself in his arms.

Eighteen

"*O*kay, so you can move pretty fast when you feel like it." Eugenia knew she sounded breathless. She could not do much about it. She *was* breathless. Her pulse was racing, and her palms were tingling, too.

"Motivation is the key," Cyrus said. "At the moment, I'm highly motivated."

His face was hewn from solid shadows. There was just enough light seeping in from under the door to make his eyes gleam. She could feel the heat and the strength in him. She also sensed the depths of his determination.

"This is no way to resolve an interpersonal conflict," she warned.

"You follow your theory of personnel management," he said against her mouth. "I'll follow mine."

"I thought I told you that you couldn't use sex to get me to do what you want."

"What if what I want you to do is have sex with me?"

"Oh. Well, I guess that would be an exception."

"Figured it might be." He kissed her, hard and deep.

There was no point talking to him, Eugenia thought. He was not in a mood to listen. She put her arms around his neck and kissed him back.

The now-familiar flash of excitement and wonder zipped through her, making her shiver with anticipation. She clenched her fingers in his hair.

Cyrus groaned, took one step to the side, and pulled her down onto a nearby padded lounger. She fell on top of him, her legs tangling with his. He was rock hard beneath her thigh.

He put one hand into the opening of her robe. The fabric parted easily. She sighed when she felt his warm fingers on her breast. When he drew his thumb across her nipple, she tried to say his name aloud. It came out as a muffled, half-swallowed exclamation. She sank her nails into his shoulders.

"Damn," he growled. He shifted his mouth to her throat. "Lady, you're dangerous."

Only with you, she thought fleetingly. *Why is that?*

The uneasy question popped into her head out of nowhere. It evaporated instantly as the heat built between them.

She fumbled with the buttons of his shirt until she could flatten her palms on his bare chest. She loved the feel of him, she realized. And the scent of him. And the strength in him.

Oh, lord. What if she just plain loved him?

Impossible. It had all happened too quickly. This could not be love. It was sex. Wonderful, exciting sex, to be sure, but still just sex.

She was still in control of herself. She had not put her heart at risk.

Or had she?

Once more the disquieting thoughts vanished in the smoke created by the flames of mutual desire. Eugenia let them go. The last thing she wanted to do was analyze her confusing emotions for this man tonight.

Cyrus seized a fistful of her nightgown and hauled it slowly, deliberately up to her waist. She sat astride him and unbuckled his belt with shaking fingers. He sprang, fully erect, into her hands.

He cupped her gently. She could feel her own dampness on his palm. Her head fell back. She had to swallow a cry that would otherwise have been audible upstairs in the bedroom where Rick slept.

She cradled Cyrus's heavy erection and squeezed carefully, awed by the sheer size and weight of him. He tensed beneath her. When he eased two fingers into her, she melted the way glass did in a furnace. Suddenly she was white-hot. She bent her head to drop wet kisses onto his shoulder.

She was dimly aware of the beat of the rain on the transparent walls that surrounded them. The night formed a cocoon of darkness around the deeper shadows inside the sunroom.

When Cyrus finally thrust into her, taking his time about it, filling her completely, she almost screamed with the pleasure and intense satisfaction of it.

His hands clamped around her thighs. He held her so that she could no longer move. "I want to feel you come."

He pushed himself a little deeper into her.

"Now," he whispered. "Come now."

She gasped. Her body clenched as tightly as a fist as the climax swept through her. He pulled her face down to his and silenced her cries with his mouth.

Before the last of the deep, twisting shivers had finished uncurling inside her, he levered himself up and turned her onto her back. He pinned her to the cushions while the shudders generated by his own release pounded through both of them.

Cyrus looked into the darkness beyond the glass-domed ceiling of the sunroom. Things were going to be very different after this adventure with Eugenia was finished.

No, that was the problem. Things would not be any different at all.

Things would go back to being the same as they had always been before Eugenia crashed into his life.

No more discussions of art with an arrogant, high-browed snob who could not resist falling into full lecture mode at the drop of a museum catalog.

No more toe-to-toe arguments with a stubborn, self-opinionated woman who thought she knew more than he did about the security business.

No more losing his temper or his self-control.

No more hot sex with a lady cat burglar.

The list went on, he realized. And it got more depressing.

No more talking to someone who understood him as no one else ever had.

A chill of dread went through him, chasing away the warmth and satisfaction of the recent lovemaking. He did not believe in premonitions, he reminded himself. He dealt in facts. He knew how to face them squarely. Everything on the long list of things that would vanish when Eugenia walked out of his life was a simple fact.

He shoved the whole list aside. He did not have time to think about the future tonight. He had other, more immediate problems.

He tightened one arm around Eugenia. "Where were we?"

"Arguing, I think." She stretched languidly on the

lounger. Her hand rested warmly on his stomach. "You were saying something about how much bigger and stronger you are."

"And you said something about being faster."

"Right. Faster." Satisfaction purred in her voice. "But we hadn't gotten to the brainy part yet. That's where I really shine, you know."

"Doesn't matter. The theory that brains are better than brawn is nothing but a myth put out by smart people with no muscles. In the real world, brawn beats brains every damn time."

"I'm not going to leave the island, Cyrus." She leaned over him. "Not until we find out what's going on here."

He looked at her, aware of the determination that radiated off her. She was accustomed to taking care of herself. Accustomed to giving orders, not taking them. Definitely not the kind of woman a man could order back into the wagon.

Maybe he should let her stay, he thought. After all, she had some rights in this, too. On the plus side, he would be able to keep an eye on her here.

Excuses, excuses.

Common sense told him she would be better off back in Seattle.

"This situation may turn dangerous," he said carefully. "I want to be sure you're safe."

"I'm safer with you than I would be alone in Seattle," she said smoothly. "You're an expert on security, remember?"

"Hell. You're not going to make this easy for me, are you?"

"Nope." She brushed her mouth against his jaw. "In fact, I'm going to make it impossible."

"If you think you can use sex to control me . . . ," he said.

"Yes?"

He groaned. "You may be right."

Her bare foot slid up the length of his leg. He could have sworn he felt himself stir. *Impossible. Christ, I'm too old for this kind of fast turnaround.*

The phone on the nearby glass table rang, shattering the whispery darkness. Eugenia's foot stopped moving. Cyrus propped himself up on his elbow and grabbed the receiver.

"Colfax here."

"It's me, Jacob Houston. I gotta talk to you."

The tension in Jacob's voice brought Cyrus to full alert as little else could have done at that moment. He shook off the lingering effects of Eugenia's touch and sat up on the side of the lounger.

"What's wrong, Houston?"

"I just got back from Rhonda's place. Something's happened."

"What were you doing at her house at this time of night?"

"I'm trying to tell you. I called her after you left. Told her she ought to get in touch with you. I wanted her to take you up on your offer to help her. We talked a long time."

"What did she say?"

"She finally agreed. Said she'd call you in the morning. Then she asked me to go over to her place and pack up some stuff she left behind. So I did."

"In the middle of the night?"

"I'm a night person," Jacob said. "I was up."

"Go on." Cyrus eased himself away from Eugenia. He got to his feet, adjusted his briefs, and zipped his chinos. "What happened?"

"That's what I'm trying to tell you. Her place is a mess." Jacob's voice rose with thin urgency. "All the drawers pulled out of the dresser. Everything in the kitchen yanked out of the cupboards and thrown on the floor. It looks like someone vandalized it."

"Local kids?"

"Maybe, but after what happened to Rhonda at the marina, I'm not so sure. This is crazy, but it almost looks like someone went through her place looking for something."

"Any idea what that something could be?"

"No. I keep telling you, Rhonda doesn't even know why someone tried to kill her, so she sure won't know why anyone would break into her cottage. Hell, maybe it was vandals. Think you could tell the difference?"

"Probably." Cyrus considered the possibilities, including the one that he was being set up. "I'll swing by your place and pick you up. We'll go back to Rhonda's together and take a look."

"Okay." Jacob sounded greatly relieved. "Thanks. I'll be waiting for you here in my cabin."

Cyrus slowly replaced the receiver.

Eugenia knelt on the lounger, adjusting her robe. "What's going on?"

He considered his words carefully. "Jacob says someone vandalized Rhonda's cottage."

"Why didn't he call Deputy Peaceful?"

"I don't know." Until he'd had a chance to check out the situation, he did not want to alarm her. "Probably because he's so anxious about Rhonda he's not thinking clearly."

He switched on a lamp and turned to look at her. Dark hair was tousled into a frothy cloud around her face. Her eyes were still hot with the aftereffects of the lovemaking. She had gathered the robe around her but one bare foot peeked out from beneath the hem.

Possessiveness coiled deep within him, a fierce,

primitive thing that shocked him with its strength. He felt the air leave his lungs in a rush.

"What are you supposed to do about vandalism?" Eugenia asked.

With an act of raw willpower, Cyrus forced himself back to the problem at hand. "I don't know. But I think I'd better take a look. Houston sounded nervous. For better or worse, he's sort of a client now. It's company policy to keep clients calm."

"I'll come with you." Eugenia slid off the lounger. "Give me a minute to get into some clothes."

"No." He shoved his fingers through his hair to straighten it. "You stay here. If I take you, I've got to wake Rick and tell him what's going on, too. Then he'll want to come with me. There's no sense in all of us running around the island at this time of night."

She hesitated, clearly dubious. "Well . . ."

"I'll be back in an hour," he said easily. He kissed her on the mouth as he went past her through the door. "Got to grab my jacket. It's upstairs in my room."

He went quickly up the glass staircase and along the balcony to his bedroom. His .38 was right where he had stashed it the day he had arrived, in the bottom of his duffel bag. He removed it, grabbed a full clip, and then tossed his black leather jacket over his arm to cover the gun.

Eugenia was waiting at the bottom of the stairs. Her eyes were huge in the shadows. She did not so much as glance at the jacket he carried.

"Cyrus?"

Something in the tone of her voice made him go very still inside. "Yeah?"

"Promise me you'll be careful."

He grinned slowly. It was nice to have someone worry about you, he decided. "Count on it."

* * *

There were no lights in the windows of Jacob's cabin, but the faint glow from the attached workshop caught Cyrus's attention as he turned into the drive.

There was no phone in the workshop. Jacob must have called from the cabin. He had said nothing about going back to work at his furnace. In fact his conversation indicated he had not been working at all that evening. He claimed he had talked to Rhonda for a long time on the phone and then gone to her cottage to pack her things.

Cyrus brought the car to a halt and hit the horn once, briefly. There was no response.

He sat behind the wheel for a moment, studying the scene in front of him. A frisson of electricity ruffled the hair on the back of his arms. After a while he reached inside his jacket and took out the .38.

Gun in hand, he got out of the car and moved into the shadows of the nearby trees. The rain had stopped, but water still dripped from the heavy branches. He winced when several cold drops splashed on the back of his neck. There were times when the detective business was not the glamorous, thrill-filled career it was cracked up to be, he thought.

The glow from the glassmaking furnace beckoned through the windows of the workshop. Fire always got your attention, Cyrus thought. He studied the scene for a long moment, but saw no movement inside the workshop.

He turned to the darkened cabin. Jacob had said that he would be waiting inside the cabin, not in his workshop.

He drifted through the wet trees, circling around to the back of the small house. When he could see the rear door, he moved out from the cover of the branches and flattened himself against the log wall.

Keeping his back pressed to the logs, he reached out and tried the doorknob. It twisted easily in his hand.

He took a deep breath, let it out halfway, positioned himself so that the logs provided some protection, and pushed the door wide. It slammed open, revealing the shadowed interior of the single room.

"Houston? You in there?"

When no answer came, Cyrus groped around the edge of the door, found a switch.

Light from the dingy overhead fixture flooded the one-room cabin. Cyrus examined the scene through the doorway.

The interior of the small house looked like a gutted fish. Every drawer stood open. A heap of well-worn flannel shirts lay on the floor where they had been tossed after being ripped from the closet. Even the refrigerator had been emptied of its contents.

There was no sign of Jacob.

A whisper of sound directly behind him was the only warning Cyrus had that he was not alone in the dark.

He reacted instinctively, dropping flat to the damp earth.

The whisper became a harsh rush of air. A split second later something very heavy struck the side of the log cabin. It thudded into the wood at the point where Cyrus knew his head would have been had he not moved.

A man hissed in the darkness. "Goddamn it."

"You missed him, you idiot." The second voice came from the trees. "Hit him. Hurry. Shit, he's moving."

Cyrus saw a pair of snakeskin boots out of the corner of his eye. He rolled toward them, striking them with the full weight of his body.

"*Bastard.*" The man in the boots staggered back

under the impact, but managed to stay on his feet. He swung again, wildly this time.

The long length of metal whizzed over Cyrus's head. He caught a glimpse of a face sheathed in a dark ski mask as he flung himself to the side.

He levered himself off the ground and brought the gun up in the same motion. Light spilling from the cabin glinted on the barrel.

"Two strikes and you're out," Cyrus said softly.

"Jesus." Ski mask froze.

"He's got a gun," the man in the trees yelled. "Run."

"I didn't sign on for this." Ski mask dropped the length of metal he had been wielding, spun around, and fled three steps into the trees.

Cyrus slowly lowered the gun.

The sound of scurrying to the left told him that the second man had also decided that discretion was the better part of valor.

He waited in the shadows of the cabin wall until the receding footsteps indicated his assailants had made good their departure.

He glanced down at the long metal object on the ground. It was the blowpipe Jacob had used earlier that afternoon. He picked it up and went swiftly toward the workshop.

At the doorway he paused. The night was chilly, but the fiery furnace had heated the workshop to an uncomfortable temperature. The smell of whiskey was strong in the air. Cyrus saw an open bottle standing on a nearby shelf. He was almost certain it had not been there earlier in the day.

The sight of the flames in the glory hole made Cyrus uneasy. He pondered the interesting question of how one went about shutting down a glassmaking furnace.

It occurred to him that Eugenia might know the answer. He could call her from the cabin.

He saw Jacob just as he turned to leave. The big man was sprawled facedown in the shadows beneath a workbench. A pair of heavy metal tongs lay beside him.

Cyrus set down the blowpipe and moved quickly into the room. "Houston."

Jacob groaned at the sound of his name. "Huh?"

Relief shot through Cyrus. He went down on one knee beside the big man. "What happened?"

"Dunno." Jacob twisted awkwardly, raised his head, and peered up at Cyrus with bleary eyes. His broad face contorted with pain. "Colfax. What are you doing here?"

"You called me, remember?" Cyrus probed Jacob's skull gently.

"Ouch." Jacob flinched and gingerly touched his head. "Shit, that hurts."

"Sorry. Looks like someone hit you with those tongs."

Jacob blinked rapidly. "I sort of remember. I think there were two of 'em. Came up behind me inside the cabin. Right after I called you."

"They were still hanging around when I got here."

"Guess they didn't hit me as hard as they thought. I was dazed, but I remember 'em talking. They complained about how heavy I was when they dragged me in here." Jacob sniffed. "What's that smell?"

"Whiskey. Wouldn't have thought you'd want to drink while you work around this sucker." He gestured toward the nearby inferno.

"I never drink when I'm working glass." Jacob struggled to get to his feet. "Hot in here. What the hell? Damn, the *furnace.*"

"I take it you didn't fire it up?"

"Hell, no. I quit for the night right after you and Ms. Swift left." Jacob lurched forward with an awkward but purposeful motion. "Got to shut it down."

"Good idea." Cyrus eyed the whiskey bottle again. "Any idea why someone would want to set fire to this place?"

Jacob turned to scowl anxiously over his shoulder. "Set fire to it? Are you crazy?"

"That's what it looks like to me. I'd say the whiskey was window dressing. I can see the headlines in the local paper: *Drunken glassmaker accidentally burns down workshop and cabin.*"

Fear flared in Jacob's eyes. "And himself while he was at it. Goddamn it, Colfax, they meant me to die in the fire, didn't they?"

Cyrus hesitated and then decided there was no point trying to put a delicate spin on the situation. "Sort of looks that way."

"I knew I shouldn't have let you go off by yourself tonight." Eugenia set the teakettle on the glass-topped halogen stove and opened a cupboard to take down several mugs. "My God, Cyrus, you could have been killed."

"Hush." Cyrus, sprawled in a kitchen chair, raised his eyes meaningfully toward the ceiling. Jacob was upstairs, moving a hastily packed bag into one of the spare bedrooms. "Houston is already agitated enough as it is. No point making him any more twitchy."

"What about me?" She poured tea water into the pot. "I'm plenty twitchy."

He grinned briefly. "No, you're not. You're as cool as an iced latte." It was no lie. When he had arrived at Glass House ten minutes ago with Jacob in tow, she had hardly blinked. It was nice to have a woman around who was prepared for any contingency.

It was nice to have Eugenia around, period.

"What is Deputy Peaceful going to do about this?" Eugenia demanded.

"Not much he can do. Neither Jacob nor I could identify those two men who attacked us. He's going on the assumption that some really nasty vandals came over from the mainland. He says it's happened once or twice in the past. Kids get drunk, steal a boat, and go looking for trouble."

She studied him closely. "You didn't tell Peaceful about any of the rest of it? That Daventry and Nellie may have been murdered and Rhonda may be in danger?"

"What do you think?"

She sighed. "I think Peaceful would have thought you were nuts if you told him two or three people had been murdered here in recent weeks and he never even realized it."

"Yeah, that's sort of the conclusion I came to, too. In all fairness to Deputy Peaceful, I have to admit that I didn't believe anyone had been murdered around here recently, either. What's more, I'm still not sure anyone was. There is no hard evidence of foul play."

"Jacob is terrified," Eugenia noted.

"I know. Not just for himself. He's worried about Rhonda. One thing's for certain."

"What's that?"

"There were two men at Jacob's house tonight. Which seriously damages my earlier theory that the killer, if there is one, is a local person."

She frowned. "Why?"

"Because it's pushing things into the realm of fantasy to imagine that two thugs like the ones I ran into tonight have lived undetected here on Frog Cove Island for any length of time."

"It is a little improbable, isn't it?"

"Yeah. Not impossible, mind you, just improbable." Cyrus sipped his tea. It was hot and oddly soothing. It struck him that he was enjoying Eugenia's fussing tonight. *Don't get too accustomed to it,* he warned himself. "And if we assume that they aren't local folks, then it's a good bet that Peaceful was right when he suggested that they had a boat waiting somewhere to take them off the island."

Eugenia drummed her fingers on her mug. "I suppose it's unlikely that a couple of murderers would use the ferry to come and go from the scene of the crime."

"Very unlikely."

"Especially when it meant that they would have to sit around until tomorrow morning to catch the eight o'clock ferry in order to make good their escape."

Cyrus considered that. "Again, unlikely, but not impossible. The ferry will be much busier than usual tomorrow because of the tourists who will be arriving to attend the first day of the Daventry Workshops Festival. It would be easy for two people to blend in with the crowd."

"I hadn't thought of that."

"Ah, but I did." Cyrus grinned briefly. "That's why I get the big bucks. And just to be on the safe side, I'm going to make arrangements to cover the ferry angle, on the off chance that those two might try to slip aboard."

"What arrangements?"

"I've got a plan."

"Somehow that does nothing to calm my nerves."

"Funny. It does wonders for mine. I always feel better when I know I've got a plan. I'm a real methodical kind of guy."

She wrinkled her nose. "All right, tell me about your plan."

Jayne Ann Krentz

"I'll give you all the details as soon as Rick gets down here."

"I'm here," Rick said from the kitchen door. He yawned as he finished buttoning his shirt. "What's this about a plan?"

Cyrus eyed him thoughtfully. "How would you like to experience one of the more boring aspects of the investigation business?"

Rick's mouth snapped shut in the middle of the yawn. His eyes lit with enthusiasm. "Sure. What do I do?"

"It's called a stakeout. Here's how it works." Cyrus leaned forward and rested his forearms on his thighs. He clasped his fingers loosely together as he concentrated. "You and I are going to escort Jacob Houston off the island on the ten o'clock ferry. One of my people, guy named Paul Stredley, will be waiting for us on the mainland."

"Go on," Rick said.

"Stredley will take Houston off our hands, and then he'll go collect Rhonda Price in Seattle. He'll see to it that the two of them are kept safe until this is over."

"That's all I get to do?" Rick's disappointment was obvious. "Take the ferry with you and Jacob?"

"No, that's not quite all." Cyrus smiled. "I'll return on the next ferry. But you'll stay behind. You're going to do surveillance on every boat that arrives from this island for the rest of the day. Get the license numbers of every car carrying one or two males. Also, keep a special eye out for a pair of walk-ons."

"I thought you didn't get any descriptions," Eugenia said.

He shrugged. "I haven't got much, but I've got something. Two men of medium build, one of whom may be wearing a pair of snakeskin boots, a flannel shirt, and jeans." He looked at Rick. "Got that?"

Rick glowed with excitement. "Sure."

"Try to look inconspicuous while you're hanging around the ferry terminal. Spend some time in the coffee shop or pretend to fish off the pier."

"I've got an idea," Eugenia said. "He could take some brushes and paper from the studio upstairs and pose as a watercolor artist. People are always sketching the ferries."

Cyrus raised one brow. "Not a bad idea."

Rick grinned. "Think those two dudes will actually be dumb enough to take the ferry?"

"You never know."

"What about the house measurements?" Rick asked. "We didn't get a chance to finish the basement."

"They'll have to wait. I'll finish them up later."

Eugenia glanced at him. "I'll help you."

"Thanks," Cyrus said.

"What about you, Eugenia?" Rick looked at her. "What are you going to do while we're gone?"

Eugenia fixed Cyrus with a determined expression. "I'm going to do exactly what I planned to do all along. I'll attend the arts festival. It will give me the perfect opportunity to have some casual conversations about Nellie with several of the local artists."

Cyrus took one look at her and knew he would never be able to talk her out of the idea. On the positive side, he told himself, she would be reasonably safe amid the crowds at the festival. He would only be gone for a few hours. How much trouble could she get into in that length of time?

He did not really want an answer to that question, he thought.

"Try to be subtle when you question people," he said. "It usually works better that way."

"I am nothing if not subtle."

Nineteen

"**I** create images of the raw forces of power and sex." The young man hovered over Eugenia as she examined the sculptures displayed in the booth.

"I see," Eugenia said. "Power and sex."

"Reduced to the essentials."

She nodded. "Essentials."

According to the sign above the booth, his name was Kevin Lanton. He was James Dean lean and intense in a pair of ripped jeans and a flannel shirt. There was something about artists, she thought. Even though she had dealt with them for years, some part of her never ceased to romanticize them.

She responded to them, even when she did not always respond to their work. There was an engaging, single-minded purity to them.

Regardless of individual temperaments and character traits, on some level they all had one thing in common. Their work was vitally important to them. It was their refuge and their passion. In some cases, she suspected, it was their link to sanity.

The most brilliant artists she had met were at the mercy of the forces that drove them to create. They lived on the edge. But the very act of creation allowed them a unique moment or two of exultation that was denied to others. She knew they paid a price for that moment in the fire, but sometimes they produced something that allowed others to experience, however briefly, the heat from the flames.

Not unlike her relationship with Cyrus, she thought. A deep wistfulness swept through her. There would be a price to pay when the relationship ended, but in the meantime she was living in the heart of the fire.

All right, she thought, strictly speaking, she was not exactly living in the heart of the fire at that precise moment. It was ten-thirty in the morning, and she was making her way through the crowded aisles of booths that lined Harbor Street.

Cyrus and Rick, together with Jacob Houston hidden beneath a blanket in the backseat of the Jeep, had left two hours earlier on the first ferry of the day.

The festival-goers had begun arriving in droves on the return trip.

The local artisans and craftspeople who comprised the Daventry Workshops had been ready for the influx of potential customers. Banners waved jauntily in the breeze. At least three dozen colorful booths displaying pottery, glass, paintings, woodworking, sculpture, and textile art had been set up on the main thoroughfare.

Interspersed among the booths were several stands that featured roasted corn, strawberry shortcake, sandwiches, espresso, and soft drinks.

Even the weather had cooperated. The rain had finally stopped. The annual Daventry Workshops Festival was off to a flying start.

Her investigation, however, Eugenia thought, was not going quite so well. Thus far she had talked to only a handful of the local artists. She had learned nothing new. Most had met Nellie Grant in passing, but it was obvious that none of them had been close enough to her to care deeply about her death.

Eugenia forced her attention back to the array of metal sculptures displayed on the table. She could almost hear Cyrus's verdict. *Looks like a bunch of rusted-out license plates welded together.*

"Fascinating." She stroked the edge of one badly corroded plate. "You've found a way to use some of the most symbolic artifacts of our culture to illustrate the potential for both creation and destruction inherent in the forces of power."

"And sex," Kevin reminded her.

"Assuming there is a difference between the forces of sex and power." Eugenia reminded herself that she had a goal here at the festival, and it was not to get sidetracked with conversations about artistic theory. But it was hard to avoid them. She loved this kind of argument. "It's seems clear to me that the energy that fuels one, fuels the other."

"Well, maybe. But you've got to consider the end results."

"Not if you're trying to illustrate the elemental nature of the forces." She was grateful that Cyrus was not around. He would be howling with laughter by now. "You're the one who said he wanted to take a minimalist approach to the subject. Why bother to create two dynamics if there is only one?"

"I'm not so sure there is just one."

"I think it's obvious. You can see it in glass."

"I don't work in glass," Kevin snapped. "The medium is too damn fragile to convey raw power and sex."

"I disagree." She was getting carried away, she warned herself. She really did not have time for this. "What better medium to represent power and sex than one that is both liquid and solid? Glass is a substance that is both strong and vulnerable. It is literally born in fire yet takes shape only when it cools. It illuminates the quintessential nature of all elemental forces."

Cyrus's eyes would definitely have glazed over by now, she thought.

Kevin shook his head. "Glass is too attractive to represent power. Power is raw. Power is ugly. Power is bestial."

"Nonsense. Power is simply transparent and invisible until it is given form and direction. It can't be raw or ugly or anything else. It simply exists, like the wind—" Eugenia broke off abruptly. This was ludicrous. She could not afford to waste any more time. "Look, this is very interesting, and your work is, uh, extremely intriguing. But I wanted to talk about something else."

"Like what?"

"Did you know Nellie Grant?" In spite of the promise she had made to Cyrus, she had been forced to abandon subtlety half an hour earlier when she had first started questioning the artists. It had become quickly apparent that no one was going to respond to the indirect approach. Not that she had made any headway with the direct method, she thought grimly.

"Daventry's last live-in?" Kevin gave his James Dean shrug. "Yeah. I met her at a couple of the parties."

"She was a friend of mine."

"Is that so?" Kevin had obviously lost interest in the conversation now that they were no longer discussing his art. "Too bad about her getting washed overboard. Never could figure out why she went sailing that day."

Eugenia tensed. "Why do you say that?"

"The weather was bad. She must have known it would be dangerous. Some people think she was depressed because of Daventry's death and went out to commit suicide. But I saw her at the party that night. She didn't look like she was seriously in love with Daventry. She looked kind of pissed, if you want to know the truth."

"Any idea why?"

"No. I didn't talk to her. I just saw her from a distance. She was going upstairs for something."

Kevin turned away to greet another potential customer before Eugenia could ask any more questions.

She waited a moment and then decided it would be pointless to push Kevin any further.

She swallowed a sigh and turned to walk down another row of booths. She was wasting her time, she thought.

Two potters and a textile artist later, she was more discouraged than ever. Yes, they had all met Nellie. No, none of them had known her well. None of them had seen anything out of the ordinary at Glass House the night Daventry had died. Most freely admitted that they had been drinking heavily at the party.

She was in the process of removing her wallet from her purse to pay for a stiff double shot of espresso, when she noticed the window of the Midnight Gallery a few feet away. Fenella Weeks had changed the display for the festival. The undersea wildlife paintings were gone. In their place was an edgy, intriguing seascape.

It was one of those rare works of representational art that managed to cross the boundaries. On the surface it was a simple seascape, complete with crashing waves, but underneath it was a great deal more. It had depth and passion and a fierce, vital quality that pulled her to it.

Kevin Lanton had tried to convey the essence of raw power and sex in his license plate sculpture, Eugenia thought. But this picture actually succeeded in accomplishing the goal. It had been executed in shades of green that reminded her of thick glass.

She had never seen Cyrus's fireplace, but she knew intuitively that the seascape would be perfect for it.

She dropped her wallet back into her purse and stepped up onto the sidewalk. She did not take her eyes off the seascape as she walked slowly toward the Midnight Gallery window.

She waited for the picture to become ordinary and dull. But the closer she got, the more compelling it became. By the time she was at the door of the shop, she knew she was going to buy it for Cyrus.

The chimes above the door rang merrily as she let herself inside.

The gallery was empty. Hardly surprising, Eugenia thought. The booths in the street were the main attraction this morning. Few people wanted to browse indoors when they could be strolling through the displays that had been set up outside.

"Fenella?" She glanced toward the rear of the gallery, but there was no one behind the counter. She wondered if Fenella had popped out to get herself a latte or to survey the competition.

The black curtain that concealed the back room stirred slightly in the breeze that blew in with Eugenia. It settled back into place when she shut the door.

"Fenella? It's Eugenia Swift. I want to ask you about the seascape in the window."

There was no response. She stepped around the end of the counter and pulled aside the heavy curtain. The

Jayne Ann Krentz

interior of Fenella's back room was crowded, like most gallery and museum back rooms, with pictures and objets d'art that, for one reason or another, were not on display.

Framed paintings were stacked against one wall. A collection of small, hand-carved seagulls perched on a piece of driftwood. Some nondescript pottery sat bunched together on a table.

Eugenia glanced around curiously and then started to step back out of the room. She caught the glint of glass out of the corner of her eye.

She stopped breathing for a few frozen seconds. Then, very slowly, she released the curtain. It fell silently behind her. A deep gloom descended on Fenella's back room.

Eugenia did not turn on the overhead fixture. Enough light slithered around the edges of the curtain to enable her to see the objects on the shelves.

She took one step forward and then another, moving deeper into the dusty storage room to get a better look at the thing that crouched in the far corner. When she was close enough to see it clearly, a queasy, disoriented sensation passed through her. She felt as if she had brushed up against a ghost.

She came to a halt and stared at the piece. It was crafted from sharp fragments of glass and scarred remnants of old metal. It twisted in on itself as if it were a living creature that fed on its own rage and craziness.

Eugenia's skin cooled with shock. She had seen this artist's work before in Daventry's gallery of ex-lovers. Her intuition told her that whoever had created this monstrous thing was capable of murder.

The shelf on which the sculpture hunkered was too high to allow Eugenia a close look. She glanced around and saw a small step stool.

She dragged the stool across the room and positioned it in front of the high shelf. Quickly she climbed to the top step and carefully reached out for the mass of ragged glass and seething metal.

She had to brace herself to pick it up, not simply because the sharp edges made it dangerous, but because some part of her fiercely resisted. She did not want to touch the horror.

She flinched when her fingers closed gingerly around the shards of glass and metal. She could feel the sick fury in it. The sculpture was heavy. Glass always surprised you with its weight, she thought.

Carefully she turned it, angling it to look for a signature. She found it on the bottom of the base.

Fenella Weeks.

"Oh, my God." Reflexively, she tightened her grasp. She felt a cold, burning sting on the tip of one of her fingers. A dark red drop of blood welled.

"Damn."

She strained to listen for the door chimes that would surely ring at any second to announce that Fenella had returned.

An eerie silence came from the other room. She could hear the noise from the art fair, but it seemed distant, as if the festival were taking place in a parallel universe.

A fine trembling started in her hands. Hastily she set the sculpture back down on the shelf. It was a relief to let go of it.

Another drop of blood appeared on her nicked finger.

She looked at it, shocked by the sight. She wondered if she had accidentally walked into some macabre fairy tale where the heroine pricked her finger and disaster ensued.

If Cyrus were here, he would tell her to get a grip on her imagination.

The thought steadied her.

She jumped down from the step stool, took a deep breath, and reached into her purse for a tissue. She found one, tightened it around her bleeding finger, and rushed toward the curtain. An overwhelming need to get out of the shop knifed through her.

If being cool was the first rule of the detective business, don't panic had to be the second. Of course Cyrus probably did not need a rule like that, she thought as she pulled the curtain aside. He would never panic.

The outer shop was still empty, but through the plate glass window in front she spotted a familiar figure wending her way toward the door. Fenella was dressed in a loose, gauzy black dress decorated with an exotic motif. Weighty earrings composed of metal and bits and pieces of other things swung above her shoulders. She carried a foaming latte cup in one hand.

Eugenia knew she could not get out of the shop without being seen. Whirling around, she bent over the nearest piece of studio glass, a muddy-looking, grayish blue bowl.

The chimes over the door tinkled with a terrible, grating cheerfulness. Eugenia shivered.

"Eugenia." Fenella sounded surprised but pleased to see her. "I didn't see you enter the shop."

"Good morning, Fenella." Eugenia straightened and turned. She summoned up what she hoped was a reasonable facsimile of a smile. "I thought you might be getting some coffee."

Fenella made a face as she walked toward the sales counter. "I enjoy festival days, but they aren't good business days for me. The crowds tend to stay outside where the booths are, especially when its sunny. Can't blame them. Was there something you wanted?"

For an instant Eugenia's mind went blank. All she wanted was to escape. Belatedly, she remembered the reason she had wandered into the shop in the first place.

"The painting in the window," she said brightly. "The seascape. I'm not a big fan of that kind of thing, but that one is special. I think Cyrus might like it."

"It's very good, isn't it?"

"Yes." Eugenia made herself walk calmly toward the door. "Another local artist, I assume?"

"Yes, of course. I told you, I only feature local artists. The painter's name is Brad Kolb. Wonderful technique."

"Fascinating use of color. Great depth without excessive detail."

"Yes, indeed."

Eugenia opened the door. She wanted to run, but she made herself toss Fenella a breezy smile, instead. "When Cyrus gets back this afternoon, I'll mention it to him."

"So that was him I noticed driving onto the early ferry?"

"He's taking his nephew back to the airport." The cover story sounded utterly inane, Eugenia thought. One would have expected a trained detective to come up with a more detailed explanation for leaving the island. But Cyrus had insisted that simpler was always better.

"I'll put the Kolb painting in the back until you can return with Mr. Colfax."

Don't hold your breath, Eugenia thought. "Thanks. I appreciate it.

Fenella's thin, unnaturally arched brows lifted in amusement. "It will be interesting to see if he likes it. I'm afraid it might not be *pretty* enough for his, uh, tastes."

Jayne Ann Krentz

Anger surged out of nowhere. This was no time to leap to Cyrus's defense, Eugenia thought. Nevertheless, she had to resist an inexplicable urge to defend his taste in art. "I'm sure he'll like it."

She escaped through the door and hurried out onto the crowded sidewalk. She needed an espresso and a quiet place to think.

Ten minutes later, plastic cup in hand, she made her way back to where she had parked her car. She got in behind the wheel, took a fortifying sip of the double shot of espresso, and made herself go over everything from the top.

The truth was, when it came right down to it, she did not really have very much to explain the adrenaline that had shot through her when she had discovered Fenella's signature on the ugly glass and metal sculpture. She had reacted on a gut level, the way she always did to art. It was time to step back and look at the situation objectively.

Okay, so Fenella Weeks may have been one of Daventry's ex-lovers, she thought. Big deal. The group was hardly an exclusive one. Nellie had never spoken of the relationship, so presumably she had either not known about it or not cared.

Fenella had never mentioned her past relationship with Daventry, either. She had even claimed that she did not know what the views were like from Glass House. But maybe that was not so surprising or even suspicious, Eugenia thought. She knew herself, that if she had ever made the mistake of sleeping with Daventry, she would have wanted to deny it, too.

She took a sip of the espresso and drummed her fingers on the steering wheel.

Daventry had had a reputation for openly mocking his old flames, usually by denigrating their artistic talent. But he had apparently kept quiet about Fenella.

Why?

The unanswered question hovered in the atmosphere.

Eugenia felt her stomach tighten with fresh tension. First things first, she thought. If Cyrus were here, he would probably tell her to verify all the facts before she leaped to conclusions.

The only real fact she had was the piece of savage sculpture she had found in Fenella's back room. It was possible—improbable, but possible—that, in her anxiety, she had made a serious mistake. Perhaps the artist who had created the monstrous thing in Daventry's gallery was not Fenella, but someone who worked in the same medium.

Eugenia decided that it was time to take another, closer look at the sculpture in Glass House. She had to be sure.

She finished the last of the espresso and tossed the cup into the small litter bag. Her fingers shook when she inserted the key in the ignition. It occurred to her that it had not been very smart to add a dose of caffeine to the adrenaline that was already swirling through her bloodstream.

Another handy tip for the amateur detective, she thought as she slammed the Toyota into gear. Watch the coffee intake when you're dealing with a murderer.

Possible murderer, she corrected herself as she drove out of the marina parking lot. No one had any real proof that Daventry had been killed.

But if he had been murdered, and if Nellie had witnessed the crime, it would explain a great deal.

The trip back to Glass House was interminable. The warning squeal of her car's tires on some of the twisting turns told Eugenia that she was driving too fast. Twice she made herself slow down to a more reasonable speed, but by the time she rounded the last curve she was treading hard on the accelerator.

She roared into the driveway of Glass House, braked to a furious stop, and leaped out of the car.

She fumbled with the new code for the front door before she finally managed to let herself into the mirrored hall. Flinging her purse down on the nearest glass table, she raced up the staircase to the third floor without bothering to remove her shoes.

She was breathing heavily by the time she reached the gallery that housed the artwork crafted by Daventry's ex-lovers.

She made herself take a deep breath before she opened the door.

The windowless chamber was as dark as an Egyptian tomb. Cold, stale air rushed out to envelope her as she stepped into it. She found the wall switch and quickly pushed it.

The dramatically arranged spotlights winked on, revealing each item in the bizarre collection while leaving the space around them in jet black shadow.

She walked slowly through the forest of black glass pedestals, never taking her eyes off the horrific glass-and-metal thing at the far end. It crouched in its glass cage, waiting for her. The sharp glass shards imbedded in it gleamed malevolently in the eerie light. The darkness that surrounded the pedestal seemed far more dense and impenetrable than the gloom that flanked the other displays.

Got to watch that overactive imagination, Eugenia thought. It would have been nice to have had Cyrus with her. His laconic, low-key attitude toward this kind of thing would have been a better tonic than the caffeine she had dumped into her system.

She reached the last pedestal and looked at the evil

sculpture through the clear glass shroud of the display case.

The same artist. It had to be the same one. Her intuition was never wrong when it came to recognizing technique and style.

She unlatched the display case and reached inside as if she were putting her hands into the cage of a dangerous reptile.

Her fingers closed tentatively around the ugly sculpture. The sharp edges bit into her palms. She lifted it out of the case and started to turn it sideways so that she could see the signature on the base.

"It's my work, of course," Fenella said lightly from the doorway. "But, then, you already know that, don't you?"

Eugenia froze. The edges of the sculpture dug into her skin. The pain broke the spell that had gripped her at the sound of Fenella's amused words.

Clutching the sculpture very carefully in both hands, she turned toward the door.

Fenella was starkly silhouetted by the bright sunlight that bounced off the mirrored walls of the atrium. The darkness of the gallery made it impossible to see her face, but it was obvious that she held an object in her right hand.

"Yes. I already knew that." Eugenia was relieved to hear her own voice. It sounded infinitely more calm and controlled than she felt. "But I had to be certain."

"I realized what had happened when I saw the drops of blood on the floor of my back room." Fenella closed the door of the chamber, cutting off the outside light. "I was afraid that you would be trouble. I hoped you would simply go away without getting the answers you wanted, but you kept pushing."

She took a step forward. As she did so her right hand passed through the edge of a beam cast by one of the display lights. Eugenia saw the gun. For a few seconds she could not breathe.

"There's no point killing me," Eugenia said. "I can't prove anything."

"I tried to tell myself that at first. Right after I realized the mistake I had made when I sold Rhonda's painting to you."

"You knew Rhonda had not painted that picture."

"Well, of course I did," Fenella said, disgusted. "Rhonda has no talent. When she asked me to sell the painting because she needed the money, I assumed she had stolen it from some off-island gallery."

"But after I bought it, she told you that it had been painted by Nellie Grant. That's when you knew you had a problem, didn't you?"

"When Rhonda got back to the island that day and discovered that I'd sold the picture to you, of all people, she came unglued. She told me that you were a friend of Nellie's and that you would probably recognize her work."

"I only wanted to find out what had happened to Nellie."

"I couldn't allow you to start asking too many questions about her death," Fenella said. "I was afraid they would lead to . . . other things."

"You killed her, didn't you?"

"No." Fenella sounded genuinely surprised. "I planned to get rid of her, but it proved unnecessary. She took care of the problem herself by getting washed overboard on the way back to the island."

"Why did you want her dead?"

"She saw me the night of the party," Fenella said. "She was watching from the door of this very chamber. She heard the argument I had with Daventry."

"You quarreled with Daventry that night?"

"Lost my temper with him, I'm afraid. And Nellie Grant saw me push him down the staircase."

"That's impossible. She couldn't have seen anything from the doorway of this room. She would have had to go out onto the balcony and look straight down."

"No," Fenella said. "All she had to do was look straight across to the opposite wall."

"My God. The mirrors."

"Exactly. They're designed to reflect the staircase from floor to ceiling. I happened to glance at that wall as Daventry fell. I could see Nellie just as clearly as she saw me."

"What happened?"

Fenella sighed. "I must admit, I panicked and ran. I thought she would call Peaceful Jones. But nothing happened."

"She didn't go to the authorities," Eugenia said. "She left the island that night."

And came to Seattle to see me, she added silently. Why had Nellie done that? On that last visit to the condo, she had said nothing about having seen Fenella Weeks push Daventry down the stairs.

"She took one of Daventry's boats from the marina," Fenella said. "I didn't know what she intended, but since she had not gone to the cops, I had to assume that she meant to exploit the situation."

"Exploit it? How?"

"I thought that she would probably try to blackmail me. But she died before she could make any threats."

"When she was reported missing in the storm, you thought it was all over and that your secret was safe."

"Yes," Fenella said. "But then I got a nasty shock. That disgusting Leonard Hastings tried to blackmail me. Can you believe it? It turned out that he had also seen me push Daventry. He was lurking upstairs in one of the second-floor rooms at the time."

"My God," Eugenia breathed. "You killed him, didn't you?"

"I paid him off until I could come up with a plan. Eventually I decided the easiest thing to do was to replace some of his heart medication with some stronger stuff. Meditation Jones was very helpful. She told me about the various illegal drugs that could kill a person with Leonard Hastings's heart condition. She had no idea how I used the information, of course."

"How did you get the drugs?"

"From a street dealer in Seattle." Fenella chuckled. "It was not difficult."

"With Hastings dead you thought you were finally in the clear again."

"I told myself that this time I was safe," Fenella said. "But then you showed up. I knew that you had been a friend of Nellie's. She had mentioned you several times. I got worried."

"Why did you try to kill Rhonda Price that night when she came to find me at the restaurant? Had she seen you push Daventry, too?"

"Rhonda?" Fenella gave the name a derisive twist. "Of course not. She's just a stupid little no-talent. She was too drunk that night to have noticed anything, even if she had been standing right there beside me."

"Then why hit her and shove her into the marina?"

Fenella sucked in air. "She made me very angry when she told me that it was one of Nellie's paintings she had given me to sell."

"I don't understand."

"*That painting was a link to what had happened that night.* It was bound to make you ask more questions."

The sudden wild rage in Fenella's voice sent shock waves to the far end of the gallery. They crashed against Eugenia.

"Yes," Eugenia said. "I see what you mean."

"I knew that if you recognized the painting you would be more convinced than ever that something was wrong. You would probe more deeply into the situation. Who knew where it would all lead?"

"And you now had two deaths to cover up, not just one. You could no longer feel safe."

"I started having bad dreams," Fenella said. There was an eerie, fretful quality in her voice now. "What if Hastings had left a note somewhere? What if he had talked to someone? Where had Nellie Grant gone the night of Daventry's death? Did she tell anyone about me before she died?"

"So many unanswered questions," Eugenia whispered.

"Yes." Fenella's voice sharpened. "And I was afraid that, because of the painting, you would ask too many of your own."

Eugenia whistled softly. "In other words, you tried to kill Rhonda because she had unwittingly shown you that you were vulnerable."

"Silly little Daventry whore. I didn't really set out to kill her. Frankly, I don't care if she lives or dies. She knows nothing. I simply followed her to the restaurant to see what she was up to that night."

"And when she went running out the back door, you were waiting?"

Fenella took a step forward. The movement caused the fabric of her black dress to rustle and slither in the shadows. "I took advantage of the moment to smack her good with a length of board that happened to be close at hand. She deserved it."

Eugenia stared at her. "You hated Rhonda. Not just because she had made you nervous by producing one of Nellie's paintings, but because she was one of Daventry's ex-lovers."

"Five years ago that bastard, Daventry, tossed me

aside for a series of little no-talents like Rhonda Price," Fenella said harshly.

"Why?"

"Why? Because I frightened him, of course." The edgy amusement returned to Rhonda's voice. "He knew I had a great talent, but he was afraid of it. It was too big for him. Too strong. He knew he could not suck it out of me the way he did with all the others. Deep down, he was terrified that I would destroy him."

Eugenia glanced at the horrific glass and metal sculpture in her hands. She thought she understood why Daventry had become uneasy about Fenella's artistic talent. She looked up again. "When he walked out on you, you vowed to make him pay, right?"

"Oh, yes. *Yes,* I promised myself that he would pay."

"One question. Why did you wait five years?"

Fenella uttered a grating, high-pitched laugh. "Because it took me that long to create a truly satisfying way to destroy him. I am an artist, after all. The destruction of Adam Daventry had to be a masterpiece."

"Excuse me? It took five years to come up with the brilliant idea of shoving him down a flight of stairs? No offense, but that doesn't sound all that creative."

"I didn't intend to kill him that night," Fenella snapped. "We quarreled. I got very angry. I lost my temper and I shoved him. Hard. He was stoned on some of his special drugs. He lost his balance and fell. But I never meant to do it."

"I see."

"Why would I want to murder him when he was paying so well for his crime against me?"

"How was he paying for it?"

Fenella moved close to another beam of light. "I was blackmailing him."

"With what? Daventry didn't fear anyone enough to pay blackmail. He would have laughed in your face."

"He didn't laugh at me," Fenella said proudly. "He paid through the nose to keep me quiet."

"I'm impressed. What did you have on him?"

"For five long years, I kept close tabs on Adam Daventry. He was so damned arrogant that he never guessed I was there in the shadows, waiting and watching. He thought that I was out of his life because he had ended our affair. But I was closer to him than he ever knew. Closer than any of his whores. And when he made his great mistake, I was ready."

Eugenia went very still. She thought she knew what was coming, but she also knew it would be folly to try to one-up Fenella. The other woman's ego was her only vulnerable point at that moment.

"Okay, I'll bite," Eugenia said. "What was Daventry's big mistake?"

"A few months ago when he became interested in ancient glass, he began to dabble in the underground art market. His contacts with the people who provided him with his special drugs led him to other people who knew how to get hold of very dangerous, extremely valuable things."

"Things such as what, Fenella?"

"In this case, a piece of very old glass known as the Hades cup."

Eugenia said nothing, but she took a very deep, very shaky breath.

Fenella laughed softly. "You know about glass, Eugenia Swift. You're an expert. Surely you're aware of the legends surrounding that cup."

"I've heard a few of them."

"People have died because of that glass. Daventry had been warned that the former owner of the cup would gladly kill to get it back. He had to protect his secret. Only a handful of people knew that he possessed it. He never realized that I was one of those people."

"Until you popped up out of the past and began to blackmail him."

"You should have seen his face when he discovered that I had moved to the island and opened my gallery." Fenella giggled. It was not a pleasant sound. "I told him that the information that he was the new owner of the Hades cup was contained in a letter that would be mailed to certain parties if anything ever happened to me. It was a lie, of course."

"There is no letter?"

"I could hardly trust anyone else with that sort of information, now, could I?" Fenella said it as if Eugenia were not very bright. "But Daventry believed me."

"He was willing to pay you for your silence?"

"Oh, he tried everything else first." Scorn burned in Fenella's words. "He told me we could take up where we had left off. Claimed that he had come to realize that I was the most brilliant artist he had ever known. The fool actually thought he could seduce me."

"But you made him pay, instead."

"Yes, I made him pay." Fenella's voice shook with fury. "Hundreds of thousands of dollars."

"Until the quarrel at the top of the stairs."

"It was all very ironic in a way."

"What do you mean?" Eugenia asked.

"He once told me that the thing that attracted him to artists was their unpredictable temperaments. He enjoyed the fire, he said. He liked to see them in a temper. It excited him."

"In the end, he died because you lost your temper with him."

Sharp Edges

"Yes," Fenella whispered. "And now, you must die also."

Eugenia realized that she needed a serious distraction and she needed it immediately. She remembered the tears that had welled in Jacob Houston's eyes when he had learned that he had inadvertently destroyed his own creation.

"You know something, Fenella? You really do have talent." She took a step closer to the light. She wanted Fenella to see that she still held the sculpture. "Too bad you can only produce monstrosities."

"That's not true," Fenella shouted. "My work is far too brilliant for you even to begin to comprehend. Put down my *Flower.*"

"Whatever you say." Eugenia raised the ugly glass and metal sculpture and hurled it to the floor.

Fenella screamed.

Glass shattered. Metal shrieked as it scraped against a mirrored surface.

Fenella pulled the trigger.

· 2 9 3 ·

Twenty

The shot slammed into the wall beside Eugenia. She forced herself to move through the fear. She only had a few seconds during which Fenella's attention would be focused on the destruction of her *Flower*.

She dove for the cover of the dark shadows near the floor and crawled on hands and knees to the nearest black glass pedestal.

"Damn you, damn you, damn you." Fenella's voice rose in a keening wale of anguished fury. "You know nothing about art, Eugenia Swift. Nothing."

Another shot cracked loudly in the room. Eugenia huddled behind the pedestal and cringed when a glass case shattered. Shards rained down onto the floor beside her. Something heavy fell off a stand and grazed her thigh.

She listened to Fenella prowl through the maze of display stands.

"Stupid bitch. Stupid museum director. You think you know art? You haven't got a clue about the true nature of art. Only another artist can know art. And you're no artist. None of Adam Daventry's whores were artists."

Another glass case exploded. Not a gunshot this time, Eugenia thought. Fenella had smashed it.

"Were you one of Daventry's whores, Eugenia Swift? Were you one of these silly bitches who called themselves artists?"

More glass shattered. Something heavy and fragile cracked when it struck the tile.

"No-talents, every last one of you."

Another display case dissolved into shards.

"My talent terrified Daventry, you know," Fenella crooned with delight. "That's why he turned to these whores. He couldn't handle my talent."

Another case fractured when Fenella struck it with the gun.

"He could not take the fire of real genius," she shouted.

Eugenia realized that Fenella was working her way systematically through the pedestals. She was destroying the display cases and the art inside.

It would only take a minute or two for the enraged woman to reach Eugenia's pedestal.

She waited tensely until Fenella hammered the next display case.

"Superficial. Pedestrian. Amateurs, all of you," Fenella screamed as glass exploded.

Under cover of the noise of breaking glass, Eugenia rose to a crouch.

"Where are you, Eugenia Swift? You can't hide much longer." Fenella smashed another case. "I'm going to destroy all of Daventry's whores, and that includes you."

Eugenia listened to Fenella's footsteps. She was coming down the aisle on the right. Fortunately, she appeared to be going about the destruction of the art in a methodical manner. The nearest case on left and then the one on the right.

Left, right.

Left, right.

Daventry had certainly had a lot of women artists in his life, Eugenia thought. At the moment, approximately four more of them stood between her and a bullet.

She edged around the corner of the pedestal, moving to put it squarely between herself and Fenella.

The footsteps came closer. Fenella was moaning in rage now. The sound had the same effect on Eugenia's nerves that the gun had on the glass. It turned them into jagged shards.

Fenella smashed another case. Another piece of art struck the tile. Something soft this time.

Left, right.

Fenella was less than three feet away now. Eugenia peeked around the edge of the pedestal and saw an upraised arm silhouetted against a narrow beam of stark white light. The gauzy black dress drifted like a gossamer shroud.

"Stupid Daventry whore. Did you believe his lies, too? Of course you did. They all did."

For that single instant Fenella's back was turned. This would be her only chance, Eugenia decided.

She lunged forward from her crouched position with all of her strength. Fenella shrieked in fury as Eugenia slammed into her.

The impact carried them both toward the floor.

The arc of the fall was halted by a jarring thud when the back of Fenella's head struck the edge of a display case. The gun clattered loudly on the nearby tiles.

Fenella went limp as she hit the floor. She lay unmoving. Eugenia fell on top of her. The shock of the impact took away her breath.

When she recovered enough to scramble to her feet, she realized that Fenella was unconscious.

Deputy Peaceful Jones passed solemn judgment as he watched his wife straighten the small clinic. "Real sad situation."

Meditation sighed as she put away her instruments. "A very strange aura. The color was malignant. Dark and muddy. There was no clarity in it at all."

Cyrus looked at them and decided there was nothing more to say.

The authorities had taken Fenella Weeks to the mainland in a helicopter. She had been awake, but not what anyone could call lucid. Cyrus had heard her babbling about a bizarre scheme to kill all of Daventry's previous lovers. It was all she could talk about. Meditation Jones said that she was lost somewhere inside herself.

Peaceful had supervised the management of the crime scene with surprising efficiency. Eugenia gave a quiet, detailed statement. When it was finished, Peaceful shook his head.

"Imagine her thinking she could blackmail someone like Daventry. Man like that wouldn't have given a damn if she revealed one of his old scandals."

"You wouldn't think so," Eugenia said.

Something in her voice caught Cyrus's attention. She did not meet his eye.

"Wonder what she had on him," Peaceful mused.

Eugenia cleared her thorat. "I think it had something to do with a shady art deal."

"Wouldn't surprise me." Peaceful grimaced. "I'll bet most of Daventry's art deals were on the shady side."

* * *

"Are you sure you're all right?" Cyrus asked as he bundled Eugenia into the Jeep. Her strangely quiet mood worried him as nothing else had in a long time. "Maybe I should take you back to Seattle to see your own doctor."

"No." Eugenia buckled her seat belt with unnatural care. "I'm not ill. Just a little shaken."

"Damn. You and me both." Cyrus got in beside her and put on his dark glasses with grim precision. "It's a wonder I'm not having hysterics."

A reluctant smile tugged at the edge of her mouth. "That would be an interesting sight. Somehow I can't imagine you having hysterics, regardless of the circumstances."

"Everyone has his breaking point." Cyrus put one hand on the wheel and the other on the back of the seat. "I think I may have reached mine today."

"Not likely."

"Damn it, Eugenia, you could have been killed by that wacko." He backed the Jeep out of the space and headed for the main road.

"You don't have to spell it out for me." Her voice sounded oddly detached. "I was there. Saw the whole thing."

"Why in hell did you go racing off to Glass House by yourself after you found the sculpture in Fenella's back room?"

"I told you, I had to be sure that Fenella was the artist who had created both of those sculptures. After I left the gallery, Fenella realized I was on to her. She followed me."

He gripped the wheel very tightly. "You should have waited until I got back to the island."

"If you're going to yell at me, I want out, here."

"Damn." He had not meant to yell at her. It was the last thing he wanted to do. But he did not know how to explain that the remains of the fear in the pit of his stomach made it difficult to maintain full control.

She had nearly died.

He made himself concentrate on the winding road. Since he could not trust himself to carry on a civil conversation, he sank, instead, into his dark thoughts.

He had nearly lost Eugenia today.

Too many loose ends left.

He could have lost her forever.

Loose ends.

Christ. She had almost died

What about the loose ends?

A strained silence settled over the front seat of the car. Eugenia did not break it until they were halfway back to Glass House. Then she stirred and turned her head to look at him.

"It's looking more and more as though I was wrong about Nellie having been murdered. Fenella claimed she didn't kill her, and for some reason, I believe her. Maybe Nellie really did get washed overboard."

"She was in a rush to return to the island that day to collect her things. She wouldn't have been as careful as usual," he agreed gently. "She might not have paid attention to the weather forecasts."

Eugenia sighed. "It still doesn't feel right, but I can't see any other logical explanation."

"Then you have to let it go."

"I suppose so." She kept her attention on him as he drove. "I told Peaceful that Fenella did a lot of ranting and raving when she cornered me in the gallery."

"I know." Cyrus flexed his hands on the wheel. "She must have really flipped."

"Thank God."

He glanced at her, startled. "What do you mean?"

Eugenia stared out the window at the waters of the Sound. "If she hadn't gone off the deep end and decided to destroy all of the artwork in the chamber, I wouldn't have had a chance."

He could almost feel the shudder that went through her. It passed straight through him, too, twisting his guts in the process. "You don't have to remind me."

"She said a lot of things. I didn't repeat all of them to Peaceful exactly as she said them."

"It's a wonder you can remember anything that she said, given what was happening at the time."

Eugenia cleared her throat. "I'm glad you see it that way. Because that's the excuse I plan to use if the authorities ever come back to ask why I didn't mention the exact nature of the blackmail threat."

Cyrus frowned. "You said it had something to do with a shady art deal."

"That much was true enough. What I didn't add was the name of the piece of art involved in the deal."

He took his foot off the accelerator and gazed blankly at the road ahead. Then he turned his head to stare at her. "Are you telling me that Fenella Weeks knew something about the Hades cup?"

"She said she discovered that Daventry had acquired the cup with the assistance of the people who helped him get his designer pills."

"Hell." He tried to fit the pieces of the puzzle together in a different way. "Maybe Fenella was after the cup. That might explain a couple of things."

"No, I don't think she cared about the cup at all. Her only goal was revenge. She seemed content with the success of her blackmail scheme."

"Until the night she shoved Daventry down the stairs."

"It wasn't a crime of opportunity, as you thought," Eugenia said quietly. "It was a crime of passion."

"I don't suppose she happened to mention where Daventry hid the damn thing."

"I don't think she knew or cared about the hiding place." Eugenia paused briefly. "But she did confirm that he was obsessed with the cup and that he knew there was a risk in owning it."

"It's got to be somewhere in that house." Cyrus put his foot back on the accelerator. "Daventry would have kept it handy so that he could see it whenever he wanted." A sudden thought interrupted his chain of logic. He glanced at Eugenia. "Can I assume that you've finally decided to accept the fact that the Hades cup exists and that Daventry had it?"

"I have to admit that Fenella's comments made a very strong impression."

He breathed deeply. "Given the way in which they were delivered."

"Yes."

"If it's any comfort," he said, "I don't think you need to be concerned about the authorities coming after you because you neglected to mention the Hades cup to them."

"No, I guess not." She smiled wryly. "As far as the experts in the art world are concerned, the cup doesn't even exist."

"And you're one of those experts who believes it's a myth. Obviously, you value your professional reputation too much to want people to think that you would listen to a crazy person's demented ravings about a mythical piece of glass."

"Right."

Cyrus paused. "Okay, so what's the real reason you didn't mention the cup to the authorities?"

"You know the answer to that."

A sudden sense of lightness unfurled deep inside him. She had done it for him.

"You kept quiet about it because of me, didn't you?" he said carefully. "You wanted to give me a chance to find it."

She shrugged but said nothing.

He took one hand off the wheel and put it on her thigh. "Thanks, Eugenia. I owe you."

"I was just trying to hold up my end of our bargain."

"Yeah. Sure. Well, thanks, anyway." The bright warmth died away, leaving Cyrus with a strong inclination to brood. He forced himself to concentrate instead on the host of fresh questions that the day's events had raised. "We've got a lot of loose ends, you know."

"Yes." She frowned. "We do, don't we?"

"Let's see what we have. Daventry was murdered and Nellie witnessed it. She left the island in his boat that night."

"She came to see me, but I'm still not sure why."

"She gave you one of the *Glass* paintings," Cyrus reminded her.

"And we've since turned up two more of them." Eugenia glanced at him. "Those paintings of Nellie's keep appearing in this thing, don't they?"

"They sure as hell do," Cyrus said. "I wonder why."

"Each one is a portrait of a piece of glass in Daventry's collection," Eugenia said slowly. "Maybe the missing one is a picture of the Hades cup."

"Even if it is, where does that leave us? There's no value in a painting of the damn thing." He paused. "But if someone thought there was, it might explain why Jacob's and Rhonda's cabins were searched."

"It would be more logical to search Glass House, wouldn't it?"

"Not if you had a reason to think that the paintings

had been removed," Cyrus said. He broke off to wrestle with that problem.

"Well?" Eugenia demanded.

"On the surface it looks like we've got two separate scenarios going on here."

"I see what you mean. Fenella Weeks was clearly responsible for one set of incidents stemming from Daventry's death and the steps she took to conceal it."

"Right," Cyrus said. "But the Hades cup provides a link. Still, I think it's safe to assume that Fenella was acting alone and had her own crazy agenda. She wasn't interested in Nellie's paintings."

"So who else would be looking for them?"

"Good question." And possibly a very dangerous one, he thought. But why would anyone go after a picture of the cup rather than the cup itself?

Eugenia flattened her palms on her thighs and rubbed them against the fabric of her black jeans. "What do we do now?"

He did not like the uncharacteristically subdued tone in her voice. "We go back to Glass House, where you will take a long, hot shower while I open one of those very expensive vintage bottles stored in Daventry's wine cellar. Then I will cook dinner for you. After that, we'll talk about what we do next."

She gave him a sidelong look. "You're going to cook dinner?"

"Think of it as a dining adventure."

"Cyrus?"

"Yeah?"

"Would you please stop the car? I think I'm going to be sick."

"If this is about my cooking—"

"No. *Please.*"

"Damn. I should have realized. I wondered when it

would hit you." He pulled the Jeep to the side of the road and cracked open the door.

By the time he reached her, she was already out, bent over, clutching her midsection. He held her gently as the spasms wracked her body.

When it was over he handed her his handkerchief.

"I'm sorry," she whispered. Tears streamed down her face. "This is so embarrassing. I never cry."

"It's a good sign. Better to let it out now than to bottle it up inside. The ones who keep it contained have the most trouble later."

"You sound like you know what you're talking about."

He remembered the first murder victim he had found. The killer had used a knife and then lain in wait for the first cop on the scene.

In the end, there had been a lot of blood, his own, the killer's, and the victim's. It had all mingled together in the dirty alley. He had survived with a scar and the knowledge that he had killed a man.

Then he recalled the stain left on the ground by the blood that had pooled around Katy's body. He thought about the deep, wrenching guilt of knowing that he had failed to protect her from Damien March.

"Yeah," he said. "I do."

She buried her face against his shoulder and cried for a long time.

The phone rang just as Cyrus dumped the pasta into a pan of boiling water. He studied the directions on the side of the empty package as he reached for the receiver. "Colfax here."

"It's me." Rick sounded tired but excited. "I'm ready with my report."

Cyrus heard the muffled sounds of traffic. "Where are you?"

"In Mr. Stredley's car. He picked me up at the ferry dock a few minutes ago. We're on our way to the airport."

"Good." Cyrus glanced at his watch. "Plenty of time to make your flight. Let's have the report."

"I copied down all the license numbers of all the cars that had two men in them. There weren't very many. Only seven in all. I gave the list to Mr. Stredley. He says he'll turn them over to Mr. Yates to trace."

"Nice going. I appreciate the help, Rick."

"I also got a look at almost all of the walk-ons. None of them wore snakeskin boots, though."

"Part of the job is to weed out the dead ends."

"Want me to stick around to do some more weeding?" Rick asked eagerly.

"You've got a job waiting for you, remember?"

"I remember. But, Cyrus?"

"Yeah?"

"I'm thinking of going into the security business."

Cyrus grinned and stirred the pasta. "You didn't get bored?"

"No way."

"We'll talk about it later."

"I'm serious," Rick insisted.

"So am I. Tell you what, if you're still interested in the security business after the end of your freshman year, I'll give you a job at Colfax Security next summer."

"For real?"

"You ever known me to be anything else except real?"

Rick paused. "No. Never."

"Let me talk to Stredley."

The pasta boiled over five minutes later, just as Cyrus finished checking on Rhonda and Jacob.

"Damn." He tossed down the phone, turned off the halogen burner, and grabbed the pot holders.

"What's wrong?" Eugenia asked from the doorway.

"This never happens with tuna sandwiches." He glanced at her out of the corner of his eye while he poured the pasta into a waiting colander.

She looked remarkably normal. Her face glowed from a recent hot shower. Damp tendrils of dark hair bobbed around her ears. The rest of the thick mass was caught up in a large clip on top of her head. She had put on a sweater and a pair of loose, flowing trousers.

"It was very nice of you to cook a meal from scratch," she said.

"That's me, Mr. Domestic." He set the empty pan down on the counter. "How are you feeling?"

"Much better, thanks. The hot shower helped. Want some help?"

"No, I'm in complete control here."

She glanced at the pasta. "That's what they all say."

"Sit down and drink your wine."

"Okay, I can handle that."

He went to work serving the pasta and salad he had prepared. "I just talked to Rick and Stredley. Rick's on his way home, and Stredley tells me that Rhonda Price and Jacob Houston are safely registered in a Portland hotel under false names. Quint will schedule people to keep an eye on them until this is over."

Her eyes widened. "That will cost a lot, won't it?"

"Yeah."

She groaned. "I was afraid you'd say that."

"Don't worry about it. I can afford it."

"Did Rick or Mr. Stredley have anything else to tell us?"

He hesitated. "Rick says he wants to go into security work."

Eugenia gave him a quick, knowing smile. "Like uncle, like nephew."

He grinned, unable to contain the tide of satisfaction that had flowed through him at Rick's words. "He'll probably change his mind a hundred times in the next four years."

"Maybe. But maybe not. I see a lot of you in him." She looked at him over the rim of her wineglass. "You know something, Cyrus? You'd make a terrific father."

He did not know what to say to that. It hit him hard that the only kids he wanted to father at that moment were hers. But it did not seem an appropriate time to bring up the subject.

"I've been thinking," she continued.

"Forget it." He carried the plates to the table and set them down. "I told you, no thinking until you've had a chance to rest."

"You and Rick never got to finish comparing the measurements of the rooms here in Glass House with those on the architect's drawings."

"So?"

She met his eyes. "I don't think I'm going to be able to sleep very well tonight. Why don't we finish the job?"

"Fine by me." He sat down.

Eugenia looked at the meal he had put in front of her. Her expression brightened for the first time since he had brought her back from Peaceful's office.

"Where did you get the idea of putting tuna on top of pasta?"

"It was sheer, culinary inspiration," he said modestly.

* * *

Three hours later, Cyrus found what he was looking for, a discrepancy of nearly three square feet.

"Well, what do you know." He surveyed his surroundings as he retracted the tape measure. "The wine cellar."

"This was where we found Leonard Hastings that first night." Eugenia examined the array of bottles. "Do you think he knew something?"

"Who knows? Maybe he figured that with his boss dead, it would be okay to help himself to some of this expensive wine. Read me the dimensions of the east wall again, will you?"

She leaned over the drawing. "Fifteen feet, four inches."

"Yeah, this is it. The actual wall is only twelve feet at the base." Cyrus put down the tape measure and began to haul dusty bottles out of the storage racks.

"What are you looking for now?"

"I'll bet three of my best aloha shirts that Daventry built a hidden safe somewhere in this wall."

Most of the black glass mirrors on the wall behind the wine racks were grimy and clouded with a layer of dust. But when Cyrus got all of the bottles out of the last rack, he found some smears and fingerprints at the edges of the glass where two of the mirrored panels met.

"Good heavens, you don't really think it will be this easy, do you?" Eugenia sounded awed.

"You call this easy?" He picked up a massive, old-fashioned wine opener. "Stand back."

"Cyrus, wait, you can't just smash that wall. It will cost a fortune to repair it. If there's a safe behind the mirrors, there must be a trick to opening that section."

"Probably is, but I don't intend to spend all night looking for it."

He swung the wine opener against the mirrored panel.

Eugenia put her hands over her ears and winced in pain as glass cracked and shattered. Belatedly Cyrus realized that she had heard far too much breaking glass that day.

"Sorry," he said. "You okay?"

"Yes." Her eyes widened as she stared past him into the opening. "Oh, my God, look. You were right. There *is* a safe."

Cyrus leaned down to take a closer look at the computerized locking mechanism. A searing disappointment stormed through him, draining away his incipient triumph. "Damn."

Eugenia looked briefly amused. "Don't tell me you don't know how to open a safe?"

"Opening this one won't be a problem." He unlatched the door of the safe. "Whoever was here last left it unlocked."

"That does not bode well, does it?"

"No. Someone else got here ahead of us." He had been so sure that the cup would be hidden here in Glass House.

She touched his shoulder. "I'm sorry, Cyrus."

He said nothing, but he was aware of the warmth of her fingers. Silently he opened the safe door.

Eugenia's hand froze on his shoulder. "There's something inside."

He frowned at the glimmer of light on a steel frame. "A painting."

He reached into the safe and pulled out the framed picture.

"The fourth *Glass* painting." Excitement built in Eugenia's voice. "I didn't notice this piece in the collection in the main vault, though." She bent closer, her expression tense with concentration. "It's old.

Very old. Or else a reproduction. I've never seen anything quite . . . Oh, lord, it isn't . . . ?"

"Yeah." Cyrus studied the intricately carved figures that struggled to free themselves from the glowing red- and amber-colored glass. "It's not just some old vase. It's the Hades cup."

Twenty-one

"No. Wait. Let her go. *Let her go.*"

"Cyrus, wake up."

The panic rolled through him in a wave that left every nerve raw, every sense screamingly alert. He felt the hand on his shoulder and flung himself to the side to avoid it.

"Cyrus, listen to me. You're dreaming. Wake up."

"What the . . . ?" He opened his eyes and stared up at Eugenia, who was leaning over him.

Her hair was in a tumbled cloud around her face. Moonlight glinted off her cheekbones and revealed the shadowy concern in her eyes. Her nightgown dipped low over her breasts.

"You had a nightmare," she said when she saw that he had focused on her.

"You can say that again." The last of the adrenaline shuddered through him. He sat up slowly and raked his fingers through his hair. Sharp fragments shifted unpleasantly in the ebbing tide of the dream.

"Damn."

"Are you all right?"

"Sure." He shoved aside the covers and got to his feet.

"Take some deep breaths," Eugenia advised urgently.

"Right. Deep breaths." He made his way into the adjoining bathroom, switched on the light, and turned on the cold water.

Eugenia came to stand in the doorway. "I thought I was the one who would have nightmares tonight."

"Consider yourself lucky." He bent over the washbasin and splashed water on his face.

"What were you dreaming about?"

He jerked a towel off the nearest bar and buried his face in it. Snapshots of fear and helplessness flashed through his head. "Can't remember. You know how it is with dreams."

She reached out to touch his bare arm. "Was it about Katy?"

The gentleness in her voice disturbed him for some reason. "No." He realized that he hadn't dreamed about Katy for over a year. The sense of responsibility was still there, as well as the need to avenge her, but somewhere along the line he had stopped seeing her blood in his nightmares.

"Then it was about me, wasn't it? I was afraid of that. You're feeling responsible for what could have happened today."

He tensed. Two guesses and she had got it right. In this short span of time she had come to know him better than Katy or Rick or anyone else, including his grandparents.

"I nearly got you killed this afternoon," he said.

"Bull. I nearly got myself killed this afternoon. It had nothing to do with you. As you pointed out earlier, if I had stayed in town and waited until you returned from the mainland, the whole thing would never have happened."

He slowly lowered the towel and looked at her. "You really believe that, don't you?"

"It's the truth." She folded her arms and leaned against the edge of the door. "I won't let you take the responsibility for the mess I got myself into this afternoon."

"You won't let me?"

"Absolutely not." She smiled faintly. "You've already got enough on your plate. No need to add a guilt complex about me."

"You're amazing."

She stood on tiptoe and kissed his cheek. "So are you."

He did not move when she stepped back. "I know I'm an idiot to bring up the subject, but I've been wondering what happens next."

"You mean, your next step in the search for the Hades cup?"

"I'm not talking about that damned piece of glass," he said. "I'm talking about us."

Her eyes were fathomless and infinitely deep. "Oh."

"As I recall," he said very carefully, "back at the beginning of this thing you noted on numerous occasions that we had nothing in common."

"I did say something along those lines, didn't I? I believe you agreed with me at the time and later went on to imply that you thought I was an arrogant, condescending, highbrowed snob."

He held up a hand. "In my own defense I must remind you that I also pointed out that we did share a mutual interest in one particularly interesting subject."

"Sex."

He winced. "When you boil it down to a single word, it sounds a little shallow, doesn't it?"

"Yes, it does. Interesting, but shallow."

He held her eyes. "It occurs to me that maybe we were both wrong. We may have made some rash judgments based on poor initial impressions."

"Quite possible." She smiled. "Where are you going with this?"

Forget it, he thought. He was already out of his depth. These kinds of conversations were not his forte. And this was not the time to talk about the future. There might never be a time to discuss it. In which case, the best advice was to keep his mouth shut.

"I'll tell you where I'm going with it." He tossed the towel aside and moved toward her. "I'm going back to bed. With you."

She put her arms around his neck. "Sounds like a plan."

She was still smiling, but he thought he detected a shadowed disappointment in her eyes. What had she wanted him to say? he wondered. He did not think it would be a good idea to ask. He might not like the answer.

He fastened his mouth on hers, carried her to the bed, and set her down amid the rumpled sheets. The urgent rush of desire hit him with such force that he nearly fell on top of her. He could see the desire in her eyes as she reached up to pull him to her.

She wanted him. It was enough for now.

The scented heat of her body enveloped him.

He pulled aside the neckline of her nightgown and took her breast into his hand. His thumb grazed across her nipple. She cried out and arched up into him. He reached down and flattened his palm against her. She was already wet.

He sucked in his breath when he felt her grasp him.

Her touch was gentle and infinitely exciting. He stroked her until she shivered, and then he eased a finger into her. Her buttocks tensed. Her hips came up off the bed.

He parted the damp, clinging folds, guided himself to her, and drove deep into her tight, hot body.

She raised her knees and clenched her thighs around him. He was aware of the exact moment when the pure, cleansing fire of their shared passion burned away the last fragments of the dream.

Eugenia woke shortly before dawn. For a moment she lay very still, uncertain what had brought her out of a surprisingly sound sleep.

Then she remembered the *Glass* painting she and Cyrus had found. There was something about Nellie's picture of the Hades cup that bothered her.

Cyrus stirred beside her. He shifted one heavy leg over her thigh. "You awake?"

"Yes." She turned her head on the pillow. "I was thinking about the fourth painting. Why would someone leave it in Daventry's hidden safe?"

Cyrus yawned. "It may be the thief's idea of a bizarre joke."

"Do you really think that whoever stole the cup from the safe, assuming someone did take it, left the picture to mock the next person who came along looking for it?"

"It's not beyond the realm of probabilities. The Hades cup has traditionally attracted some very weird characters. But there are other possibilities."

"Such as?"

He regarded her with a thoughtful expression. "It's interesting that Daventry took the risk of showing the Hades cup to Nellie. He must have trusted her."

She shrugged. "I think he trusted his own ability to

lure and hold young, pretty artists. He probably felt in control of Nellie. He was a very arrogant man, Cyrus."

He nodded. "Any way you slice it, the next step is to focus on the members of the Connoisseurs' Club. Since the cup is gone, they are now the most likely suspects."

"You never give up, do you?"

He smiled fleetingly. "One of my Grandpappy Beau's favorite stories was the one about the tortoise and the hare. Slow and plodding wins in the end."

"Know what I think?"

"What?"

She propped herself on her elbow. "I think you like to give people the impression that you're the slow, plodding type because it suits your purposes. Puts folks off guard. Makes them underestimate you."

He considered that and then shook his head. "Nope, I think it's the real me."

"Don't give me that. You're the guy who rides in out of the desert on a big horse and proceeds to clean out the bad guys."

He did not smile. "Don't make me out to be some kind of hero, Eugenia."

"But that's just what you are." She leaned over to brush her mouth against his. "And to think that I had almost given up trying to find one."

A long time later he felt her stir against him. "Cyrus?"

"Yeah?" He curled his fingers in her tangled hair.

He was still grappling with what she had said earlier. He'd been called a lot of things in his time, including dependable, reliable, and steady. But no one had ever called him a hero.

"I want to take another look at that picture we found in the safe," Eugenia said. "Last night in all the excitement, I concentrated on the cup, itself. But there's something about the background. Something familiar."

"Familiar?"

"It's the colors. I don't want to say anything more until I've had another chance to look at it."

Forty-five minutes later Cyrus carried the painting into the kitchen, where Eugenia was hard at work on the espresso machine. She turned her head to study the picture of the Hades cup.

The morning light revealed nuances of color and craftsmanship that, in her disbelief and excitement last night, she had failed to note. Nellie really had been a very talented artist, she thought.

"The cup was done with the same technique that Nellie used when she painted the other three pieces of glass," she said after a minute.

Turning, she leaned back against the counter. She allowed her eyes and her other senses to move over the picture, looking for the things that made it different from the other three in the *Glass* series.

"Well?" Cyrus waited expectantly.

"The background was done in a hurry and not with the same painterly technique as the cup, itself. You'll notice that Nellie didn't use the glass vault as a setting this time."

Cyrus eyed the picture. "It's different," he agreed.

Eugenia stepped closer to the painting. She reached out to touch the thick swatches of acrylic paint. "I think she painted over the original background. And she did it in a hurry."

"The paint does look a little heavier in some places than others."

"Not her usual painterly approach," Eugenia said. "In the background she's used the acrylics as if they were watercolors. Quick, fast, sweeping strokes. Minimal impressions. She didn't play with the light, the way she did in the others in the series."

"Go on." Cyrus glanced at her. "You said something about the colors."

She smiled slightly. "Your eyes don't appear to be glazing over the way they usually do when I talk about art."

"You have my full and undivided attention this time."

Eugenia's brief amusement vanished. "I can see that."

She turned back to the picture. She warned herself not to jump to conclusions. Intuition was all well and good as far as it went, but with things this serious, she needed to stick with facts. She had to use logic.

She drank in the colors and the abstract shapes that surrounded the Hades cup. A disorienting lightheadedness swept through her.

Impossible.

"There's an impression of fire around the cup," she whispered hesitantly.

Cyrus looked dubious. "Maybe. Lot of red and orange. What about it?"

"It makes sense. Glass is born in fire. It would be a logical background. But the other colors, the ones Nellie used on the perimeter of the picture . . ." She trailed off, still shocked by her own conclusions.

Cyrus scowled at the picture. "Lots of green and yellow."

"Not yellow. Amber." Eugenia gripped the edge of the counter behind her. Memories of Nellie's last visit flashed through her mind.

The unfinished wall next to her fireplace stuffed with thick, fluffy pink insulation. The stacks of hand-painted glass tiles waiting to be grouted into place around the hearth.

"*I can't wait to see how it looks when it's finished, Eugenia. It's going to be spectacular.*"

Eugenia swallowed twice before she found her voice.

"I recently finished redecorating my condo, Cyrus. Those are the exact shades of green and amber that Nellie used to paint the glass tiles that surround my gas fireplace."

"So?"

"I told you that the last time I saw her was the day she died. She stopped by my place to tell me that she was going back to Frog Cove Island to get her things. My living room wall was still open near the fireplace. There had been a mistake with the wiring."

"What are you saying?"

She took a deep breath. "I know this sounds crazy, but it would have been easy for her to stuff an object the size of the Hades cup through the opening in the wall and conceal it behind the wallboard.

Cyrus looked stunned. "Are you serious?"

"The insulation would have concealed it and cushioned it while the contractor finished covering and painting the wall." She raised her eyes to meet Cyrus's gaze. "I never understood why Nellie traveled all the way from Frog Cove Island for that short visit and then went all the way back to pack her things. It made no sense."

He watched her. "Are you telling me that you think she hid the cup in your *wall?*"

"Yes." Eugenia met his eyes. "And she repainted the background of this picture to tell me where to look for it."

"Why stick it in Daventry's hidden safe, where you might never have found it?"

Eugenia shook her head slowly. "She must have assumed I would find it."

"Why would she leave a clue for you?" Cyrus tossed his hastily packed duffel bag into the back of the Jeep.

The overriding urgency that gripped him had sprung, fully grown, from the revelation that the Hades cup might be in Eugenia's house. He could feel more of the jagged pieces of the puzzle slamming into place. They were sharper than broken glass and they could cut more deeply.

Eugenia stuffed her red leather suitcases into the trunk of her Toyota. "I don't know."

"Hell, you didn't even believe that the Hades cup existed. Why didn't she tell you about it? She must have known you'd be interested in something like that."

"You're the one who keeps saying that the cup is dangerous." Eugenia dropped the garment bag that matched the suitcases into the trunk. "Maybe she figured that the less I knew, the safer I would be."

"Bullshit." Cyrus walked to the Toyota and closed the trunk lid. "It wasn't your safety she had in mind. If she wanted to protect you, she would never have hidden the cup in your house. With friends like that, trust me, you don't need enemies."

"She was very tense that day."

"She had just witnessed a murder and stolen a piece of glass that could get her killed. She had a damned good reason to be nervous." He took Eugenia's arm and steered her to the driver's side of her car.

"She went back to the island that afternoon, though," Eugenia reminded him as she got behind the wheel. "Why would she do that if she had just stolen the cup? She should have been concentrating on getting herself as far away as possible from the scene of the crime."

"I can think of one real good reason," Cyrus said. He shut the Toyota door. "To fake her own death at sea."

Shock washed through Eugenia. "Oh, my God. Do you really think . . . ?"

Cyrus looked at her through the car window. "She was a woman with two very big problems. Like I said, not only was she a witness to a murder, but she had stolen an object that could get her killed. She needed to disappear."

"But she would have contacted me, Cyrus."

"I'm sure she will contact you. When the heat dies down and she's ready to retrieve the cup." He straightened. "See you at the ferry dock. Drive very, very carefully."

Eugenia got out of the car and went to stand at the ferry rail. The brisk breeze off the water snapped at her black windbreaker and whipped her hair into a froth. Behind her, Frog Cove Island receded swiftly into the distance.

She sensed rather than heard Cyrus come up behind her. He did not touch her. He rested his forearms on the rail, linked his fingers, and looked out over the gray-green waters. He had put his battered leather jacket on over a fuchsia and green aloha shirt that was covered with a mass of hibiscus flowers. The crisp breeze ruffled his dark hair, revealing the flecks of gray at the temples.

He looked as centered and relaxed as always, but she could feel the hunter's readiness in him. It hummed just beneath the surface. She stared at his powerful hands. Memories of those strong, incredibly sensitive fingers on her body brought a rush of heat deep inside her.

She wondered what would happen if they found the Hades cup. For the first time it seemed a real possibility. Would Cyrus disappear from her life once he had it in his hands?

The thought brought a wave of melancholy. She struggled valiantly to squash it.

"Regardless of whether or not we find the cup, I want you to know that Colfax Security will look for Nellie Grant," Cyrus said.

His words jarred her out of the depression that was gathering around her. "Do you really think that Nellie is alive?"

"Put it this way, I think there's a very good possibility that you were right when you said you didn't think she had drowned in a boating accident."

"But I assumed she had been murdered. I never had any reason to believe that she might have faked her own death."

"One way or another, we'll find out what happened."

Eugenia believed him. "What about Jacob Houston and Rhonda Price?"

"I think they'll be safe once we put out the word that all four of the Nellie Grant paintings have been located. Whoever searched their cabins must have been looking for the pictures."

Eugenia gripped the rail very tightly. "If you're right, that means that someone knows that one of the paintings holds a clue about the location of the Hades cup."

There was a long silence from Cyrus. For a moment she thought he hadn't heard her. When he did respond, she knew that he had already arrived at the same conclusion.

"Yeah," he said finally, "I think we can assume that someone knows about the importance of the fourth *Glass* painting."

"Who?"

Again he took much too long to answer. "Could be one of the members of the Connoisseurs' Club."

She could tell that he did not really believe that. "Or?"

"Damien March."

Eugenia was suddenly aware of the chill in the wind. She hugged herself very tightly.

After a moment Cyrus put his arm around her shoulders and pulled her against his side.

They stood together at the railing until the ferry drew close to the docks.

Cyrus stopped just inside the front door of the condominium, dropped his duffel bag and two of Eugenia's suitcases on the floor, and gazed around with deep curiosity.

He thought he'd grown accustomed to the veneer of sleek sophistication that Eugenia wore so easily. Once he'd discovered the intelligence, the earthy passion, and the strength beneath the surface, he'd ignored the fancy trappings. But the glossy decor of her home was a glaring reminder that she inhabited a very different world than the one in which he moved.

"Damn. It's definitely you," he said.

Eugenia grimaced. "That doesn't sound like a compliment." She opened the hall closet and hung the garment bag inside.

He walked through the hall to stand in the arched opening that framed the living room. He studied the expanse of white carpet. "Should I take off my shoes?"

"Please." She stepped out of her loafers and kicked

them into the coat closet. Then she slipped her feet into a pair of soft, black ballet-style slippers. "You can put your things in here."

He felt the weight of the gun he wore beneath the jacket. "I think I'll hang on to my jacket, if you don't mind. It's a little cold in here."

She glanced at him in surprise. "I didn't notice. I'll be glad to turn on the heat."

"Don't bother." He stepped out of his moccasins and used his big toe to push them into the closet. "I'll be fine."

She hesitated, as if not quite certain what to do with him now that he was right there on her turf.

He smiled slightly. "Guess I clash with your decor, huh?"

"Don't be ridiculous." She glanced toward the arched opening. "Well, I suppose you want to look at the fireplace."

"Yeah."

"It's in the living room." She went past him into the white-carpeted room beyond the hall.

He followed slowly, glancing at the various pieces of studio glass on display. "Your own private collection?"

"Yes."

He nodded. The white-on-white condo with its elegantly restrained touches of color and its refined lines were infused with a stark purity that worried him.

"You know something, Eugenia? You live in an art gallery."

She gave him a strange smile. "Funny you should say that. I was just thinking the same thing. I never noticed the similarity until today."

He looked at the left wall and saw the fireplace. "I see what you mean about the colors in the tiles. They are the same as the ones in the painting of the cup."

"I told you so. The picture over the fireplace is the one Nellie gave me the last time I saw her."

He glanced at it and then walked across the room to examine the hand-painted tiles that surrounded the gas fireplace. "Which part of the wall was open the day Nellie was here?"

"The lower section just to the right of the fireplace."

He shoved his hands into the back pocket of his chinos. "Might as well get to it. Got a hammer and a large knife?"

She groaned. "I have a feeling that this is going to hurt me more than it does you."

"Colfax Security will pay all the repair costs."

Her brows rose. "I take it you haven't done any redecorating lately. The repair costs are the least of it. The real problem is getting a contractor out for such a small job."

"You're right. I haven't done any redecorating recently." No point in it, he thought. A man who lived alone and ate a lot of tuna fish didn't waste a lot of time and energy on fancy interior design work.

Ten minutes later, armed with a hammer and a utility knife, Cyrus got a fix on the location of the studs behind the wallboard. When he thought he had them pinpointed, he crouched and went to work on the lower section of the wall.

Eugenia flinched at the first blow.

"You're not going to cry, are you?" he asked as he aimed the utility knife.

"If you only knew how much time and money I put into that wall."

"Relax." He angled the knife for another cut.

A few minutes later he pulled the first square of

wallboard free and set it down. Fluffy pink insulation billowed forth.

Cyrus reached inside the wall and probed carefully.

A knock on the door made Eugenia turn. "Who in the world? It must be the manager. Probably saw my car in the garage and wants to know why I'm back from my vacation so soon. I'll be right back."

"Keep her out of this room. I'd just as soon not have to explain the hole in your wall . . ." He trailed off as his questing fingers touched an object enfolded in what felt like protective bubble wrap.

He heard the door open. A woman's voice rose on a soft wail.

"Eugenia, oh, God, I'm so sorry . . ."

"Nellie. You're alive. I don't believe—" Eugenia's voice broke off with alarming abruptness. "Oh."

"Well, shit," Cyrus said very softly to himself.

Then he heard another voice, cultured, plumy, laced with condescending humor. He had not heard that particular voice in three years, but he had not forgotten it. He would never forget it as long as he lived.

"Good evening, Ms. Swift. Kindly close the door and lock it, or I will blow your brains and those of Ms. Grant all over your very nice white walls."

Twenty-two

"No, please, Colfax, don't bother to get up." Herding Eugenia and a pale woman with flame-red hair ahead of him, Damien March came to stand in the arched opening that divided the living room from the hall. His patrician features registered icy amusement at the sight of Cyrus half-sprawled on the floor. "I insist. I much prefer you where you are."

Cyrus abandoned a belated effort to scramble to his feet. He slumped back into a reclining position against the gaping wall and looked at Eugenia. She stood, frozen, beside the redhead. Her face was rigidly composed, but he could see the shock in her eyes.

He turned back to Damien and smiled humorlessly at the other man's elegant white linen sport coat, perfectly tailored blue trousers, and handmade Italian leather shoes. In addition to a gun, which he held in his right hand, he carried a pricey-looking leather briefcase.

"Still got that GQ look, I see. Been a long time, March."

"Unfortunately, not long enough. I would have preferred that we never met again. Speaking of clothing, however, I must ask you to remove your jacket." Damien shifted the gun closer to the nape of Eugenia's neck. "I feel obligated to point out that it was a fashion mistake."

"You would know." Cyrus watched Eugenia's eyes narrow faintly as he tugged off the leather jacket and tossed it aside.

Damien tut-tutted at the sight of the hibiscus-and-palm-covered shirt. "I see you still favor the casual look. And no gun. Really, Colfax, you're remarkably underdressed for the occasion."

"Eugenia doesn't like guns."

Damien chuckled. "How convenient."

Eugenia clenched her hand into a small, angry fist. "I'm rethinking my stand on the issue."

"Don't blame yourself, Ms. Swift. Even if Colfax had been armed, it wouldn't have done him any good. He would have had to shoot through you to hit me. I know him very well, and I can assure you that he lacks the guts to do anything so outrageous as to kill an innocent woman."

"Unlike you?" she retorted.

"I admit I do not trouble myself with archaic and outmoded concepts of honor that tend to stand in the way of my own success and survival. I am a realist, Ms. Swift. We realists take a more pragmatic view of the world."

"You're a vicious, cowardly thug, not a realist," she shot back. "There is a difference."

"If you believe that, my dear, then you very likely still believe in fairy tales."

"Oh, I do. Otherwise how could one explain the existence of monsters such as yourself?"

Cyrus stirred slightly. "I don't think this is a real good time to argue with him, honey."

"He's right, Ms. Swift. This is not the best moment for a discussion of the very fine line between good and evil." Damien watched Cyrus with amused but watchful eyes. "As I said, I would prefer never to have seen you again, Colfax, but given the situation, there was no choice."

"It was inevitable," Cyrus said. "I was pretty sure you wouldn't have the common decency to be dead."

"And you would never have stopped looking for me."

"Nope."

Damien gave a small, resigned sigh. "I knew I would have to do something about you eventually. You and your bloody, plodding, single-mindedness. You would have found me, sooner or later."

"Yeah."

"Well, I suppose I can't complain, can I? Your talents always were limited by your charmingly quaint notions of duty and responsibility. But I must admit that what you do, you do with unwavering determination."

"Gosh, thanks."

"I don't believe you've met Ms. Grant." Damien inclined his chin in the redhead's direction. "Allow me to introduce you. Nellie, my dear little thieving bitch, this is Cyrus Chandler Colfax."

Cyrus studied the dull defeat in Nellie's aqua eyes. She looked exhausted and scared.

"Thought you were lost at sea," he said.

"Ms. Grant tried to fake her own death." Damien chuckled again. "But she wasn't quite clever enough to pull it off, were you, my dear? My people found her a couple of days ago in a rather tacky hotel room in Las Vegas."

"How did you find her?" Eugenia asked.

"It wasn't difficult." Damien smiled. "She was preparing to auction off the Hades cup, you see. She was rather careless in her choice of contacts. One of them worked for an acquaintance of mine. He came directly to me."

"I don't understand." Eugenia glanced quickly at Nellie. "What is this about an auction?"

Nellie's eyes brimmed with tears. "I was a fool."

"Yes, you were, my dear," Damien said. "But you proved useful in the end, so don't be too hard on yourself."

"What, exactly, is going on here?" Eugenia demanded.

Damien smiled. "It's a long and somewhat complicated tale, Ms. Swift. You see, I knew that Colfax was on the trail of the Hades cup. I made certain that he heard the rumors of its theft and resale on the underground market. I knew he would pay close attention."

Cyrus groaned. "You made sure I learned of the rumors because you wanted me to find the cup for you, didn't you?"

"In a sense, I've been your client for some time now." Damien looked more amused than ever. "As the victim of a rather unusual, rather private theft, I could hardly go to the police. I wanted someone on the case who would have a strong, highly motivated reason to find my missing cup."

"Me."

Damien gave him a smile that dripped with condescending approval. "Yes, you, Colfax. I knew that once you heard the cup had surfaced you would be hot on the trail in hopes that it would lead you back to me."

"Damn. I was afraid of that."

It had always been a possibility, Cyrus thought. Nevertheless, it was irritating to learn that he had been used. Still, it was not as though he'd had a lot of options. One way or another, events had come together to lead him to Damien, just as he had sensed that they would. Unfortunately, the meeting was taking place under less than ideal circumstances.

"I'm happy to say that you performed the task with your customary unflagging perseverance," Damien continued. "You managed to discover that Adam Daventry had bought my cup. But by the time you realized he was the new owner, he was dead, wasn't he?"

"Yeah," Cyrus said. "Sucker got shoved down a flight of stairs before I could get to him." Out of the corner of his eye he saw Nellie flinch.

Damien gave him a pitying look. "I had followed your progress at a discreet distance. I admit I was curious about your alliance with Ms. Swift. I know she's an expert on glass, but you didn't require her expertise to locate the cup or to identify it. When I learned that Daventry had left his glass collection to the Leabrook, however, things fell into place."

"What do you mean?" Eugenia asked.

"As the representative of the Leabrook, you were given unrestricted access to Glass House. Which was exactly what Colfax needed. All he had to do was find a way to attach himself to you and he was inside." Damien paused with what was no doubt meant to be a droll, lascivious wink. "So to speak."

Eugenia stared fixedly at Cyrus. "I see."

"What confused the issue for me, Ms. Swift," Damien continued, "was your peculiar interest in Ms. Grant. I did not understand, at first, why you purchased her painting in that pathetic little island gallery."

Eugenia frowned. "Why did that surprise you?"

Cyrus glanced at her. "Don't you get it? He figured the real reason you took advantage of the chance to stay in Glass House was because you had also heard the rumors about the Hades cup."

"What?" Eugenia stared at Damien. "But that wasn't true. I didn't even believe the cup existed until very recently. I went to the island to find out what had happened to Nellie."

Nellie's head came up. "You went to look for me?"

"I thought you were dead," Eugenia said gently. "But I didn't buy the accident story. I believed you'd been murdered."

"And you wanted to find out who had done it. Oh, Eugenia. I never realized—" Nellie broke off on a sob.

"I beg your pardon, Ms. Swift." Damien gave Eugenia a charming smile. "I naturally assumed that it was the cup you were after. I admit it never occurred to me that you might want to investigate Ms. Grant's supposed death. After all, she was just a foolish little artist who happened to have worked for you. Why would you care what became of her?"

"I doubt if you would understand," Eugenia said.

Nellie's flame-colored hair tumbled forward as she bowed her head. "I'm so sorry, Eugenia."

"Don't cry, Nellie." Eugenia reached out to touch her.

March tightened his fingers on the gun. "Don't move, Ms. Swift."

Eugenia stilled, the hand she had been about to put on Nellie's shoulder frozen in midair. "You're a very loathsome creature, aren't you, March?"

"It depends on your point of view," Damien said.

Cyrus saw the mutinous expression in Eugenia's eyes. "Eugenia. No."

He did not inhale until she reluctantly lowered her hand.

"Best listen to him, my dear," Damien said softly. "He knows me very well."

"He's going to kill us," Nellie whispered in a broken voice.

"Now, now, now, Ms. Grant," Damien scolded. "No need to be so pessimistic. I told you that as long as everyone cooperates, there's no reason we can't all arrange to walk away from this and never see each other again. Live and let live is my motto."

"Except when someone becomes a liability the way Katy did," Cyrus said.

"Ah, yes. Little Katy." Damien shook his head with mock regret. "She was a problem. She had not only helped me arrange the theft of the Hades cup three years ago, she also knew about my plans to disappear. I had no intention of taking her with me into my new life, of course. She wasn't really my type."

"You used her," Cyrus said very softly.

"You know, I've always wondered why you felt the need to avenge the silly little slut. She betrayed you without a moment's hesitation."

"You seduced her, you son-of-a-bitch."

"It didn't take much effort, I assure you. Do you know, she told me once that she married you because you made her feel safe and secure. But then she discovered that safety and security can become extremely boring after a while."

Cyrus felt the familiar anger, but it was as old and cold as the affection he had once had for Katy. She was gone, and so was most of what he had felt for her. Only the task of avenging her remained.

"So you offered her excitement, is that it?" Cyrus asked.

"Which she mistook for true love and enduring passion." Damien's fine mouth twisted with scorn. "She began to cling. When she discovered that I planned to vanish with the cup, she became hysterical."

"You killed her," Cyrus said. "Shot her down in cold blood. Made it look as if she'd been the victim of a carjacking."

"I had no choice. She would have gone straight to you, Colfax, the way she always did when things went wrong."

"She knew too much," Cyrus said.

"She did, indeed." Damien smiled his alligator smile at Nellie. "Just as Ms. Grant does."

Nellie raised her head. She focused on Eugenia. "I tried to stall him. I did my best."

"You told him about your *Glass* series, didn't you?" Eugenia said.

Nellie shut her eyes. "I had no choice. When his goons found me, I had to tell them something. They promised to do terrible things to me if I didn't talk."

"Hush," Eugenia said. "It's all right. I understand."

"Ms. Grant concocted quite a story," Damien said. "She told me that Daventry instructed her to paint certain clues into the portrait of the Hades cup. Clues that she, herself, did not comprehend, but that an expert in glass would understand."

Cyrus frowned. "Clues?"

Nellie's lips trembled. "It was all I could think of on the spur of the moment. I told him that Daventry had never told me where he hid the cup, but that he had wanted to leave a record of its location in case something ever happened to him."

Damien smiled ruefully. "It was a rather clever story. I believed her because I knew that Daventry was very anxious to leave a lasting monument to himself. It made sense to me that he would want his greatest treasure, the Hades cup, to be associated with the

Daventry collection after his death. To do that, of course, he had to leave a record of its location."

"But an obvious record would have been dangerous." Cyrus looked at Nellie. "Your little story wasn't entirely a lie, was it? The only difference was that you were the one who left the clues in the painting, not Daventry."

Nellie nodded forlornly.

Cyrus turned back to Damien. "So you went looking for the four paintings."

Damien nodded. "Unfortunately, by the time my people got to the island, one of the *Glass* pictures had appeared in a gallery and had been sold. I realized that someone had already taken the paintings from Glass House and intended to sell them for cash."

"Rhonda Price?" Cyrus suggested.

"Yes." Damien's eyes hardened. "But by the time my people figured out what had happened, she was gone. They went to her boyfriend's house and found nothing. Unfortunately, they ran into you, Colfax."

Eugenia looked at Nellie. "Why did you take the Hades cup in the first place?"

"It was stupid, I know, but I couldn't resist." Nellie closed her eyes for a few seconds. "I saw Fenella Weeks push Daventry down the stairs. That night, after Deputy Peaceful and the others left, I realized that, with Daventry dead, I was the only person on the face of the earth who knew that the Hades cup was in the hidden safe in the wine cellar. I also knew where Daventry kept the combination."

"What about Fenella Weeks? Weren't you a little worried about her?" Cyrus asked. "She knew you were a witness to the murder."

"Fenella was crazy." Nellie's shoulders moved in a listless shrug. "I could have dealt with her. She wasn't the reason I faked the boat accident. I was more concerned about the cup. I knew it was dangerous."

"And since you were an obvious person of interest for anyone who came looking for the missing cup, you decided to disappear," Cyrus said.

Damien's brows rose. "Ms. Grant's biggest mistake was in believing that she could be a player in the big leagues of the private art market."

"A little goldfish in a sea full of sharks, as my Grandpappy Beau would say," Cyrus muttered.

"Precisely." Damien smiled broadly. "And I was the first shark on the scene."

Eugenia frowned at Nellie. "That night after Daventry died, you repainted the background of the Hades cup portrait. You brought the cup here to Seattle and hid it. Then you faked your own death on the way back to Frog Cove Island. But why did you leave the painting in the safe?"

Nellie caught her trembling lower lip between her front teeth. For a moment Cyrus thought she would fall apart right there on the carpet. Instead, she appeared to rally slightly.

"I knew that what I planned to do was very dangerous," she said. "If . . . if something happened to me, I wanted you to have the cup for the Leabrook, Eugenia."

"You expected me to find it?"

"You were my friend. You gave me that job when I needed it. You encouraged my art. You tried to warn me about Daventry."

"But how on earth was I supposed to find the hidden safe?" Eugenia demanded.

"It was only a matter of time," Nellie said. "The information about the hidden safe is in Daventry's will. But I figured that it would take months, maybe a year or two, before the lawyers actually got around to finalizing the details of such a huge estate. If, for some reason, I didn't make it back to Glass House to get the picture out of the safe, someone would open it and find *Glass IV*. When you saw it, you'd know it was my work and you'd figure out the clues."

"Why not leave the Hades cup, itself, in the safe?" Cyrus asked.

Nellie's red brows drew together. "Because I was afraid that one of the members of the Connoisseurs' Club or maybe Fenella Weeks would find it. They all knew that Daventry owned the cup, and they must have figured it would be hidden somewhere in Glass House. I had to get it out of there before one of them went looking for it."

Eugenia eyed her thoughtfully. "What if one of them had found the painting?"

"The clues would have meant nothing to them," Nellie explained. "They would have recognized the cup, but that was all."

"But you knew that I would recognize not only the Hades cup, but my own fireplace wall."

"I knew you would start asking questions." Nellie's eyes drifted to the open wall next to Cyrus. "You would remember the last time I came to see you, and you would wonder what I had tried to tell you in the painting. You always had incredible intuition. You would have put it all together eventually."

Cyrus settled his shoulders more comfortably against the wall and laced his fingers across his stomach. "What you didn't expect was that she would start asking questions about your death shortly after you disappeared."

Nellie's expression held painful bewilderment. "No. No, I didn't expect that."

"It never occurred to you that she blamed herself for having introduced you to Adam Daventry in the first place," Cyrus continued coldly. "It never struck you that she was afraid you had been murdered because you had seen or heard something in Glass House that put you in danger."

More tears coursed down Nellie's face. "I knew Eugenia was kind, but how could I have guessed that she would care enough to find out what had really happened to me? No one's ever given a damn about me."

"I hate to interrupt such a touching scene," Damien said. "But this is all becoming somewhat maudlin."

He sounded dangerously bored, Cyrus thought. As usual, Damien got restless when he was not the center of attention. "What happens now?"

Damien's gaze narrowed with anticipation. "You will finish your little home improvement project, Colfax. Get the cup."

Cyrus hesitated.

"Now."

Cyrus shrugged and reached into the thick, springy insulation. He probed until his fingers touched the object covered in bubble wrap. He paused.

"Well?" There was a thread of urgency in Damien's voice now. "Is it there?"

"Something's in here." Cyrus put his other hand into the wall and eased the bubble-wrapped object out of its nesting place.

"Don't give it to him," Nellie wailed. "He'll kill us all once he has it."

"Shut up," Damien ordered. "Hurry, Colfax. I don't want to waste any more time retrieving my property."

"It's not your property," Eugenia said forcefully. "I hate to sound like Indiana Jones, but the Hades cup belongs in a museum. Specifically, the Leabrook."

"It belongs to me," Damien said with gritted teeth. "Give it to me, Colfax."

"Take it easy, March. It's heavy, remember?"

He had forgotten just how heavy it was, Cyrus realized. Beneath the thick plastic covering, he could see the muted glow of blood-red glass.

"Be careful," Eugenia said with unexpected urgency.

A fine time for her professional passions to surface, Cyrus thought. What was it with these arty types? Eugenia seemed to have temporarily forgotten that she was standing at the wrong end of a gun held by a man who would have no qualms about pulling the trigger.

Cyrus twisted slightly to draw the plastic-wrapped cup through the hole in the wall. "Forget about the damned cup, Eugenia. In case it has escaped your notice, we've got a few more pressing problems . . . Oops."

The thickly wrapped cup slipped from his hands and rolled slowly, ponderously across the carpet. For an instant the other three seemed paralyzed. Under other circumstances Cyrus would have found their expressions of incredulous horror amusing.

"You dropped it!" Eugenia gave a half-stifled shriek. She took what was obviously an instinctive step toward the cup, hands outstretched.

Nellie gasped.

"*You clumsy fool,*" Damien shouted. "That cup is nearly two thousand years old." He shoved Eugenia out of the way and swung the barrel of the gun toward Cyrus. But his attention was distracted by the tumbling bubble-wrapped package on the carpet.

Cyrus already had one hand back inside the fluffy pink insulation. He wrapped his fingers around the grip of the gun he had stashed there when he'd realized who was at the door.

He aimed as best he could in that awkward position and pulled the trigger.

The bullet tore through the layers of insulation and smashed into the upper right side of Damien's chest.

Nellie screamed.

Damien squeezed off a single shot as the impact spun him back against the wall.

He dropped the gun and the leather briefcase and slid to the floor.

An eerie silence fell. It would not last long, Cyrus thought. The neighbors were probably already frantically dialing 911. He got to his feet and walked to Eugenia.

"You okay?" He did not take his eyes off Damien.

"Yes." Her voice was barely audible. She tried again. This time the words came clearly. "Yes, I'm fine. Thanks to you. Oh, my God, Cyrus, are you all right?"

"Yeah."

"You're bleeding."

Cyrus became aware of the cold fire in his left arm. He looked down. "It's okay. He just nicked me."

Eugenia whipped off her scarf. "Nellie, call 911."

Nellie stared, open-mouthed, at Damien. "Is he dead?"

"Call 911 right now, Nellie." Eugenia wound the scarf around Cyrus's upper arm.

"Ouch," he said.

"Sorry." Eugenia tied the scarf. "You should lie down. Shock, you know."

"I'm not going into shock. It's only a flesh wound."

From out of nowhere, tears sparkled in her eyes "Cyrus, you could have been killed."

Her frantic concern did more to dampen the pain in his arm than anything the medics would have with them, but he did not think this was the time or place to tell her.

He walked across the white carpet and came to a halt a short distance from the fallen man.

Damien stirred slightly. He opened shock-dulled eyes and stared up at Cyrus with chilling hatred. "So you won our little game after all."

"It's the old story of the tortoise and the hare, as my Grandpappy Beau would say." Cyrus pulled out his handkerchief and reached down to scoop up Damien's gun. "You're the hare. I'm the tortoise. I just keep slogging forward until I get where I'm going."

"You and those goddamned sayings of your grandfather's." Damien coughed weakly. "Did he ever tell you the one about old sins casting long shadows?"

A fresh chill settled in Cyrus's stomach. He crouched beside Damien. "Yeah, he did."

Damien's eyes closed slowly. "It's true, you know. You could have made a fortune. Better yet, you could have had real power. You could have taken it all, you stupid son-of-a-bitch."

"So you went for it, instead?" Cyrus asked.

"Yes. But I made one mistake. Thought I could control the shadow. . . ."

Damien's head fell to the side. He did not move again.

Cyrus rose and scooped up the leather briefcase. It was just the right size for a laptop computer. When he unlatched it, he saw the glint of a black metal case.

He reached into his jacket and pulled out the phone. Quint Yates answered on the first ring.

"I need you here in Seattle, Quint. Take the next plane out of Portland."

"I'm on my way."

Eugenia put her hand on Cyrus's shoulder. He closed the phone and touched her fingers.

He looked at the blood that stained Damien's elegant white linen sportcoat. It was the color of the Hades cup in reflected light.

Twenty-three

Cyrus was brooding.

Eugenia was worried. He was back into his self-contained mode. The grim aura that enveloped him had grown steadily darker after the emergency room staff and the police had finished with them. But it was not until he had returned from a two-hour meeting with Quint Yates that his mood had become truly bleak.

She wondered if she ought to phone the emergency room and ask about delayed shock syndrome. Cyrus did not appear to be in shock, but given his controlled demeanor, it was impossible to tell what was going on below the surface.

The future of the Hades cup had not yet been resolved. At the moment, it was housed in the Leabrook. Possession might be nine-tenths of the law, but whoever had written those words of wisdom had not taken into account someone of Cyrus's unrelenting tenacity.

Unable to face her blood-stained floor and the hole in her wall, Eugenia had checked herself and Cyrus into a downtown hotel. She had taken charge because Cyrus appeared oblivious to the problem of where they spent the night.

He did not show any interest in what was going on around him until she picked up the phone to order dinner from room service.

At that point he had emerged from wherever he had been inside his head.

"Forget room service," he said. "The food is always cold."

Pleased to see some response, she had not argued. "All right. We'll go out."

They had walked a few blocks to one of the eateries in the nearby Belltown neighborhood. It was a balmy evening, and many of the cafés on First Avenue had put tables out on the sidewalk. Trendy people dressed in a lot of black, pale neutrals and denim ate tapenade on crusty bread and drank chilled chardonnay and locally brewed beers.

Eugenia chose one of her favorite cafés. The hostess recognized her and found a table at the rear of the crowded restaurant.

After a few minutes, Eugenia gave up trying to concentrate on the menu. She put it down with a snap and leaned forward slightly. "Are you sure you shouldn't be in bed?"

"What?" Cyrus did not look up from his own menu.

Eugenia leaned closer and pitched her voice a bit louder to overcome the background hubbub. "I said, maybe you should be in bed."

He finally raised his eyes to meet hers. She thought she saw a flicker of humor. It didn't last long, but she was vastly relieved to see even a glimmer of something besides the enigmatic remoteness that had been there all afternoon.

"I love it when you get swept away by your obsession with my body," he said. "Don't worry, I promise we'll get to bed eventually. But first I need food."

"I'm not talking about sex, and you know it." She flushed, horrified by the way her voice had risen. She glanced around quickly, afraid that someone at one of the other tables might have overheard. But no heads turned.

Cyrus definitely looked amused now. "Are you sure?"

"For heaven's sake, you were wounded only a few hours ago." She frowned at his left arm. The sleeve of a fresh aloha shirt, this one covered with pink flamingos, covered a neat white bandage. "You shouldn't be exerting yourself."

"I don't think eating will put an undue strain on my arm." He paused as the waiter arrived at the table. "What are you going to have?"

She glanced impatiently at the menu. "The grilled ahi, please. Medium rare. Wasabi on the side."

"Make it the same for me, I'm in the mood for tuna fish." Cyrus handed his menu to the waiter. For the first time he appeared to notice the glass of wine in front of Eugenia. "And a beer."

Eugenia drummed her fingers on the table while the waiter dutifully wrote down Cyrus's selection.

"What's wrong?" Cyrus asked when they were alone again.

"Do you think you should mix alcohol with those pain pills the doctor gave you?"

"Probably not. But since I haven't taken any of the pills, it's a moot point."

"You didn't take the pills?" Eugenia was aghast. "But doesn't your arm hurt?"

"Nothing a bottle of beer won't fix."

She sank back in her chair. "I give up."

"Good. Let's change the subject."

She braced herself. "I suppose you want to talk about the Hades cup."

He shrugged. "I'll get to that later. It's safe enough at the Leabrook for now."

His indifference to the cup did nothing to alleviate her anxiety. Instead, it threw fuel on the fires of her growing unease. Something was very wrong. "Out with it before I go crazy."

"Out with what?"

"Whatever it is that's bothering you." She reached across the table to touch his hand. "Look, a certain degree of anxiety and depression is quite normal after what you've been through today."

His eyes widened slightly in surprise. "I'm not depressed. I'm thinking."

"From where I'm sitting, it's hard to tell the difference." She hesitated. "You're dwelling on the past, aren't you?"

The waiter returned to the table with the beer at that moment. He started to pour it into a glass. Cyrus waved him off.

When the waiter disappeared again, Cyrus picked up the bottle and took a long swallow. "Speaking of the past, you were right about Katy."

"I was?"

"She did betray me. I guess I just never wanted to look at it that way because it meant facing the fact that she hadn't loved me enough to resist Damien March."

"Cyrus, I'm so sorry."

"She needed me in some ways." He studied the label on the beer bottle. "But need isn't the same thing as love, is it?"

Jayne Ann Krentz

Eugenia hesitated. "I think there's some degree of need wrapped up in love. There are a lot of things mixed in with love. I have a hunch that the right combination of elements varies from one person to another. That's probably why it's impossible to define."

He nodded. "Sort of like art."

"Yes." She smiled wryly. "You can't describe it, but you know it when you see it."

"The problem is, until you do see it, you don't really know what it looks like, do you?" His eyes were very green. "So you make mistakes."

"Yes."

"I made a mistake with Katy."

"It's over, Cyrus. You've avenged her. Let the past go."

He rolled the bottle between his hands. "There's something you should know."

Eugenia held her breath. "What's that?"

"I let Katy go a long time ago. But that didn't mean I could forget about Damien March. Two different things, even though they were linked. Does that make sense?"

"Yes. Old emotions are one thing. Justice is another matter altogether. Just because the first had faded didn't mean you could ignore the second."

He drank from the beer bottle and then set it down with great precision. "You're a highbrowed, fancy-talking museum director. How come you understand me so well?"

"You left out intuitive. I'm a highbrowed, fancy-talking, *intuitive* museum director."

"I thought your intuition only worked with art."

"Trust me, Colfax, you're a real work of art."

He did not smile. "So you figure it's this intuition of yours that makes it possible for you to understand me?"

"Well, no, I don't think that's the real reason I sometimes comprehend you."

"What's the real reason?"

She propped her elbow on the table and rested her chin on the heel of her hand. "This is important to you?"

"Yeah. It is."

She chose her words carefully. "I suppose it's because, deep down where it counts, we've got a lot in common."

His expression lightened briefly. "I wasn't sure you had figured that out."

So it was not the past or the Hades cup that had pitched him into this strange mood. It was their relationship that occupied his thoughts. She did not know whether to be relieved or more anxious than ever.

She waited in an agony of suspense, but Cyrus lapsed back into brooding silence. When she could stand it no longer, she cleared her throat.

"Was there something else you wanted to say?" she asked gently.

"Yeah."

Here it comes. She was suddenly dangling over a cliff above a very deep river. If he said good-bye and told her it had been fun she did not think she could be held responsible for her actions.

Cyrus gazed at the beer bottle as if it were a crystal ball.

If he said he saw no long-term future for the two of them, she would launch herself across the table, rip off his aloha shirt, and tear it into little pieces.

Cyrus took another swallow of beer.

If he said nothing at all, she would go crazy.

Cyrus poured more beer down his throat.

Eugenia crumpled her napkin in her fist. She started to get mad. Here she was, suffering untold agonies of suspense, and he was sitting there, drinking beer, completely oblivious to her pain. It was not fair.

She had been right back at the beginning, she thought, fuming. He was not her type. There was no way she could have fallen in love with this man.

Fallen in love.

She closed her eyes. Lord, that was exactly what she had done. She had fallen in love with a man who wore loud aloha shirts and liked to hang bland seascapes over his fireplace. A man whose eyes glazed over when she discussed art.

It was too much. It was all she could do not to throw herself down on the floor and pound her fists in frustration.

She opened her eyes and took deep breaths. "Lucky for you, I am a sophisticated woman who would never make a fool of herself in public."

Cyrus cocked a brow. "Huh?"

Eugenia thought about kicking him under the table to see if it would jump-start the conversation.

"Well?" She was shocked by the thread of breathlessness in her voice. "What was it you wanted to say?"

"March was blackmailing Zackery Elland Chandler."

"What?" Wine splashed on the table in front of her. Hastily she set the glass down and tried to reorient herself. So much for her incredible intuition. She pulled herself together with a heroic effort. "You're sure?"

"Quint found a whole file devoted to it on March's computer. The name of the file was 'Shadow.'"

She recalled the briefcase Cyrus had quietly concealed in her hall closet when he heard the sirens. He had opened it for a moment, just long enough for her to glimpse the black metal object inside. Later, in the busy chaos that had followed the arrival of the police, she had forgotten about it.

"No wonder you didn't mention the computer to the police."

"I couldn't take the chance." Cyrus looked at her with a steady gaze. "I didn't know what would be on the hard drive. When March said something about old sins casting long shadows, it hit me that he could be the blackmailer."

"You kept quiet to protect your father, didn't you?"

Cyrus shrugged. "March is dead. No one needs any more evidence against him."

"What happened to the computer?"

"After Quint erased the Shadow file, he arranged for the cops to find it.

"Why not just toss it into Elliott Bay?"

Cyrus looked at her. "Because, among other interesting tidbits, the files contained the names of the two goons who searched Rhonda's and Jacob's cabins."

"How in the world did you figure out that March was blackmailing Chandler?"

"Process of elimination. He was one of the few people in the world who could have known that Chandler was my father. I never told him, but Katy must have."

"I see." She thought about that. "Who else knows that Chandler is your father?"

"Quint Yates, you, and me."

She stared at him. "That the whole list?"

"Yeah."

A rush of warmth went through her. He had confided the biggest secret of his life to her. That had to mean something.

"Other people may know now," she said carefully. "The private investigator your father hired, for one. And the lawyer who was involved. Lord, Cyrus, there's no telling who may figure out the connection. One way or another, your father still has a problem."

"Yeah. Me."

"Chandler will probably keep looking for you until he finds you. Even if the blackmail threats stop, he can't ignore you any longer."

"True." Cyrus's mouth curved in a humorless smile. "He knows I'm a potential liability."

"So? What are you going to do?"

He shrugged. "Who says I have to do anything? The problem is Chandler's, not mine."

She sighed. "You can't go on dancing around the issue like this. It's got to be resolved."

"You're wrong. I don't have to resolve a damn thing."

"If you really felt that way, why are you brooding tonight?"

"It's been a long day."

She woke up shortly after midnight, aware that she was alone in the bed. It took her a few seconds to remember that she was in a hotel room. Then she saw the dark shadow that was Cyrus standing at the window. He had his back to her as he looked out over the city. His broad shoulders cut off most of the glow of the late-night lights.

"What is it?" She sat up against the pillows. "Does your wound hurt?"

"Not bad. I took one of the pills."

"In other words, it hurts like heck."

"It'll be all right when the pill kicks in."

She drew up her knees and folded her arms on top of them. "Stop fighting it, Cyrus."

He did not pretend that he did not understand. "What the hell am I supposed to say to him?"

"I don't know. I guess you could start by telling

him that the blackmailer is dead. Let him take it from there."

Cyrus made a fist and rested it on the frame of the window. "If he offers me money to keep me quiet . . ."

"You'll spit on his shoes and walk out the door."

He turned slowly and walked back to stand beside the bed. He stood looking down at her. "Yeah, that's just what I'll do."

She reached out, caught his hand, and squeezed gently. "This is a big occasion. Be sure to wear your best aloha shirt."

He opted for the electric blue and yellow one with the brilliantly hued reef fish swimming in circles.

The neatly tailored, gray-haired woman seated at the desk in the outer office eyed the fish with a deeply wary expression. "May I ask if this is in reference to a wildlife issue? If so, I can arrange for you to receive one of Mr. Chandler's position statements."

Cyrus leaned forward and planted his hands on her desk. "Tell Mr. Chandler that Cyrus Colfax from Second Chance Springs wants to see him. I represent a voting block of one."

"I beg your pardon?"

"Just do it. I think you'll be amazed at the results."

The receptionist lifted her chin. "Mr. Chandler is expecting his wife at any moment. They plan to do lunch together."

"I won't stay long. Tell him I'm here, or else I'll announce myself."

The woman glanced around quickly, but there was no one else in the vicinity. Cyrus had deliberately chosen to time his arrival for noon. He knew that Chandler usually worked through lunch while most of his staff left the office.

The woman behind the desk seized the phone and

spoke quickly. "I'm sorry to interrupt you, sir, but there's a Mr. Colfax from someplace called Second Chance Springs to see you. I don't think he's with any of the usual groups. . . . What?" She looked at Cyrus, clearly baffled. "Yes, I'll send him in, sir."

She put down the phone very slowly. "Mr. Chandler will see you."

"I was pretty sure he would." Cyrus crossed the carpet to the closed door that guarded the inner office. He was surprised by the cold emptiness in his gut. Eugenia would have had an explanation for it.

The thought of her had a warming effect. He turned the knob and opened the door.

"I know we've got a legal claim to the cup, Tabitha." Eugenia reached the far end of her office and paced back across the Oriental carpet. "But I think we should relinquish it."

"I don't believe I'm hearing this." Seated behind the desk, Tabitha peered at her over the rims of her reading glasses. "The Hades cup may be the most important piece of ancient glass that has turned up in the past fifty years."

"Don't you think I know that?"

"Yet you're seriously suggesting that we give it up to some anonymous collector who can't even offer hard proof that he once owned it?"

"Not can't. Won't." Eugenia came to a halt in front of the desk. "But Cyrus vouches for him, and I think we should take his word on this. He says it belongs to his client. He feels a responsibility to return it to him."

"That's ridiculous." Tabitha narrowed her eyes. "Let this client, whoever he is, come forward and talk to our lawyers."

"He won't do that. I told you, Cyrus says he's very

eccentric. Has a thing about his anonymity. But he has a legitimate right to the cup."

Tabitha shook her head in disbelief. "I'm amazed to hear you arguing in favor of handing over the Hades cup. I would have expected you to fight tooth and nail to keep it."

Eugenia smiled ruefully. "You don't know how hard this is for me, but I feel it's the right thing to do under the circumstances. Cyrus risked his life for that cup. In the process he saved Nellie and me. He also saved Rhonda Price and Jacob Houston."

"Hmm, there is that, I suppose. On the other hand, if it hadn't been for you and the auspices of the Leabrook, he might never have found the cup in the first place."

Eugenia almost laughed. "You're wrong, Tabitha. Believe me, sooner or later, Cyrus would have found it."

Zackery Elland Chandler's pose said it all, Cyrus thought. Chandler stood resolutely, protectively, in front of a framed picture of his wife and children. His *legitimate* wife and children.

The glaring California sunlight from the window behind him threw his face into unreadable shadow. It also outlined the aggressive, determined line of his shoulders and the fierce angle of his jaw.

It was a jaw that Cyrus had viewed often enough in his own mirror. He'd seen Chandler's picture hundreds of times in newspapers and on television, but he had never been able to detect anything more than a fleeting family resemblance. In person, though, it was much more obvious. It sent a jolt through him.

"Who the hell are you?" Zackery asked.

"Not the guy who's been blackmailing you. His name is Damien March. He's dead."

Nothing showed on Chandler's face. "Dead?"

"Very."

"Goddamn it, this is another extortion attempt, isn't it? You're here to take this Damien March's place, aren't you? Well, you're wasting your time. I won't give you a bloody dime, let alone access to political favors."

The cold feeling in Cyrus's stomach intensified. "I didn't come here for money or access."

"Who are you?"

"I thought your receptionist told you. My name is Colfax. Cyrus Chandler Colfax from Second Chance Springs." He paused. "I believe you knew my mother."

For a few seconds there was no response. Then Zackery moved away from the glare of the sun.

Eye color was something else that was hard to discern in grainy newspaper photos or on TV. For the first time Cyrus saw the color of his father's eyes. They were green.

"Are you claiming to be my son?" Zackery asked.

"Afraid so."

Zackery stared at Cyrus's eyes. "Damn. It's true. You *are* my son."

"It's not as though we won't get anything out of the deal, Tabitha." Eugenia resumed her pacing. "If we play this right, the publicity could be incredible. The Leabrook will get credit for assisting in the recovery of the Hades cup."

"Hmm."

"We'll call in the press." Sensing the lack of enthusiasm, Eugenia waved her arms a few times. "We'll get photographs. It'll make a terrific feature story for the local papers. I bet it will do wonders to arouse interest in the Cutting Edge exhibition."

"You've got this all plotted out, haven't you?"

"What's more, if we time it right, the story will hit the media just before the annual Leabrook Foundation reception. The Board will be thrilled."

"Unless, of course, they find out that we could have legitimately claimed the cup as part of the Daventry collection but chose to give it up, instead," Tabitha said dryly.

Eugenia winced. "Yes. Unless they find out about that part." She took a deep breath. "Tabitha, we have to let it go."

"This is important to you, isn't it?"

"I know I'm asking a lot. Probably a lot more than I have any right to ask. But I honestly think we should let Cyrus have the cup. It's a question of professional ethics."

"As long as we don't submit to blood tests, there's no hard proof for anyone to find," Cyrus said. "My mother put a false name on the birth certificate. She claimed that the father of her child had disappeared and that there was no way to contact him."

"Yes, I know. I wonder why she did that?"

"She was very young," Cyrus reminded him. "She wanted to protect you."

"From whom?"

"My grandfather. He was the old-fashioned kind. He'd have gone after you with a shotgun. She probably would have broken down and told him the truth eventually, but she died in a car crash when I was a few months old."

Zackery's hands tightened on the edge of the desk behind him. "I recently learned of her death. I'm sorry. More sorry than I can say."

"There are others who know. I can vouch for the people I've told. They can be trusted to keep the secret. You'll have to worry about the ones on your end. But if you think they'll keep quiet, we should be okay."

Zackery narrowed his eyes slightly. "Are you telling me that you intend to keep quiet about this?"

"I have no reason to tell anyone."

Zackery did not respond directly to that. "You said this March was a murderer?"

"He confessed to it in front of me and two other witnesses."

"Whom did he kill?"

Cyrus hesitated. "My wife. Her name was Katy."

There was a long pause.

"Christ." Zackery ran a hand through his hair. "I hadn't realized."

"Yeah, I know."

"Did he kill anyone else?"

"It wouldn't surprise me. Two days ago he set up a scenario in which he tried to kill me and two other people."

Zackery studied him with deep curiosity. "You're alive."

"Things worked out okay."

"What's wrong with your arm?"

Cyrus glanced down at the slight bulge of the bandage beneath his shirtsleeve. "March got off a shot before I got control of the situation."

"I see." Zackery eyed him thoughtfully. "What is it, exactly, that you do for a living?"

"Why?"

"I'm interested. You know much more about me than I know about you."

Cyrus looked at him. "Well, I didn't go into politics."

"All right, all right, you win." Tabitha flung her glasses down onto the polished surface of the desk.

"The Leabrook has an unblemished reputation for integrity. If you feel that reputation will be forever tarnished if we maintain possession of the Hades cup, we have no choice but to relinquish our claim."

Eugenia flopped down into the nearest chair, exhausted from the argument. She gave Tabitha a misty smile. "Thanks. I owe you one."

"Yes, you do. But sooner or later, I expect you'll repay me." Tabitha grinned. "You always do."

"I don't suppose you'll believe me when I tell you that until those blackmail notes started arriving on my computer, I never knew you existed," Zackery said.

"Doesn't really matter, one way or the other."

"You're wrong. It matters." Zackery leaned back against the desk and folded his arms. "How long have you known the truth?"

"Since I was twenty one."

"Who told you?"

"There was no one around who could tell me. I found out on my own."

Zackery's mouth tightened. "Why didn't you contact me?"

"Didn't seem to be much point."

"But now you claim that you've come to rescue me from a potential campaign nightmare. In my business, no one ever does anything without expecting something in return."

Shit. He's going to try to buy me off.

Cyrus could feel the anger gathering inside, a great, roiling storm that, if not controlled, would wreak unknown damage. He had to get out of there. Now.

"I think that's about all there is to say." He turned toward the door.

It opened just as he reached for the knob. An attractive woman in a tasteful pastel suit smiled curiously at him.

"Excuse me." She glanced at Zackery. "Bernice isn't at her desk. I didn't know you were with someone, dear. I'll wait outside."

"Come on in, Mary." Zackery smiled. "I want you to meet my eldest son."

"How do you do?" Mary offered Cyrus her hand. "I've been looking forward to meeting you. So have Jason and Sarah. Zackery has told us all about you. Or at least as much as he's been able to discover. You know, the resemblance is amazing."

Twenty-four

*E*ugenia was waiting for him at the airport. It only took him a second to pick her out of the crowd at the gate. She was dressed in a black calf-length skirt and a snug black knit top. She wore a turquoise blue silk scarf around her throat. Her hair was pulled back in the familiar sleek knot.

She looked sophisticated, rakish, and terribly arty.

She gave him a radiant smile when she saw him. Cyrus came to a full stop, blocking the flow of deplaning passengers. He ignored the grumbling and the mutters behind him. He could not take his eyes off Eugenia.

No one and nothing in his life had ever looked as good as she did waiting for him tonight, he thought. Ignoring the crowd that swarmed around them, he dropped his duffel bag at his feet and pulled her into his arms.

It was a long time before he raised his head. "Did I ever tell you that the first time I saw you I thought you looked like a lady cat burglar?"

She tilted her head back. Her eyes gleamed. "Funny you should say that. The first time I saw you, I thought you looked like the tough, relentless marshall in an old-fashioned western. The kind who met the train at high noon and shot it out with the bad guys."

"In spite of the shirt?"

She fiddled with one of the buttons of his color-splashed shirt. "You can't hide behind a shirt, Colfax. Come on, let's go home. The cleaning company did an incredible job. There's still a hole in my wall, but I can live with that. The blood is gone and so is the crime scene tape."

Home. The word fused several circuits in his brain for a few seconds. Take it easy, he thought. She was speaking casually. Lightly.

She took his hand as they walked through the terminal. "How did it go?"

"Chandler called a press conference late this afternoon. Announced he had a son he had never known existed. Said he was delighted to welcome me into the family. Even told the reporters that I had thwarted a blackmail attempt."

"Thwarted?"

"It's the sort of word politicians use."

"I see."

"It'll be a two-day wonder in the California papers, at best. Got to hand it to Chandler. Guy knows how to do damage control. I have a hunch he'll win the election."

"What else did he tell the reporters?" Eugenia asked.

"He claimed full responsibility for the affair with my mother. Says he wishes she had tracked him down and told him that she was pregnant. Said he would have done the right thing by her because his parents would have insisted on it."

"How did it go over?"

"The press ate it up. The potential for rumors and scandal was nipped in the bud."

"Don't be so cynical," she said. "It's a very touching story. Do you believe him?"

"Are you kidding?" Cyrus grimaced. "Old Z. E. Chandler, senior, would have gone ballistic if there was any suggestion that his son marry a nobody from Second Chance Springs. At the very least, he would have tried to buy my mother off or coerce her into getting an abortion. The real problem for Chandler would have been my grandfather."

She smiled. "I can imagine that Grandpappy Beau would have had a few things to say about the situation."

Cyrus nodded. "But the public will buy the story. Chandler's a politician, Eugenia. He's good at looking you in the eye and getting you to believe him."

"He's your father. Cut him some slack."

He tightened his hand around hers. "One thing I'll say in his favor."

"What's that?"

"When crunch time came, he refused to pay blackmail. You have to respect that in a man."

"Yes." She slanted him a knowing glance. "You do."

Cyrus had left Los Angeles one step ahead of several reporters seeking interviews. On the flight back to Seattle, he had called Quint and issued instructions to his staff to ignore all inquiries from journalists. Now that everything was out in the open, he knew the story would fade quickly.

In the meantime, he had other problems. Like his entire future hanging in the balance, for example. What the hell was he going to do if he could not convince Eugenia that they belonged together?

Her car was waiting in the short-term parking lot. Cyrus tossed his duffel bag into the back of the Toyota and looked at her across the roof.

"Want me to drive?" he asked.

"No, thanks. You've been through a traumatic experience. It's not every day a man meets his long-lost father. The least I can do is drive you home from the airport and pour you a beer." She opened the door and got behind the wheel.

He got in beside her, buckled his seat belt, and concentrated on the novelty of being coddled. It had been a long couple of days, he thought. He was tired. More so than he had realized.

"I had a long talk with Tabitha while you were gone," Eugenia said as she drove out of the airport parking garage. "She agreed to relinquish the Leabrook's claim to the Hades cup. You can return it to its rightful owner."

Cyrus tried unsuccessfully to stretch out his legs. "Talked her into it, huh?" He stifled a yawn.

"Yes." She shot him a quick, searching look. "You don't sound surprised, thrilled, or even very grateful."

He shrugged. "I wasn't worried about a battle over the Hades cup. I knew that, in the end, you'd do the right thing."

"*What?*" Her voice rose on a note of outraged incredulity. "You think I went to bat for you just because I thought your client had a better claim to that damn cup than the Leabrook does?"

He slouched down, leaned his head against the back of the seat, and closed his eyes. "Yeah."

"That is pure, unadulterated *crap*. I did it because I love you. Do you hear me, Colfax? I gave up the Hades cup for you. I would not have done that for any other man on the face of the earth. It seems to me that you could at least show a little appreciation."

For a split second he thought he had fallen asleep and slipped into a dream. He opened his eyes and saw the red glare of the taillights on the car ahead.

Not a dream.

He turned his head to look at Eugenia. She was staring grimly through the windshield, gripping the wheel as if she wished it was his throat.

"Are you by any chance trying to tell me that our relationship has progressed beyond the point of sexual obsession?" he asked.

"What if it has?" she snapped.

"Be a major relief to me," he admitted. "Means I can tell you that I'm in love with you, too."

An acute silence descended. For several miles Eugenia appeared to be concentrating fiercely on her driving. They were nearing the Western Avenue off-ramp before she spoke again.

"Where does this leave us?" she asked.

He smiled at the tension in her voice. "We make plans."

She switched on the turn signal. "Plans? What kind of plans?"

"Nothing you have to worry about. I shift the headquarters of Colfax Security to the new Seattle office, and I move in with you."

Her mouth opened and closed and then opened again. "Just like that?"

"I'm a simple kind of guy. I don't believe in complicating things any more than absolutely necessary."

She smiled at the windshield. "Okay."

Two weeks later the only thing missing on the night of the Leabrook Foundation reception was Cyrus.

Other than that, Eugenia thought as she strolled among the guests, everything had come off perfectly. The Leabrook had been decorated in an Art Deco motif that perfectly suited the magnificent glass collection it housed. The masses of flowers were arranged in several highly sculptural vases that dated from the early 1930s. A small quartet filled the air with the sounds of *Le Jazz Hot*. Waiters, most of them part-time actors in local fringe theaters, carried trays of champagne. In their sleek black and white costumes, they looked as if they could have been working on board the *Aquitania* during an Atlantic crossing between the wars.

As always, the Leabrook collection of rare and spectacular glass was the main attraction. It glowed in the carefully lit display cases, fragile but powerful links to the past that never failed to enthrall Eugenia.

There were third-century B.C. Hellenistic bowls that had once held exotic unguents for an Egyptian priest. Across the room was a fourth-century bottle that a Roman matron had used for her perfumes. In another wing there were exquisite twelfth-century beakers and flasks that had once belonged in a medieval nobleman's household.

Brilliantly decorated fifteenth-century Venetian glassware gleamed inside other cases. Eighteenth-century English and Irish crystal blazed in still others. In the new wing, the one that had been constructed after Eugenia became the museum's director, was an array of contemporary studio glass that took the ancient craft into the realm of art.

In keeping with the theme, Eugenia had chosen a slim, emerald green 1930s-style satin gown. It was cut to expose a great deal of her back. Her only regret was that Cyrus was not around to appreciate it.

He had left two days ago to return the Hades cup to its reclusive owner. He had phoned yesterday to say that he expected to make it back in time for the reception, but two hours before she was due to leave the condo, Quint Yates had called.

"He asked me to tell you that he's going to be a little late," Quint said.

"Is something wrong?"

"Nope."

"Then why is he going to be late?" Eugenia asked patiently.

"Didn't say." Having delivered his message, Quint apparently saw no reason to dawdle on the phone. He hung up in Eugenia's ear.

"A wonderful turnout." Tabitha paused beside Eugenia and surveyed the crowd with satisfaction. "You were right about the publicity, my dear. The timing was perfect. I admit it will take me a while to get over the loss of the Hades cup, but I suppose the excellent public relations will comfort me."

"It's bound to ensure good ticket sales for the Cutting Edge exhibition next month," Eugenia said.

"Indeed. I must say, that Jacob Houston piece you brought back from Frog Cove Island is amazing. I'm delighted that the Leabrook will be the first museum to display his work. Can we get any more for the exhibition?"

"Don't worry, I talked to him just yesterday. By the way, he told me that he and Rhonda Price are going to get married."

Tabitha frowned. "I trust the wedding won't impact his work schedule."

Eugenia grinned. "I don't think we'll have any problems getting our glass. Rhonda has appointed herself his business manager. She's got big plans for him."

"Hmmph. Probably intends to triple his prices."

"At the very least."

Eugenia noticed Nellie standing with several members of the Leabrook Foundation Board. She lifted her glass of champagne in salute. Nellie smiled and then turned back to charm the elderly, white-maned man who was trying to discreetly peer down her dress.

Tabitha followed Eugenia's gaze. "Do you think we did the right thing in giving her back her job until she gets her art career off the ground?"

"Relax. She's the heroine of all that publicity we got, remember? Of course we had to give her back her job."

Nellie's role in the tale of the Hades cup had been altered somewhat at Eugenia's insistence. Tabitha and Cyrus had argued for a while, but in the end, they had abandoned the effort. By the time the police and the newspapers had gotten the story, Nellie was portrayed as the daring young artist who had hidden the Hades cup to protect it from a crazed dealer named Fenella Weeks.

"Speaking of heroic figures," Tabitha said, "I believe I see Mr. Colfax."

"Cyrus is here?" Eugenia swung around, her pulse kicking into high gear. "Where?"

"He just walked through the door." Tabitha's eyes glinted with amusement. "Hard to miss him in that shirt. I thought you told me he had broken down and rented a tux for tonight."

Eugenia's heart lifted at the sight of Cyrus in a dazzling red and blue aloha shirt spattered with parrots. He had already seen her and was heading in her direction. He did not appear to notice the crowd as it parted for him the way small yachts part for an aircraft carrier. His eyes were on Eugenia.

He carried a large, heavily wrapped object in his hands.

Eugenia frowned. "He did rent a tux. It's hanging in the closet. He must have come straight from the airport. Excuse me, Tabitha."

Tabitha gave her a knowing smile. "Run along, my dear."

Eugenia set down her champagne glass and slipped into the crowd.

They met midway across the floor.

Eugenia looked into Cyrus's green eyes. "What kept you?"

"This." He handed her the bulky package he had brought with him. "Took me a little longer than I expected to talk my client into donating the Hades cup to the Leabrook."

"Donate . . . ?" She realized her mouth was hanging open. She glanced down at the package and then looked up again. Out of the corner of her eye she noticed several heads turn. "Good heavens, Cyrus, are you telling me that he agreed to let the Leabrook have it?"

"Yeah. Said you were right. It was too important to belong to any individual collector." Cyrus winked. "Plus, which, I sort of convinced him it was safer in a museum."

Eugenia laughed. "Tabitha will kiss the ground you walk upon."

"Nothing like a satisfied client. Sorry I didn't have time to go home and get the tux."

"Don't worry about it. I've been a little busy, myself, today."

"Yeah?"

"I picked up our honeymoon trip tickets." She straightened the collar of his brightly patterned shirt. "I thought we'd go to Hawaii."

His eyes were very green and very deep. He

Jayne Ann Krentz

touched the side of her cheek. "A honeymoon implies a marriage."

"Yes, it does, doesn't it?"

"I take it this is a yes to the question I asked before I left?"

She smiled, as sure and certain as she was when she looked into the depths of brilliant, glowing glass.

POCKET BOOKS
PROUDLY PRESENTS

FLASH

JAYNE ANN KRENTZ

Available now in hardcover from
Pocket Books

Turn the page for a preview of
Flash. . . .

Eight years earlier

Jasper Sloan sat in front of the fire, a half-finished glass of whiskey on the arm of the chair beside him, a thick file of papers in his hand. Page by page he fed the incriminating contents of the folder to the ravenous flames.

It was midnight. Outside a steady Northwest rain fell, cloaking the woods in a melancholy mist. The lights of Seattle were a distant blur across the waters of Puget Sound.

In the past his Bainbridge Island home had been a retreat and a refuge for Jasper. Tonight it was a place to bury the past.

"Watcha doin', Uncle Jasper?"

Jasper tossed another sheet to the flames. Then he looked at the ten-year-old pajama-clad boy in the doorway. He smiled slightly.

"I'm cleaning out some old files," he said. "What's the matter, Kirby? Couldn't you get to sleep?"

"I had another bad dream." There were shadows in Kirby's intelligent, too-somber eyes.

"It will fade in a few minutes." Jasper closed the half-empty file and set it on the wide arm of the chair. "I'll get you a cup of warm milk."

The dozen books on parenting that Jasper had consulted during the past several months had given conflicting advice on the subject of warm milk. But the stuff seemed to be effective on Kirby's bad dreams. At least there had been fewer of them lately.

"Okay." Kirby padded, barefoot, across the oak floor and sat down on the thick wool rug in front of the hearth. "It's still raining."

"Yes." Jasper walked into the kitchen and opened the refrigerator. He took out the carton of milk. "Probably stop by morning, though."

"If it does, can we set up the targets and do some more archery practice?"

"Sure." Jasper poured milk into a cup and stuck it into the microwave. He punched a couple of buttons. "We can do a little fishing, too. Maybe we'll get lucky and catch dinner."

Paul appeared in the doorway, yawning hugely. He glanced at the file on the chair. "What's goin' on out here?"

"Uncle Jasper's getting rid of some old papers he doesn't want anymore," Kirby explained.

Jasper looked at his other nephew. Paul was a year and a half older than Kirby. Instead of the overly serious expression that was Kirby's trademark, Paul's young gaze mirrored a hint of his father's reckless, aggressive approach to life.

Fletcher Sloan had bequeathed his deep, engaging blue eyes and his light brown hair to both of his sons. In the years ahead, when the softness of youth would give way to the harsher planes and angles of manhood, Jasper knew that Paul and Kirby would become living images of the dashing, charismatic man who had fathered them.

He also had a hunch that, given the strong forces of their two very different personalities, there would be problems as both boys entered their teens. He could only hope that the parenting books he was buying by the palette-load these days would guide him through the tricky years.

Jasper was relying on the books because he was only too well aware of his inadequacies in the field of parenting. His own father, Harry Sloan, had not been what anyone could call a strong role model.

Harry had been a devout workaholic all of his life who had had very little time for his sons or anyone else. Although ostensibly retired, he still went into the office every day. Jasper sensed that the day Harry stopped working would be the day he died.

Jasper poured a second cup of milk for Paul. He would have to take things as they came and do the best he could. It wasn't like there was much choice, he reminded himself. Fortunately, there were a lot of books on parenting.

He watched the digital readout on the microwave as it ticked off the time. For a disorienting moment, the numbers on the clock wavered and became years. He counted backward to the day, two decades earlier, when Fletcher had entered his life.

Flamboyant, charming, and slightly larger-than-life, Fletcher had become Jasper's stepbrother when Jasper's widowed father had remarried.

Jasper had few memories of his mother, who had died in a car crash when he was four. But his stepmother, Caroline, had been kind enough in a reserved fashion. Her great talent lay in managing the social side of Harry's life. She was very good at hosting dinner parties at the country club for Harry's business associates.

It had always seemed to Jasper that his father and stepmother lived in two separate universes. Harry lived for his work. Caroline lived for her country club activities. There did not appear to be any great bond of love between them, but both seemed content.

Caroline's only real fault was that she had doted on Fletcher. In her eyes her son could do no wrong. Instead of helping him learn to curtail his tendencies toward reckless irresponsibility and careless arrogance, she had indulged and encouraged them.

Caroline was not the only one who had turned a blind eye to Fletcher's less admirable traits. Six years younger than his new brother and eager for a hero to take the place of a father who was always at work, Jasper had been willing to overlook a lot, also.

Too much, as it turned out.

Fletcher was gone now. He and his wife, Brenda, had been killed nearly a year ago in a skiing disaster in the Alps.

Caroline had been stunned by the news of her son's death. But she had quickly, tearfully explained to Jasper and everyone else involved that she could not possibly be expected to assume the task of raising Paul and Kirby.

Her age and the social demands of her busy life made it impossible to start all over again as a mother to her grandsons. The boys needed someone younger, she said. Someone who had the patience and energy to handle children.

Jasper had taken Paul and Kirby to live with him. There had been no one else. He had committed himself to the role of substitute father with the same focused, well-organized, highly disciplined determination that he applied to every other aspect of his life.

The past eleven months had not been easy.

The first casualty had been his marriage. The divorce had become final six months ago. He did not blame Andrea for leaving him. After all, the job of playing mother to two young boys who were not even related to her had not been part of the business arrangement that had constituted the foundation of their marriage.

The microwave pinged. Jasper snapped back to the present. He opened the door and took out the mugs.

"Did you have a nightmare, too, Paul?" he asked.

"No." Paul wandered over to the fire and sat down, tailor-fashion, beside Kirby. "I woke up when I heard you guys talking out here."

"Uncle Jasper says we can do some more archery and maybe go fishing tomorrow," Kirby announced.

"Cool."

Jasper carried the two cups to where the boys sat in front of the fire. "That's assuming the rain stops."

"If it doesn't, we can always play Acid Man on the computer," Kirby said cheerfully.

Jasper winced at the thought of being cooped up in the house all weekend while his nephews entertained themselves with the loud sound effects of the new game.

"I'm pretty sure the rain will stop," he said, mentally crossing his fingers.

Paul looked at the closed file on the arm of the chair. "How come you're burning those papers?"

Jasper sat down and picked up the folder. "Old business. Just some stuff that's no longer important."

Paul nodded, satisfied. "Too bad you don't have a shredder here, huh?"

Jasper opened the file and resumed feeding the contents to the eager flames. "The fire works just as well."

In his opinion, the blaze worked even better than a mechanical shredder. Nothing was as effective as fire when it came to destroying damning evidence.

Five years later

Olivia Chantry poured herself a glass of dark red zinfandel wine and carried it down the hall toward the bedroom that had been converted into an office. She still had on the high-necked, long-sleeved black dress she had worn to her husband's funeral that afternoon.

Logan would have been her ex-husband if he had lived. She had been preparing to file for a divorce when he had suddenly jetted off to Pamplona, Spain. There he had gotten very drunk and had run with the bulls. The bulls won. Logan had been trampled to death.

Trust him to go out in a blaze of glory, Olivia thought. And to think she had once believed that a marriage based on friendship and mutual business interests would have a solid, enduring foundation. Uncle Rollie had been right, she decided. Logan had needed her, but he had not loved her.

Halfway down the hall she paused briefly at the thermostat to adjust the temperature. She had been feeling cold all day. The accusing expressions on the faces of the Dane family, especially the look in the eyes of Logan's younger brother, Sean, had done nothing to warm her. They knew she had seen a lawyer. They blamed her for Logan's spectacular demise.

Her cousin Nina's anguished, tearful eyes had only deepened the chill inside Olivia.

Uncle Rollie, the one member of Olivia's family who understood her best, had leaned close to whisper beneath the cover of the organ music.

"Give 'em time," Rollie said with the wisdom of eighty years. "They're all hurting now, but they'll get past it eventually."

Olivia was not so certain of that. In her heart she knew that her relationships with the Danes and with Nina would never be the same again.

When she reached the small, cluttered office, she took a sip of the zinfandel to fortify herself. Then she put down the glass and went to the black metal file cabinet in the corner. She spun the combination lock and pulled open a drawer. A row of folders appeared, most crammed to over-flowing with business correspondence, tax forms, and assorted papers. One of these days she really would have to get serious about her filing.

She reached inside the drawer and removed the journal. For a moment she gazed at the leather-bound volume and considered the damning contents.

After a while she sat down at her cluttered desk, kicked off her black, low-heeled pumps, and switched on the small shredder. The machine whirred and hummed to life, a mechanical shark eager for prey.

The small bedroom-cum-office with its narrow windows was oppressive, she thought as she opened the journal. In fact, she hated the place where she and Logan had lived since their marriage six months ago.

She promised herself that first thing in the morning she would start looking for a bigger apartment. Her business was starting to take off. She could afford to buy herself a condo. One with lots of windows.

One by one, Olivia ripped the pages from the journal and fed them into the steel jaws. She would have preferred to burn the incriminating evidence, but she did not have a fireplace.

The zinfandel was gone by the time the last entry in the journal had been rendered into tiny scraps. Olivia sealed the plastic shredder bag and carried it downstairs to the basement of the apartment building. There she dumped the contents into the large bin marked *Clean Paper Only*.

When the blizzard of shredded journal pages finally ceased Olivia closed the lid of the bin. In the morning a large truck would come to haul away the contents. The discarded paper, including the shredded pages of the journal, would soon be transformed into something useful. News-print, maybe. Or toilet tissue.

Like almost everyone else who lived in Seattle, Olivia was a great believer in recycling.

The present

Jasper knew that he was in trouble because he had reached the point where he was giving serious consideration to the idea of getting married again.

His attention was deflected from the dangerous subject less than a moment later when he realized that someone was trying very hard to kill him.

At least, he *thought* someone was attempting to murder him.

Either way, as a distraction, the prospect was dazzlingly effective. Jasper immediately stopped thinking about finding a wife.

It was the blinding glare of hot, tropical sunlight on metal reflected in the rearview mirror that got Jasper's attention. He glanced up. The battered green Ford that had followed him from the tiny village on the island's north shore was suddenly much closer. In another few seconds the vehicle would be right on top of the Jeep's bumper.

The Ford shot out of the last narrow curve and bore down on the Jeep. The car's heavily tinted windows, common enough here in the South Pacific, made it impossible to see the face of the person at the wheel. Whoever he was, he was either very drunk or very high.

A tourist, Jasper thought. The Ford looked like one of the rusty rentals he had seen at the small agency in the village where he had selected the Jeep.

There was little room to maneuver on the tiny, two-lane road that encircled tiny Pelapili Island. Steep cliffs shot straight up on the left. On Jasper's right the terrain fell sharply away to the turquoise sea.

He had never wanted to take this vacation in paradise, Jasper thought. He should have listened to his own instincts instead of the urgings of his nephews and his friend, Al.

This was what came of allowing other people to push you into doing what they thought was best for you.

Jasper assessed the slim shoulder on the side of the pavement. There was almost no margin for driving error on this stretch of the road. One wrong move and a driver could expect to end up forty feet below on the lava- and boulder-encrusted beach.

He should have had his midlife crisis in the peace and comfort of his own home on Bainbridge Island. At least he could have been more certain of surviving it there.

But he'd made the extremely rare mistake of allowing others to talk him into doing something he really did not want to do.

"You've got to get away, Uncle Jasper," Kirby had declared with the shining confidence of a college freshman who has just finished his first course in psychology. "If you won't talk to a therapist, the least you can do is give yourself a complete change of scene."

"I hate to say it, but I think Kirby's right," Paul said. "You haven't been yourself lately. All this talk about selling Sloan & Associates, it's not like you, Uncle Jasper. Take a vacation. Get wild and crazy. Do something off-the-wall."

Jasper had eyed his nephews from the other side of his broad desk. Paul and Kirby were both enrolled for the summer quarter at the University of Washington. In addition, both had part-time jobs this year. They had their own apartment near the campus now, and they led very active lives. He did not believe for one moment that both just happened, by purest coincidence, to find themselves downtown this afternoon.

He did not believe both had been struck simultaneously by a whim to drop by his office, either. Jasper was fairly certain that he was the target of a planned ambush.

"I appreciate your concern," he said. "But I do not need or want a vacation. As far as selling the firm is concerned, trust me, I know what I'm doing."

"But Uncle Jasper," Paul protested. "You and Dad built this company from scratch. It's a part of you. It's in your blood."

"Let's not go overboard with the dramatics," Jasper said. "Hell, even my fiercest competitors will tell you that my timing is damn near perfect when it comes to business. I'm telling you that it's time for me to do something else."

Kirby frowned, his dark blue eyes grave with concern. "How is your sleep pattern, Uncle Jasper?"

"What's my sleep pattern got to do with anything?"

"We're studying clinical depression in my Psych class. Sleep disturbance is a major warning sign."

"My sleep habits have been just fine."

Jasper decided not to mention the fact that for the past

month he had been waking up frequently at four in the morning. Unable to get back to sleep, he had gotten into the habit of going into the office very early to spend a couple of hours with the contents of his business files.

His excuse was that he wanted to go over every detail of the extensive operations of Sloan & Associates before he sold the firm to Al. But he knew the truth. He had a passion for order and routine. He found it soothing to sort through his elegantly arranged files. He knew few other people who could instantly retrieve decade-old corporate income tax records or an insurance policy that had been canceled five years earlier.

Maybe he could not control every aspect of his life, he thought, but he could damn sure handle the paperwork related to it.

"Well, what about your appetite?" Kirby surveyed him with a worried look. "Are you losing weight?"

Jasper wrapped his hands around the arms of his chair and glowered at Kirby. "If I want a professional psychological opinion, I'll call a real shrink, not someone who just got out of Psych 101."

An hour later, over lunch at a small Italian restaurant near the Pike Place Market, Al Okamoto stunned Jasper by agreeing with Paul's and Kirby's verdict.

"They're right." Al forked up a swirl of his spaghetti puttanesca. "You need to get away for a while. Take a vacation. When you come back we'll talk about whether or not you still want to sell Sloan & Associates to me."

"Hell, you too?" Jasper shoved aside his unfinished plate of Dungeness crab–filled ravioli. He had not been about to admit it to Kirby that afternoon, but lately his normally healthy appetite had been a little off. "What is it with everyone today? So what if I've put in a few extra hours on the Slater project? I'm just trying to get everything in order for the sale."

Al's gaze narrowed. "It's not the Slater deal. That's routine, and you know it. You could have handled it in your sleep. If you were getting any sleep, that is, which I doubt."

Jasper folded his arms on the table. "Now you're telling me I look tired? Damn it, Al—"

"I'm telling you that you need a break, that's all. A weekend off isn't going to do the trick. Take a month. Go veg out on some remote, tropical island. Swim in the ocean, sit under a palm tree. Drink a few margaritas."

"I'm warning you, pal, if you're about to tell me that I'm depressed . . ."

"You're not depressed, you're having a midlife crisis."

Jasper stared at him. "Are you crazy? I am not having any such thing."

"You know what one looks like, do you?"

"Everyone knows what a midlife crisis looks like. Affairs with very young women. Flashy red sports cars. A divorce."

"So?"

"In case you've forgotten, my divorce took place nearly eight years ago. I am not interested in buying a Ferrari that would probably get stolen and sent to a chop shop the first week I owned it. And I haven't had an affair in—" Jasper broke off suddenly. "In a while."

"A *long* while." Al aimed his fork at Jasper. "You don't get out enough. That's one of your problems. You lack a normal social life."

"So I'm not a party animal. So sue me."

Al sighed. "I've known you for over five years. I can tell you that you never do anything the usual way. Stands to reason that you wouldn't have a typical, run-of-the-mill midlife crisis. Instead of an explosion, you're going through a controlled meltdown."

"For which you recommend a tropical island vacation?"

"Why not? It's worth a try. Pick one of those incredibly expensive luxury resorts located on some undiscovered island. The kind of place that specializes in unstressing seriously overworked executives."

"How do they manage the unstressing part?" Jasper asked.

Al forked up another bite of pasta. "They give you a room with no phone, no fax, no television, no air conditioner and no clocks."

"We used to call that kind of hotel a flophouse."

"It's the latest thing in upscale, high-end vacations," Al assured him around a mouthful of spaghetti. "Costs a fortune. What have you got to lose?"

"I dunno. A fortune maybe?"

"You can afford it. Look, Paul and Kirby and I have already picked out an ideal spot. An island called Pelapili. It's at the far end of the Hawaiian chain. We made the reservations for you."

"You did *what?*"

"You're going to stay there for a full month."

"The hell I am, I've got a business to run."

"I'm the vice president, second largest shareholder, and the chief associate in Sloan & Associates, remember? You say you want to sell out to me. If you can't trust me to hold the company together for a mere month, who can you trust?"

In the end, Jasper had run out of excuses. A week later he had found himself on a plane to Pelapili Island.

For the past three and a half weeks he had dutifully followed the agenda that Al, Kirby, and Paul had outlined for him.

Every morning he swam in the pristine, clear waters of the bay that was only a few steps from his high-priced, low-tech cottage. He spent a lot of time reading boring thrillers in the shade of a palm tree, and he drank a few salt-rimmed margaritas in the evenings.

On days when he could not stand the enforced tranquillity for another minute, he used the rented Jeep to sneak into the village to buy a copy of the *Wall Street Journal*.

The newspapers were always at least three days old by the time they reached Pelapili, but he treasured each one. Like some demented alchemist, he examined every inch of print for occult secrets related to the world of business.

Jasper thrived on information. As far as he was concerned, it was not just power, it was magic. It was the lifeblood of his work as a venture capitalist. He collected information, organized it, and filed it.

He sometimes thought that in a former life he had probably been a librarian. He occasionally had fleeting images of himself poring over papyruses in an ancient library in Alexandria or Athens.

Cutting himself off from the flow of daily business information in the name of relaxation had been a serious mistake. He knew that now.

He still did not know if he was in the midst of a midlife crisis, but he had come to one definite conclusion: He was bored. He was a goal-oriented person, and the only goal he'd had until now on Pelapili was to get off the island.

Things had changed in the last sixty seconds, however. He had a new goal. A very clear one. He wanted to avoid going over the edge of the cliff into the jeweled sea.

The car was almost on top of him. On the off-chance that the driver was simply incredibly impatient, Jasper tried easing cautiously toward the shoulder. The Ford now had room to pass, if that was the objective.

For a few seconds Jasper thought that was what would happen. The nose of the Ford pulled out into the other lane. But instead of accelerating on past, it nipped at the fender of Jasper's Jeep.

Metal screamed against metal. A shudder went through the Jeep. Jasper fought the instinct to swerve away from the Ford. There was no room left on the right-hand shoulder. Another foot and he would be airborne out over the rocky cove.

The reality of what was happening slammed through him. The Ford really was trying to force the Jeep over the edge of the cliff. Jasper knew that he would die an unpleasant but probably very speedy death if he did not act quickly.

The green Ford was alongside the Jeep now, preparing for another nudge.

Jasper forced himself to think of the situation as a business problem. A matter of timing.

His timing was really quite good when it came to some things.

He slid into that distant, dispassionate state of mind that came over him whenever he concentrated on work. The world did not exactly go into slow motion, but it did appear in very sharp focus.

The goal became crystal clear. He would not go over the side and down the cliff.

The path to that goal was equally obvious. He had to go on the attack.

He was intensely aware of the physical dimensions of the space around him. He gauged the distance to the upcoming curve and the speed of his own vehicle. He sensed the driver of the Ford had nerved himself for another strike.

Jasper turned the wheel, aiming the Jeep's bumper at the Ford's side. There was a shudder and another grating shriek of metal-on-metal. Jasper edged closer.

The Ford swerved to avoid the second impact. It went into the next curve in the wrong lane. The driver, apparently panicked by the thought of meeting an oncoming vehicle, overcorrected wildly.

For an instant Jasper thought the Ford would go straight over the edge of the cliff. Somehow, it managed to cling to the road.

Jasper slowed quickly and went cautiously into the turn. When he came out of it he caught a fleeting glimpse of the Ford. It was already several hundred feet ahead. As he watched, it disappeared around another curve.

The driver of the Ford had obviously decided to abandon the assault on the Jeep. Jasper wondered if the other man, assuming it was a man, had lost his nerve or simply sobered up very quickly after the near-death experience on the curve.

Drunken driving or maybe an incident of road rage, Jasper told himself. That was the only logical explanation.

To entertain for even a moment the possibility that someone had deliberately tried to kill him would constitute a sure sign of incipient paranoia. Kirby would have a field day. Probably drag Jasper off to his psychology class for show-and-tell.

Damn. He hadn't even gotten the license number.

Jasper tried to summon up an image of the rear of the green car. He was very good with numbers.

But when he replayed the discrete mental pictures he had of the Ford he realized he did not remember seeing a license plate.

A near accident. That was the only explanation.

Don't go paranoid on me here, Sloan.

He spent most of the warm, tropical night brooding on the veranda of his overpriced, amenity-free cottage. For a long time he sat in the wicker chair and watched the silver moonlight slide across the surface of the sea. He could not explain why the uneasiness within him increased with every passing hour.

He had put the incident on the island road firmly in perspective. He knew that it was illogical to think for one moment that anyone here on Pelapili had any reason to try to murder him. No, it was not the brush with disaster that afternoon that was creating the disturbing sensation.

But the restlessness would not be banished. He wondered if he was suffering from an overdose of papaya, sand and margaritas. The problem with paradise was that it held no challenge.

A two in the morning he realized that it was time to go back to Seattle.

Look for
Flash
Wherever Books Are Sold
Available Now in Hardcover from
Pocket Books